"*A CRY OF ANGELS* IS JUST THAT—A RESOUNDING HALLELUJAH FOR A TROUBLED WORLD ... A STRONG, FRESH BREEZE!" —*Minneapolis Tribune*

"It has sparkle, gusto, pathos, comedy and drama ... written with an expertise that must be ranked among the finest" —*Chicago Sun-Times*

"A memorable tale of a boy who becomes a man once he learns to answer his own angel's cries ... a vivid array of characters who are drawn with such warmth and vitality that they will keep living in your imagination long after the story is over" —*Literary Guild Bulletin*

"We find ourselves wondering why delightful novels like this aren't written any more, and grateful that this one has come along to fill the void!" —Christopher Lehmann-Haupt in *The New York Times*

"IT WILL MOVE YOU, TICKLE YOU, AND JUST PLAIN ENTERTAIN THE HELL OUT OF YOU ... A WONDERFUL NOVEL, GREAT-HEARTED AND ALIVE!" —Larry L. King

"THOROUGHLY DELIGHTFUL ... PURE FUN" —*Washington Post*

A CRY
OF
ANGELS

Jeff Fields

BALLANTINE BOOKS • NEW YORK

Library of Congress Catalog Card Number: 73-91623

ISBN 0-345-28204-3

This edition published by arrangement with Atheneum Publishers

Manufactured in the United States of America

First Ballantine Books Edition: September 1975
Second Printing: June 1979

First Canadian Printing: October 1975

A CRY
OF
ANGELS

The storm broke and thrashed along the river in the summer darkness, with water slanting, leaves flying, trees bent and writhing in the wind.

Beyond the metal crying of Dirsey's beer sign, wrenching violently on its pole, behind the rattling, windows of the rough board and tarpaper building crouched at the mouth of Twig Creek, work-stained men in clay-crusted brogans stood silently in the yellow light and watched the drunken Indian dance in the circle of beer bottles on the floor.

Round and round he circled and swayed, a seven-foot giant in khaki clothes, his long hair brushing the flypaper coil, arms outstretched, heavy boots squeaking the boards.

Lightning slashed across the late August sky, tree branches sprayed the roof.

The Indian was aloft, soaring now, moving slowly to the rhythm within him, mumbling his wordless chant.

"Unh-huh . . . unh-huh . . . unh-huh."

He was finally home, after four months of his legendary rambling trips on the road. With considerable reluctance my great-aunt had sent me to guide him back to the boardinghouse. Normally Miss Esther forbade me to go anywhere near Dirsey's place, but

1

when word had come after supper that the Indian was back in town, she sighed and nodded acquiescence: "Better for the boy to lead him out of Dirsey's tonight than for me to have to pay him out of jail in the morning."

A man at the bar started to sway and clap. The farmers and quarry hands began to take it up, dirty overalls and rock-dusted caps swaying back and forth tauntingly in the light.

"Unh-huh . . . unh-huh . . . unh-huh."

Jutting black bands of hair shrouding his eyes, the Indian clamped his felt hat on tight. Head tilted back, he stared glassy-eyed through half-closed lids. The great body bounced and dipped, rolls of fat bobbing on the Sam Browne belt he had taken off a cop in Memphis.

"Hallelujah!" someone shouted, and they were all laughing and clapping. They slid out of booths and off of stools and everyone crowded around. One dared another to touch him.

"Leave him alone," ordered Dirsey. "He pays his way. Stand clear and leave him alone."

I crawled up on a stool at the end of the bar to see over the heads of the men, straining through the smoke and dimness for his eyes. They were still glazed. Full of pain. And danger.

Suddenly he scooped the twelfth bottle of beer off the bar and turned it up, chugalugging, the frosty liquid foaming between his great thick lips. He bent over and set the empty down with the others, completing the circle on the floor. The monotonous chant was beginning to die. I knew now it wouldn't be long.

"Aiiiiiiiyah!"

He was rigid, staring frozen-eyed from a puffed red face. I jumped down and took cover behind the bar.

"Aiiiyah!"

With a savage kick a bottle went skidding under the booths. A startled farmer jerked up his feet.

"Aiiiyah! Aiiiyah! Aiiiyah!"

2

BOOK ONE

1

"EARRR'UHL . . . EARR'UHL . . ."

The voice sang softly in my ear, wafting on the scent of Tube Rose snuff. It was Farette, the boardinghouse cook, waking me up.

"Aw, Farette, no . . . please."

"I got a dipper of cold water," came the voice coaxingly. "You set up and drink it, it'll wake you up. You lay dere, and I'll po' it down yo' back. Dat'll wake you up too . . .'

I pulled the pillow around me. "I was up late, Farette, I had to bring . . ."

"I was up late myself! I don't need no excuses. What I need is you outa dat bed and wakin' folks up."

It was no use. I threw off the pillow and sat up. *"Dere* he is . . . !" Farette stood beaming, a wiry little black woman with an assortment of pigtails laced across her skull.

She handed me the dipper. "Now hurry and go get 'em up, and don't forget about the new boarder." She closed the door.

The new boarder! The schoolteacher! I jumped out of bed and climbed hurriedly into my clothes.

Like everybody else in the boardinghouse, I had been aching to meet the girl who had come to marry Jayell Crooms. She had arrived the night before to begin her stay with us until Jayell could get them a house built, which was to him as important a prerequisite to a proper marriage as the wedding ceremony, if not more so.

All we knew about her was her name, Gwen Burns, that she and Jayell had met that summer while he was on the campus of the girls' college she went to in Atlanta, designing a small art center, and that she had already been hired to teach at Quarrytown High.

All the boarders were puzzled by the abruptness of Jayell's engagement, coming so quickly as it had on the heels of his broken romance with Phaedra Boggs. Jayell and Phaedra had courted for two violent years before they called a halt, and now, a mere three months after the end of that tempestuous affair, old Jayell was committed to another girl.

One of the boarders, Mrs. Metcalf, an incurable romantic, said there was no accounting for true love, it just blooms, and two people can know at first glance that they are right for each other and nobody else. It had happened that way with her and her late husband. At a house party given by a mutual friend, they had met one morning on the path to the privy, and he had tipped his hat and allowed her to precede him, and she knew in that moment that that man was made for her!

Miss Esther, more practical, said Jayell was just on the rebound from his breakup with Phaedra Boggs. It was as simple as that. Why else would he have taken the commission to design that art center in the first place? Despite his wild reputation he was still known as one of the most brilliant young architects in the state, and his services were constantly in demand, but none of the previous offers had lured him out of town, had they? No, sir, he was just so tore up over the Boggs thing he had to get away for a while, and when he got there he was ready for the first skirt that swished at him.

Fine, said jaunty little Mr. Rampey, cocking his derby, that answered for Jayell all right. Hell, it was just like Jayell to get carried away in the heat of the moment. That's the way he had joined the Marine

Corps! But what about the girl? Unless she was too ugly to walk the streets in daylight, or too dumb to read a newspaper and know that a truce had just been signed in Korea and pretty soon the place would be swarming with eligible young men, what kind of girl would latch onto Jayell . . . give up what Atlanta had to offer to move to Quarrytown?

That stumped them all.

Quarrytown was a granite-producing center in Georgia, a cluster of bleak buildings around a town square on a southern finger of the Blue Ridge Mountains. It drew its life from profitable holes sunk in the profitless cotton fields of the surrounding county. Once the town's economy had depended almost entirely on Roe Cotton Mill on the Little Iron River, and a sprawling mill village had grown in the hollow north of town where the boardinghouse was now located. It was here in 1855 that a pair of half-mad Italian brothers named Poncini sunk the granite quarry that put the town in the tombstone business, and eventually made paupers of them. That quarry never did produce enough tombstones to pay, and only caused them disruption. Although the Civil War started the Poncinis on the road to bankruptcy, it was the poor-grade granite that actually finished them off. But during Reconstruction other entrepreneurs began to cast a speculative eye toward the foothills' higher outcroppings, and by the turn of the century the county was pockmarked with the straight-sided holes, and the town had found itself an industry.

Given the somewhat higher-paying jobs in the quarries and finishing sheds, white people began moving out of the settlement to suburbs south of town, and left their shacks and mill jobs to the blacks who were pouring in from the country. Eventually, with the industrial boom following World War Two and newer, ultramodern textile plants crowding in from the Carolinas, Roe Mill began losing money. When old man Morgan Roe finally died, his heirs sold the mill to the wealthiest man in the hollow, a black undertaker named "Doc" Harley Bobo, who had already managed

8

to acquire most of the other property in the hollow. Under Doc Bobo's ownership, and near-slavery wages, the mill had not only survived but flourished.

So by that August of 1953, the hollow, long since populated mostly by black people, had become a dismal, shadowy world the people uptown referred to as the "Ape Yard," with only a handful of whites, in addition to those of us at the boardinghouse and Jayell Crooms, still living there. Up to that time Jayell was the only voluntary resident, the rest were just too poor to move anywhere else.

"Breakfast! Breakfast is ready!"

One of the chores I enjoyed least at the boardinghouse was ringing the breakfast bell. Since most of the old people were up before dawn, it was a useless ritual. And on this particular morning, the sound was unkind to the ears of someone who'd been up half the night wrestling a drunk Indian. But Miss Esther insisted on it for formality's sake, so, starting at the top of the stairs, I made the rounds, swinging the small brass handbell and stopping to make sure each boarder was awake before moving on.

"Breakfast, Mrs. Porter."

"Thank you, Earl."

"Breakfast, Mrs. Bell."

"Thank you-u-u . . ." Mrs. Bell always sang it out. She had a nice, musical voice.

"Breakfast, Mrs. Cline."

"I'm up! I'm up! *Been up!*"

"Breakfast, Mr. Rampey."

"Yeah, sport, comin' right down."

"Breakfast, Mr. Burroughs." Wait. No answer, of course. Open the door and give a quick rattle. "Mr. Burroughs—breakfast!"

"What? Oh—oh, great God!" Hurled upright on the quivering bed, blinking, working his white moustache *"Oh—great—merciful God . . ."*

Mr. Burroughs was our newest boarder. His children had taken him away from the farm out in the Four Forks community because they worried about him living alone. Then they'd sold the homeplace,

9

robbed him, he said. Bandits. And once a month he went to them to reap vengeance, preparing for those visits as though girding for battle, methodically brushing his hair and cursing softly into the mirror.

"Breakfast, Mrs. Metcalf."

"Good morning, Earl."

I opened Mr. Woodall's door and shook him awake. He was too deaf for the bell.

The last door on the hall was Mr. Jurgen's. I stopped and got ready. Look sharp here or get a cracked skull.

Mr. Jurgen was the type who would say, all right, he was awake, then roll over and go back to sleep. Then he would grumble the rest of the day about not being waked for breakfast. So I had strict orders from Miss Esther to get his feet on the floor before I left. A dangerous assignment, but one I secretly relished. It almost made the early rising worth it. Mr. Jurgen, an old-maidish retired bookkeeper, behaved as if age had distilled his faults alone, and he had arrived a nuisance, a bother, a tattler, and a snippity nag. He and I never got along.

"Breakfast, Mr. Jurgen!" I gave the door a kick and started the bell in a hard, steady rhythm.

Finally a muffled voice said, "All right, I'm awake."

I kept the bell swinging. "Breakfast, Mr. Jurgen. Time to get up, sir."

"I heard you! I'm awake!"

With my unemployed hand I took up a knocking on the door. "Get up, Mr. Jurgen. Time to *rise and shine,* sir."

The voice was a screech. "I said I'm awake, I'm awake for Christ's sake!"

Phase three. Propping a knee against the door, I let my toe alternate with the knocking of the fist, both still backed by the full orchestration of the bell.

"Get-away-from-that-goddamned-door!"

Aha! Backing off now, keeping an eye on the door-knob, I matched my voice to the Salvation Army persistence of the bell.

"Break-fast! Break-fast! Don't want-a miss your breakfast! Break-fast! Break . . ."

10

The door jerked open and his metal trash can scored another dent in the opposite wall. I was already taking the stairs three at a time.

I had forgotten to ask Farette which of the empty downstairs rooms had been assigned to the new girl, but I had no trouble finding it. She was leaning in the doorway in a white and gold kimono, her arms crossed, staring at me.

A strikingly beautiful, red-haired girl, she was a glorious sight to come upon in the dark, cavernous hallway of our boardinghouse.

She leveled cool blue eyes on me. "Don't tell me. It's *Midsummer Night's Dream,* and you're Puck. Right?"

"Ma'am?"

She snapped her fingers. 'No, it's some kind of initiation for me. You don't really do this every morning."

"Yes, ma'am, every morning. Miss Esther's orders."

"Well, I may get used to it, but I doubt it. Morning's not my best time."

"Some don't," I said, smiling. "There was one lady said she'd sooner take a room at the asylum and commute."

She didn't laugh.

"I'm Earl," I said. "I was supposed to get a taxi and meet you at the bus station last night, but something important came up."

"I understand. It's all right, I managed to get a cab all by my little self—although it wasn't easy convincing the driver that this was where I wanted to come. He seemed to think I was crazy."

I shrugged. "Don't mind that, people uptown have funny ideas about the Ape Yard. It's not so bad after you get used to it."

"I couldn't see much at night, but what *is* that awful smell?"

"Oh, that's the old Poncini quarry down the hill, but you'll get used to that too. Those of us that have lived down here awhile don't smell it at all."

11

She lifted an eyebrow. "What a strange kind of community pride."

"Jayell says you'll be teaching eighth grade. I'll be in your class this year!"

"Oh . . . really."

I nodded. "I'm only thirteen. I guess you figured me to be a little older."

"No, not really."

"Oh. Well, I know I'm *taller* than average. I've got this friend, Tio, and I'm taller than he is. Tio's about average. I guess bein' skinny makes me look smaller."

"Tell me, are you always this talkative?"

"No, I'm usually pretty quiet," I said. "Oh, I almost forgot, Jayell said to tell you he couldn't meet you himself because he got tied up out at the Fundeburk place and couldn't get away. They're tryin' to get a roof on and this rain is giving them a fit."

"Oh, well," she said, "as long as it's something—really important . . ."

"Ma'am?"

"Yes?"

"Are you really going to marry Jayell?"

She looked at me. "What do you mean by that?"

"Ah, well—it's just hard to picture somebody like you coming all the way from Atlanta to marry Jayell, I guess. You know, a lot of folks figure old Jayell to be a little—looney."

"Oh, do they now?"

"You know, the way he is, and the houses he builds. People say, the houses are crazy, he's got to be a little crazy. 'Course, I don't think so at all."

"My, what a comfort to have your confidence in my fiancé's sanity."

"No, I was talking about the houses. They're sound as a dollar. I help him build 'em sometimes. Jayell is a little crazy, and no doubt about it, but everybody thinks a lot of him."

She put her fingers to her temples. "I'm still asleep, that's what it is."

"Ma'am?"

She swung her head slowly. "None of this is really

12

happening. I'm dreaming. It's the result of a wild send-off party, a long bus ride, the ghastly specter of this dismal town looming up at me out of the dark, and a restless night in this barn of a house. That's what it is, right, Puck?"

It was my turn to look at her. Maybe I was wrong about her. She sounded just like Jayell.

Her eyes drifted to Mrs. Cline's crippled fern across the hall. "I just need time to absorb it all: what I've done, what it means . . . the change from Atlanta, the new life, the town, moving from a sorority to this place . . ."

"Sure, it'll take time. It was hard for me to get used to it too. But you'll get to like us. You know, you were kind of a pig-in-a-poke for us too."

Her shoulder came off the doorjamb. There was a hard, flat edge to her voice. "As for you, I've had just about enough. Now you listen to me. I know Jayell has some strange affinity for this place, but I only came here to humor him, and only until I can get him out of here. Personally, I find nothing romantic about living in a slum, with Negroes for my neighbors. This house is utterly depressing, and old people get on my nerves"—she leaned so close I could tell she smoked—"but not nearly so much as nosey kids who chatter about things that don't concern them! *Do* we have an understanding!"

"Ye-yes, ma'am."

" 'Ma'am' is a professional Southern term that is outdated, shopworn and phony. My name is Gwen at home, Miss Burns at school—preferably neither, whenever you can manage it. Do you have that too?"

"Yes—Gwen."

"Then-why-are-you-still-standing-there?"

I started away, then came back. "Uh-well, there was something . . . oh, I know what it was. Farette said to be sure and ask how you wanted your eggs."

She sighed. "A piece of cinnamon toast will be fine."

"I don't think Farette knows how to make that."

"Is that it, then? Eggs? Have we no other choice?"

"Well, you get to pick bacon or sausage, and there's

13

other things like grits, fritters, sliced tomatoes . . ."

"Please, I have a weak stomach in the morning. Just plain toast. Plain toast and coffee, okay?"

"We don't have loaf bread. Farette makes drop biscuits."

She pointed a red fingernail at my nose. "One egg! Poached!"

I shook my head.

"She doesn't know how to do that either," she said. I nodded.

"Help me, Puck!"

"Well, you can get it scrambled or fried. Most people take fried."

"All right! My God, I wouldn't want to completely disrupt the household! Tell Farette I will happily accept a fried egg and be most grateful! Now, if you will kindly disappear from my sight I'll get dressed and try to start this day!"

She closed the door and I started away, then stopped. I came back again and knocked. She peeked out, clutching her robe.

"Hard fried or gooshy?"

Her mouth tightened into a fine white line, and she slammed the door in my face.

Ear-r-r-r-l!" Miss Esther's voice crackled through the ceiling. I dashed into the kitchen and gave Farette the teacher's order. "Hard fried," I ordered for her, "definitely hard, with crinkledy edges," and I looked around for Miss Esther's coffee. Miss Esther had to have a cup of coffee in the morning while she dressed. Farette stood at the stove sullenly stirring a bubbling pot of grits.

"Farette, where's her coffee?"

Farette rapped her wooden spoon on the edge of the pot. "Ain't had time to be studyin' no coffee. I been on my knees wipin' up the mud I just foun' on that floor that *some*body tracked in here last night!"

Ay, Lord. I forgot.

One of my great-uncle Wylie's last acts of drunken extravagance was to buy Farette a new kitchen linoleum, a white one with cabbage-sized roses she picked

14

out herself. And no one, not even the immaculate Mrs. Bell, approaching it from outside without carefully scrubbing their feet.

"Farette, I'm sorry. I was so beat after I got home I guess I just forgot. Please, just give me the coffee. I'll mop the whole floor tonight, I promise."

Farette grudgingly pulled down a cup and poured the coffee. "Don't see why we don't just bring in pigs to raise and be done with it."

"Ear-r-r-r-r-l!"

I dumped in sugar and gave it a stir, splashing the hot liquid on my fingers in the process.

"G-o-d . . ."

"Watch now, you don't cuss yo'self out of breakfast! You know I don't feed no blasphemous mouth."

I grabbed the coffee and ran for the stairs.

Miss Esther was sitting up in bed, waist deep in her bulbous feather mattress with pillows shocked up behind her.

"Running late this morning, Mr. Whitaker."

"Yes, ma'am."

"Mr. Burroughs?"

"He's on his way."

"Mr. Jurgen?"

I grinned. "Most especially."

"Well, maybe he'll arrive by dinnertime. Don't suck your thumb, you're too big for that." I took my scalded thumb out of my mouth. Having heard the morning report, Miss Esther sniffed with satisfaction. The morning was right, the day on course. She elbowed her pillows into order and prepared to taste her coffee.

It was strange to me even then that a dilapidated house of off-cast old people could be run with such discipline and order. And probably no one could have managed it but Esther Whitaker Cahill.

I had been brought to live with my great-aunt when I was a little over five years old, after my mother and father were killed in a tenant-house fire in North Carolina. There were other relatives scattered nearby, and many of them far better off than Miss Esther, but

15

she was the only one who showed an interest in taking me in.

There was no family tree, as such, among the Whitakers. It was more like a plant bed, with each member springing from common soil, but having little else to do with each other. A disjointed clan of farmers, carpenters, mill hands and preachers, given to wasteful living, bad marriages and early deaths, their one shared family trait was a tendency not to do very well at whatever career they chose.

Esther Whitaker had high hopes of escaping that crowd and starting a new line when she took Wylie Cahill out of Duke University and eloped with him to Morehead City. Wylie was flunking his way out anyway, and she saw no cause to delay the vice-presidency awaiting him in his father's insurance company.

But Wylie never became the insurance tycoon his father and bride envisioned. Wylie was an outdoorsman who preferred hunting partridges to selling policies, and he spent his days rambling the countryside in his roadster, slapping backs at church barbecues and swapping stories over a bottle of shine at country stores, completely forgetting appointments to snatch his shotgun from the boot if he saw a sharecropper in the field with a hunting dog that looked like it knew its business.

Miss Esther would put her hands on her hips, mimicking him: " 'Insurance is a hell of a game to sell folks anyhow,' he would say! 'You got to get a man to bet you the price of the premium that he'll die before the next premium is due. It's hard to get a man to bet you he'll die before the month's out. Then he gets tired of losing month after month and having to pay the premium, and pretty soon chucks it altogether.' "

With that business philosophy and his natural habits, great-uncle Wylie managed to lose every agency his father gave him, each loss causing him to be banished farther south, and when his father finally died and he

16

inherited the company, it was no real challenge to him to lose that too.

By the time they were reduced to the storefront independent agency in Quarrytown, Miss Esther was hardened to the fact that instead of escaping to the Cahills, she had simply naturalized another Whitaker. As their financial condition worsened they began trading houses, living on the profits as they traded down, until they ended up in the two-story house with the shaded yard in the mill village hollow. Then the mill changed hands and the blacks started moving in and they were stuck. There was no profit in a sale after that.

They had one son, Vance, and his mother started in on him early, with piano, special tutoring, careful selection of his friends—but again the Whitaker genes came home to roost. Vance grew fat, took to wearing loud clothes and shied away from the daughters of prominent granite families to hang out at the square dances at Taylorsville. Urged to join social clubs in high school, he became a Future Farmer and talked artificial insemination at the table. In time he traded his piano in on an electric guitar, his years of lessons serving only to make him the only member of the Quarrytown Troubadors who could read music.

When, as a second-string lineman, Vance inadvertantly recovered a fumble and scored the touchdown that gave Quarrytown its first Class-A Championship, and his father his fatal heart attack, Miss Esther threw up her hands.

Inconsolably grieved, Vance dramatically announced that he was quitting school to understudy a tobacco auctioneer in North Carolina. Miss Esther packed his bags without a word.

Vance had since married, and now lived with his wife and their twins in Durham. They had only been to visit Miss Esther once in the eight years I had lived with her, but every year Vance did send a Christmas card, sometimes with a five-dollar bill inside, sometimes with a picture of the twins. Sometimes both.

17

On Wylie's death Miss Esther found herself in the classic widow's bind: too old to remarry, too young for a pension, too inexperienced to work, and too proud for welfare. All she had was the peeling two-story house in the growing Negro section and a good name in the community. It was one of her friends at a missionary-circle meeting who first asked Miss Esther if it wasn't lonely for her in that big house, and whether it wouldn't be a comfort to her to have the woman's aging mother occupy one of the empty bedrooms. She would be compensated, of course. Miss Esther did indeed find that a comfort, and Mrs. Deedee Cline moved in.

That let down the gate. It seemed half the church had an aging relative crowding them out of bedroom space, and the siege on Miss Esther's was mounted. Before long it was an informal nursing home, though Miss Esther preferred to call it a boardinghouse, and Farette was hired full-time to do the cooking and cleaning.

All her life a battler, and surrounded by nothing but weaklings, Miss Esther now found charges worthy of her energies. Old people. People forgotten by those who run the world, people with nothing going for them but their wills. This kind of battle Miss Esther understood, and she threw herself into it, with fire.

At Miss Esther's there was stroke and hum to a day, clash and conflict, a baiting of personality to keep its anger, its vanity, its pride alive. It was never allowed to become one of those places where old people sit and listen to the ticking away of their lives. At Miss Esther's there was humor, there was individuality, there was respect, all radiating from her own bullfiddle personality. "Don't you lay down on me!" was her threatening bedside manner, and she got them up, time and again.

Into this atmosphere she accepted me as she accepted the death of one of her boarders, a fact to be dealt with, to be fitted into the total thrust of order. But I was young, and needed little attention, so she tucked me away in the household and left me to grow, so long as I caused no trouble.

I did cause trouble at first, and a good deal of it. For a while Miss Esther thought she was going to have to ask the state to take me off her hands, and she couldn't be blamed for that; even Dr. Breisner thought I was going to need treatment.

But, of course, that was all in the first dark, turbulent winter—before that magical time when the giant Indian loomed in the doorway—with his fierce, scowling eyes, skin the color of old china, and dried rat's blood on the soles of his boots.

"Well," Miss Esther was saying, "did you meet the new schoolteacher?"

"Did I? She's the reason I'm late." I raised the shades.

She blew on her coffee, watching me closely. "What'd you think of her?"

"I'd say she's made to order for Jayell Crooms. She couldn't even make up her mind on what she wanted for breakfast!"

Miss Esther chuckled. "Yep, Yayell marries that one, he's in for a lively time."

"What'd Jayell want her to stay down here for? I'd think somebody like that would be a lot happier in an apartment uptown."

"Well, of course she would! *I'd* be a lot happier uptown! Anybody would but Jayell. He said he knew she wouldn't, so he's looking for a lot over in Marble Park, but since he's goin' to keep his shop down here and keep on buildin' houses for these blacks and country folks, he says it won't hurt her to get to know the kind of people he's goin' to be dealin' with. And too, I think he's testing her a little."

"Testing her?"

"Rubbing her nose in the kind of life she's going to have if he marries him. Jayell comes from a mighty poor family, and it's poor people he's wantin' to help. She might have just a little too much gloss to suit him."

19

"Hnh! I'd say he's goin' to have a time rubbing any of it off."

Miss Esther smiled. "Could be you're right, Mr. Whitaker. Could be you're right."

"It's sure hard to figure, a girl like that falling for Jayell Crooms."

"Well, I hear he caused quite a stir up at that college, had 'em all flocking around him. The head of the school made a big to-do over the building he drew up for him, had other architects over to look at it, trumped him up for some kind of genius, had him speak to the art classes, that kind of thing. And you know Jayell, the way he talks, the way he looks, I expect he was quite a change from all those professors with the button-down collars, especially at a girls' college where there ain't a whole lot of competition. It ain't too hard to figure them little small-town gals goin' crazy over him. At that age they'll fall in love with anything strange."

"I wonder what it's like, being in love."

"I wouldn't know. All I ever had was Wylie, and that was more like owning a dog. Who sugared this coffee?"

"I did . . . one spoonful . . ."

"Well, get Farette to show you the difference between a teaspoon and a tablespoon." She shivered and set the cup on the bedside table. She looked up sharply. "The others haven't met her yet, have they?"

"Not this morning. Didn't they see her when she got in last night?"

"It was past their bedtime. Besides, it's more proper they meet at breakfast"—she threw her feet over the side of the bed and felt for her scuffs—"which, by the way, we don't want to miss."

"Miss Esther, you think it was a good idea letting her come here? I don't know how the boarders are going to take her."

Her eyes narrowed mischievously. "Like a dose of medicine, is my guess. From what Jayell told me about her, and what I saw last night, I'd say she's just what this crowd needs right now. Wake 'em up a

20

little, get their minds off themselves. There's been entirely too much achin' and complainin' around here lately. And havin' a teacher around awhile might do you some good too, from what I saw of your grades last year. Let's get to breakfast."

"Ah—I'm not too hungry this morning. I think I'll run out to the Fundeburk place and let Jayell know she's here."

"He knows. He'll come when he's ready."

"He might have forgot—you know how he is when he's workin' . . ."

"There's a place waiting at table, mister!"

"Yes, ma'am."

I stopped at the door. "Oh, I got Em Jojohn home all right. He's sleeping it off now."

Mis Esther shook her head. "Just try and keep him away from the house a few days. That girl's got enough to get used to."

'Yes, ma'am."

2

I TOOK A DEEP BREATH AND HEADED FOR THE DINING room.

Places at the table were claimed by the boarders on arrival at Miss Esther's, and held for life. With the exception, of course, of the transient Mrs. Porter. No place suited her, and no sooner was she seated than she was prevailing on someone to swap. The sun was in her eyes. Her chair had a bit of a "rick." Or, couldn't she sit near the hall, as she was expecting a telephone call.

My place, when I was forced to take it, was between Mrs. Bell and Mr. Rampey. Mr. Rampey was a good soul, but a spot finder. On his plate, his glass, the silverware, somewhere at every meal he found a little speck of something and summoned Farette in a rage. She gave up inspecting his dinnerware beforehand because that left the offending speck no place to hide but in the food—and that upset the others.

Still, I was in a more enviable place than the teacher, because she was next to Mrs. Cline. Once Mr. Rampey found his particle he was satisfied, but Mrs. Cline's taste reports went right on through the meal. "Now, I can't taste the beans at all today," she would say, or, across the table to Mrs. Bell, "Can you taste this creamed corn, Lucia? Well, I can't. It just has no taste to me whatever." Sadly, "It's so awful not to be able to taste anything." Brightening then, reassuring us all, "Now I can taste the beets, they're good." Mrs. Cline, our oldest boarder, lived in a room stripped bare except for a bed and a marble-topped night table on which a photograph of her husband in his casket stood surrounded by stalky African violets. She was near ninety now, and fragile-looking as a glass cobweb. She seemed always at death's door, tugging, and just too weak to get it open. At least, that's what we thought, until Em Jojohn, of whom she was terrified, delivered something one day and looked in her room without knocking; she hoisted a heavy potted plant, dirt and all, and splintered the doorjamb above his head.

I saw Gwen about to pass the sausage to Mrs. Metcalf, and tried to warn her, but couldn't get her eye quick enough.

"Oh! My goodness, no." Mrs. Metcalf recoiled in laughing horror. "None of that for me. I'm allergic, you know."

"Oh, really?"

"Why, my, yes, if I took so much as one little bite of pork I'd be flat on my back in the hospital. I can't eat acid fruit, green vegetables, milk or any kind of dairy, and if I so much as touch a piece of beef my ankles swell out to here."

"I'm sorry."

"Listen, last Thanksgiving I tried a boiled onion— you remember, Nadine—well, I couldn't get my breath! Mr. Rampey had to help me to my room! And for days after, I had this peculiar swimmy feeling, and saw these spots. Awfulest thing I've ever been through! I thought it would be all right, boiled, don't you know. But, oh, let me tell you didn't I suffer—ha-ha—from, oh, that boiled onion!"

Gwen looked at the woman's empty plate, empty cup, undisturbed dinnerware. "Well, what can you eat?" she asked.

Mrs. Metcalf folded her hands in her lap and shrugged. "Nothing," she said.

The teacher looked around the table, but nobody else wanted to get into it.

"Awww-riiight!" Miss Esther, announcing her arrival. She nodded good morning to everyone and took her place at the head of the table. "I hope the introductions have been taken care of," she said to Gwen.

"Said what? Said what?" croaked poor deaf Mr. Woodall.

Miss Esther turned to him. "I said *good morning, Mr. Woodall!*"

The old man nodded and smiled. "And to you, Miss Esther."

Her eyes traveled around the table and stopped on the allergic and abstaining Mrs. Metcalf. With iron in her voice, she barked, *"Eat,* Portia!" Mrs. Metcalf jerked upright and immediately began serving her plate.

"Tell us, Miss Burns, have you and Jayell set a date yet?"

"Sometime next summer, if we can decide on a house by that time."

"Oh, then you'll be with us for the winter."

"Perhaps," Gwen said, with a hint of petulance in her voice. "Of course, I haven't heard from Mr. Crooms in more than a week. I assume our plans haven't changed."

Mr. Rampey chuckled. "If you ain't heard from Jayell in the last five minutes the plans could be changed."

"Mr. Rampey . . ." Miss Esther was interrupted by

a knock on the window behind her. She leaned back and threw up the sash. It was Wash Fuller, the black man who lived across the road.

"Sorry to trouble you, Miss Esther," he said, "but my dog Jincey is up under your house. Do you mind if I beat on this pan to get her out?"

"Not at all, Wash. Do you want me to stomp on the floor a little?"

"If it wouldn't be no extra trouble."

So Miss Esther got up and stomped around on the dining-room floor as she continued the conversation. "Where was I? Oh, yes, have you decided where you're going to live?"

"No, not yet. I passed a beautiful suburb on the way in last night.'

"That would be Marble Park. Jayell figured you'd like it up there." Stomp Stomp. *"Yoooo—Jincey! Get out of there!"* Underneath, Wash Fuller could be heard crawling along beating on the pan. "Well, I don't know if they'd let Jayell build one of his houses up in Marble Park. Pretty straight-laced folks up there."

"These grits are flat," said Mrs. Cline, "no taste whatever. She must not have put any salt in them."

"Well," said the schoolteacher, "Jayell and I have differing views on . . ."

"Mr. Rampey, would you swap with me?" asked Mrs. Porter. "There's a naked colored child on that porch over yonder. I can't eat and look at that."

"Marble Park is not bad," said Miss Esther. Stomp. "If you can stand the strain. Too many Joneses up there for my taste, if you know what I mean." Stomp. *"Get from here, dog!"*

"Ah, ha!" shouted Mr. Rampey, scooping a forkful of scrambled eggs and wavering a long knobby finger. "Look there, now, what is that? Farette!"

The little cook came running frm the kitchen, snatched the fork from his hand, replaced it with another one, and retreated without a word.

Gwen closed her eyes and put her napkin to her

lips. I forked another sausage patty, beginning to be glad I came.

"Jayell's got different views from a lot of people," chirped Mrs. Cline. "I guess you know by now he's got his . . . ways . . ."

Gwen picked up on that as if she had been waiting for it. "All people of exceptional ability have their . . . 'ways.' They only seem curious if you don't understand them."

"You feel you know Jayell well enough to take him on, then, do you?" said Mrs. Porter.

The girl took a sip of coffee. "I know that we're compatible. We lived together almost the whole time he was on campus."

Seven old people turned to stone.

Mrs. Metcalf cleared her throat but nothing came.

Mr. Woodall lived in a world of soft buzzing voices, which for the most part he happily ignored. Only two things got his attention: a sound loud enough for him to hear clearly, and a dead silence. He now cupped a hand to his ear. "Said what? Said what?"

"Is—uh, is that the way they're doing things at the colleges these days," asked Mrs. Porter, "living together before they're married?"

"It's the way they're doing it everywhere," said the girl, "and always have. We're just not so hypocritical about it anymore."

"Well," crooned Mrs. Metcalf, "I've known Jayell since he was a boy. I know he wasn't raised that way."

Miss Esther stood at the window watching eagerly as the tension built. "The thing about Jayell," she said, stomp, "is that he needs to be led. With a good woman a-hold of him, he'll come out of his wildness. How you coming, Wash?" There was a tap on the window and Wash Fuller appeared holding the dog in his arms. He waved his thanks and went away. Miss Esther didn't see him. Her concentration was fixed on the proceedings at the table.

"That's true," said Mrs. Bell, "a good woman's influence can sometimes work wonders with a man."

"That's true enough, especially in Jayell's case," said

25

Mrs. Metcalf. "I know what happened when his mama died."

Mrs. Cline tapped Gwen's arm. "Are you a Georgia girl, honey? You don't sound like a Georgia girl."

"You mean, because I don't have a Southern accent?" said the girl, distracted but obviously pleased. "I know, people tell me they'd never know I was from Georgia. I suppose it's because I'm from Atlanta."

"Atlanta's in Georgia," stated Mr. Jurgen.

"Atlanta is *not* Georgia," she smilingly corrected him. Then, turning again to Mrs. Metcalf, "What was that you were saying about Jayell's mother dying?"

"Oh, well, like I said, I've known Jayell since he was a little boy. They lived right next door to us, just down by the creek down there. It was a pitiful family. His daddy was a ledgehand at one of the quarries, that is, when he worked. Lay drunk most of the time. If it wasn't for his mother and her sewing I expect they'd all have starved. Jayell was the only child they had, and oh, such a precious little boy. Used to go set and draw while the other mill young'uns was rippin' and snortin' and gettin' in devilment. Day after day I'd see him settin' on the bank in front of his house, that little blond head bent over his tablet, drawin'. And smart! His teachers said they never saw anything like it. Always in his books, and settin' and drawin'. His mama would walk him uptown to check art books out of the library. I remember one Christmas she bought him a whole set of books on art, ordered 'em special from Atlanta, and, Lord, you never seen a happier child! Had to come over to my house and show 'em to me three or four times. I used to brag on him a lot, you know. But then she died, and he just went to pieces."

"Went to pieces?"

"Started to act plumb crazy. He was startin' to high school about then, and at a wild age anyhow, and when she died he cut loose. He'd always had a trigger temper, jumped the man at the furniture store one time for sayin' something hateful to his mama when he wasn't no more'n twelve or thirteen. Busted a lamp over that man's head! Well, when she died he started gettin' in one scrap after another, he broke windows, he stole things, he took his daddy's car and wrecked it. He got throwed out of school several times, but he always went and begged for 'em to let him back in. His mind was made up to go to college, you see. 'Course, everybody else said he was goin' to jail. 'Specially his daddy. He and Jayell had a time of it. Billy Crooms was always onto Jayell to lay out of school and work. He was plannin' on Jayell quittin' altogether just as soon as he was old enough, but Jayell was having none of that. They got into it time and again over it till finally Billy just throwed Jayell out of the house. Jayell got Luther Pierce to rent him that little place by the creek and started him a fix-it business. You'd see him down there three, four o'clock in the morning fixing somebody's chair or alarm clock and poring over his books. He stuck it out too, and finished high school when he was just past sixteen. Made the highest marks they said anybody'd ever made in Quarrytown High."

"Ah, but a hell-raiser," laughed Mr. Rampey. "You remember that thing about the water tower?"

Mrs. Metcalf put her hands to her mouth. "Oh, I'd almost forgot about that!"

Mr. Rampey continued eagerly. "One night he and some boys had been drinkin', and he got 'em to lower him from a rope on the water tower and painted this great big picture of the school superintendent and his wife, without any clothes on, and he had 'em . . ."

Miss Esther cut in. "I don't think we need all the details, Lester." Stomp.

"Anyhow," laughed Mr. Rampey, "the likeness was so exact there couldn't have been any doubt whose work it was, even if Jayell hadn't been fool enough to sign it."

The table roared with laughter, everybody except Gwen, who sat listening, frowning.

"Farette," called Mrs. Cline, "did this sausage come seasoned or did you season it?"

27

Farette put her head in the door. "It come seasoned, Miz Cline."

"Well, it's certainly not seasoned enough." She lifted her eyebrows at me. "I can't tell if it's hot or mild."

"I don't think Jayell would have got in half the trouble he did," said Mrs. Porter, "if he wasn't so all-fired cocky. He always knowed he was the sharpest tack in the carpet, and expected folks to take notice of that."

"Now, that's a fact," said Mrs. Metcalf. "I know the time he's accused of gettin' Sheriff Middleton's daughter in trouble, when the sheriff come bustin' down to see him it was Jayell that flew into the greatest fit of temper; he was astounded that anybody would think him that stupid! He took on so the girl finally broke down and confessed it was Harvey Oates's boy that done it." She turned to Mrs. Bell. "Whatever become of them? I know he used to work at the telegraph office."

"What astounds me," said Gwen, sighing, "is that genius is never recognized by those closest to it. That's one reason I chose to become a teacher. To think of the undiscovered potential that must go to waste . . ."

"Oh," said Mrs. Metcalf, "there wasn't no question about Jayell's potential! With all the awards and honors he won? Why, the whole town was behind him. They got him scholarships to go to Georgia Tech—several of the civic clubs raised money. I guess that's why it was such a disappointment to them that he didn't turn out like they thought he ought to."

"How do you mean?"

"A millionaire," said Mr. Rampey, "buildin' mansions for millionaires. They couldn't understand him chuckin' it all and comin' back to the Ape Yard to break his back buildin' houses for sharecroppers and colored folks."

"Well," sighed Gwen, "with a background like that it's no wonder he's never found himself. With a little understanding and proper guidance . . ."

"Oh, he's found hisself, all right," said Mr. Rampey.

28

"Jayell knows exactly what he wants to do—and he's doin' it."

"I don't understand you all," said Gwen, looking around at them. "Here is a man reputed to have the most intuitive head for architectural design since possibly Wright himself, who, when he was on our campus, had students and professors sitting at his feet! And yet he buries himself in this town, wasting his talents on, as you say, sharecroppers and colored people, and you find nothing unusual in that!"

My eye fell on Miss Esther, who stood by the window keyed-up, eyes sparkling, watching closely, still absently stomping the floor off and on for the long-gone dog.

The girl's voice rose. "You all seem to regard him as some harmless but slightly demented creature who's playing some extraordinary game!"

Mr. Rampey cleared his throat. "Now, wait a minute . . ."

Mrs. Bell put a hand on his arm. "I think we should change the subject, now, don't you?"

"Young lady, I believe you've misunderstood us," said Mrs. Metcalf.

"I think the misunderstanding has been on your part," the girl shot back.

"Uh—please." Mrs. Bell was leaning forward.

The girl fairly shouted, "Here is an absolute genius, and you talk about him like he's some kind of fool!"

The volume having gotten to a level to attract Mr. Woodall again, he cupped a hand to his ear:

"Said what? Said what?"

"I can't eat." Mr. Jurgen shoved aside his fork.

"Well, come to think of it," said Mr. Rampey, "he's both, a genius and a fool, you just got to know which one you're talkin' to."

Ohhh . . ." Gwen threw down her napkin.

'*Yoo,* Jincey!" Miss Esther clapped her hands.

'Have you decided, Miss Burns," Mrs. Bell was saying eagerly, "what kind of house you and Jayell are going to build?"

29

"I may not wait for that! I might just move in with him at the shop—tonight!"

She shoved away from the table and was getting to her feet when suddenly there was a shout from outside, the back door slammed, and in the next instant a compactly built young man was leaping through the door, his shaggy blond hair flying. Gwen gave a little squeal as he crushed her against his dirty denim clothes and whirled her across the room, burying his sunburned, boyish face in her neck, kissing her lips, her hair, her shoulders.

"Better ease off, Jayell," Miss Esther chuckled. Stomp. "There's coronaries in this room."

"You can quit stomping now," reminded Mr. Rampey.

"Jayell!" The girl struggled out of his arms. "My GOD—what . . . where have you been!"

Jayell released her and stalked around the table watching her, his sleepless eyes glistening deep in their darkened sockets. "My God, look at her . . ." He bent over Mr. Rampey's shoulder. "Ain't she sump'n, Ramp? What'd I tell you, huh?" He turned his head and whispered something in Mr. Rampey's ear, and the old man burst into laughter.

"Jayell!" Gwen was furious. "Why didn't you write, why didn't you call? Do you realize it's been over a week . . ."

"A thousand reasons, princess." He limped toward her and stopped, resting his weight on the slightly shorter left leg that cocked his hips at an angle, and looked her up and down. "And not one of them good enough.' And suddenly he was kissing her again.

"Not here," she said, pulling away, "come . . ."

"No time."

"Let's go to my room where we can at least . . ."

"I missed you," he said, squeezing her shoulders as if to reassure himself that she was real, "missed you awful bad."

She tried to calm her voice. "I missed you too, Jayell." She glanced at the others, who sat watching

30

contentedly as though they'd paid to see the show. "Please, let's get out of here."

"Ain't she fantastic!" Jayell cried.

"Jayell, will you please stop displaying me like a side of beef! For heaven's sake, will you come . . ."

"Sorry, honey, I just can't. I've got boys waiting in the truck."

"What!"

Jayell turned and picked up a sausage patty and bit into it. "Critical. Got to get a roof dried in before the rain starts up again or I'm going to have a house full of water."

"Well, at least sit down and rest a minute. You look like you haven't slept for days. It's a miracle you're not dead of pneumonia! Look at your shoes, they're soaked!"

Jayell winked at Mr. Rampey. "How quick they start giving you hell, huh, Ramp. Oh, God!" Suddenly remembering, he lifted a mud-caked brogan and looked at it and stuck his head into the kitchen. "Sorry, Farette, I'm sorry, darlin'." There was an angry rattle of pans in the kitchen. "I better get out of here."

"Jayell, it's Sunday . . . I've just arrived . . ."

"I know, honey, and I'm sorry, but believe me, this just can't wait. I'll make it up to you, I promise." He kissed her quickly. "Pick you up at seven o'clock. "Wear something pretty, now." He was halfway out the door.

"Wait! At least tell me how to dress . . . where are we going?"

Jayell looked at her, puzzled by the question. "You said yourself—it's Sunday. To church, of course." And he was gone.

The girl looked down at the benevolently smiling faces, back at the empty door. Tears of frustration welled in her eyes. She touched a hand to her forehead and turned to leave—and bumped headlong into Mr. Burroughs, groping in on his nickel-mounted cane.

31

"Careful, miss!" he cried. "Don't hurt me! I'm going to see my children and I need my strength!" Gwen drew back from the towering figure, then tried to squeeze by. He seized her arm and demanded, "Have you children, young woman?" She bit her lip and shook her head, edging. "Good! Have none, then! What good is a family? Bloodsucking kin? You can have mine at a good price, I'll tell you! When I was slaving at that farm for them from dawn to dark it was 'papa' this and 'papa' that. Couldn't slam a door without knocking three of 'em down! But let me get a few years on me and they sell my homeplace from under me and start diggin' up the shrubs and killin' one another over the dishes!"

With a wrench the girl pulled free and backed into the hall, sobbing. She kept it up all the way to her room.

Mr. Burroughs stood blinking after her, slowly re-settling his teeth.

"Mighty high-strung, ain't she?" ventured Mr. Rampey.

"I know what's wrong with that one," said Miss Esther, and she threw back her head and bawled, "Far-rette! *Where's the Cardui?*"

After breakfast I filled a lard can with leftovers from the table and made my way down to the ramshackle garage and climbed the stairs to the loft. Em Jojohn was still asleep, the flimsy iron cot bowed under his weight. I got a fire going in the trash burner and put the coffee on to heat. After Miss Esther's dining room, the loft was balm for the soul.

The garage sat in the woods between the boarding-house and Teague's grocery on the next dirt street down. Nearby was the well and the ruins of a burned-out house, the chimney and crumbled foundation barely visible through the devouring undergrowth. The garage had been unused for years until the Indian stumbled on it, sulphured out the rats and moved into the loft. We furnished it with a cot, a second-hand trash burner, an army footlocker and a lady's

32

dressing table with the mirror gone, plus one of Miss Esther's lawn chairs. I brought him a Coca-Cola calendar and a Lone Ranger bread poster to decorate the walls.

I suppose I liked it best because it was alive, almost at one with the wind and the trees. Aunt Esther's was a heavy, solidly constructed old house, so insulated you couldn't even hear the rain. But in the loft there were insects buzzing, birds lighting on the tin, creatures ticking in the walls, the worry of wind and the sounds of old timbers stretching themselves in the afternoon heat, the startling bang of a pecan hitting the roof.

Instead of the sterile odors of furniture polish and sachet, the loft had a warm, animal smell, mixed with the scent of khakis overdue for the wash, a ham hanging overhead from a wire, the musty creek-water smell of fishing gear, the clayey smell of his canvas traveling bag, and a banana somewhere, getting too ripe. And on winter mornings, after spending the night there, as I sometimes did, to wake to the sound of snow spitting at the roof and the smell of strong chicoried coffee and fatback sizzling in the skillet was something not soon forgotten.

It was always good being in the loft. I would go there sometimes, even when Em was on the road, to dodge chores or get out from underfoot at the house, which I was ordered to do often, or just to be alone. I suppose everyone, at some time, has a Place, or dreams of one. The loft was mine.

Em Jojohn yawned and turned on the groaning cot. I got up and stood out of the way. Those first few mornings after a trip on the road, Em asleep was an uncertain animal. He opened his eyes and looked at me.

"Am I in hell, or Georgia?" he rumbled.

"Georgia," I said, playing the game.

Em shook his head. "That devil done tricked me again."

While Em ate I plied him with questions about where he had gone this time, most of which he answered with a simple headshake. "Florida? Did you go down to Florida this time? Worked a fishing boat maybe."

Negative.

"Up North then, bet you went up to New York or someplace."

Em made a face. *"Sheeee!* New York. Went to New York oncet, that'uz enough. Worst hell hole you ever see. Never comes a morning in that place—just gets light and dark, with people hanging around from the night before. Street maggots. Deliver me from that place."

Em opened up some then. He had just rambled up through the Carolinas, he said. Unloaded trucks at a warehouse in Greensboro for a while, cropped some tobacco on the coast, tied some reinforcing steel in a bridge in Virginia.

"Did you have any trouble?" I would have known the answer even if I hadn't noticed the fresh raw scar on his neck. Em always had trouble. It dogged him like his shadow.

"Nothing to speak of."

"Where'd you get that?"

"Ah—" Em rubbed the scar. "Outside of Richmond one morning. I was walking along minding my business and the blue boys stopped me. Wanted to lock me up for a check-out. You know how it is."

I knew. Em the drunk, the brawler, the heckler had spent time in "crossbar hotels" from Washington to Pascagoula. Violence was simply part of his abrasive nature, as natural as his breath. Sometimes he instigated it himself as a sociable attempt to relieve boredom, but most often it just came at him by some strange attraction I never understood. People moved away from him almost instinctively. A sleeping dog would lift his head at his scent, lay back his ears, and the next moment be standing at the end of his chain, salivating, gnawing the air. That, added to his enormous size and dubious color, made him suspicious to police everywhere. He had been in so many conflicts with small-town deputies that the mere sight of a badge started him backing and bristling.

"What happened?" I asked. "Did they lock you up?"

He shook his head, reflecting. "I don't like to be locked up." His mood was darkening. I knew the limit and asked no more questions. He ate in silence.

Em was from an obscure tribe in eastern North Carolina. Hadn't any name, he claimed at first. When I pressed, he said they'd been called several names; the last he heard, they were petitioning to be called Lumbees. Asked to teach me some Indian words, he said they hadn't any language either. And that was about all he would ever say about being an Indian.

Em had just turned up at the boardinghouse one day about seven years ago asking if there was work he could do for something to eat. Standing in the doorway, he was so large he blotted out the sun. I hid under the table. Miss Esther said if he didn't go away she'd call the police, and slammed the door in his face.

She busied herself in the kitchen until she was calm again, then looked out the window and made a little sound in her throat. She jerked the door open again and there he stood. This time she used language I hadn't heard her use since Wash Fuller's dog came to hide in her kitchen. The Indian stood resting his weight on one foot and took the abuse like he was used to it, and waited for her to expend herself. When she did, her humor returned. "Aside from scaring people to death, just what kind of work do you do?"

He was an ironworker before he got too heavy to climb the iron, he told her. Now he took whatever he came across. Lately he had been killing rats.

"Well, we've got the rats," Miss Esther said. Indeed, most of the houses in the Ape Yard were infested with them, big ones, that turned and sized you up before they scuttled away. She would feed him until he cleared the place.

She brought him a plate of leftover catfish, but the Indian backed away and shook his head. "Can't eat fried food," he said, "bad stomach." Miss Esther snorted and offered him what was left of the ham

35

hock. Another headshake. "Too much fat. What you got in the way of greens?"

Miss Esther was aghast. "Well, this is my first encounter with a bum on a diet. Next thing, you scoundrels will want menus posted on the blessed door!" But she rummaged in the safe again, and this time brought him a bowl of beans and boiled potatoes. The Indian's cheeks parted in a broad, uneven smile. He stepped off the porch and settled himself under one of the fig bushes. But before eating he held up his fork, inspected it carefully, jabbed it in the ground a few times and wiped it on his shirt. The back door closed with an emphasis that rattled the china.

He became a familiar sight around the place with his traps and poisons, and after the rats were gone he began a cleaning operation. When the yards and garden shed were spotless, he invaded the house. He took on the attic, a mass of mildew, cobwebs, and all the indescribable junk attics accumulate, and in two days it was immaculate. He cleaned every room in the house, moving furniture and clearing closet shelves, scouring and dusting and stacking back exactly as it was. He even scoured the black off of Farette's seasoned skillets, which put him on slim rations for a while.

But for being such a stickler for neatness, he never gave a thought to himself. His shirt cuffs were buttonless and flapping, his pants always wrinkled, and his belt buckle continually working toward one hipbone or the other. The single exception was his army-surplus paratrooper boots, which he kept polished to a mirror shine. Every night he carefully washed away all traces of mud or rat's blood and worked in another coat of wax. When we went frog gigging or scrounging in the dump for scrap iron, he protected them from getting scratched by tying them around his neck. When he gashed his big toe to the bone on a piece of broken glass one day I said I supposed then he would put them on. He shook his head and wound the bleeding toe in a rag. "Toe'll cure up. Boots won't."

The business about the bad stomach, I discovered,

was a fraud. It was simply one of the repertoire of tricks he used to get his way, to make people deal with him on his terms. Em never gave an inch on anything. He did exactly as he pleased, when it suited him to do it, and he could be depended on for nothing more. He would be responsible to no one but himself. "To do anything you don't want to do or be anyplace you don't want to be is a sign of low character," he said, "in fact, it's a downright sin agin' nature."

He dealt with people as little as possible, and only then when it was unavoidable, or when he wanted something from them. Anything smacking of officialdom turned him cold. He refused to be listed, numbered, or have his name appear in anyone's files, even to the point of not applying for a driver's license, a temptation he avoided simply by not learning to drive. Faced with the absolute necessity of having a Social Security card for construction work, he at last relented, and applied, under the name of George Washington. Once, while doing my homework, I absently scribbled his name on the edge of the page. When he saw it he grew restless, kept looking at it, and as soon as my back was turned he tore it off and stuffed it in his pocket. It was *his* name, part of him. Because I accepted Jojohn as he was, and expected nothing of him, he and I got along.

He liked the Ape Yard, and the black people there liked him, but he seldom ventured uptown. Before long he had beaten down a path to the garage from the street below, turning off by Teague's grocery and coming up the deep gulley from the rear, thus avoiding the house. This route he used mostly when drunk, or when coming home in bloody rags from one of the river joints, or when he just didn't feel like being seen from the house. He did chores around the place and came to the house occasionally for meals, but kept mostly beyond the wild grown hedges. Then, if he didn't show up for a few days and no bursts of country music from his portable radio came over the trees, you could assume Em was on one of his trips, and look for him when you saw him coming.

The only trouble was, those trips seemed to do something awful to him, and for two or three nights after his return he went through a special kind of agony. To endure it, or release it, I never knew which, he always got drunk, bitter, vicious, roaring drunk, during which time he would lash out like an animal suffering in a trap, at me or anybody else. In the daytime he seemed all right, his old self. but at sundown it would come on him again, and he would change from the Em I knew to some frightening creature in torment, hurting so bad he was dangerous to be near. When he'd gotten himself tanked up and stumbled off into the woods, there was nothing I could do, despite my deep hatred of the woods at night, but follow him along the darkened riverbank until the frenzy abated, and, when it was safe enough, try and lead him home.

When he had finished eating, Em rolled a smoke from his Prince Albert can and worried out a belch. "Well, now that you've pumped me dry, what's been happenin' around here?"

"Nothin' much," I said, "except for the school-teacher."

"Schoolteacher?"

"Yeah, guess what—she's come here to marry Jayell Crooms!"

Em put down his cup. "Where'd that big a fool come from?"

"Atlanta, he met her while he was at the college this summer."

"College! Jayell? And ain't much goin' on, he says!"

"Yeah, the college hired Jayell to design this little art center for them. It was written up in the *Star* and everything. And while he was up there he met this girl and they fell in love. She's at the boarding-house now."

"How's old Phaedra Boggs takin' all that?"

"They say she didn't take it too good."

"Well, yer teacher must be sump'n else to pull him away from that Boggs gal. She's rough as a cob, but there ain't no finer lookin' woman nowhere. Boy, that's some gal!"

"Well, the teacher ain't all that bad lookin' neither. Kinda pinchy about the eyes, but she's got good legs."

"Legs! Listen to him. What you know about legs, boy?"

"I know more'n you give me credit for."

"Oooooh, man." Em stretched himself out on the cot. "Talkin' 'bout legs, mine's still achin'. Had to walk that last stretch from Little Holland yestiddy. How 'bout you breakin' along and lettin' me rest 'em a little."

I got up to leave. "Oh, by the way, Jayell's been asking about you. He sure needs some help gettin' Lilly Waugh's house finished up."

"Lilly Waugh's house? Y'all ain't done with that one yet?"

"Well, he lost three months bein' up at the college, just runnin' back to do what he could on the weekends, and on her house it's been mostly just me and him since she won't let his black boys set foot on the place."

Em's eyes were closed. "Don't know's I want to set foot on Lilly Waugh's place agin, neither. That woman gives me the fan-tods."

"Well, anyhow it's all done now but the trim work. if you change your mind you can let him know tonight—" I stopped, remembering Miss Esther's admonition to keep him away a few days. But then, I thought of the girl in the hall, and looked at Em, and I couldn't resist it. Besides, church might be good for Em that night, with him just back off the road. "He's coming to take her to church tonight. *To church*, Em." I took the cigarette from his dangling fingers and stubbed it out. "Sure would be good to go to *church* again, wouldn't it, Em? Bet you haven't been the whole summer."

"Church." Em smiled sleepily. "Some peculiar things happen in church. You know, some years back I went

39

in this little backwoods church in Tennessee—just passin' by one Sunday e'nin' and thought I'd drop in for services. Well, I noticed one of the front pews was missing, and I seen that when folks had to walk around that place they'd kind of shy away from it, wouldn't even steps on the nail holes in the floor . . ."

I started cleaning up the breakfast things. It was one of his long rambling stories I had heard a dozen times before. I emptied the coffee cup and rinsed it out and repacked Farette's lard can.

". . . so I ast somebody, 'Why's that pew been took out, and them folks actin' so skittish around that place?' Well, they didn't want to talk to me about it right off, me bein' a stranger, I guess. You know how mountain folks are . . ."

I closed the screen door and tiptoed down the stairs, his voice trailing.

"But finally they told me. Some years back, they said, there was a deacon, man by the name of Hoover, they said, that suspected his wife of carryin' on with another member of the church. Well, one night, right in the middle of services . . ."

I lost his voice in the afternoon hum and crick of the woods. If there's one thing I can't stand, it's to hear a story over and over again.

3

TRUE TO HIS LORD, JAYELL ARRIVED PROMPTLY AT seven o'clock. Gwen Burns swirled into the parlor in a crisp white dress, complete with hat and gloves. When she saw me waiting on the couch, all decked out in my sport coat and clip-on bow tie, she looked surprised but said nothing.

When I followed them out and got in the back of

the truck, she looked even more surprised—and said something.

"All right, what the hell's going on here?"

"Oh, him?" said Jayell. "It's all right, Miss Esther said he could go."

"Jayell! This is our first time together since I arrived. I've already seen more of him than I've seen of you!"

"Aw, what's it going to hurt to give the boy a lift to church? He don't go enough as it is. Wasn't for me and the Indian he'd probably never darken the door."

Gwen sighed. "Whatever you say, dear."

She would find that Jayell took his fundamentalist credo seriously. Unpredictable as he was, his wildness was just as often counterpointed with the beliefs his mother instilled in him as a child. He had taught shop at the high school, and although he kept a whiskey bottle under his desk, he submitted to a request by the Holiness preacher's boy and started the whole year's classes with devotionals. He slept on a cot in the rear of his workshop, sometimes with a woman, once with two, limped along the streets in unironed clothes, gambled and caroused with the worst kinds of people, black and white, drank and fought with Em and the quarry ledgehands along the river joints, but he never, ever missed church. He turned down a lucrative contract to build a guest cottage for a rich quarry owner's wife, and instead built a beautiful little Catholic chapel, free of charge, for the Italian stonecutters at Glenshade. He devoted an entire summer to crafting animal bunk beds, again without pay, for the orphans at Tucker Village, but while the Jaycees were waiting at the banquet to name him "Man of the Year," he was being hauled drunk and naked from the post office platform with a lady who traveled with a gospel quartet.

I saw Gwen was carrying a Book of Common Prayer. "Are you Catholic?"

"Episcopalian"—she slammed the door until it caught—"and you're all Baptists, I suppose."

"All but Mr. Rampey. He's a lapsed Lutheran. Oh,

41

and Mrs. Metcalf, she's a Christian Scientist. She takes a drink now and then, but she swears it's *not* for medicinal purposes."

"I should hope."

"Myself, I've never joined any church."

"I'll pray for you."

"Oh, that ain't to say I don't attend. I attend a lot, thanks to Jayell and Em. Miss Esther don't care which ones, as long as they're fairly hardshell."

Actually I'd never spent enough time in any one church to develop a preference. Mostly I went with Em, and that exposed me to quite a variety. Usually we visited the off-brand tabernacles out in the country, crossing denominational lines without favoritism, except for those with a little extra whoop and holler, or maybe an all-night sing. At Miss Esther's church uptown, historic Pinnacle Baptist, it was tame as bathwater. The minister spoke softly, the congregation listened politely, and when somebody joined the church they just strolled down the aisle and shook the preacher's hand and the congregation voted them in, and, well, there just wasn't anything to it at all.

Whereas at our churches a man had to wrestle the devil to get his salvation, with tears and self-denunciations, and when he got down the aisle the preacher struggled with him, and then the congregation came for a turn, and when it all got done, that man knew he was SAVED. The only part of services Em couldn't take was Communion. Whether it was the pomp and silver of historic Pinnacle Baptist or the grape Kool-Aid and oyster crackers of Lamb of God Pentecostal, it sent Em away fighting the heaves.

"I hope," said the schoolteacher, "there is an Episcopal church in town."

"Oh, yeah," I said, "just the other side of the square. It's a little one, though."

"It's probably hardshell too. That's one of those cheap clip-on ties, isn't it? They all look the same."

We were backing down the driveway when the hedge shattered open and a large figure bore down on us, waving his arms.

"My God!" gasped the girl.

"It's Jojohn," said Jayell, hitting the brake, "when did he get in?"

Em pounded alongside and leaned breathlessly in the window. "Goin' to church, I bet!"

"Don't tell me!" said Gwen.

"Mind if I catch a ride? 'Scuse me, ma'am, we ain't met. Em Jojohn. I look after the place. Don't mean to crowd in, now."

"Let all be welcomed into the House of the Lord," I said, happily, scrambling to make room in the back. Em plunged over the side grinning, and took off his hat and smoothed his hair. "Been lookin' forward to meetin' you, ma'am." He had on fresh khakis and his trouser legs were pulled down neatly over his boots. The girl was cutting glances at Jayell, but he wasn't seeing them. Across the road Wash Fuller was on his knees poking in the culvert with a rake. "Maybe he and that shy dog would like to come too," she said.

Em hummed happily to himself as he rolled a smoke. He offered her one. She declined with thanks.

Rounding the square, Em turned on his knees and shouted into the wind, "Seen a poster comin' in yestiddy, where the Parkins Family is at Four Fork Calvary this week . . ."

"The Parkinses," said Jayell with interest, "the ones with the kid that cuts such a commotion?"

"The same," Jojohn replied.

Without a word Jayell made a sharp right at the ice plant. When we passed the GRANITE CENTER OF THE WORLD sign at the cemetery, Gwen became suspicious. At the city limits she turned sideways in her seat and said, "We are going to the Episcopal church!"

Em spoke up quickly. "Aw, ain't nothin' happenin' there, little lady. You'll enjoy Calvary, them folks at Four Forks knows how to praise!"

Gwen abruptly slid over and shot a foot to the brake pedal. The treadless old pickup squalled off the road and scampered to a sliding halt in the yard of a granite shed.

There was heavy silence.

43

Em said tentatively, "You got a grab in that right front wheel, Jay."

Gwen sat tight-lipped, staring straight ahead. "Get out, both of you," she said. "I have had enough for one day."

There was another long silence.

Finally Jayell turned and looked over his shoulder, deadpan, and said, "Okay, Em, you're on your own. If she says go, you go."

Em read his look. He nodded, and solemnly pulled on his hat. He climbed out of the truck and beckoned me to follow. Beside the truck, he stopped and removed the hat again. Penitently, great shoulders leaning, he rested a foot on the running board, and his voice rumbled softly in her ear. "Miss, I reckon you think we're the wildest bunch you ever come acrost. Well, we are, and there's no excusin' us. If we're loud, if we got no manners, it ain't 'cause we don't like you, it's 'cause we're a little dazzled by you, and I guess it was our ignorant way of trying to cover up. You're the brightest penny ever to come down the slopes. I don't know what it is you see in that crazy clodhopper sittin' beside you, but I can sure see what he sees in you, and the last thing I'd want is to cause him embarrassment in your eyes. I want you to know I'll make no more trouble for you, and if any man does, all you got to do is point him out."

Em stepped back and pulled on his hat. "I know I shouldn't have led you off like that, but well, Jayell's daddy always loved that little church—he was baptized there, you know—and I thought you'd like to see it."

Surprised, Gwen turned to look at him, then at Jayell.

"One small favor, though," Em added quickly, "If you don't mind. I'd be more'n grateful if you'd let the boy ride back with you. It's most a three-mile walk and, well, they give him a lot of sulfa drugs when he was little and it weakened his knees."

The girl sat a moment longer. Finally she sighed.

44

"Oh, I suppose it's too late to get to the Episcopal service anyway. Get in."

Em lifted me bodily over the side of the truck and scrambled in after me. Jayell put the truck in gear and a moment later we were buzzing down the highway.

"Wait'll you hear this Parkins family," Em was yelling over her shoulder, "they got a kid plays the banjo like you never seen!" And he rambled on and on until we drove into the yard of the little concrete block church.

I was only half listening, preoccupied with the outlandish notions of Jayell's father, ten years dead of radiator booze, crossing the threshold of *any* church, and that incredible business about sulfa drugs and weakened knees!

Jayell wasn't saying a word.

We pushed into one of the back pews, next to a smiling lady who was fanning herself and a coatless old gentleman beside her. He sat expressionless, staring, his hands limp in his lap and his white hair wafting gently in the breeze. The lady gave Em a long, hostile look, then smiled at Gwen. "We're the John Hoopers," she said, "nice to have you." Gwen thanked her and the lady patted my hand.

The pianist stopped playing and Mr. Hooper applauded until his wife grabbed his hands. A few people looked around but quickly straightened up. The Hoopers were well known. Em and I had seen them on previous trips. So Em felt qualified to explain, in a voice like a tuba, "The old man's a little off!"

"Mr. Hooper has had a stroke," Mrs. Hooper explained icily.

Gwen drew smaller in her seat.

The minister took the rostrum and explained that, once again, the sermon would be omitted and the service would be turned over to the Parkins family for their wonderful message in music. And as the plate was being passed he reminded everyone that this was a special offering to be used in the furtherance of the Parkinses' ministry. It was hard to tell whether he was telling them to give extra, or to hold off for the church's regular offering, but while he was speaking Mr. Parkins was tuning up his guitar in a most mournful manner.

The Parkinses sang a couple of songs, him on the guitar and his wife accompanying him with the tambourine, and then she sat at the piano and invited the church to join in. The congregation warmed right up, clapping and singing along. A few got in the aisles and swayed and snapped their fingers. A church always enjoys a chance to sing with professionals. Mr. Hooper clapped from the end of one hymn to the start of the next.

Finally Mr. Parkins strummed for attention and held up his hands.

"Dear Christian friends, the Ghost has truly been on this revival."

Amens.

"Yes, this has been a week we shall long remember. And now, once again, we'd like to present our pride and joy, the union of my wife, Clara, and me in Jesus. Here he is—our only begotten son—*Lit-tle Timmy Parkins!*"

His wife had been working the knobs of the powerful guitar amplifiers, sending warbling tones reverberating, and on the cue electronic screams crescendoed to ear-splitting frenzy.

A side door opened and a small boy sprang onto the platform, bringing a rush of gasped ooh's and aah's.

He was about seven years old, dressed in a shimmering white sequined outfit with buckskin fringes, gold shoes and a gold bow tie. His long hair was bleached as white as his clothes, and around his neck hung a gold banjo hardly bigger than a ukulele.

Mrs. Hooper made an ecstatic gesture to her mouth. "Did you ever?" she gasped.

"Never," said Gwen.

Little Timmy propped a foot on a pulpit chair and struck a chord, the light sparkled on little gold crosses on the ends of his shoelaces.

46

"Let's go home to Je-sus!" he cried, and he cut loose with "I'll Fly Away," singing in a high, ringing voice, his parents accompanying him on piano and guitar, and joining in on the choruses.

Now the crowd really shook itself loose. Little Timmy picked up the tempo, raising the banjo high on his chest, his amplified voice climbing like a siren. He dipped and ducked and danced and bobbed, his white hair flying, fingers tearing at the banjo. When he approached the last verse his father lifted him and stood him on a disc mounted on the top of the piano, then flipped a switch; revolving under a colored spotlight, Little Timmy had added tap dancing.

The crowd was beside itself, eyes closed, heads shaking. The clapping and shouting was joined by stomping and murmuring, starting up front and working its way back to us, and the murmuring built to a roar.

"They're talking in tongues," Jayell explained to Gwen.

Em sat clutching the back of the pew, rolling his eyes aloft, the rumbling chant deep in his throat.

Gwen clutched a hymn book to her breast and stared at Mrs. Hooper, who was developing a twitch. Her husband, still clapping, roamed unmolested up front. All around us the chorus of voices grew.

Abruptly Mrs. Hooper closed her eyes and issued forth a long, low moan. Gwen pushed closer to Jayell. Suddenly the woman gave a cry and lurched on her side and commenced thrashing about in the pew. "The Ghost is on her!" I yelled excitedly.

Gwen racked her hymn book and shoved us toward the aisle. "Then let's get out of here," she said, "and give them room to work!"

"Wasn't that something?" I cried, breathless with exhilaration, as we came down the steps. "Let's see your Episcopalians come up to that!" Then I stopped, the elation breaking, as I saw Em already outside by the truck.

Arms outstretched, he was deep in the throes of

his dance, a silhouette slowly turning in the moon-light.

Em said nothing on the way home. He sat, in the heavy brooding silence, watching the country roll by. I had hoped that going to church that night would make a difference, maybe distract him some from that awful black mood of his first couple of days home, but it hadn't. If anything, it had only seemed to make it worse. As soon as he touched ground at the boarding-house he demanded a five-dollar loan from Jayell and struck out straight for the river.

Jayell was saying something about it being so early he was going to take Gwen for a drive and to tell Miss Esther to leave the door unlocked, but I was only vaguely listening, and made no answer.

I got down and followed Em, bracing for another bad night.

4

"COME ON, EM, SOMEBODY'S GOING TO CALL THE law!" The Indian tore loose from my grip and hurled himself back at the squeaking fence. In the glare of streetlight on the other side, the big collie dog was frenzied with fury, fangs bared, climbing the wire. Jojohn howled back at him, waving his arms, the great blubbery face taunting, tormenting. The dog leaped to bite and Jojohn reached over the fence, grabbing for the bristling neck. The collie snapped for the extended hand and the Indian sagged his collar and lifted high the startled animal, swinging around and holding him firmly at arm's length.

"Let him go, Em! Turn him loose!" I pushed and shoved and pleaded, but it did no good. He stood watching the dog plunge and kick, snorting for breath in the strangling collar. Lights came on in the house and the Simmons woman came running. She beat at him with a rolled newspaper. "Put him down! You put Sonny down this minute or I'll call the po-lice, you crazy . . ." With a sudden twist of his body Em hurled the big dog against the side of a passing truck. The truck slowed down, the perplexed driver looking around. The yelping animal scrambled to his feet and disappeared over the hill full stretch, shaggy coat heaving, not looking back.

I got Em pulled away and turned into the rutted clay of Sunflower Street. The Simmons woman was still screaming, following us along the wire.

The porchlight came on at the boardinghouse, two houses down, and boarders were crowding to the rail. As we approached the house, Em turned and started straight for the front yard. "No, Em, come on around this way." He shook me off and tried again for the steps.

Miss Esther pushed through the boarders and leaned over the banister, waving us off. "No, no, not up here! Take him away, take him on around!"

Em stopped before them, wavering, uncertain. I shouldered him off the steps. He stumbled to the corner of the porch and stopped to catch his breath. With a foot braced against the bricks I got him pushed away and moving again. He staggered, tripped over the spigot and we both went down the bank.

"As long as there are drunks, there'll be little boys to lead them home," said Mrs. Porter. "It's a pity."

"Come on, Em, get up." I pulled on his arm and he rolled over with a groan and got to his knees. "Come on, get up from there!" He struggled to his feet and jerked away. I reached for him again and he put a hand against my face and shoved me into the hedge.

"My God, somebody do something!" It was Gwen's voice.

"Keep away," said Mr. Rampey. "When he's like that, can't nobody handle him but the boy."

With the blood hot on my face I scrambled out of the prickly hedge and rammed him hard as I could from the rear. He lurched, then suddenly whirled and lifted me high in the air. Beneath me those wet black eyes glistened in the porchlight. The quivering fingers sank deeper and deeper in my ribs. I was fighting for breath. "Em," I gasped, "for God's sake!"

He dropped me and turned away. I got to my feet and held my aching ribs. "Come on. All right, come on now." I took his arm gently, and he let me lead him around the hedge to the garage in the woods.

When I returned to the boardinghouse Gwen was in the hall with the others. She looked a little pale. "Well, he seemed dangerous to me," she was saying. "Earl, are you all right?"

"Fine," I said, trying to smile. I coughed and felt a sharp pain in my side, and wondered if Em had cracked a rib. He had never hurt me during those spells, but he was coming closer. I brushed past everybody and climbed to my room.

"Aw, he gets on a tear like that every time he comes home," said Miss Esther. "I don't pay no attention to it."

"Well, I don't know why you even put up with it. He's liable to hurt somebody," Gwen said.

"*Pshaw*, he's all bluster. It's an aggravation, I'll grant you, but the boarders have got kind of attached to him. They feel better having somebody like that around with the sorts we got in this neighbornood, if you know what I mean. And, I got to say, he's been good for the boy. I remember what he was like before the Indian came."

I remembered too.

I remembered the lady in the brown suit who brought me south on the train. I asked her about the angry red patch on her ankle, and she said it was ringworm, and it was killing her. And I remembered the dark, cavernous hallway and the curious, withered faces, and Miss Esther standing there in a polka-dot dress. She was thinner then, and wore a ring with an oval green stone—and I could tell from that first moment that my coming was a bother to her.

And I remembered the long mornings in my room after Farette had made the bed, and the afternoons sitting by the bookcase in the hall, listening to the strange voices, or sitting in the powdery dirt under the house playing with match-box cars and watching raindrops plunk in the sandy puddles.

But most of all I remembered the nights—and the dream. It was hell, right out of the picture Bible, with swirling flames, black smoke. There was crashing and thunder, the walls were shaking, my mother was screaming. A monster was there, and I thought he was killing my father. I could hear my father's screams of agony. I was coughing. I couldn't see. Flames were sweeping up the walls, across the floor. My father was dying, I could hear it, and then my mother was a demon herself; beyond the blackness and smoke I heard her screaming fiendishly, ". . . the boy! Get the boy!" And then the door crashed open and the instant it did my smoldering bed leaped up in flames. The devil was coming for me through the smoke, enormous claws reaching out, and when they touched me I felt flames climbing up my arm. I could smell my own flesh burning . . .

Mr. Jurgen in the next room kept complaining to Miss Esther about the noises I made while I was dreaming and she put in a night light, but it didn't help. Finally I made a tent of the quilts so no one would hear me if I dropped off to sleep and started making the noises, and I lay awake sweating under the suffocating quilts until dawn.

I was told I had to be quiet because there was someone very sick down the hall. It was the lady in the corner room. As the weeks passed she dissolved into a skeleton with heavy eyebrows and chin whiskers. And there was the smell. It stayed a long time after she died.

Then Farette said I wasn't eating right, and Miss Esther scolded me for sleeping so much in the daytime. Late one night I felt sick but was afraid to tell anybody. The room went green under the night light and I tried to get out of bed but couldn't, and realized in half-waking horror that I had dirtied the bed. Miss Esther was calling me but I couldn't wake up.

There were people around me in white coats pushing a sharp spike in my spine.

When I awoke there was an elderly Negro man in a white coat and I tried to get away, but he held me and kept saying he hadn't hurt me and wouldn't hurt me, and yelling over his shoulder until Dr. Breisner came in.

The Quarrytown hospital was a small building with only twenty beds, and they needed mine. Dr. Breisner said he would let me go home early if I would drink lots of fluids and stay in bed until he came to see me. I left with Miss Esther, avoiding her eyes because of what I had done to her bed. But she was all smiles and bought me a paint set and said she would spend more time with me. Farette made me a banana pudding.

There was talk about prolonged stress and adjustment and brain dehydration, and Miss Esther was at the end of her rope. She didn't see anything left to do but send me to Tucker Village, the county orphanage. Dr. Breisner said they had a good clinic there, and being with other children might help me.

When I heard that I grew quiet, and made every effort to cause no more trouble. I was too quiet. The boarders said I still wasn't "right." I tried not to think about that, or anything. In order to keep awake at night, I climbed out on the roof and huddled by the drainpipe in the cold, and slipped out after breakfast to sleep in a straw fortress I made in the gulley. As the weeks passed, senseless, meshing, it all went out of me; the ache, the longing, even the horrible dreams. There was only the gray wallpaper of my room.

Then, in the early spring, two weeks before my sixth birthday, Em Jojohn came to the kitchen door.

I wouldn't go near him for days, making it a point to stay out of his way as he went about his business of killing rats, but I began to feel those dark, evil eyes following me. He had a way of turning up places I was going to be, of being behind the corner I was rounding.

One afternoon in the gulley I suddenly awoke with my nose and lungs on fire. I scrambled up the bank and came face to face with the Indian, squatting up-wind of the garage.

"What is that?" I said, wiping my watering eyes.

"Burnin' sulphur."

"What's it for?"

"Rats."

"Is that how you kill 'em?"

The Indian looked at me. "Naw, that drives 'em out. Then I grabs 'em and bites their heads off." I couldn't tell if he was joking. He was such an ugly, scowling creature. "How come you sleep in that gulley?"

"I—I can't sleep in my room."

"Why not?"

I shrugged.

"You live here with your grandma?"

"She's not my grandma, she's my great-aunt."

"Where's your folks?"

"Dead."

The Indian pointed to the skin graft on my arm. "That how you got that?"

I reached down in the gulley for my shirt and quickly pulled it on. The pink, pimply patch of grafted skin ran from my left shoulder to just above the wrist. I couldn't straighten that elbow out all the way, but otherwise it didn't bother me. That is, not until I started to school. I soon learned to wear long sleeves, even in summer.

"How'd you like to help me kill some rats?"

"Huh?"

"If you can't sleep anyway, you might as well be helpin' out some. Come back tonight after supper."

"Tonight?"

"Sure. Night's the best time to kill rats."

"I ain't supposed to be out after dark."

"You mean you're scared of the dark." He waited. I didn't answer. "Well, that's understandable, but if you know how to take keer of yourself there ain't nothin' to worry about."

"Are you—scared of the dark?"

"With all the things layin' to wait to grab you, all the ghosts and ha'nts walkin' about? Hell, anybody with *sense* is scared of the dark! You just got to know how to deal with 'em." And the Indian gave me my first lesson on what were, to him and me, the very real creatures that lay beyond the dark.

Up to that time they had been vague beings that inhabited the dark corner under the stairs, and waited under my bed for a hand to drop over the side. They darted for me just before I hit the light switch and made them disappear, and crawled along the weeds at the edge of the yard when I took out the garbage at night.

But as the Indian began to sort them out for me, they became real working ghosts, with their own identities, character traits and working habits. And to my collection the Indian added those that cried in the wind when someone died, that hovered in the woods like fireflies, stalled cars at crossroads where they wanted to get out, and sat on buried treasure and made people sick that came too near. He knew the ones that sucked breath from sleeping people, the harmless ones that just liked to watch through windows, and those that, when angered, could snag and tear your flesh and make you think it was a splinter or a nail.

I was awestruck. How, then, did a wanderer like him, a rat killer who actually spent his working hours in the dark, keep from being swallowed up by them!

Simple, he said. His big weapon was Belief. A person couldn't lug around enough charms or chants to get by all of them, as different ones required different liturgy. But the one thing that stopped them all was simply *believing* in them. That was rare flattery. The worst of them couldn't stand up to that. *He* never slighted a spook by calling it a tree limb waving at the window, or a cat prowling on the garage. He *knew* what it was, and they knew he knew, and went away satisfied. They didn't have to prove nothing to *him*. Everybody wants respect, he said, dead or alive.

Of course, that was the way you handled the really fearsome ones. There was another kind, the feisty little creepy ones that just liked to slip about and scare, and they had to be dealt with differently. That crowd needed a firm hand. If you showed proper courtesy, and felt them still hovering about, then a good cussing, flat out and loud, was what took care of them. "It shames a ha'nt to be cussed at," he said, "tucks him right in and sends him away."

And what impressed me most about this lecture was the conviction that the Indian wasn't fooling. He believed every word he said. He convinced me then, and I never had reason to doubt him later. He didn't know who was in charge of the other world, he said, and one lifetime wasn't enough to sort it out. In the meantime any superstition or religion was fine. He didn't trust any faith to tell the whole story, and hadn't the vanity for doubt.

I sat thinking about it, in a glow of indescribable relief.

"Well," he said finally, "what about them rats?"

"Yeah," I said eagerly, "I'll come back." Then I had second thoughts. "At least, I'll help you catch 'em. I ain't bitin' no heads off."

"Hey! You think I'd let you be gnawing 'em up without no experience? Hell, you ain't even got your teeth filed down." The Indian shook his head in a way that plainly put me down as the biggest fool, by far, he ever met. "Come after supper," he said in dismissal, and rose to check the garage.

I came back, and tagged after him night after night, helping him set his traps and poison his biscuits, watching in macabre fascination as he lunged on a cornered rat the size of a rabbit and danced on it by lantern light. And, oddly, drenched in the horror of the whole ghastly business, in real ugliness, real blood, real striking out at the despicable shadowy creatures, my own night terrors began to pale. Each corpse laid something to rest.

55

It was with considerable apprehension, however, that I watched him take that first live one from a trap, and I was greatly relieved to see that he did not, in fact, bite its head off.

But, I must admit, there was disappointment in it too.

And I gained a new respect for the ferocious survival instinct of rats. Once Em set a steel drum in the shed near a shelf that showed droppings, and filled it with water and poured on a layer of cottonseeds. The seeds rode the top deceptively, and each morning he pulled a drowned rat from the barrel.

But one morning there was a recent catch, and as we entered the shed I could hear the rat squirming in the barrel. When we approached, our presence seemed to increase his fury. He bared his teeth and squealed at us and thrashed harder through the water, his claws scoring the sides of the rusty drum. We stood and watched as, ears twitching, he swam round and round, squealing, lunging, scratching at the steep metal sides. The minutes dragged by, his strength was going, but still he fought, raising his head higher as the fat little body sank deeper in the water, and he continued to fight, struggling fishlike with the stronger muscles of his back until there was only the head moving in the cottonseeds, giving violent shakes, snorting water.

Far beyond the strength of the body was the will to that last instinctive spark, and only when that was used, and the powerful life force extinguished, did the blunt little snout sink below the surface. There was the unshakable feeling that the rat didn't drown. He was dead before that.

With the Indian I wandered farther and farther from the yard. We met Tio and other black boys, went fishing with them and had maypop battles, dug caves in the red hills, scrounged the dump for scrap iron, and stole watermelons from the farms across the river, hiding in cornfields and gouging out the warm hearts with our hands. We slept when we felt like it, mostly in late afternoon, and ate on the same schedule. At the boardinghouse they took little notice of my absence, glad to have me out from underfoot and no longer running up doctor bills.

After a night of rat hunting and breakfast before sunrise, we would burst from the garage for long, loping walks through the blue steel dawn, stopping in the Ape Yard to pass the time with a white-haired old black man leaning on his gate, mumbling low, so as not to wake the village, trudging along the marsh grass, listening to the river discover morning, or up through town before anyone was about, clapping our hands to hear the sound bounce off the darkened buildings. Em was always feeling for echoes. We rambled and searched the surrounding hills shouting in the wind, stomping devil's huts, beating trash piles to flush a snake. Nothing of consequence but feeling air and motion, a breaking of time, something centering inside me.

Em got me to climbing trees, despite my weak arm, claiming his weight made us even in the races. Once, on a dare I climbed to the top with my good arm tied to my belt. He could dare with such sarcasm, such persistence that you would kill yourself to prove him wrong. One dizzy June day, under his taunts and jeers, I actually crossed from one tree to another! Riding the limber top, swaying back and forth, rocking on the wind, I forgot myself in the giddy moment of exhilaration and anger and suddenly plunged away and crashed into the other's branches. Later when I looked at the height and realized what I had done, I was so shaky I had to sit down.

He taught me to swim that summer in an abandoned quarry fed by springs. And again, as always, the goading, the challenging, bobbing below me and spouting like a whale: "Come on, Early boy, when you the most scared, that's the time to *dive!*"

The pressure of leg muscles tightening, the vertigo, the far-away glistening water . . . the instant of almost committing myself . . . then settling back, to the safety of heels planted, giving up . . . and running and climbing down the side to a lower ledge and jumping off onto the jeering head, sinking it . . . the Indian bellowing and thrashing water, the sounds bouncing back from the granite walls, then both of us shouting, our voices ringing around us . . . echoings of joy.

On winter nights we piled slabs in the heater until the flue sucked and roared and glowed bright red around the damper, and I shook the wire corn popper over the top while Em practiced his hand shadows on the wall, at which he was terrible. "Look, it's a rooster, don't you see it?" I saw nothing but the blobby shadow of locked hands, and said so. Waggling a thumb then, persisting, "There now, there's his comb—you see him now, then, don't you?"

Other times he made things, at which he was better. With a broom handle, wire and tines from a discarded pitchfork he could turn out a better frog gig than you could buy at the hardware store, or whittle a wild cherry gun, a kind of plunger made from reeds that could fire a green cherry with enough force to raise a blister from across the room. But his masterpiece, bar none, was the leather belt he made for me, hand tooled and studded with the green jewels he shot from the bottoms of Mason jars with Tio's BB gun.

Sometimes in the early fall afternoons I would find him sitting in the weeds behind the garage, his head against the clapboards and smoke curling lazily from his cigarette as he watched the sun build amber fires in the treeline. When I asked him what he was doing, he would only say, "Washin'." In those times I left him alone.

By Christmas I was sleeping through the night, and the Indian and I were friends.

And now my friend Em Jojohn, who had found my demons and so deftly torn them from me, lay in his own night of agony, unable to articulate, nor I to understand, the dark terror that tormented him.

58

5

THE NEXT MORNING, STILL SHAKEN FROM HER VISIT
to church and the chaotic scene with Em, Gwen
skipped breakfast, pleading a faculty planning session
at the school, where she would be teaching eighth-grade
English and civics. When Miss Esther asked me if
she was satisfied with our Episcopal church, I had to
admit that we went to Four Forks. That worried her.
"How'd she take all that shoutin' and jumpin' around?"

"Oh," I said, "before it was over she was up and
shoutin' too."

Miss Esther seemed surprised, but greatly relieved.
As soon as the breakfast dishes were cleared away I
went by the loft for Em, hoping that the morning had
done its job.

It had. He was his old self, standing at the window
railing at the birds that woke him, and he wolfed
down the ham biscuits I brought him as though he
hadn't eaten in a week. He was still reluctant to go
to the Waugh place on Wolf Mountain to do the painting Jayell wanted done, though, and it was only after
careful consideration of the fact that he was flat broke,
in debt to Jayell for five dollars, and of the many dry
days ahead without booze money that he eventually
got the best of his superstitious nature. He sighed
and clamped on his hat, and we made our way down
into the sprawling, gullied ruins of the Ape Yard.

To know the Ape Yard, in its essence, you had only
to know the Poncini quarry.

At the very bottom of the hollow, down past the
small block of stores that made up the Ape Yard's
main street, on the last rise of ground before the final
slope toward the river, sat the great maggoty hole of

the original quarry. Abandoned when the Poncinis went broke, the quarry was three-quarters full of seepage, and sat still collecting rubbish, rainwater and outhouse drainage, and giving off a smell that had them complaining across town when the wind was right. The city had tried draining it and filling the bottom with granite slag and earth, but that only raised the smell closer to the surface. The old quarry seeped full again, and no ordinances could keep out the garbage and trash. In summer, trucks came with drums of chlorine and lye, but still the quarry remained what it was, a foul, gaseous sore in the earth.

And around that quarry, in the larger basin of the Ape Yard hollow, was its counterpart in human life.

Below the quarry, where twisting, rust-colored Twig Creek emptied into the Little Iron River, it was the worst. There the ground was mushy even in dry spells, and when the rains came down the slopes in spring, water stood at the porches for weeks on end. Children sat idly watching a stranger pass—spindly, clay-colored children with raw, expressionless faces, to whom play was a perpetual, listless roaming. If there was an egg in the house it went to the working man. Children sopped hoecake in the grease. Sometimes there was a can of dogfood to fry. Women brush-broomed the porches slowly, scuffling heavily on bare, callused feet. Their men sat in the yards and rubbed their hair, tinkered with machines, wandered off somewhere.

From there the crumbling shanties climbed the hogback hills in row after row, to Sunflower Street on the north, and up across the railroad to the warehouses on the southern rim that marked the beginning of Quarrytown. On the east it was bordered by Wolf Mountain, overlooking the river, and to the west by the fairgrounds, where the main rain-gutted road led into the hollow. Scattered among the plum bushes and winding dirt paths stood the tarpaper shacks and fading clapboard houses with washtubs on the wall and old cars on jacks under chinaberry trees, none of them having seen repairs since Doc Bobo bought them. All shared the same look of ruin and decay.

In the taverns there were men who would tell you they knew what was wrong with the mill, with the world, and could fix it in a day if they were in charge. They had made that payment, the company's books were at fault. The man read their meter wrong. Household bills came at them like a pestilence and their families were gluttonous maws of need. They spent their paychecks quickly, clutching at luxuries, before responsibility came to take them away. They believed every ad and bought with abandon, mumbled their sins in the finance company confessionals, promised to do better, and when the "repo" man came for the outboard motor they hid it among the neighbors.

And there were those who accepted their condition as if it were divine appointment, and even found a kind of grace in it. They white-washed their picket fences and raised pretty flowers in painted truck tires, lived on religion and pinto beans, paid their bills and got their praise. They were the "good niggers," like Ralph Martin, a foreman at the mill, who lived three streets down. He had had a son killed in Korea and had kept a flag flying from a pole in his yard with a light to shine on it at night, until some pranksters tore it down. He wrote a letter to the *Star* and they printed an editorial about it. His wife came up and got Miss Esther's copy to send to her sister in South Carolina.

There were the Lupos, below us on the curve that led around and up to the cemetery. Hobart Lupo lived on fruit-jar whiskey and headache powders and liked to slap his wife. They came down the road one Saturday afternoon and every few yards he would stop and slap her. She was drunk too, and every time he would slap her she would stagger off a few yards and then come back and walk beside him until he stopped and slapped her again. I watched them go all the way home that way. One day another couple was visiting them and the four of them were out on the porch and suddenly Hobert slapped his wife and she would have gone over the rail if the other man hadn't caught her. Then the other woman said something about it and Hobert slapped her too, and the man laid Hobert out with a Coke bottle. It was weeks before Hobert was up and about again, and I never found out who that couple was because they never came back.

And there was the saucy black woman named Clara Kitchens who had moved into a two-room shack that once stood across the street from us. "Hot Kitchens" she was called and after she moved in the crowd with the bright-colored, high-powered cars began to congregate heavily at night, and the boarders began to complain about the noise. It was said she drank anything, even liquid shoe polish strained through bread. Once, after an unusually quiet weekend, one of the boarders, Mrs. Bell, was sitting on the porch and heard crying from the shack. She found two infants alone in the house, a boy and a girl. They were under a baby crib turned upside down and the boy was almost dead. After the welfare people came and took the children, Miss Esther personally supervised Em's destruction of the shack and sat around for days waiting for the Kitchens woman's return. But she was never heard from again. Fortunately, for whatever reason, nothing was heard from Doc Bobo about the destruction of his property either.

There were the young boys I grew up playing and fighting with, like Skeeter, Carlos and little Jackie James, who now worked for Jayell. There was Grandma Tyne on the river, who traded Em and me peppery sausage biscuits for fresh-caught perch. And old Aaron Tim, ninety years of age and still climbing the slopes each morning in search of day labor to support his retarded daughter.

But the one thing all of the people in the Ape Yard had in common was that they were trapped, caught in that basin of poverty and servitude to Doc Bobo in the hollow, and held in place by the weight of the white structure beyond. For them, escape seemed futile at the outset.

Without education there was no horizon, no plan, no organization to their lives, and consequently no hope of dealing with the world beyond the Ape Yard rim. There was only the dullness of the hollow's endless days, the brutal terror when Doc Bobo's "dog boys" came in to bring a troublemaker into line, the murderous release of a Saturday night, lashing out at home, unleashing their fury with moonshine, devouring their own.

And Monday morning, once again treading the paths to the aged brick building of shuddering looms, lint-matted windows and fiberglass slots of sky, while the elderly, the women and the children climbed to the shading oak at Cooper Corner to wait for odd jobs in town or in the fields. All of their faces once again masked in that look of grief, of ancient, ingrown, hopeless anger.

That was the Ape Yard. Its color the unrelieved red of the sunbaked slopes. Its sound a clatter, the ragged burr of old engines, a fight somewhere in the squat gray houses, a curse, a calling, an unexplained wail in the night. Its mood, eternal despair.

Of course, that vision of my world came later. At the time I saw it through the eyes of a boy, in that half-remembered time when we were dreamers.

Jayell Crooms's shop on Twig Creek was a small wooden building surrounded by mountainous piles of scrap and salvage lumber. It was only about nine o'clock, but a dozen boys were already at work as Em and I approached. In the dust and din Jayell lunged among them shouting above the saws and planers, seizing work from them in despair and impatience.

"Wood butchers! You're nothing but a bunch of wood butchers! Look at this . . ." He shoved aside a small boy in floppy overalls and dragged a gleaming maple secretary to the middle of the floor. "You got tired of sanding, you piled on a little extra varnish, huh, Jackie? That will not go, gentlemen!" He snatched a nail from his pocket and walked around the secretary, raking deep X's in the surface. "Now, after you sand out those marks we'll try for a proper finish."

He stopped beside Skinny Skeeter, a boy so thin he looked about the same from front or side. "Not a bad-looking coffee table, Skeeter." He picked it up and turned it over in the light, running his hand over the finish, sighting the joints. "Not bad, not bad at all." The boy adjusted his glasses with a sigh of relief, then his face clouded in sudden horror as Jayell spun and hurled the table against the wall. It fell to the floor with one leg hanging.

Jayell shook his head. "Not a bad-*looking* coffee table, but it's really a piece of junk! You know why?" He poked a finger in the boy's ribs. "Bad glue-joints! I've told you, the wood better break before your glue joints! That's like the damned stuff you buy in stores; it looks good but falls apart the minute you get it home. You will not put junk in my houses!" He roamed the floor, exhorting, condemning, explaining: "Feel the wood, feel what it wants to be. Measure twice, cut once, that's the rule, huh? But think, think, think, many times, before you even measure!"

He stopped at the lathe and put his arm around the heavy shoulders of Carlos. "You know how the Eskimos carve, Carlos? They believe the thing they're carving, the image, is already locked inside the ivory, and when they carve they just let it out. Huh? So, a stick of wood can be a fine table leg, or just a club to beat people over the head with, can't it? You make me a table leg, Carlos. You make me a club and I'll beat you over the head with it, huh?"

He was determined to make builders of them. He would take these poor black boys from the Ape Yard and build his dream. There was no more sense in people living in monotonous shacks just because they were poor than in two wealthy people sharing a mansion.

There were materials enough if used properly, the cost could be controlled, and if he could develop enough designs and show what could be done with "only a minuscule of imagination," he could redirect the housing trend in this country away from opulent, unused space for the rich and small wooden cells for the poor.

"Look at automobiles!" he would say. "Every year they get bigger, for people who stay the same size. The same thing's happening in housing. Only the poor can't afford those big cars, any more than they can afford the big houses, and they're the ones with the larger families. So what's the solution? Simple! The Japanese discovered it centuries ago. You make imaginative use of what you've got. They use rice-paper walls to create illusions of extra rooms, of added space; they paint, they decorate. If five little black kids have got to share an eight-by-ten room, do you just throw 'em in there like animals in a cage? No, you disperse some colors, you put in little plywood partitions. A little girl won't mind bein' cramped in an isolated corner if she gets to crawl to it through a bright-colored tunnel; it becomes her own little hidden, secret place. But these goddamned builders have got to care! They've got to use a little imagination! And, hell, they can still make a profit. These things can be produced on a mass basis the same as those match-box things they stick in the suburbs. And once I get enough designs developed, I'm going to show them how to do it. Houses are being priced right out of poor people's hands. In twenty or thirty years they're all going to be living on the government, and that's a crime! It's a crime! I'm going to tap that market. I'm going to show them what can be done. Let other people build the goddamned mansions."

That was the dream Jayell had come home to pursue after visionary thinking of that kind had brought his architectural career to so abrupt an end in Atlanta.

He had started out promisingly enough. At Georgia Tech he was a straight-A student. He devoured his courses, sat in the library until it closed, then spent most of the night in the offices of the architectural firm to which his major professor had recommended him. His college years passed quietly enough. The only explosion of impulsive behavior had come the night after final exams of his sophomore year. He had just turned eighteen, and to celebrate that and the end of the term, he got gloriously drunk, went to a rousingly good war movie, and shortly thereafter, still in a fever of patriotism, joined the Marine Corps.

He was discharged a year later after winning a bet, in another state of intoxication, that his barracks building at Parris Island was so flimsy that he could drive a tanker truck straight through it. With a left leg two inches shorter than his right and a healed fractured skull (which many were convinced only added to his later troubles), he returned to finish his studies at Tech.

After graduation he went to work full time for the architectural firm in Atlanta, and somehow managed to stay with them three years until he got his license.

As long as Jayell stayed at the drawing board there was no trouble. His knowledge of engineering and his artistic talent amazed and delighted his employers, and as he was assigned to work on the new, modernistic buildings going up in the rapidly growing city, his reputation grew among other architects. But his first love was residential architecture, and he returned to it whenever he could. The only problem was Jayell couldn't get along with people, in the office or out of it. In his final year, when he was doing more outside supervising and dealing more directly with contractors and clients, he managed to antagonize everyone.

If a change was needed, he wanted the contractor to implement it; he didn't see the need for meetings and consultations, no matter how often he was lectured. And if an addition a client wanted would ruin the design, Jayell told him so, in no uncertain terms. Added to that was Jayell's barely concealed, and growing, animosity toward people who could afford hundred-thousand-dollar houses, who only wanted something gaudier and more expensive than what their neighbors had—an extravagant waste, brought home hard whenever he drove through Atlanta's mushroom-

66

ing slum sections. Finally, Jayell infuriated contractors, clients and his bosses when it was discovered he was stealing leftover materials from jobs and doing a nonprofit weekend home-improvement business.

The final break came when one "ghastly monstrosity" of a home for a city councilman kept growing in deformity before him, his ideas for it aborted, twisted, discarded as too outlandish, the firm bowing to meet the demands of the councilman's wife, until one midnight driving past it, Jayell, again drunk, suddenly stopped and made what alterations he could with a sledgehammer. Then, still not satisfied with his work, he succumbed to the desire to repeat his Marine Corps performance, and was wresting control of a tanker truck from the startled man refueling a nearby service station when a patrol car picked him up.

The councilman agreed not to press charges if Jayell's firm assumed all damages, which they did, seeing no point in suing or jailing the departing Jayell. Indeed, they forgave him enough to later recommend him to the college that wanted an art center and didn't have the money for what they envisioned. Jayell Crooms can give you what you want on the money you've got, they were told, if you can get him, and if you'll grant him complete autonomy on the final design and stay the hell out of his way. They had, and they had been delighted.

Jayell had lost no time in returning to Quarrytown. First he tried teaching high-school shop for a year, but his unorthodox methods caused him trouble from the start. He taught a curriculum of his own devising, refusing to check rolls or give written tests. Instead of lecturing safety, he would simply pull a cigarette from a student's mouth and drop it down his collar. On his desk he placed a jar of formaldehyde in which a human thumb hung suspended from a string, contributed by a man he once worked with, he explained to the class, who got careless with power tools.

Still bitter from his experience in Atlanta, he refused to concede an inch to the school system. He ignored policy and principal alike, dismissed the school board as America's Club of Fools, would not file reports or attend meetings of any kind, refused even to speak to a parent, and would throw a sassy student bodily out the door.

When at the end of the year he decreed only two items built in the shop of even acceptable quality, and methodically smashed the others to kindling, both Jayell and the school agreed that they had had enough. He returned to the Ape Yard and the shop by the creek, where he taught high-school dropouts and chain-gang graduates like Carlos a trade in exchange for their labor.

Jayell saw me and came down the shop, scowling. "Well, you decided to show up today, did you? Look where the sun is! We could have done a half-day's work!"

"You said to get Em if I could; well, it took some doing but I got him. Now you can work us or send us home, but don't point no suns to me!"

Jayell clapped me on the head and laughed. "I swear, Early boy, you get more like Em every day. Let's go paint a house."

Em was already in the back of the truck dozing under a tarpaulin. Jayell leaped in the truck and I barely pulled in beside him before we were bounding down the road. Jayell was in high spirits; he hummed a country song in the blast of air that whipped over the shuddering windshield, the points of his collar fluttering like bat wings in the breeze. Jayell had chiseled the top off the cab when he bought the truck from Speck Turner. It was useless against the rain anyway, since Speck, a high-living black plumber who subcontracted work from Jayell, drove it home drunk one night, firing holes through the roof with his .44 Magnum.

"Look at that!" Jayell nudged my arm and pointed to a triangular-shaped house against the hillside with a slanting roof. A small stream meandered down the hill, poured across the slate roof and fell in a sheeting waterfall past the staggered front window. The young couple who lived there had wanted a honeymoon house under a waterfall. Every contractor in the county had laughed. "They said I'd never waterproof that roof! Hah!"

Building mostly for the poor had advantages other than allowing him to experiment on small structures and use salvage materials, Jayell said. Wealthy people had to have houses that looked pretty much alike; it wasn't safe to deviate too much; and in certain cases, like in suburban developments, they couldn't deviate at all, but had to preserve a certain community look. But poor people didn't have that problem, or a reputation to worry about, or a job they might lose for being considered peculiar. Besides, they had the worst lots: a patch of swampy bottomland, a craggy half-acre on the side of a hill, and that offered a greater challenge, and provided for wider experimentation.

Jayell's guiding principle was to shape the house to fit the terrain. He built toad-stool houses on pilings in the middle of swamps, wedge-shaped houses in ravines; he arched rooms over a stream on a farm in Lenox County, and made a flowing, bladderlike thing without steps, inserted with dozens of tiny windows, for the old Patterson woman who was going blind. He ran roofs to the ground, fitted beam supports into the hills, cantilevered porches toward the Georgia sunsets, and for a large crowded family, counter-weighted whole walls that could be shifted by hand. And every step of the way he drove his shop boys brutally, excusing no mistakes, inciting them to learn with a force that the white boys making desks and what-nots in the high-school shop had been able to tolerate only a year.

But Jayell's major problem was that he was simply no businessman. His operating capital was a drawer full of promissory notes, and payments when his customers could make them. He scoured the countryside for salvage lumber and used only the cheapest materials, secondhand when he could get it, but still he was running into trouble. Smithbilt Corporation, one of the large developers that fattened on the postwar housing boom, was interested in what Jayell was doing (they had openly copied some of his designs for lake retreats) and had tried to entice him to work for them in construction, promising that he could experiment at their expense, and that they would test the marketability of his plans. Sometimes Jayell seemed ready, questioning the possibilities in great detail. Later he would say he didn't have enough designs worked out, that he hadn't done enough experimentation on his own. Or, in the heat of some new creation, he might just order the Smithbilt representative off the job, shouting that the company only wanted to steal more of his ideas.

On our way to the Waugh place on Wolf Mountain, the truck lurched noisily through the rundown eastern edge of town. Suddenly Jayell remembered he had to stop at I. V. Tagg's office over the pawnshop. Tagg was a CPA who made a determined effort to keep Jayell's books in order. Still humming, Jayell scrambled up the stairs and burst into the office; seeing no one in the dusty, cluttered room he shouted, "I. V., damn your rotten soul, come out here!"

The frail little man hurried out of the bathroom hooking on his glasses. "What is it, Jayell, for God's sake what is it this time?"

Jayell pulled an envelope from his pocket and waved it in the bookkeeper's face. "The Internal Revenue people, they say we've not paid our withholding. Will you put me out of business; is that your intention?"

The bookkeeper sighed. "Jayell, I can't pay your taxes from my own pocket. Have you checked the bank balance lately?"

"My God, are we flat again?"

"And three returned. I called Maudie Fisher at the bank and she's agreed to hold 'em until tomorrow noon, but she's getting tired of this."

Jayell slapped his pockets. "Here, wait a minute." He pulled a check from a wad of time sheets. "Here, that's the last one on the college job. Will that clear us?"

Mr. Tagg looked at it. "Well, it'll take care of Maudie, but not the Internal Revenue."

"But they'll get their money. Don't they always get their money?"

"Eventually, but I've told you, Jayell, the taxes withheld from wages must be deposited monthly. They don't want you operating with government money. It should be put in a separate account."

"What the hell's the use of opening two accounts when we can't keep money in one? Talk to 'em, I. V., tell 'em we've got to have more time. They've got to bend with us a little."

"Jayell, you've got to remember who you're dealing with. This is the federal government, they don't have to bend with anybody. And how am I to figure taxes if you keep trading work for supplies and paying people out of your own pocket? You never withhold the proper amounts, you can't even get the correct social security numbers. I got a new list back from Baltimore this morning."

The veins stood out in Jayell's neck. "All I know is there are ragged sons of bitches all over these hills living in their own houses for the first time in their lives, put together with stuff most builders throw away, and we done it without red tape or any help from the federal government, and in the process a few black boys learned a trade who might otherwise end up on the welfare rolls. It seems to me the federal government ought to be told to remember who they're dealing with!

"Jesus," said Jayell, clumping back down to the truck, "for every man who tries to do, there's a hundred to hold him back."

Em Jojohn sat up and looked around, and seeing we were not at our place of work, cocooned himself in his tarpaulin again.

"Look at him," laughed Jayell. "Would you believe he's the one who finally got me started on this? We were down at Dirsey's one night, right after I'd left the high school; figured I was washed up by that time, everybody thought so. And I was carrying on

71

about the shape housing was in, how I'd like to just start a company to build houses like this, and he looked at me and said, 'Why don't you do it?' Just like that: *'Why don't you do it?'* Hah! Crazy son of a bitch." Jayell reached back and slapped the tarpaulin and slipped into a one-block short-cut up One-Way Street and headed out toward Wolf Mountain.

6

LILLY WAUGH'S FARM WAS LOCATED AT THE VERY TOP of Wolf Mountain, which rose out of the rolling foothills at the back of Quarrytown and overlooked the town and the Ape Yard.

By driving back and forth between Quarrytown and Atlanta on the weekends during the summer he was at the college, Jayell had kept his construction business going as best he could. But the Waugh house, almost finished when he was called away, had been largely neglected. Building that house had been a pain. Since none of Jayell's black shop boys were allowed up there, Jayell concentrated on his other houses during those weekend visits and ran by to work on the Waugh house when he could. Now it was all finished except for the outside trim work, but Lilly Waugh said she wasn't moving in a stick of furniture until the house was completely done.

Pete Williteer, the elderly Negro sharecropper who lived on the Waugh place and looked after Miss Lilly, was waiting for us at the jobsite. He had talked a reluctant Jayell into building this house by promising him ten acres of Waugh land on the northeast slope, just above the Ape Yard, and agreeing that Lilly Waugh would not set foot on the job.

"Gon' finish up today, Mr. Crooms?" Pete Williteer asked, smiling.

"Just touch up the paint and be gone," said Jayell. "How's the old woman?"

"Fine. And she likes it, 'specially likes them high board fences. She sho' is anxious to get in it."

Privacy had been the central theme of the Waugh house. It was a miniature feminine fortress. Even the doors had blind entrances. "Yeah? What'd she say about it?" asked Jayell.

"Ain't said nothing. But I can tell she likes it."

"Well, just keep her away one more day."

Pete Williteer nodded. "I got to go over to Little Holland today. Need anything before I do?"

"No, we'll be okay." When Williteer had gone, Jayell got out the paint cans and rousted Jojohn.

The big old Waugh house sat on the crest of the mountain surrounded by tall, broken oak trees. The Waughs had been rich people before the Depression. Mrs. Cline remembered the parties they used to give, with the house all lit up and shiny new automobiles winding up through those trees. Miss Lilly brought her whole class home from finishing school one weekend for a houseparty. Then they lost it all, and Mr. Waugh shot himself. But Mrs. Waugh kept spending and donating money on the old grand scale until she died, and Lilly was left almost penniless, and subsequently became a recluse.

She stayed on at the Waugh farm, and with the help of Pete Williteer raised a few acres of cotton to keep them going, and to my knowledge, never set foot off the place.

I'd never seen her, but Em had; he said she walked straight and tall like a man, and had deep blue eyes that looked out of slits of waxy skin, and always wore an ankle-length white dress and bonnet.

It was obvious why she wanted to get out of the old house. It was literally falling in, and the roof was damaged in several places by falling limbs from those fire-gutted oaks. The fire department had tried to get Miss Lilly to have those trees cut down. They said the reason the trees had been hit by lightning so many times was that they sat on a hill surrounded by open

73

fields. Miss Lilly ordered the fire chief off her place with a pistol. Her grandfather had planted those trees.

Em had, to me, a much more plausible explanation. He said it wasn't the trees drawing the lightning, it was Miss Lilly. God was trying to kill her because she was a witch.

Checking the fields and woods to make sure she was nowhere about, Jayell got a paintbrush and started to work. After half an hour or so, he grew impatient. "Hell, you two can finish this up, I need to get another one started. Just take it easy on the trim and don't get sloppy."

When he had gone, Em and I settled into a more comfortable working pace, taking frequent breaks with the water jar, and finally stopping to nibble on wild fox grapes we found growing along a pine log. At least I ate them. Em wouldn't touch anything that grew within a mile of the Lilly Waugh place. He lit a smoke and rummaged in his pocket, and began unwinding fishing lines from the spool he carried. "I wonder if that creek down yonder has got any bream in it big enough to eat," he said. I wondered about that, too, but I knew we really ought to stay on the house. "I know what we *ought* to do," he said, "but what do you *want* to do?" Naturally, we set off to see about the bream.

Moving downstream, we dropped our hooks around the wooden pilings of an old bridge where he was sure there were congregations. Em crooned to the fish and waggled his line, snatching out his hook every few minutes to check the worm. He was about the worst fisherman I ever knew, but how he loved to fish. We sat in the late-morning warm of creek rot and silence, broken only by the steady wash of current against the pilings and Em plunking his sinker from spot to spot, to get their attention, he said. By eleven o'clock I had hooked and thrown back two small perch. Em was playing his line from the bridge when suddenly he caught something that put up a terrible fight. It was an eel. Em forfeited the line in roaring frustration. "Well, damnit, then, I think I'll have a swim." And setting his Vaseline jar of matches on the rail, he somersaulted into the water. We had a good long swim, and, our wants taken care of to Em's satisfaction, returned once again to the unfinished ought.

The pine thicket behind the Waugh place was like an oven, and though our clothes had quickly dried when we came out of the creek, by the time we had finished touching up the final trim work we were soaked through again and steaming.

The Waugh house seemed docile enough sitting across the field, and I wondered vaguely if the old terror of the Waugh place wasn't just another of those time-embellished tales that grew up about eccentric people. She was probably just a quiet little old lady who talked to her flowers. I started to mention this possibility to Em, and found him frozen, a paper half-filled from his tobacco can, staring past me. I turned and saw her standing at the fence. And she was nothing like that at all.

At least six feet tall, feet apart, she stood glaring from the shadow of her bonnet, one fist against her hip and the other dangling a big revolver.

"Uh-huh," said Em, and he went crashing through the brush.

"Come here, boy," she ordered. The voice was harshly masculine, but with an unnatural squeak, like green shucks being pulled off corn. Steadying my legs, I cautiously approached the fence. Up close she was even more striking. Her hands were long and spidery, and seemed to leap about on their own. One sprang to a post and crouched there. She had too much hair for her small head, and there was something defiant about the way she let it stream down her back instead of tying it up in a bun the way old people are supposed to. But most discomforting to me were her eyes, flat little blue disks that alternately drifted unfocused, then ganged up and bore down on you. "What are you doing down here?"

"Jayell Crooms hired us to help on this house."

"Who's that hiding in the bushes?"

"Em Jojohn, he's helping too."

"He a nigger?"

"No," I said, "he's an Indian."

"Looked pretty dark to me."

"Well, maybe you got bad eyes."

The eyes zeroed in on me, burning. The revolver trembled in her fist.

"Run, boy, run!" came the voice from the woods.

"We're hired hands on Jayell Croom's payroll," I said, "and you got no call to come around threatening us with a pistol."

"I never threatened nobody, and don't you go sayin' I did!"

"Then what you doin' with the gun?"

"Don't look her in the eye, Earl!"

"I was going to shoot some dogs when I saw somebody sneaking around down here, and come to investigate. There's been stealing lately."

"Well, I've never set foot on your property, and he ain't neither."

"See to it you don't. Now get your work done and get on away from here." She turned and started back toward the house.

"Ma'am, wait a minute! What was that you said about the dogs?"

She stopped and turned around. A strange little smile touched the corners of her mouth. "My bitch got run over yesterday. I'm going to do away with the puppies."

"You're going to shoot 'em because they got no mama?"

"You tend to your business, I'll tend to mine."

I jumped the sagging fence and landed in front of her, a move so unexpected it startled everybody, including me. Em started out of the woods. "Give them to me," I said, "I'll take 'em off your hands."

"That's foolish. They ain't even weaned."

"I'll bottle feed 'em."

"They'll die."

"Well, at least I can try. It's better than shooting them before you even give 'em a chance!"

She hesitated, mulling it over.

"Give 'em to him," called Em. "Ain't no skin off yours one way or t'other." She shot him a sharp glance and he took an uncertain step toward the woods.

Miss Lilly took a lace handkerchief and pinched at the corner of her mouth, the blue disks floating. "What'll you give me for 'em?" she said.

"Give for 'em? What are they worth if you're going to kill them anyway?"

"*Nothing,* to me. The question is, what are they worth to you?"

I couldn't believe my ears. "But, I've got no money, and couldn't get any to buy dogs with!"

The old woman eyed me cannily. "Then maybe you and the big 'un would like to do some work for 'em."

"Yes, ma'am," I said eagerly, "we could do that! I'm good at chores . . ."

"Got a few big pieces of furniture to move down here from the big house. Too much for Williteer. You-all do that and maybe I'll give you the dogs."

Em and I looked at each other. The thought of setting foot across the threshold of the Waugh place threw a chill on the whole proposition. "Shoot the dogs," voted Em.

"No," I said, "I'll help you."

"You can't lift nothing."

"I know what I'm doing." I was already walking toward the house.

"Come back here!" yelled Em.

Miss Lilly caught the drift, and turned to follow me.

"Come back here, I said!" I kept walking. Once I glanced back; he was still at the fence, mumbling, shaking the wire, fretting and cursing to himself. But by the time we reached the yard he was trudging along up the hill, looking warily about.

Milss Lilly opened the door to an upstairs bedroom and it was obvious why she wanted it evacuated. There was an enormous tree limb hanging through a hole in the wall. The rain had peeled the wallpaper

77

and left a large brown stain on the floor, from which she had rolled back an oval hooked rug.

The furniture was of the old solid oak, elaborately scrolled variety that has no redeeming qualities except that it's "in the family," and *been* in the family, and therefore can't be got rid of, and travels from generation to generation, with the taste of some unschooled and ignorant pioneer girl tormenting every subsequent bride until it meets one with the guts to throw it out. Or smart enough to sell it to the fools who pull U-Hauls and hang out at auctions. Miss Lilly hated it, I could tell by the way she looked at it, but there she was, locked in the tradition, starting it on its way.

"Looks like you could of emptied the drawers," groaned Em, heaving a bureau away from the wall.

"They are empty," she said.

"Oh, God."

"Pick up now, don't you scar the floor!"

"Pick up, hell, I ain't gettin' no rupture rasslin' this junk!"

We maneuvered it through the door and Em got under it trying to lift the rusted rollers over the steps of the stairs. Miss Lilly hovered about fussing and fretting as though we were moving an invalid aunt. When it was dragged across the field and into the new house Em was ready to strike a bargain. "Give him one dog for the bureau, and do what you want with the others."

"Nothing doing, Em," I said.

And Miss Lilly was quick to take my side. "All or none."

Next we wrestled down a dresser with flapping wing mirrors and an overstuffed chair so large Em was moved to comment on the inordinate obesity of the Waugh line. Then he cut his hand knocking the bed apart. "Now look! Just look at that!" He stepped out and let the high headboard crash to the floor and examined his bleeding palm by the window. "Right across the lifeline," he said woefully. "I knew I should'a never set foot in this place."

Miss Lilly lifted her dress and tore a strip of cloth from somewhere underneath. But Em backed away in horror. "Get away from here! Wrop it in that thing hit'd rot off at the elbow!"

"Get blood poisoning, then, see if I care. Just don't you get blood on my furniture."

When the room was emptied she took a key from her pocket and locked it as casually as if she were leaving for the day. She moved to the other rooms, the kitchen, choosing what else she wanted dragged to the new house. When the last items were moved we were both eager to get out in the open air. I drew a drink from the well but Em shook his head. He kept his cut hand closed in a protective fist. Miss Lilly came and stood on the back steps. She said nothing.

"Well, we'll go now," I said. "Where are the puppies?"

Still she said nothing. She stood with her head tilted to allow the sun to her face.

"Ma'am, the puppies . . ." Then the realization hit me.

I looked back at her, still standing with her face to the sun. "Em, there ain't any puppies. There never was any puppies!"

"What?" Em rubbed his bleeding hand on his pants. "Where's the dogs, old woman? Look, we ain't got time to . . ."

A spidery hand leaped to her apron pocket and suddenly the pistol was leveled at his nose. The blue eyes blazed from the funnel of her bonnet.

I struggled to keep my voice steady.

"Let's go home, Em. It don't matter. Come on, it's gettin' late."

Em was outraged. "What do you mean? She said she would give you the dogs! We moved the goddamned furniture so she wouldn't kill the dogs!"

"Never mind about the dogs. Let's go."

"You mean that crazy old woman . . ." She was eyeing him curiously, as though he were some animal that had suddenly started speaking. "She ain't crazy.

79

She's just puttin' on. She knew what she was doin'."

I pulled him close, trying to keep my voice down. "Em, if there wasn't any dogs to shoot, why'd she bring a gun down to the fence in the first place?"

Em stopped blustering. I could see the logic taking hold. He looked at me, and back at Miss Lilly. If she wasn't going to shoot dogs, there was the very real possibility that she had fully intended to shoot us, and when she found we weren't prowlers, decided to trick us into the work.

The anger drained out of Em's face. We started backing away. At the edge of the field we broke and didn't stop running until we were across the fence and into the safety of the woods. When we looked back she was gone. The old house looked undisturbed and calm.

But the more I thought about it, the madder I got. "No, she set the whole thing up, made pure fools out of us."

Em's mood, on the other hand, seemed to reverse. "Aw, let it ride," he said. "She only done it 'cause she hadn't no money. Pulled it off, too, she did."

"Now look who's taking up for her," I said.

"Craziness was all she had to bargain with. She's proud, and folks like that would rather cheat and steal than beg."

"She didn't have to beg. She could of asked it as a favor."

"That's the same as beggin' if you got no way of payin' it back. 'Sides, you can't take no pride in somebody doin' you a favor. But now, you trick somebody, outsmart 'em, well, that ain't nothin' but good business. You can take pride in that." He sauntered along shaking his head, chuckling, whipping at milkweeds with a stick.

With a full afternoon before us and nothing to do, we decided to stop off at Mr. Teague's for a frozen Pepsi and pass a little time with Tio. Through some malfunction, Mr. Teague's drink box had one corner that froze drinks solid. I have never encountered another one with that characteristic, though I still look for it in every box I open. He could have charged double, even triple for those drinks, and got it. I have known boys to sit on his curb for hours waiting for their drinks to freeze.

Alvah Teague's gray brick wedge of a grocery store had sat on that knoll in the Ape Yard longer than anyone could remember. It had been there, and run by Mr. Teague's grandfather, when it was hardly more than a trading post in the hollow north of what was to become the town. Captain McIntosh's mule-mounted cotton farmers supplied themselves at the store before they forded the Little Iron and shot up half a regiment of Union regulars at the battle of Social Rose. When Alvah Teague inherited it, people were still riding half a day by wagon to shop there. That was before Roe Mill changed hands, and the infamous quarry was dug, and everyone who could moved out.

Now supermarkets were climbing the foothills—there was a new one opening in Galaxy Plaza that afternoon—and Teague's place was dying. The half-moon lettering, *Teague & Son*, had peeled to mere tracings on the window. The floor sloped dangerously under the meat cases, and the pine bench along the outside wall, worn slick and grainy by generations of weather and overalls, was empty of Saturday loafers.

As we neared the store Em suddenly stopped and pointed to a tennis shoe swinging from under the front awning. Putting his finger to his lips, he crept to the corner of the store, then pounced forward and yelled, *"Hyaaah!,"* simultaneously giving the canvas awning a violent shake.

There was a startled cry, and a skinny black boy dropped down from the awning, swinging by his knees from the crossbrace. Hanging upside down, he shook a wrench in the Indian's face. "You ain't no funnier'n you ever was, Jojohn. Now, put me back up. I'm just about done."

"Ain't you gon' say you glad to see me?"

"I'm 'on hit you where you live with this crescent wrench, you don't put me back up."

81

Em sighed and lifted him back on his perch and helped himself to peanuts from the parching machine. "What you makin' now?" he asked.

"Automatic awning raiser. Raises and lowers the awning without cranking."

"That mus' be a help," Em said.

"Ain't no other store got one."

Tio Grant was my age, though slightly smaller and considerably bonier, with a felt hat with square holes in the crown permanently affixed to his head. He wore the hat with everything—or with nothing, as when we went inner-tubing on the river. It was his trademark, he said.

Tio had lived with Mr. Teague since his mother died, when he was five years old. She used to do the little hunchbacked grocer's washing and ironing and what other little housekeeping was required in the three rooms over the store, and Mr. Teague gave him an apple or a cracker and let him play in the store while his mother worked upstairs. On slow days he began letting her drop the boy off while she went to work elsewhere, and soon Tio became a familiar sight around the store, scurrying to fetch things from the shelves and scattering sweeping compound before Mr. Teague's broom. Sometimes Mr. Teague let him wear a pinned-up apron with a stub of pencil stuck in the pocket. After the Grant woman died of pneumonia, it came as no real surprise to anyone when Mr. Teague marched down to the neighbor who had taken the boy in, and fetched him and his belongings back to the store. Tio had been there ever since, despite the fact that Mr. Teague threatened to throw him out about every other day.

Tio and I had started hanging around together shortly after Em came to the Ape Yard, and I suppose, next to Em, we were each other's closest friends. Everybody in the Ape Yard liked Tio, but living with Mr. Teague had made Tio a little too white for the other boys. Mr. Teague dressed him better than most of the black boys at old Pelham Grace School on the river, demanded better grades from him, and brought him up sharp in private if he forgot the difference between politeness and hang-dog cringing when dealing with people uptown. I knew what it was like. My being from the Ape Yard was plenty enough to keep my classmates in Quarrytown at a distance from me. I suppose it was that peculiar position we shared of not really belonging to either community that made Tio and me hit it off so well.

The only real fistfight we ever had was over the question of race.

It started when I discovered in geography class that my height was exactly that of the average African pygmy, and the teacher had me stand up and demonstrate it to the class. It was one of the few times I was ever taken notice of in class, and I was pretty excited. So that Sunday when Tio showed up, I was carrying Em's frog gig, dressed in a bath towel with my body coated with mud, all set to play pygmy.

Tio balked at the idea.

"Man, you can't be no pygmy. Pygmies are black, everybody knows that."

"What difference does that make? I'm the right size for it."

"Never work. Now, I can be the pygmy, but you'll have to be sump'n else."

"What are you talking about? I'm the only one the right size for it. The *exact* size for it, whereas, *by the book,* you are at least two inches too short! It's just as bad to be the wrong size as the wrong color."

Tio was unmoved. "I'll grow into the right size; you ain't never going to be the right color."

Neither of us would budge. I thought Tio was being uncommonly stubborn, even for him. We had both been Japanese samurai without any problem. But, of course, that had been *his* idea.

Finally he hit on what was to him the perfect solution: "Tell you what," he said, "I'll be the pygmy—you can be a midget."

"What!"

"What's wrong with it! A pygmy gets to hunt with a spear and be wild. Whoever heard of a wild midget!"

But Tio had that look on his face that always gave me a knot in the stomach, the look that said that, as usual, he had found a hole in my argument and was just about to hang it around my neck.

"Earl, you know as well as I do that stunted black folks are called pygmies. Stunted white folks are called midgets. Now, if my folks choose to hunt dangerous animals and live wild and free, and yours end up in the circus—makin' folks *laugh*—that ain't no fault of mine."

I think it was at that point that I proceeded to show him how wild my folks could be.

The awning raiser was only the latest of Tio's time- or money-saving projects. He was constantly inventing devices or devising methods to improve operations at the store. He had salvaged a paddle-fan, with one paddle missing, from the back of the barbershop, installed it in the ceiling and got it working again. Unevenly, but working. He argued with the wholesaler's driver about the most efficient way to stock the storeroom. He initiated countless new methods for checking the inventory, several of which did save time, but none of which were simple enough for Mr. Teague to understand. He was good, and Mr. Teague depended on him more and more. He could butcher a side of beef, he knew the price of every article in the store and with Mr. Teague's arthritis getting worse, Tio was doing practically all of the bookkeeping. For the most part, Mr. Teague gave his inventive mind free rein, and sometimes had cause to regret it. When the city installed the new parking meters around the square uptown, Tio was soon caught protecting Mr. Teague's Model-A truck with a homemade jimmy key. The judge let them both off with a warning. "Got a mind like a damned hummingbird," Mr. Teague would say, "flits and spurts around, you never know *where* it's going to light!"

Tio dropped to the ground and carefully ordered his toolbox, then stood back admiring the odd structure of angle braces and garage-door springs mounted under the awning. "Now, ain't that beautiful?" he said.

"Takes my breath away," said Em.

Tio dragged us inside to point out other recent improvements: a rotating display of canned goods, tilted shelves that allowed the next item to slide to the front to replace the one removed, the rebuilt motor in the meat case.

"You ain't messed with the drink box, I hope," I said.

Tio grinned. "I know when to leave well enough alone." We opened our Pepsis and covered the sputting ice with our mouths. "Come on out back," he said. He led us to the rear loading dock and pointed out a derrick with a swinging platform operated by a winch and chain. "My automatic freight elevator," he said. "Watch this." He levered a sack of potatoes onto the platform and winched it aloft into the second-floor storeroom. He pulled another lever and dumped it off.

"Not bad," Em admitted.

"And that gridwork runs the length of the store. Mr. Teague can't lift like he used to. I got the idea watching 'em move beeves at the packing plant. 'Course, I made a few modifications."

"Course."

"Got to know what you're doing, though. The wholesaler's driver tried it, and it threw him out down here." Tio made a wry mouth and dipped a thumb at his crotch. "Hey, I never showed you the awning raiser!" He hopped to the ground and ran up the stairs leading to the three rooms he and Mr. Teague shared over the store. "Y'all go back around front."

We returned to the front of the store. Tio was leaning out of the upstairs. "Now, here's how she works," he said. "There's a lever mounted up here just inside the window. You pull it down, the counterweights fall, which shifts those rods along that axis and lowers the awning, and at the same time cocks the springs. So then, if you want it raised, all you got to do is flip it . . ."

"*Tioooo!*" The front door burst open and Alvah

Teague lurched onto the sidewalk, a wispy, thin little man with large ears and watery eyes and his galluses riding high on his rounded back. In his seventies, Mr. Teague was at an age when the mind sometimes skips a beat, and familiar words begin to hide, giving him a tendency toward long stares and vague answers. His hearing was starting to go, too, reducing his voice to a mumble, except when he was shouting, as he was doing now. *"Where is he? Where is that scoundrel now?"*

"Got him treed," said Em, pointing.

"Up here, Mr. Teague," called Tio.

Mr. Teague backed up until he could see that high. "Where you been? I told you to wake me at two o'clock!"

"It ain't two o'clock yet."

"Don't argue with me! Get down here and lock the store!"

"You want me to lock the store?"

"If you can spare the time from your other affairs."

"What for?"

"We're going to the Grand Opening of that new Valley Farm market everybody's talking about!"

"Aw," said Tio, "what you want to go there for?"

"Because, from all accounts it's going to put me in the poorhouse and relieve me of you and my other aggravations, and I'm going to pay my respects! Earl, get in the truck and help me steer. That wheel's gettin' too stiff for me."

"Tio can drive," I said.

"I know Tio can drive! It's what converted me to Christianity! *Em, get outa them peanuts!"*

Em dropped the lid of the parching machine and squirmed on the tailgate with a double handful. I got under the wheel and Mr. Teague squeezed in beside me, got settled, and turned the engine over.

"Hey, just a second," yelled Tio, "look at this." He flipped the awning lever. Nothing happened. He flipped it again, and again. Same result. Mr. Teague was worrying the truck into gear. Tio threw his arms in disgust and ran out and down the outside stairs.

He made the tailgate just as we were backing away from the curb.

But as we turned to start up the hill, the old canvas awning suddenly contracted against the wall with such a prodigious, dust-clouding wallop that several passers-by jumped into the street.

We crossed the railroad and drove into Quarrytown, on streets that still showed patches of brick, into the four blocks of stores that made up the main business district, around the tree-shaded square with its Confederate soldier at attention, and out past the poolroom with its loafers at ease. The Little Holland highway, like most roads leading out of Quarrytown, was strung with corrugated metal granite sheds, their broad doors open to the light and air. Stonecutters, broad-backed men with features as sharp and gray-dusted as the stone they carved, guided the hammers and cable saws to satisfy that peculiar craving of man, who is content to mark his birth with a piece of paper, but wants his death recorded in stone.

The largest granite firm in town was Blue Light Monuments, owned by William Thurston, president of the Granite Association. The new shopping center was located on open acerage adjoining one of the largest Blue Light sheds, on land leased from Thurston, just inside the city limits.

With Mr. Teague pumping the bleeding brake and both of us riding the wheel, we managed to guide the old jalopy to a jolting halt in the field next to Galaxy Plaza. The parking area was jammed with milling crowds. A miniature carnival was in operation—kiddie rides, candied apples, a man shooting dogs from a cannon. We moved to the edge of the crowd listening to the mayor's welcoming speech in front of the Valley Farm store. A man gave Tio and me free balloons.

When the mayor had finished his speech, lauding the new supermarket as "the most modern unit of the fastest growing food chain in the United States," and congratulating the company official, a man in a blue serge suit and buttondown collar, for electing to locate it in Quarrytown, "the crossroads of the Emerging New South," he and Miss Quarrytown High cut the ribbon, then picked it up and pretended to cut it several times more for the *Star* photographer. Then the mayor led the people inside, he and Miss Quarrytown High pushing a decorated cart on a ceremonial shopping tour with the photographer ranging around them popping flash bulbs like a giant lightning bug on a leash. The crowd fanned out through the aisles, pointing, marveling, leaving the children behind to jump up and down on the magic mats that made the doors pop open. Mr. Teague squeezed through the maelstrom, dodging the doors, nodding to people he knew, and once inside, stopped cold.

The old man stood blinking in the fluorescent glare, the celestial sweep of music. He was dwarfed in sudden pyramids, shelves of goods higher than his head. The aisle stretching away before him held more foodstuffs than his entire store, and there were others, hills of them under the signs and streamers; bins of hardware, a housewares section, a complete drugstore displayed along the wall.

Mr. Teague moved down the aisle, fingering, touching labels, ticking off the numbers of different brands. He stopped to wave his hand in the fog of open dairy cases, to peer in the upright freezers. At the end a white enameled meat market ran the entire width of the store. A half-dozen men in paper-boat hats ran up and down filling orders, and behind a glass wall others operated on the blocks. Unbelieving, Mr. Tague moved to the counter, piled high with cellophaned chickens and preweighed slabs of meat. He lifted a package and read the blue-stamped price, tilted his glasses and examined it again. "That's sirloin, mind you," he whispered to Tio, *"sirloin* going for that price!" A young man in a spotless apron appeared at the counter. "Help you with something, sir?" Mr. Teague looked at him, waved his hand absently, put down the package and moved away.

At the produce department he stopped to lift bars of packaged tomatoes, nearly the same size as billiard balls, and to examine the okra, pole beans, asparagus, all of a uniform length and all encased in see-through wrap under the slanted mirrors.

He had to rove every aisle, finger every stacked display. It seemed hours before we finally moved past the weighing station and out past the clacking registers. At the door, the man in the blue suit stepped out of the cubicle office. He looked at Mr. Teague's apron and smiled and put out his hand.

"I'm John Ramsey, regional vice-president," he said, "nice of you to drop in." Mr. Teague gave him a vague stare. "Well, now that you've seen us, what do you think of us?" The man folded his arms complacently. He had confronted a lot of small grocers.

Mr. Teague looked puzzled, trying to place something. He stood looking out over the store. Finally it struck him, his eyes grew wide. "It's the smell!"

"Beg pardon?"

He pointed an accusing finger. "Your store's got no smell!"

"I'm afraid I don't . . ."

"And how can it have any, when you got everything embalmed in plastic? People like to get to the food, man, sniff a little, pinch a little. Even your meat market's got no smell, it's more like a damned hospital! And your produce, everything portioned out that way, that's the way you feed livestock, not people!"

"Our methods," said Mr. Ramsey quietly, "are dictated by efficiency in handling volume merchandise. People don't want to take the trouble to punch and poke and feel and weigh. They haven't the time anymore. They want to be fed in the quickest possible way in the least amount of time. That's what we're doing. The little grocer on the corner had his day, Sir, and a fine day it was, but this," he waved his arm, "this is tomorrow."

"Then all I can say is God help us," said Mr. Teague. "God help us all." He started for the door and jumped back when it sprang open for him, and went out muttering and shaking his head.

Em put his arm around Mr. Teague's shoulder. "Didn't seem much to me, Alvah . . . All your place needs is dressin' up a little! Here, let me tell you what you oughta do . . ."

7

AUGUST ENDED, AND WITH IT, THE LAST DAY OF SUMmer freedom. The day after Labor Day I dutifully greased down the sprigs of my new haircut, found a pair of socks that would stand exposure on the gymnasium floor for calisthenics in P.E. class, and with Gwen Burns beside me on that first day, walked over to College Avenue to enter the bewildering fracas of high school.

In those days, we attended elementary school through the seventh grade, then moved up to high school as "sub-freshmen" in the eighth. Quarrytown High, the only white school in town, was an old brick building with white cornerstones that stood crumbling majestically a block from town. On its left were the band-room annex and the gym, and behind, below the little barrackslike shop building, in a natural hollow between the school and the courthouse, was the Granite Bowl, the football stadium with granite seats fitted into the hillsides.

Gwen tugged me down the long cement-apron walkway, past club initiates in grotesque makeup and inside-out skirts—boys shining shoes and getting paddled, girls sweeping leaves and chanting club creeds—and into the crowded hall to the principal's office to fill out the forms to get me enrolled.

Back in the hall again, Gwen stood hugging her notebooks, surveying the tumult, her eyes lit with ecstasy.

"Oh, Earl, it's finally happening! I just can't wait!"

And she hurried off to take charge of her own home-room and left me to find my way through the halls jammed with girls in see-through blouses and rustling crinolines and boys fingering ducktails and greeting each other in jovial obscenities with honking male teenage voices:

"Blow boy!"

"Fish mouth!"

Stiff little middle fingers ranting in the air.

Overall, it was a uniformly lackluster small-town student population. In Quarrytown the children of the wealthy were sent off to exclusive prep schools in the mountains, or up North. Quarrytown High was made up of middle-class town kids mostly, who forti-fied themselves in tight little cliques and clubs; a few busloads from the country, most of whom were kin; and a scraggly fringe of lower-class poor, untalented and ugly, who sat in the corners of classrooms and waited for age sixteen to set them free.

"Earl Whitaker?" My homeroom teacher, Mrs. Barnes, looked up from the stack of registration cards. "Whitaker? Is he here?"

I raised my hand from the back of the room.

"Your enrollment card was signed by one of the teachers. Your parents are supposed to sign."

"I live with my great-aunt," I said.

She studied the card. "Sunflower Street, where is that? I don't believe I've ever heard of . . ."

"It's over by the fairgrounds," I said quickly.

"It's in the Ape Yard," corrected Benny Ford, who actually did live by the fairgrounds. "He lives in nig-gertown!"

"My God," roared another boy, "we got a coon in the room!"

Mrs. Barnes quieted the laughter and went on with the business of checking the roll. I kept my eyes down, making long, slow circles in my Blue Horse tablet. It was going to be grammar school all over again.

We spent the rest of the day finding our classes and getting acquainted with what our teachers expected of us. Math was going to be plain hell as usual, and General Science, with its physical laws and drawings of plants and engines, didn't promise to be much better, until Joe Breisner, the doctor's son, smuggled in a human anatomy book. While the teacher, Mrs. Claxton, droned on about flower pistils and stamens, we sat in the back trying to get worked up over close-up photographs of female genitals. Few of us found anything sexy in them, and a couple of the boys skipped lunch.

That afternoon, English and civics, both under Gwen Burns, proved to be the most threatening courses of all. We were going to "immer-r-rse" ourselves in great literature, majestic poetry. We would have playlets, we would have dramatic readings, we were going to make the arts "come a-lii-ve!" As for civics, there would be none of this rote learning of the levels of government, the Constitution and the Bill of Rights. We would become the government! We would elect our own mayor and councilmen, set up our own judicial system, and learn the workings of democracy firsthand!

Afterward we straggled out to the gym for a final P.E. class under Coach "Stumpy" Rayburn, who shouted us through a furious half-hour of calisthenics on the basketball court, then gathered us into a circle for a fatherly talk on the proper care and treatment of the Christian body, complete with charts on balanced diets and exhortations about sleep and exercise. After looking about to see that the girls were out of the gym, Coach also warned us about "abusing." We had to stop it, he said. It was like losing a pint of blood. And, as a Christian athlete, he believed it was a sin against the body, the temple of the soul. He finished by calling on every boy there who had indulged in the practice to be man enough to stand before the class and take an oath never to do it again.

There were several tense moments—with neck-craning and side-long glances—but it turned out all of us were pure.

"Oh, Jayell, it was wonderful," said Gwen that night on the steps after supper, "not anything like I expected."

"Yeah? What did you expect, love?" said Jayell, fanning out a match and taking a deep drag on his cigarette.

"Well, you know, half-asleep teachers, a petrified curriculum . . ."

"And it wasn't like that? Must have changed a lot since I was there."

"No, really—well, I'll admit the building's falling down and there can't be two books per pupil in the library, but the teachers are really trying, and the principal backs them up all the way."

"Old man Guest?"

"Yes, he explained that it was all a lack of funding, like all small school systems they have to operate on a shoestring, but he's wide open to new ideas, improvements of any kind."

Jayell was incredulous. "Harvey G. Guest?"

"Yes, honey. He was most receptive to the ideas I have for teaching civics, especially the student court system, he loved that."

"Well, I had trouble gettin' old Harvey Guest to even listen to a new idea. But I guess a pretty girl who'll work for nothing would make a difference."

"And there are some marvelous teachers. I met Thelma Martin, and we hit it off right away. She lives in Marble Park, and she was so excited that we may be moving up there."

"Thelma Martin, is she teaching there now?"

"Uh-huh, for two years now. Senior English, and she directs the school plays. She said you and she went to grammar school together."

"Yeah, I remember Thelma. Used to eat peas with her fingers—one at a time—like that."

"Oh, Jay!" Gwen put her arms around his legs and rested her head on his knees. "You know, I still can't believe it's all really happening. It's still like a crazy dream. Here I am in a strange town, ready to marry a man I hardly know. I suppose I should be scared to death. We really can be happy here, can't we, Jay?"

Jayell leaned down and kissed the top of her head, cradling her shoulders in his arms. "We can be. We will be."

They were quiet for a time, watching lightning bugs lifting off the lawn.

"I got another letter from the folks today, wanting to know if we've set a date yet. I think Mother suspects we're living together."

"Well, now. I can get her an affidavit with eight solid-gold signatures in no time flat. Wait, tell 'em we just—hold hands occasionally."

"Don't be snide. You know how old-fashioned they are. This whole thing came as quite a shock to them —and they still don't know what to make of you."

"Do tell. I didn't think your mother was going to let me in the yard."

"But I had my way, didn't I?" she said, looking up at him. "I always have my way."

"Always." He was leaning down to kiss her when she turned away and moved up on the step beside him.

"Jayell, what was that company you said was trying to hire you, the one that had copied some of your designs?"

"Smithbilt, out of Miami."

"Is it a big company?"

"One of the biggest in the Southeast, I guess. They got started in this area with Marble Park, and now they're throwing up subdivisions in every little town around here. They're one of those quick-build corporate developers."

"They must really be impressed with you if they're stealing your ideas.'

"Anything other than four walls, a roof and a carport is a radical idea to Smithbilt."

"What did they offer you?"

"The moon, the stars, the president's eldest daughter . . ."

"Now, Jay, be serious."

"Well, where are you going with this line of questioning?"

"I was just thinking—if you had a regular job it would help toward our own house, and . . ."

"What are you talking about? I've got a job! A hell of a job, and I've got the money for our house, enough for the land and a good start on the house anyway."

"For a start, but you can't start putting scraps and salvage in a house in Marble Park, Jay."

"You've seen my houses! Do they look like scraps?"

"Now, calm down, calm down."

"Look, we've picked out the lot in Marble Park. You decide what you want in a house and I'll start building it tomorrow! That's what's holding me up, not the money. I've got the money. Do you think you're marrying a welfare case?"

She put her arms around him. "I think I'm marrying a man who heats up a little too fast, that's what I think."

"Well, you're talking foolish. Foolish talk."

"It probably is. I just have so much to get accustomed to, Jay. The way you think, the way you live, well, it's just so different from the way I grew up. You see things where I see nothing, like this Ape Yard. It's inconceivable to me why you've lived down here all these years, why you waste your talents building those little architectural gems for people who can't possibly appreciate them, let alone afford them. It's all so completely foreign to me. But I took a chance, didn't I? I gave up my world and came to live with you."

"And to try to take me out of mine?" he said.

"That's not fair, Jayell."

"Listen, I agreed to move to Marble Park, that's all. I have lived down here because I'm free down here. There are no demands, no expectations. I work the way I do for the same reason, and I will not give that up."

"Well, for heaven's sake, I just thought of it as a

95

temporary thing, until we got on our feet. And it would mean so much to the folks . . ."

Jayell took her by the shoulders. "I made no promises, you have to remember that, not to you, not to your folks. You knew the way I lived, and to make sure you knew, I brought you down here to see it firsthand. Now you've seen me, not as some fake character in the never-never world of a college campus but as I really am, and if you can't take me as I really am, and the way I live, maybe the best thing for you to do is get on the next Greyhound."

Gwen shoved his arms away and stood up. Her voice was calm, but hot with anger. "I can do that, Jayell," she said. "Believe me, I can do that."

He arose and stood facing her. There was a long moment there in the dark, of indecision, of testing.

And, not surprisingly, it was Jayell who broke. Just as quickly as he had raised the wall, he shattered it, contrite, seizing her in his arms. "No you can't," he said fiercely. "You can never do that, you can't even talk like that!"

The porchlight flicked on and Miss Esther flung open the screen. "Bedtime, Mr. Whitaker!"

"My Lord, I'd forgotten he was here," said Gwen turning, as I slid out of the glider.

Miss Esther peered around the door toward the dark at the end of the porch. "And bring that old gentleman with you."

Without a word, Mr. Rampey got up out of the swing and shuffled sheepishly down the porch, lifted his derby to Gwen and Jayell, and followed me into the house.

"Jee-sus," I heard Gwen say.

8

FROM THE FIRST, THE GIRL HAD BEEN STRIKING SPARKS
at the boardinghouse. As we waited for Jayell to build
them a house, she made her presence increasingly felt.
She wrinkled her nose at most of Farette's meals. She
argued politics with the men, who knew nothing
about politics, which accomplished nothing and took
away the fun. She pointedly asked Mr. Woodall what
brand of cigar he was smoking, and he took the hint
and clumped to the porch. And she brought Mrs.
Cline to the edge of a stroke by calling her favorite
faith-healing evangelist a fraud. In a household devoted to the Back to the Bible Broadcast, she played
Buddhist chants on her phonograph, and would groan
and stalk off to her room the minute anybody turned
on the Grand Ole Opry.

It was the age difference, I supposed at first, but
as the days went by, I was sure it was more than that,
only I ddn't know what. Finally, one day when I
caught Jayell in one of his reflective moods, when
he might be disposed to talk about and make sense
on such matters, I asked him about it.

"Jayell, what is it with Gwen? I can't figure her out,
and nobody else seems able to either. Does she like
us or not?"

We were sitting in his truck at the end of a working
day waiting for Skeeter and Carlos to finish gathering
up tools for a jobsite. Jayell slid down in the seat
and rested his lame leg over the side of the door.
He chuckled to himself. "Oh, yeah, Earl, she likes
you enough all right, I guess. It's just that the boarders represent what she's trying so hard to get away
from. Country folks scare a brass cracker to death."

"A what?"

Jayell laughed. "Brass cracker. That's what I call these New South kids, the first-generation-off-the-farm crowd. See, Earl, the South's going industrial now. Since the war the big corporations have been racing each other down here, looking for that crop of cheap nonunion hands, the most precious crop ever produced in the South. Now everybody wants to move to the city and join up with that new middle class, and they're still trying to shake the hick image. That's Gwen, trying so hard, but still so unsure of herself."

"But I thought she was from Atlanta?"

"Oh, she is! First-generation city. Her father moved to town and opened a Firestone store! But every Sunday they get in the car and drive out to the country to see Granny and Grandpa, just twenty miles out of town, and still living in another century. That's what eats at Gwen, and the kids who are like her—that reminds her of how close to hicksville they still are. They're ashamed of that farm background and running from it as hard as they can, flooding into the cities: Charlotte, Birmingham, *modern Atlanta!* When I was in school up there, I used to laugh when I heard the brass crackers telling the Northern kids, 'Atlanta is not Georgia! Atlanta is not Georgia!' Hah! Atlanta is the essence of Georgia . . . the brass cracker capital of the South!" He shook his head. "Atlanta—that overweight 'Southern Princess,' humping her shoulders into the skyline and trying so hard to lift her skirts off Georgia soil.

"Lord, I almost drowned in it when I was up there, all that strident, nouveau middle-class striving. Ballet from New York and beatniks for the park, sharecroppers' daughters reading Zen and freeing love. Existentialists in Sears underwear. But the sophistication is as fleecy as the dogwood blooms. The roots are still deep in Georgia clay. It's still a race of farmers' sons you see on Peachtree Street.

"And that's my lovely Gwen: a hard veneer of city brass, but still pure cracker inside. Don't you worry about it, Early boy, she'll settle down. It's just a phase she's going through. Once she gets a mite surer of herself—gets up to Marble Park and established securely in the nouveau middle class, she'll loosen up."

"You think so?"

"Oh, sure"—Jayell leaned close and whispered confidentially—"you got to remember—at heart she's a good old country girl," and threw his head back against the seat, his laughter cackling out on the afternoon.

But if she loosened up in the following weeks, I couldn't tell it, and even without the problem of two classes a day under Miss Burns, it was plain from the start that this was not going to be a blue-ribbon year. The trouble started in my first class, math, with an ominous introduction to algebra, the most treacherous member of the arithmetic family I'd come across yet. Em looked in one night while I was tussling with it, cursing and throwing wads of paper, to ask if I wanted to slip out for a while. There was a marathon poker game under way at Lew Birdsong's, and when Em played poker he liked to have me around to keep an eye on the other players.

"I can't," I grumbled, "there's an algebra test tomorrow."

"Algebra?" He peered over my shoulder. "What's that?"

"Aw, it's a kind of arithmetic, only there's nothin' about it that's got anything to do with arithmetic. They use letters instead of numbers so you can't tell what's goin' on!"

"How can you do arithmetic without numbers?"

"That's what the hell I'd like to know!"

"Well, you have a good time with that. I'm goin' down to Birdsong's where they still play with numbers."

Science class would have been interesting, I suppose, if Mrs. Claxton hadn't turned it into an art class. Every picture in our biology book had to be copied off into our notebooks, and I don't care what I had to draw, from a flower to a frog, somehow it always came out looking like a map of a swamp.

Physical education was a foregone conclusion. I could never get under a high fly ball. I always seemed to run toward the boy who most wanted to tackle me, and I couldn't have hit a basketball goal if they set it on the floor at my feet. Having noted all this, along with my lopsided pushups, bony shoulders and general skinny condition, Coach Rayburn, a kindly soul at heart, gave up on me from the start, probably consoling himself with the thought that at least I was safe from the draft.

My one moment of distinction came when we got to the wrestling mat. There, for the first time, having grown up in the Ape Yard proved to be an advantage. Few of the black boys in the hollow had baseball, football or basketball gear, so what we did mostly when we got tired of rolling hoops, kicking cans, and shooting slingshots was wrestle. We wrestled for hours, up and down gullies, on creek banks, singly, in pairs, ganging up on the big ones like Carlos in "bring down the bear," and in mob free-for-alls in the sedgefields. And I learned early that in wrestling, speed, balance and being able to read your opponent were just as important as strength. On the mat I was a mad octopus, and it finally took a senior to calm me enough to pin me. Coach Rayburn was so impressed that I think if the school had had a wrestling team he would have put me on it, and started training me, and turned me into a star athlete, and the school and the world would have taken notice of me. That was a dream I had at the time, anyway. But, of course, it never happened, and Coach and I figuratively shook hands on a passing grade in P.E.

The problem with Gwen was, I had her teaching at me at home as well as at school. The boarders could clear out when she started in, but I was her student; I had to stay on the porch after supper and listen to her long discourses on literature and poetry, and "real meanings" behind passages that were written in plain enough English. To her, no author, no poet ever said exactly what he meant; he put down something else, and you had to try and dig out what he was really getting at, which seemed to me a complete waste of time.

"It's no wonder you feel that way," she said. "Look at that bookcase in the hall. Don't the people in this house read anyone but Zane Grey and Ellery Queen?"

"Well, there's Mrs. Cline's *True Detective* magazines, but Miss Esther don't like for me to read them. She makes Mrs. Cline keep 'em in her bureau drawer."

The teacher thought. "I know the school library is atrocious—what about the public library, do you ever go there?"

"Oh, no, nobody hardly ever goes there because of the librarian, Mrs. Watkins—old, snappish woman, got this big goiter. And you can't say a *word* the whole time you're in there. They say Mrs. Watkins keeps her silence rule in force even when there's nobody there but her. She don't even talk to herself. You know what I used to think? I used to think Mrs. Watkins' goiter was all of those unspoken words locked in her throat."

"Earl, you're wandering again. Listen, listen to me now as I read this verse from Browning . . ."

And so it went, with no peace: Browning, Frost, Shelley, Keats, the darkness of Poe, the verbal rainstorms of Thomas Wolfe. Em happened by one evening in time to get caught up in Twain's "Baker's Blue-Jay Yarn" and leaned on the porch and laughed until tears came to his eyes. That so enthralled Gwen that she started trying to enrich him, too, but all of her "serious" stuff went right over his head. At her insistent pleading he came back a couple of nights and sat and smoked and stared while she read, but even she could see she was getting nowhere. When Em responded to nothing else but a reading of the bounding rhythms of Vachel Lindsay, and went rocking about the yard shaking his behind, the teacher gave up and banished him from our literary circle.

By this time the boarders were unified, for the

first time, in a single purpose: they wanted her out of there. Even Miss Esther started to drop hints:

"Jayell, have y'all decided on your house yet?"

"I can't pin it down," he said. "What Gwen would like, and what I can bring myself to build! Damnit, they got codes up there!"

"You never had trouble with building codes before," said Miss Esther.

"Not structural—design. Up there they all got to *look* right to suit a committee, and what that committee likes is boxes!"

"Well," said Mrs. Metcalf, "maybe she wouldn't really like living up there."

"Oh, it's what she wants, heart and soul."

"It takes me out," said Mr. Rampey. "She took a shine to you at the college because you build the wild ones, and now you're sayin' she wants a regular house."

"I've got to find the right combination," said Jayell. "Something really good, really fine, and yet plain and old-fashioned enough for Gwen to like it. I think that's one of the reasons she insists on living in a suburb like Marble Park. She knows they won't let me go too far up there."

"Well, it seems to me the simplest thing to do would be to just sit down with the girl and let her tell you what she wants," said Miss Esther.

"I have! We've spent hours at it, and get nowhere! See, the hard part is getting Gwen to admit to her tastes. At heart she's an old-fashioned girl, the home and hearth, grandpa's-farm type, and she's not about to acknowledge that. So we made a deal. I'll build the house, something I guaranteed she'd like, and she won't see it until it's finished."

"Sounds like you're taking an awful chance," said Mr. Rampey.

"You think I can't read her! My specialty is looking inside of people and building what they really want. And you think I don't know this girl I'm going to marry?"

No one could argue that point.

102

"Well," Miss Esther concluded, "You go right on looking till you find what you want. In the meantime she's more than welcome here, and that's all that's to be said on it."

And so the thing rocked along. The girl was a nuisance to me, too, of course, but I tried to keep an open mind about her, like Miss Esther, trying not to form a definite dislike for her.

Until the day when, through nothing but her own callousness, she came so close to exposing the gentle secret of Mrs. Bell. Then my feelings about her hardened like a rock.

Among all the gradations of character at the boardinghouse, there was at least one existing polarity, that between Mrs. Porter and Mrs. Bell. They were an inseparable pair, always together, and there were no two more different people alive.

Mrs. Porter was a sufferer. We had all learned about the hell of Mrs. Porter's childhood and the hell of Mrs. Porter's marriage, and she shared with us unreservedly the hell of her declining years. Let Mrs. Porter come on the porch and a foreboding chill cut the air, all banter ceased, and one imagined bugs scurried higher in the vines and worms in the planters dived deep. Any ear that wandered near was seized on the spot, no matter if that ear had become as stony as the courthouse steps. And having heard a story once in no way disqualified you from hearing it again; rather, it solidified your standing in her circle of confidants and permitted access to even darker secrets. Thus, the plumber learned of both her father's desertion of the family and her husband's penchant for strip poker. The men who put down the linoleum knew the real reason for her brother's dishonorable discharge from the army, and the man caught repairing the furnace found out what a time she had with her hysterectomy. The mailman became so deaf at our house you had to follow him down the street to get his attention on any matter at all.

Mrs. Porter suffered greatly, but she understood that everyone else suffered too, and was ever ready

103

to share the pain. That was her attitude toward Mrs. Bell's drinking problem. She was shocked, of course, when she first suspicioned it, but quick and joyous in Mrs. Bell's defense. "Lord, she's had a hard enough time of it since they lost that farm, and little enough help she's had from her daughter and that idol-worshiping Catholic she married! You can't expect a person that's lived the quiet, sheltered life she has to forbear like somebody's had the knocks I have, praise the Lord."

With Mrs. Bell, she was able to turn outward. There had to be suffering, and if it was someone else's—and she could share—it didn't have to be on her own. And so she sat—when her aged spaniel died, when the drugstore threatened to close her account, when word came of sickness or troubles in the family, and rocked and consoled Mrs. Bell.

On the other hand, we knew next to nothing about Mrs. Bell. She moved in from the country when her husband died, and although her daughter had since married well and moved to Marble Park, she never came to visit. Mrs. Bell was the gentlest person I ever knew. A lady of impeccable manners, she moved about the house and grounds like a wisp of smoke, enshrouded always in her own quiet aura of dignity and peace. You couldn't talk *with* Mrs. Bell, for she seldom spoke, but she was always ready to listen, and you never felt uncomfortable with her; nothing about her was tense or awkward, even her way of sitting erect and still in a rocking chair. But as you talked the words simply disappeared in the silence of some bottomless well, absorbed in the nether regions of that impenetrable mind, and you found yourself simply sitting quietly, sharing her presence. To all but Mrs. Porter this hampered, and finally killed, conversation. To Mrs. Porter silence was fuel.

No one really cared that Mrs. Bell was drinking. She didn't take drugs of any kind, and as Mr. Rampey said, with a case of arthritis like hers, she certainly needed something.

It was the worst case I ever saw. She could barely

open her hands. Yet she worked daily in her vegetable garden, bending from the hips like an experienced field hand, digging her knobby fingers determindly in the soil. Once I rounded the shed and found Mrs. Bell crying. She stood rubbing her fingers over the gnarled knuckles, her upturned face bright with pain. When she saw me, the pointed jaw quickly set and she pulled a sleeve across her face. "Foolish arthritis," she said apologetically, "mustn't give in to it." And she took out her trowel and went back to her garden.

There *was* some concern among the boarders that she was drinking hard shine, although the pint jar she received from the country man once a week hardly seemed cause for alarm. She certainly never showed any effects from it, and she never smelled of anything but bath powder. If anything, it made them more comfortable to know of her one weakness, to know that she was not the absolutely unflinching personality they thought.

I was the only one who knew Mrs. Bell's real secret, and the day that Gwen Burns came so close to exposing it I knew that, somehow, we had to get that teacher away from there.

It was a showery Sunday afternoon, one of the last warm days of September. I was sitting on the front steps watching a Dixie cup wash along the gutter and half listening to Mrs. Porter recount to Mrs. Bell the latest episode in her running battle with the paperboy.

" 'I ain't gonna put it in the box,' he said, 'I ain't got the time.' And I said, 'Yes you will, young man, if you deliver my paper at all.' So then, this morning, I heard him, *whap* against the house. 'Well! Well,' I said, but by the time I got my robe on he was gone. So, I didn't do a thing in the world but pick up the phone and call Ed Davis at the *Star* . . ."

Mrs. Porter stopped as Jayell's pickup rattled to the curb. Gwen got out, laughing, turned and kissed him and came trotting up the walk in her bathing suit. Sweetness flooded Mrs. Porter's face. She gripped the arms of her chair and leaned forward to spit over the rail. Gwen tried to get by with a nod but Mrs. Porter stopped her.

"Well, Miss Burns," she said, pinching at her mouth, "been to the lake, I see."

Gwen put her fists on her hips, returning the smile. "Nothing escapes you, does it, Mrs. Porter."

"Lord, you girls nowadays have more courage than we ever did, going out in public in an outfit like that. Next you know, girls will be running buck naked, I guess."

"It's called a bikini," said Gwen evenly, "and most people consider it quite respectable."

Mrs. Porter chuckled. "My, it's a wonder to me a little thing like that'd even stay on if you tried to swim in it."

"No worry about that," said Gwen, "I always take it off before I go in the water."

Mrs. Porter glowered, blinking, but could think of nothing to say. The girl beamed in triumph. She started toward the door, then stopped at the sound of a motor turning the corner. A mud-streaked car pulled in the driveway and a farmer got out with a twisted paper bag.

Gwen let the door close and called out cheerily, "Happy time, Mrs. Bell."

Mrs. Bell, acutely embarrassed, pulled herself from her chair and made her way to the edge of the porch.

"You know," mused Gwen aloud, "I've lived in the South all my life and I've never tasted shine."

"Miss Burns!" snapped Mrs. Porter.

Mrs. Bell paid the man, took the bag and turned for the house. Gwen stepped in front of her. "That is the real stuff, isn't it, Mrs. Bell? The old stumpy hole?"

"If you don't mind . . ." began Mrs. Bell.

"Oh, don't let Mrs. Porter spook you. I'll bet that White River tonic of hers is at least ninety proof. Do you mind if I have just a taste? I'm dying to know what it's like."

"Really, I—" Mrs. Bell was trying to edge by when

suddenly Gwen lifted the sack from her hand. "Well, at least let me see what it looks like. Better look away, Mrs. Porter, you'll turn to a pillar of salt or something." She was flipping open the top of the sack. "Really, Mrs. Bell, you shouldn't be so . . ."

"No, don't!" Before I realized what I was doing I had jumped onto the porch and grabbed the sack from the girl's hand. She looked at me in amazement. "What's got into you?"

"Leave her alone!" I realized the hand holding the bag was shaking, and put it behind me.

"My goodness, you'd think I was going to . . ."

"What's in there belongs to Mrs. Bell. You got no right to be takin' it away from her." I took Mrs. Bell's arm and led her through the door and up the stairs. At her room I turned the knob for her and handed her the sack. "Why do you put up with it?" I said angrily. "Why don't you tell them?"

Mrs. Bell smiled and shook her head. "Mrs. Porter needs my alcoholism," she said, and giving my arm a light squeeze, she slipped into her room.

I went to my own room and lay down on the bed. I was still angry, angry at Gwen, at Mrs. Porter, at the weakness that despises strength and makes strength feign weakness. Why couldn't they accept her for what she was?

I was jolted out of my thoughts by a soft tap, like a fingernail, on the door. I jumped out of bed and opened it and found Mrs. Bell clutching a robe over her slip. She smiled timidly and shook her head. "I'm afraid I need your help again. Would you mind?"

Mrs. Bell led me back to her room and took the sack off the bureau. "I tried to get it open, but Mr. Bowman has such a strong grip." She pulled the jar out of the sack.

The lid was punched full of holes, and instead of whiskey it contained a half-dozen live honeybees, flicking their wings and buzzing against the glass.

It was for her arthritis. It was an old country remedy—superstition perhaps, a ritual to toughen the will, but the only thing, she said, that helped. I braced

107

the jar against my thigh and wrenched loose the lid.

She had removed her robe and moved to the window in her slip. Very carefully she reached into the jar and picked out two angry bees. Placing one under each white armpit, she stood with her hands folded, the elegant face placid, immobile, staring out at the rain.

9

As it turned out, Jayell himself solved the problem. In a drunken tear, he abruptly announced, "Hell, I know what she wants is a plain old ordinary house, so by God, why don't I just build her a plain old ordinary house! What's she want, one of your Ranchero models, a Tara, a *Magnolia Manor?*" He ripped through the drawings and magazine clippings piled on his office desk. "All right, I'll build her the ordinariest house—what do I care? She's the one got to live in it, right? Ain't that what the salesmen say? I'll build such a box it'll get the Smithbilt Silver Medallion!"

Em Jojohn chuckled. "You couldn't build a house that looked like a house."

"Here it is." Jayell snatched a picture from the stack. "This is what she really drooled over. A converted barn, that's what's big this year. A New England barn converted into a house. Je-sus, would you look at that thing!"

"You got a problem there," said Em. "Ain't too many New England barns around here."

Jayell slammed down his bottle. "My God, Em, don't you know anything? That's what makes it fashionable! People don't want the original thing, they want reproductions! Some slick advertising guy puts a gimmick like this in a magazine, and people say,

'Oh, ain't that cute?' And right away want one like it. Only when they find there ain't too many dairy farmers ready to evict their cows and fill their barns with fools, there's a new reproduction market created. Hell, it's the whole secret of the antique business. Yessir, we'll build her a barn first, and then convert into a house. Them Marble Parkers will be frog-ass green with envy!"

"Marble Park?" I said. "Are you really going to build up there?"

Jayell winked. "Made a down payment on a lot this morning. Don't say nothing to Gwen."

"How them folks going to take to having a barn up there in them ranch styles?" said Em.

"Oh, listen, no problem there. They wouldn't stand for nothing really good, of course. But some cutesy notion like this, why it'll just fit right in. Juice up the neighborhood just enough to look 'clever,' but not far enough from mediocre to make 'em uncomfortable. Be cheaper too, when you think about it. I got enough barn salvage to reproduce one *hell* of a *barn!*"

The lot Jayell had bought was at the end of one of the newly paved subdivision streets. We trooped up there, the three of us and the ragged crew from Jayell's shop, and he roved over the site, laying out the house. And from what I saw, Jayell was right; the plans he outlined would fit right in with the carefully contrived mood of architectural freedom in Marble Park. Mostly the brick split-levels predominated, plus the predictable Southern "mansions" with fluted wooden columns, but there were several scattered attempts at buttoned-down striving toward the avant-garde: two or three circular houses, a three-story obelisk with only ground-floor windows, and one fine attempt at a castle, but the sun porch gave it away. Marble Park housed the granite executives, textile managers, bankers and others of the town's elite. It was a world of frantic golf and determined bridge parties, of dollar-down cabins at Lake Lorraine. They were the country clubbers, the Little Theater boosters, symphony supporters, Friends of the Library, a scant generation from corn huskings and quilting bees, but in there solid as boat payments, Spocking their children, trying.

Slowly the house began taking shape, and it was plain from the start that this was to be the strangest house Jayell ever built. It was a perfectly conventional, heavy-beamed barn, so devoid of Jayell's usual touches, his bizarre shapes and flying angles, that it might have been lifted straight from a Grandma Moses painting, so old-timey that it seemed to age as it grew from the ground. But if the house looked simple enough to the rest of us, for Jayell it was a torment, a crucible. He was relentlessly on the move, searching out the tiniest flaws, remeasuring, tearing out and changing, yelling in frustration, scrapping whole sections and starting again.

It was always strange to watch Jayell work, the flarings of temper, the sudden peaks of happiness, the long periods of overriding confidence that dipped suddenly into melancholy, but for some reason this project seemed to challenge him as none before. He brooded over it, he began drinking more than usual when he was working, he sat in the falling night when the others had gone, slugging from the bottle he picked up each morning at Dirsey's and staring intently at the house. I crawled up on the wood pile beside him. He was wound tight, covered with sweat and grime, trembling from exhaustion, anxiety.

"Jayell, why do you suffer so?"

He spoke through gritted teeth. "God is jealous of anyone who attempts to create. It's the ultimate sacrilege."

"It is?"

"That's why artists are so miserable. It's their punishment."

"But how can you say that—you believe in God."

"You gotta believe in Him," Jayell said, "even when He's wrong."

110

"It could be they suffer because they don't eat and sleep right too."

He whirled around on me. *"Are you going home now?"*

"Yes."

And I got down and did.

Despite all the starts and stops and changes, the house moved along, and from the smoothness of its shape, the natural way it came together, no one would ever guess the strain it was to get it that way. It just seemed the only way that house could have been built. And it was a beautiful house. The rooms were of moderate size, but spacious and comfortable, and the kitchen, ringed with cabinets and little alcoves, was airy and full of light. Nowhere did a board lie even slightly out of line; windows and heavy oak doors moved at the touch of a finger; and the overhead beams joined with a seeming interweaving of grains with not a razor's thickness of gap in the joints.

The furniture was less trouble than I expected. From under his bed at the shop Jayell pulled boxes of drawings, and within days the designs were emerging from his boys' lathes and planers. The real time-consumer was finding the right fabrics and having upholstery made; for some of the accessories and ornamental hardware Jayell had to make trips to Atlanta.

Helping Jayell with the house after school and doing my homework while eating leftovers from the oven before toppling into bed, and spending as much time as I had to with Gwen Burns, was getting to be almost more than I could bear. The teacher kept her end of the bargain and never asked a word about the house, but as it occupied more and more of Jayell's time, she devoted more of her attention to me.

One night as I was pulling down the covers, bone-tired and already half asleep, she came to my room, eyes afire with excitement, and swiftly closed the door behind her.

"Earl, may I share a secret with you?"

I said of course, expecting a sure catastrophe, and

trying to clear my head enough to meet it. She came and sat on the side of the bed, looked into my eyes for a moment, and whipped out a spiral notebook.

"I want to be a writer."

She waited, and when she got no reaction from me, she said, "What's the matter, don't you believe me?"

"Well, sure, but I don't see why you keep it a secret. Mrs. Cline wants to be one too, and she talks about it all the time."

"Mrs. Cline? The one with the detective magazines?"

"Uh-huh, she wants to write up a real murder for the magazines, but they don't happen that often around here, and when one does happen she can't get out to see about it. It's real sad."

"That nice little old lady. I would never have thought it."

"But she writes all the time anyway, and it's a nuisance. Miss Esther says she's about fed up with it."

The girl was shocked. "Why would she care about a thing like that? That poor, lonely little old . . ."

"Well, she wouldn't if Mrs. Cline would write somewhere besides the bathroom. But she won't; she sits in there and writes until her legs fall asleep and then somebody's got to help her to her room."

The teacher sat and looked at me. "Earl, I can't shake the feeling that you're somehow making fun of me."

"Oh, no, it's the truth. You can ask anybody."

"All right, never mind that now, here"—she opened the notebook and handed it to me—"now just read it aloud and tell me what you think. I don't expect you to grasp it all immediately, just let it seep in and see what it does to you inside, see if it evokes a response."

I looked down at the paper and could hardly believe my eyes. There were no capitals, periods or any kind of punctuation, not even paragraphs. It was all written in one big block, without a clue as to where one thought ended and another began. I looked at her to see if she was now making fun of me.

"It's all right," she said, "it's supposed to be that

way. It's called stream-of-consciousness. Go on, read."

So I started reading, punctuating when I gave out of breath. As best I could tell, it was a dream of some sort, with the girl describing all the things she saw. There were some nice things, fields of yellow flowers and throbbing-throated birds and melting sunsets; but then the picture got disturbed with "raging thoughts, like swirling bits of tissue paper, tumbling in the whirlpool of the mind." And finally the scene opened out on a meadow, with boys and girls, and it took on a decidedly different tone. Here things got down to specifics, with "great bronzed arms" and "hot ivory bellies" and "nymphs worshiping at the steeple of life." I stopped reading.

"What's the matter? Are you embarrassed?"

Embarrassed? At that age I still had trouble buying underwear from a lady clerk at Belk's!

"All right," she said, smiling, "but tell me, what do you think?"

"I—uh, I'm not sure, I'm afraid it's a little over my head."

She leaned close. "But tell me, did you *feel* anything?"

"Oh, yes, ma'am, especially toward the end . . ."

"That's enough!" she said ecstatically. "It's enough that you *felt* something. I get so discouraged in that English class, nothing moves them! I plan the most exciting lessons, full of nuggets, I hit them with things that should make their hair stand on end! And they just sit there. Every day I come away drained, the blood sucked right out of me!"

"Well, maybe we just got a dumb class."

"No, it's the same with the other teachers, only they just seem to accept it, to go along every day drilling the facts into them, getting it back on tests, and moving them up a grade. Teaching has to be more than that, but where do you start?"

I opened my mouth, and then realized, hell, I didn't have an answer for her.

"Well"—she got to her feet—"thank you anyway, Earl, for listening—for trying." She rolled the notebook and looked at it. "It may never amount to anything, but I have to have this release. Sometimes I feel so bottled up inside. I can trust you with my little secret, can't I. You won't tell the others."

"Oh, no, ma'am, but they wouldn't care anyway—so long as you don't write in the bathroom."

It was the wrong thing to say. She stopped at the door. "Good night, Earl," she said coolly.

"Good night."

It was no use, I thought. With some people, no matter which way you step, it's wrong.

She let up on me with the poetry and literature after that, and I thought maybe she had gotten discouraged and given up on me, and I was going to have some peace. But as it turned out a few days later, she was only gearing up enthusiasm for the court system she was establishing in civics.

10

"JAYELL, YOU'RE KILLING YOURSELF." GWEN SPREAD the sandwiches and potato salad on a sawhorse trestle. Since it was Saturday, Jayell, for once, had let the shop boys knock off at noon, but he had asked me to stay and help him salvage a small barn after we finished painting on the Ledbetter house. "Why don't you quit for the weekend? I never see you anymore."

"Promised to clear away a barn this afternoon." Jayell ate silently, his eyes scanning the nearly finished house.

"The Martins have offered us the use of their boat if we want to go down to the lake tomorrow. With cold weather coming, it'll probably be the last chance we'll get to go."

"Maybe, if I can get this one finished up this afternoon. Told Ledbetter I'd give him the keys Monday, else he's liable for another month's rent. That time in Atlanta threw everything off."

"Jay, what kind of life are we going to have, with you working eighteen hours a day . . ."

"Gwen, you know I barely scratch a living on these houses. Until I get the boys better trained and get some capital built up . . ."

"I know," she said, "and that's why I can't understand why you don't reconsider that Smithbilt offer. It sounds like a wonderful opportunity."

"How do you know about Smithbilt?"

"That man—Mr. Wyche?—was by the boardinghouse this morning. Jay, they've . . ." She stopped and turned to watch a blue station wagon pulling up to the jobsite. She looked at Jayell sheepishly. "I told him you'd be here this afternoon."

John Wyche, the Smithbilt vice-president, picked his way through the construction debris. "How's it coming, Jayell?"

'Hello, John," said Jayell, glancing at Gwen.

John Wyche was a large, energetic man who had a habit of hitching his pants as he talked. "Fine-looking house you've got there. Like I told this little lady, you get more done with a half-dozen nigger laborers than we can with a crew of skilled carpenters."

"You got too many," said Jayell. "We don't use two men to carry a two-by-four."

"Exactly," said Mr. Wyche, "absolutely right. That's what I want to talk to you about, Jayell. We're just getting too big—did I tell you we're starting a new development outside of Abbeville? New mill going up there and they want five hundred houses! Got the bulldozers in there now. We got to have help. *Got* to have help." He stopped and looked again at the house. "My God, do you ever build any two alike?"

"Ain't had to yet," said Jayell, munching a stalk of celery.

"Listen, Jay, I'll come right to it. We *got* to have somebody to coordinate construction in this area. The Miami office is on my neck constantly about this territory, and with the Abbeville thing coming up, I don't know what I'm going to do. I ought to be in the office right now. This whole area is booming, and indications are it's just getting started. New plants opening every day. That means people, Jayell, and people means houses. Now, the company sees yours scattered around the hills and they keep asking me, 'Who's this fellow with such originality—who builds houses like that with a handful of niggers and utility-grade lumber, and why can't we get him on our team?' And frankly, Jayell, I'm running out of answers."

Jayell smiled. "Like I've told you, John, I've got all I can handle."

'How can you realize out of a little unit like this? In the time you put up one, we build a dozen. We're prefabbing whole sections now and hauling them to the job by truck. With override alone you could make three times what you're making now."

"We've talked about that, John. You know it's not the money."

"Jayell, don't kid me. I know you're hanging by your fingernails. Any day now you're gonna stretch a little too far and your creditors are gonna clean you out! Besides, how many of these things can you build on what you're clearing? Now, you come and get a-hold of this Abbeville thing and get it rolling, and in the meantime we'll feed some of your ideas to our boys in Miami. Let them look them over, test the marketability, and if they think you've got something, hell, we can turn 'em out by the hundreds. We're interested in the low-income housing market too. If it doesn't work out, you've made a little extra money, and you can go right on building your houses. No harm done."

Jayell looked at Gwen, whose eyes were dancing with excitement. "John, I'm just not ready yet, and I don't know how I want to handle it when I am ready. What you say is true, I am hanging by my finger-nails, but if there's any way to do it on my own, that's the way I want to go."

Mr. Wyche was scribbling on the back of a busi-

116

ness card. "Had to have my home number unlisted —wife's orders—but you can reach me here anytime." He handed the card to Jayell. "You think it over, Jayell, that's all I ask, talk it over with this lovely lady, and you change your mind, you give me a call." He turned to Gwen and took both her hands in his. "Miss Burns, it's been a genuine pleasure. Incidentally, my son, Carl, is eagerly looking forward to trying out for the senior class play this year. Now I can well understand his sudden interest." He turned and walked quickly back to his car, leaving Gwen with an expression of surprise and pleasure.

Jayell chuckled. "If a six-foot-two linebacker turns up at the tryouts, digging his toe and looking like the last man at the Little Big Horn, that'll be Carl."

"Jayell, I don't think you're being fair."

"Ah, John's all right. He just oversells sometimes."

"It sounds like a great opportunity to me. Why don't you take a breather, go to work for them awhile and put some money in the bank. Your boys can keep this going on the side, can't they? Then, when the financial pressure is off somewhat, you can attack it again. You just need a rest, Jay."

Jayell nodded. "But when you've accustomed yourself to sleeping on the floor, there's a danger in getting in a nice, warm bed. You don't want to get out again. If I had to go either way, though, I'd rather be out there with a construction gang than sitting in an architect's office, I know that."

"Jay, you have a blue-collar, with *starch* in it."

"Just a clodhopper, baby."

She put her arms around his neck. "And speaking of nice warm beds . . ."

Jayell kissed her. "Don't forget to leave your window unlocked tonight."

"Jayell, how much longer are we going to play that silly game? Why don't I just come down to the shop?"

" 'Cause your bed's got springs! Besides, I kind of like being a porchclimber. Adds excitement."

"I'm convinced Mrs. Porter's putting a glass to the wall."

"Yeah? Well, tonight I'll throw her a few moans. Do her more good than her White River tonic."

"I wonder what we're doing for *him?*" Gwen nodded toward me. I got busy picking something from my sandwich.

Jayell laughed. "We probably just put him through puberty. Come on, big ears, let's go wreck a barn."

"Hey," said Gwen, "can I come too?"

"Ah—no," Jayell said quickly, "you might get hurt. Tearing down those old buildings can be tricky business."

"Well, you can't blame a girl for wanting to get out of doing lesson plans. Will you be late?"

"No, it's just behind the cemetery over the hill from the boardinghouse. I'll stop off and see you on my way back."

"Behind the cemetery!" I said.

Jaywell shot me a glance. "Let's go." He kissed Gwen again and climbed into the truck. When we were out of earshot, I said, "The Boggs place? The barn's at Phaedra Bogg's place? No wonder you didn't want her to come along."

"Take your choice," Jayell said, "you can keep talking or you can keep your job."

I kept my job.

Why Jayell broke up with blonde, long-legged Phaedra was still a mystery to me and everybody else. She was far and away the most beautiful girl in Pollard County, in a rough-edged sort of way, and her reputation never seemed to bother Jayell; certainly it was no wilder than his, though it did run him a close second, and maybe surpassed him in certain particulars, but on balance they seemed made for each other.

As for me, I'd made every effort to avoid Phaedra ever since the time I jumped out of the hedge with a cap pistol and popped a couple of shots at her as she was passing the boardinghouse, and she took the pistol away from me and beat it to pieces against a rock.

There was another time, when I was seven and she was twelve, that we might have encountered each other, but after what happened before I was in no mood to help her. That was the night that the sheriff and a search party came by the house to look for Phaedra after she had been missing for a couple of days and her hysterical father, the cemetery caretaker, convinced the sheriff that one of the Ape Yard negroes had dragged her off to the woods.

Em wanted us to go along with the men and help look for her. He said it would be good for me. But there was no way I would be caught near the woods at night, unless they dragged me. I had pretty well conquered my ghosts by that time by using the methods Em had taught me, but for some reason I could not go near the woods at night. There was no way to describe or explain to him the paralyzing dread that came over me at the sight of a clump of trees shadowed by dark. I would watch them from the window of the boardinghouse or the loft as the sun set, wondering about it, trying to recall some past incident that might have caused it, imagining the friendly trees as I knew them in the daytime, full of birds and squirrels, but nothing seemed to help. As the long shadows moved jaggedly into the fields, as the gloom slowly descended with malformed shapes of white limbs, and the streaks of dark hung like black tinsel among the trees, the cold, nameless dread came climbing as steadily as the blood coursing toward my heart. I tried not to make a big thing of it, but when we went on a hike through the woods, or inner-tubing down the river, I always carefully calculated the time and distance to be sure we would arrive at home before dark. Fighting Em down to the loft when he was drunk, I could sometimes forget, but usually I stayed the night in the loft after I got him there. And those nights I had to get him from Dirsey's and follow him on his rampages along the river, through the nightmarish world of licking tongues, of hostile creatures that touched and rubbed and skittered away and sat watching behind trees and under branches and climbed gleefully to warn others of my approach and wait ahead in other gangs for that one moment when they could get me alone—they all come as fervently to life in my mind as they were in those early dark days of childhood.

So when the opportunity came to venture into the woods behind the cemetery in search of the girl who had busted my cap pistol, I let it pass. After half a night of searching, it was Em who finally found her, hiding in a boiler in the remains of Tyndall's still. She had run away from her father, she said, who had come home shot down on moonshine and stay-awake pills and, as usual, itching to beat somebody. He used to beat both her and her mother, Phaedra said, but since her mama had gotten sick Phaedra had to bear it all, and she was fed up. She wasn't going back home come hell or high water. Sheriff Middleton had told her she was either going home or to the girls' reformatory. She finally went home, but only after scorching Em's ears for bird-dogging her, and sinking her teeth in the sheriff's hand.

As Phaedra moved along three years ahead of me in school, having failed a couple of grades along the way, I watched in fascination as this tough, croaky-voiced girl with the stringy blonde hair metamorphosed into a sleek, full-sweatered young woman. That froggy voice mellowed into a husky burr that did things to the hair on the back of your neck, and by the time she was thirteen she sported a figure that had the teachers lifting eyebrows at each other. And as she grew older, she grew wilder. There was a different sports car or hotrod buzzing over the hill through the cemetery almost every Saturday night, many of them belonging to sons of some of Quarrytown's best families, to take her to the drive-in, to restaurants out of town, to the dances at Taylorsville—to take her anywhere, of course, but home.

Jayell met her the year he taught at the high school, and, despite their age differnce, dated her a couple of times on the sly (more to ease his own conscience for dating a sixteen-year-old, no doubt, than any fear of the school system), and he said her low academic showing wasn't because she was dumb but because she just didn't give a damn. She was a whiz in math and science, he said, and could rasp out plant names by the hour, many in Latin, and ripped into frogs with a savage curiosity. She loaded her homeroom with the jars of mosses and odorous shrubs she was always collecting from the woods, until finally her teacher, who favored delicate blooms and pretty berries, put her foot down. The trouble was, that was *all* Phaedra cared about, and she let her other grades die. She just wouldn't average out. The girl didn't know a sonnet from a soup recipe, and despite the discovery that she had an above-average singing voice, they could no more get her to join the girls' chorus than they could lure her into the home economics kitchen. The teachers concluded that Phaedra elected the extra math and science classes just to be among the majority of boys in those classes, who were, no doubt, responsible to some degree for her high grades.

One day toward the end of that year, with Jayell leaving and Phaedra on the verge of failing again, she was standing at the pencil sharpener when Charley Thurston, the son of the president of the Blue Light Monument Company, whom she had dated once or twice, and no more, happened along behind her and gave her a hard pinch on her shimmying fanny. Phaedra, apparently in a sour mood, turned and smiled and gave Charley a wink, and then knocked him over a row of desks. Charley's parents said the bridgework alone cost four hundred dollars, and Charley had played first-chair trombone. Enough was enough, the principal had said, and suspended Phaedra for the rest of the year. Phaedra had said it was plenty for her, too, and chucked education altogether.

After that she and Jayell squared off in a serious two-year courtship that had everyone predicting that they would get married or kill each other, when suddenly Jayell broke away and left for Atlanta. He would never say why, or what happened. He just wouldn't talk about it. And no one ever asked him more than once.

Phaedra was now working at Nelson's Florist shop and singing Saturday nights with the Graniteers at the dances in Taylorsville.

"Take it easy on the tin," said Jayell, "he gets to keep that." I was on the roof of the Boggses' barn with a crowbar, making more noise than progress, while Jayell carefully pried off the weathered siding. The sun was hot despite the breeze, and before long the tin was burning through my tennis shoes. The barn was down near the woods. Jayell had come in the back road to avoid the house, but I knew it was only a matter of time.

"What the damn hell are you doing?"

Jayell dropped his crowbar and turned around, and there she stood, in skin-tight cut-off jeans and a white blouse knotted below her breasts.

"What the damn hell does it look like," said Jayell, retrieving his bar. "I'm tearing down this barn."

"What for?"

"I bought it off your old man for the lumber. That all right with you?"

She squinted up at me. "You see a gray mama cat up there?"

"Saw one down near the woods awhile ago."

"Probably moving the kittens. Give me a foot up," she told Jayell. She put a foot in his folded hands and hoisted herself easily through the rafters. After a search of the loft she said, "Yeah, I guess she moved them already. Damn, looks like Papa could have told me. Now I got to find 'em before the dogs do. Help me down." Jayell reached up for her and lifted her down again and she stood for a moment, her hands resting lightly on his shoulders. Without expression she said, "How you been, Jack?"

"Can't complain."

"Got the world's poor in castles yet?"

Jayell smiled. "Still working on it."

Phaedra nodded and walked back up the hill.

We stacked the siding and tin and went to work on the framing. The little barn was tacked together with country carpentry and came apart with little trouble. In a short time we were laying out the rafters and joists.

Phaedra drifted down the hill and sat in the wheelbarrow with a handful of raisins. She sat popping them into her mouth. "What you going to do with that scrap?"

"Build a house."

"Won't be much of a house."

Jayell didn't say anything. He climbed in the wall and started knocking out studs.

"Tick Weaver asked about you the other day. Said he hadn't seen you since you got back."

"How is old Tick?"

"Still pickin' guitar half the time—drunk on his ass the rest."

Jayell laughed and shook his head. "Been meaning to look in on those fellas."

"We know, you been—tied up."

"Hey"—Jayell wiped his face with a forearm—"you suppose you could find us a drink of water?"

"Sure." Phaedra slid out of the wheelbarrow and tugged at her blouse, pulling the cloth tight across her breasts; a seemingly unconscious movement, except that I knew Phaedra. "If you want something stronger, we've got a jug in the kitchen."

"No, water'll be fine."

"You can help me carry the glasses," she said, lifting a chin at me.

I threw down my bar and followed her up the hill. She moved ahead of me in a full Phaedra walk, brown legs stroking, careful of the motion in her shorts. It was intended for Jayell, of course, and it was just as well, since it would have been lost on me anyway. I was watching that house.

Phaedra's mother lived in a hospital bed in the living room, and ruled the house with a chart and a bell. The boys who dated Phaedra never went into the house, and the few who had seen her mother in recent years said they wished they hadn't. All I knew about her illness was Dr. Breisner's comment to Miss

Esther that it was a rare skin and muscle disease. There were many terrible things about it, he said, and probably the worst was that you could have it and live a long time.

I followed Phaedra through the Boggses' back porch, a screened-in jungle crammed with every kind of vegetation from the surrounding woods, with only a narrow pathway to the kitchen between sprouting pots and cans and curtains of vines swinging from homemade trellises.

Phaedra took an ice tray from the refrigerator and ran it under the spigot. "What's she like?"

"What's who like?"

"Keep your voice down. Look, sport, I didn't get you up here to play games. You know who—that bitch from Atlanta."

"Well, she's kind of—different."

"In what way?"

"It's kind of hard to say . . ."

"Well, come on! Three tits? What?"

"Gimme a minute, will you. I don't know. The best I can say—she's from Atlanta—but just lately. You know what I mean?"

"Holy Je-sus." Phaedra said in disgust.

"No, wait. Big city, but still . . . well, let me put it this way—she's a brass cracker. Now you got it?"

Phaedra nodded. She threw up her hands. "She's a brass cracker. Hand me those glasses." She moved to the window and flicked aside the curtain. "You think he loves her?"

"Yes," I said, without hesitation, "that I can say for sure. He loves her."

I hadn't meant to be cruel, but only to give it straight and quick when I was asked, as I knew from the start the question was coming. But when she turned and looked at me, there was not the jealousy or anger that I expected, that might have made me feel better. What was in her face was completely un-Phaedralike; a sudden softening, a flash of warmth that was totally unconscious, surprise-fixed before she caught herself and the features hardened again. "Well," she said, "I hope the little bastard gets what he deserves."

I reached in the cupboard for the glasses, but my fingers were sweaty and one of them slipped. I grabbed for it and knocked it into some jars on the sideboard.

There was an immediate response from the living room.

"What's that! Phaedra? That you back there?"

"You idiot!" Phaedra snapped.

"Phaedra! I hear—you got somebody back there with you? Who've you brought in this house? You better answer me!"

Phaedra was shoving me toward the door. "Get out, get out! Go!"

I needed no encouragement. I thrashed my way through the back porch greenery and the screen door and sprinted off down the hill.

Jayell was loading the last of the lumber on the truck. He looked at me in surprise. "What's wrong with you? Where's the water?"

"I, uh, didn't get it. You ready to go?"

"Didn't get it? You were gone long enough to dig a well! What's the matter, the old lady get after you?"

"Let's get out of here," I said. "We had no business coming here."

Jayell looked up toward the house, to the shadow standing amid the sprawling green of the porch. "Yeah," he said, "I guess you're right." And he started the truck and pulled slowly up the hill, watching to see that the lumber settled and was going to ride.

11

WHEN THE POLLARD COUNTY FAIR OPENED IN November, Em and I were ready; we had saved our money for weeks.

For entertainment, Quarrytown was about as well off as most small towns. There was the Tower Theater and traveling shows that still came through occasionally in those days, including a "science show" set up in a vacant lot by a man who stood on the tailgate of a pickup and did tricks with chemicals, then mixed up bread with a liquid he said was stomach acid, and blew up a balloon with it to show how his indigestion medicine worked; and there was a hypnotist who tried to put a man to sleep in the department-store window by chanting over the radio, but the crowd kept tapping on the glass with coins and waking the subject up. And, of course, there were the preachers; one, an ex-convict who sermonized through a cell door welded into the back of his van, was so popular because of his tirades against young people that he was held over to speak at the school assembly on Monday. But without his cell door he was just a pitiful old tramp up on the stage, ill at ease, jumping every time the hall bell went off.

So when the fair came to town, everybody turned out. Em was especially looking forward to a reading from a real carnival gypsy. He considered her more professional than Madame Edith out on the highway, whom he suspected was nine-tenths Italian.

Em and I rode the ferris wheel, knocked over some milk bottles, and threw some darts, and winning nothing, splurged on more rides and then wandered through the livestock barn. We had no interest in livestock, but it was free. Em got some cotton candy

126

and I ate a couple of hot dogs, despite Em's warning that a carnival was no place to be eating meat.

We wandered down the midway and watched a sharpshooter, a tall cowboy in charcoal gray pants and a pink shirt, popping balloons around a lady in a spinning board. Then Em spied the fortune teller's tent. He hustled me toward the shooting gallery.

"Here, boy," he said, stuffing a dollar bill in my pocket, "shoot slow and make it last."

I did, taking my time choosing a rifle and remembering to count my change between each round. Half an hour later I had very carefully fired twenty times and scored eighteen hits. I put down the rifle greatly pleased with myself. The man in the booth shoved a bone-handled pocketknife at me and told me for Christ's sake to go away. One of the blades was broken but he wouldn't listen.

As I was walking away, a voice spoke from between the tents bordering the gallery. "Not bad shootin' pardner, not bad a'tall." I turned, and there in the darkness stood the sharpshooter, his pink shirt glowing like neon. He pushed back his hat and smiled. "Those sights are bent, you know."

"I know," I said. "After the first couple of shots I allowed for that."

"Well, you know about guns, do you, sport?"

"Not much, but I'm learning. Someday I'll have a hundred of 'em. I saw you with that lady back there."

"Yeah? What you think of that shootin'?"

"Did you ever hit her?"

The cowboy laughed. "Once in a while, but she always recovers." He patted me on the shoulder and his hand smelled sweet. He left it there, massaging while he talked. "You talk about rifles now, I've got a collection that'd knock your eye out! Worth upwards of twenty thousand dollars."

"Yeah?"

"Got this big elephant gun I've been offered five thousand cash for, inlaid with pure silver, once belonged to the king of Belgium. 'Course, pistols I got all over the place. Got 'em with barrels that long,

127

two little derringers you could hide in a baby's hand. Say, you know, my trailer's just back over there, how'd you like to step back and have a look . . ." Then he stopped and shook his head. "But I guess we couldn't do that. Your folks'd be wonderin' where you was."

"Oh, no," I said, "ain't nobody but Jojohn, and he's gettin' the five-dollar reading."

"Yeah?" The cowboy glanced about. "Well, tell you what, you know I've got this little rifle, sweetest shootin' little .22 you ever saw, no real use to me, I took it on a trade, and I'll bet a boy like you could really take to a gun like that." As he talked he gently pulled me into the shadow. We moved toward the rear of the tents.

"H'yeaaahh-Noww . . ."

The cowboy released me and whirled around. Em stood silhouetted against the flashing midway, his head near the top of the tents. He stepped over the ropes and the sharpshooter backed into the side of the tent. The Indian moved close and looked down on him, the multicolored lights throwing unearthly strains of light across his face. The man tensed and made a sound in his throat.

"What's goin' on here?" rumbled Jojohn.

The cowboy pressed tighter into the canvas, trembling. "Please," he whispered softly.

They stood looking at each other.

Suddenly Em became ill at ease, a little embarrassed. He moved back and tossed his head. "Go, get out of here."

"I didn't mean no harm."

"Just get out of here."

The cowboy took a step, hesitated, then turned and walked away quickly, his boots swishing through the tall grass as he disappeared in the carnival night.

"What'd you go and do that for?" I said.

"You just stay in the light and don't go wanderin' off."

"He was only going to show me his gun collection! What'd you run him off for?"

128

"Tell you all about it sometime. Hey, you want to ride that loop thing again?"

"Tell me about what?"

"You ain't all clear on the *regular* kind yet. Ain't sump'n you wanta learn about back'ards. How about the scrambler? That thing'll shake your brains out!"

"I don't want to hide the scrambler."

"Wanta see the geek eat a live chicken?"

"No, *sir.*"

"How about the exhibits—the old lady's got some canned stuff entered."

"Aw, come on, Em . . ."

"Well, what you come to a fair for if you ain't gonna do nothin'?"

"I want you to tell me about that man, and why you acted that way."

So, Em told me. Seeing that I was not to be budged, he pulled me off to the side, and there on the edge of the midway, with its whirling music and flashing colored lights, Em created another unreal world for me. At first I couldn't believe it, and dogged him with questions. He answered as best he could, describing what he knew in minute detail, and he described this horror with a strange compassion. "I don't know the whys of it, some folks are just that way, and like anybody else that's different, it's hardest of all on them. 'Course, anybody messes with a child of either sex deserves to get his head busted in."

"Then why didn't you?" I said, still shaking, unable to shake the picture in my mind. "Why didn't you kill him?"

Em thought about it; shook his head. "I don't know. It's funny, I can hit a mannish woman without no trouble, but I never could hit a womanish man." Em studied me closely. "Anyhow, you got it all straight now?"

I nodded. I didn't feel like talking.

"Good boy. Now, tell you what, you go give the hobby horses a turn, whilst I make one more stop—then we'll go."

129

Em had spied the South Sea Islands Revue.

"You go ahead," I sighed. "I'll just wait here."

"Oh, no, not here." Em looked around quickly. "You go in the exhibit barn. You'll be safe there. Just stay with the local folks and look over the booths. It'll be educational." He pushed me toward the DAIRY PRODUCTS booth and struck out for the tent where heavy women in grass skirts had just finished sashaying around to the phonograph and were filing through the flap.

I hung around RURAL ELECTRIFICATION and THE QUARRIES OF POLLARD COUNTY as long as I could, then wandered out onto the midway again.

But the fair was ruined, out of kilter; the people who ran the rides looked dirty, the music was too loud, straining at artificial excitement. There was peeling paint and weariness, grotesqueness in the canvas signs of "The Python Girl!" and "Oscar, the Dog-faced Boy," sadness in black boys pitching hard-earned pennies in dishes to win dollars, in grown people with serious faces studying kernels of corn on bingo cards . . . "under the N, three . . ." Shaggy little ponies stood with drooping heads while children clambered noisily on their backs, waiting to plod ahead in the path their hooves had worn bare in the grass. A thousand miles in a thousand towns, a mindless trek in thirty-foot circles of infinity.

Em was wrong, I told myself. I knew all about sex. I had heard the jokes, seen the little books stolen from fathers' dressers, overheard the barbershop talk. But it was always between a man and a woman. The business about the cowboy just didn't fit, threw the whole system off. There was so much I didn't know, and no answer that ever seemed final.

The music built in the girlie tent, accompanied by bursts of applause and laughter and Em's unmistakable cries. Eventually, a crescendo, with pulsating drums and crashing cymbals. Then, as it reached its climax, there was a loud scream from one of the girls, and a commotion inside the tent. A moment later Em came through the flap, propelled by two policemen,

130

his cotton candy in one hand and a glittering G-string dangling from the other. "Wait now, gentlemen, don't get anxious now . . ." Expelled through the gate, he ran back to the fence for a few indignant words at the policemen. Finally he turned and saw me.

"Oh, there you are." Then he frowned, remembering. "Thought I told you to wait at the exhibit barn."

I handed him his fallen hat. "A lot of good it would have done me, with you out here."

"Oh, yeah. Well!" He clapped on his hat and held out the cotton candy. "Want some?"

"No," I said, "let's go."

Out on the highway, cars were bumper to bumper as the second-shift people headed for the fair.

"Man, them gals was sump'n." Em looked at me in the glow of headlights. "You all right? You don't look so good."

"I'm okay."

"How 'bout that ferris wheel! Could see the whole town from up there!"

We walked in silence for a while.

"See what I got?" Em twisted the G-string to make it sparkle. "That big blonde . . ."

I stopped, fighting the sickening swells.

"What's the matter, boy?" Em grabbed my arm and the cotton candy waved close to my face, glowing pink, thickly sweet.

I lurched away and vomited beside the road.

Em took his boots out of danger and sat on the bank until I finished. He sadly shook his head. "Told you them hot dogs was tainted."

As we came down the road toward the gulley, Tio was sitting in the darkness on Teague's front step. "How was the fair?" he said.

"Same old thing," I said. "Didn't you go?" I asked, even though I knew he hadn't. Things were getting worse by the day at the store. Tio had even cut out his Saturday picture show.

"Shoot," he said, bringing out frozen Pepsis, "I got better things to waste my money on."

131

"One thing about a fair," Em said, "every year they get new gals."

"They looked pretty old to me," I said.

"That's 'cause you don't know nothin' 'bout it. Ah, that big blonde was sump'n else." Em struck a match and looked in his wallet. "Two dollars. That'll do." He got up and dusted his pants. "You kids play nice and don't fight," and he shambled off down the road.

"Where's he off to now?" said Tio.

"Deva's place, I guess. The carnival gals got him all tore up. Tio, have you ever—done it?"

"Done what?"

"You know, with a girl."

"Oh, hundreds of times."

"Yeh, well, you must have *seen* it done."

"How come I must have seen it done?"

"Well, you know, they say black people do it a lot."

"Not around me they don't. How about you?"

"Now, who's going to be doing it at the boarding-house!"

"Yeah, I see what you mean." Tio chuckled. "I'll bet you could see it down at Deva's place. Bet they're doing it right out in the yard!"

"You ever been down there?"

"Just once. One Halloween night me and Skeeter and Carlos slipped down and spread a bucket of fish under the house. *Hooo*—by the time they found 'em you could smell that place two blocks away!"

"Wish you wouldn't talk about that," I said.

"What's the matter?"

"Ate some bad hot dogs at the fair." I swigged on the Pepsi. "Look," I said, "let's just go down to Deva's and have ourselves a look."

"You mean it?"

"Damn right! We been ignorant long enough. Here I done messed around pickin' up bits and pieces, and before I can get it all straight, things are startin' to run backwards. I've heard the talk and seen the pictures, now I'm gonna see it myself and get it clear."

Up to that time I myself had never ventured closer to Deva's than the corner, when I followed Em down one night. It was in the most notorious section of the Ape Yard, and the fights and carryings on were legend. But it was the only whorehouse in town where Em was welcome. A group of white women plied an informal trade at the Gibbs Hotel, but Em hadn't been allowed in there since the night he got drunk and tore up the lobby and three paying customers. Besides, Em was a bit shabby, even for the Gibbs, and he was dark enough to make the girls uneasy. Actually, he said, he was more comfortable at Deva's, and there was a big black woman named Mae who wore a red wig and hadn't any shame at all!

Once in the cindered alley beside the two-story house, we set about plotting the best way to get in. The front parlor was full of people, but they weren't doing anything but sitting and drinking and talking. "What's goin' on is goin' on up there," said Tio, pointing to the second-floor windows.

"Maybe we could slip in the back door."

Tio opened it and peeked in, then put his fingers to his lips and motioned me back outside. "People in the hall," he said. He thought he could climb the vines up the back porch, but they were rotten and he fell in the yard with both hands full of brittle stems and dead flowers. He was ready to call it quits. "I ain't bustin' my back breakin' in no whorehouse."

"Naw, we can't quit now," I said. "You got to try something else."

"What you mean I got to try? I don't see you doin' no tryin'! You're the one wantin' to see it in the first place. I've seen dogs do it; that convinces me. You're the one wantin' all the facts; seem like to me you ought to be the one doin' some climbin'!" Tio pulled himself sullenly on a parked fender. "Git somebody *killed!*"

As we sat and thought about it a knife fight broke out across the street and men in bloody shirts were chasing one another up the road. The people in Deva's place piled out onto the front porch and milled in the yard.

Tio jumped down off the car. "Now's our chance!"

We ran to the back door and into the hall and tip-toed up the stairs. The house was surprisingly similar to Miss Esther's. There was a single bulb burning at the head of the stairs, and as we got there a door opened down the hall. We made ourselves small behind a chifforobe. A young woman came out and led a man down the stairs.

We stopped at a couple of doors and listened, but heard nothing. Then we heard noises from the end of the hall. Tio looked at me and nodded. We crept to the door and listened, and knew we had found what we were looking for. That bed was in a lot of pain.

Tio slowly turned the knob and was easing the door open when a voice behind us boomed like a cannon.

"Whut is *dis!*"

She was enormous, a heavy-jowled black woman in a tent of shimmering yellow. I couldn't get over the size of that dress, and bright to hurt your eyes. Tio was the first to recover. "Hey, Miss Deva," he said, striking a broad grin.

"What the very—how'd you all get in here!"

Tio stayed cool. Hooking thumbs in his belt, he said, "Just lookin' around. Say, uh, you wouldn't have anything our size, would you?"

"I'll give you sump'n yo' size!" And next I knew she had us both by the collar and we were being carried down the stairs, our toes barely touching the carpet. When we reached the kitchen she plunked us in chairs and took a seat at the head of the table. Propping her heavy elbows on the oilcoth she aimed a finger at Tio. "Right now, mister, whut's this all about? And gimme that much sass and I'll jerk a knot in yo' tail."

Tio swallowed. "Well," he said, glancing at me, "we were just looking . . ."

"Looking for Jojohn," I blurted out.

"Who?" Deva jangled her plastic bracelets and leaned closer. "Lookin' for who?"

"Jojohn. Em Jojohn."

"Big Em? The Indian?"

"Yes, ma'am. But we can see he ain't here, so . . ."

I was interrupted by a man in a pin-striped suit rushing into the kitchen. He leaned down and whispered something in Deva's ear. Her face changed to sudden alarm. She said something quickly and the man nodded and left. "You two don't budge," she said, and she was up and gone.

Tio and I looked at each other and started to ease up from the table, but the cook racked a boiling kettle to the edge of the stove and shook her head.

"You heard what Miss Deva said."

We sat back down.

"Fine mess," Tio said, "just fine."

A moment later Deva returned, followed by Em Jojohn. "Come on," he said, "move."

"Em, we didn't mean to cause no trouble . . ."

"No time. No time. Trouble comin'—move!" He jerked us up from the table and shoved us out the back door. As we hit the yard a pair of headlights swung in from the street. Em dived, and the three of us went over the low wall as the headlights washed the yard. "Lay flat and don't make a sound," he said.

The car killed its lights and slid to a stop among the other parked cars. Instantly, those milling about disappeared. The yard was deserted and quiet. Wherever that dark green Continental went in the Ape Yard it trailed a wake of silence. It announced the presence of "Doc" Harley Bobo.

Doc Bobo was the town's black undertaker, and one of the wealthiest and most powerful men, black or white, in Pollard County. In addition to the cotton mill, he owned almost all of the residential property in Ape Yard, plus the Starlite Café and the other four shops and taverns clustered at the foot of the hill below Mr. Teague's in the place called Cabbage Alley. It was rumored that Doc Bobo also had money in white-owned businesses uptown, particularly the loan company, an insurance agency and a used-car lot that catered heavily to black trade. It was said that no business was conducted in the Ape Yard without Doc

135

Bobo being involved somewhere in the transaction. Hit-and-run solicitors such as home-improvement outfits, lawn-furniture salesmen, and itinerant peddlers of books, kitchenware and mail-order clothes, who normally do well in black communities, all found doors closed to them until they got directed to the two-story white funeral home with the blue neon clock sign set back behind the willows and magnolias on a spacious, well-kept lawn on Oglethorpe Street. Then, if they met with Doc Bobo's approval, one of his men went out to ride with them as they made calls, and they did a booming business.

During the war Doc Bobo was the source of supply for anything on the black market, and when the county went dry, Doc became the most reliable purveyor of quality moonshine. Most of his operations were thought to be confined to the Ape Yard, but when a hot-car ring that had operated in northeast Georgia for over two years was broken, it was traced to a garage on the Little Iron River. Thirteen blacks were arrested and the case was closed. Some of the families got monthly checks. Local officials saw no reason to get involved.

Doc Bobo was highly respected among influential whites. He often boasted that Pollard County had the highest level of registered black voters in the state, and it was understood that the political faction doing business with Bobo got a bloc of several thousand extra voters standing hat in hand on election day. It was Doc Bobo who was photographed with the governor breaking ground for the new Negro school; who bustled into the school auditorium the night of the Community Chest drive, gold tooth agleam, bearing the buckets of coins that represented the Ape Yard's contribution; and who gave soothing talks to the civic clubs.

Cruising the streets in his dark green limousine, his diamonds glinting in the sun, Doc Bobo was a calming influence to the town's white people. The law wasn't needed in the Ape Yard. Doc Bobo kept the peace. His "dog boys" were on patrol. If a crime was committed anywhere of which a black man was suspected, the sheriff simply picked up the phone. The next day a black man was in jail. Or dead.

To those blacks on the raw underside of that calm, he was not a man but a force, a presence as awesome as evil itself.

The door of Doc Bobo's green Continental opened and the splendidly built black giant, Clyde Fay, stepped out, tugged his cap down to his Roman nose, and moved across the yard to the shadows of the house with the flowing grace of a dancer, which he was said to have been at one time.

Presently another car came down the road and turned in at Deva's, a battered Plymouth with fins and a torn and squeaking fender. Several black men got out laughing and talking among themselves, quarry ledgehands, judging from their leather caps and dusty overalls. One of them carried a large paper sack.

As they started for the house a horn sounded—one sharp blast from the Continental—and they stopped. A shadow was moving along the house; it stopped between them and the door. The door opened momentarily and Clyde Fay was framed in the square. The men saw him and froze. The door quickly closed again. The men dropped back and began moving away, all but the one with the sack.

The man left facing Fay began shaking like a terrified child, whining. He started backing away. He backed into the grille of the Continental and stopped. He was murmuring something, pleading. Fay moved toward him, slowly, and as he drew closer the other man suddenly cried out and snatched something from the bag. A bottle of beer whirled past Fay's head and crashed against the wall. The man broke right, but with a single bound Fay was in front of him again. The man dodged again, and again, and each time Fay cut him off. In panic the man threw another bottle, missing Fay's head by inches. Another.

Then something peculiar happened: the Continental's lights came on! They shone directly in Fay's face, blinding him. Then I heard laughter from the limousine. Doc Bobo was playing a game.

Fay's lips spread in a wide grin, and as the bottles shot at him from the darkness he continued to dodge them with no more than a swift movement of a shoulder, a flick of the head. Cursing hoarsely, the man hurled bottle after bottle, each time the bottles missing their mark and bursting and foaming down the wall. When the bag was emptied the man screamed and broke to run, but instantly Fay was on him. He threw him against the house and went to work.

The house and the street were deathly quiet; in trancelike horror I listened to the man's back thumping against the boards with each precisioned blow that Fay, standing straight, delivered to his middle. Each strike was slow and measured, and it seemed Fay would never stop. Offering no resistance, the man stood with his eyes tightly closed, emitting tiny squeaking noises like a rubber doll when it's squeezed, enduring it more like a necessary operation than the wanton brutality that it was. And it was that, the acceptance of it, that was most horrible of all. When the man started to vomit blood Fay stepped away and delivered a final blow to his temple that sent him spinning to the ground.

Fay stopped to examine his sleeves in the headlights before getting into the car. He started the engine and the Continental pulled out of the yard.

The only movement was from the crumpled pile of overalls on the ground by the chimney, where the dying man lay drawing his knees up in agony.

And only a glimpse of that, for I was being lifted bodily in the air, and with Tio under one arm and me under the other, Em Jojohn was pounding acorss the stubble field toward home.

12

By the first of March the house in Marble Park was finished, a fact that was obvious to everyone, it seems, but Jayell Crooms. He still had Em and the older shop boys on the premises from dawn to dark, and expected the rest of us to keep coming directly from school, although there was little to do but tap and scrape, carry bits of lumber from here to there, and try to look busy enough not to get yelled at. When Jayell did turn up a bit of real work, we fell on it like a pack of terriers after a rat.

The Hendersons next door, who at first looked with suspicion on the crew of black boys, gradually fell into the spirit of the surprise for Gwen, and the spirit Jayell always seemed to create around anything he was building, and eventually they began supplying us with cookies and iced tea. They were now asking daily if Jayell was ready for Gwen to see the place yet. They wanted to have a house-warming party. Thelma Martin from down the street was bursting with excitement. She and the other teachers were planning showers.

Still Jayell roamed and fretted, touching up here, scraping a fleck of paint there, finding a hundred things wrong, cursing himself for sloppiness. Under that galling pettiness, plus the double pressures I was under at home and at school, I began to lose patience. Em quit outright, and before long even the shop boys began making excuses. Finally Jayell was left alone on the job, fuming, puttering, ranting to himself. The house stood framed among the trees like a three-dimensional painting, bright and strong and beautiful, waiting for its creator to give it up. And he kept trying, and couldn't.

If Gwen was suffering any anxiety about her future home during that time, she didn't have time to show it. She was preoccupied trying to figure out, and explain to the principal, Mr. Guest, why, since the institution of her model court system in civics, our classroom had degenerated into the rowdiest and most undisciplined in the school.

It had started out well enough, an imaginative innovation in the teaching of government, Mr. Guest had said, and praised it highly to the other teachers. In our courtroom Gwen was the judge, with student attorneys and police appointed by her, and the rest of the class filled out the juries and provided the criminal element. A person could be charged with cheating, shooting spitballs, passing notes, talking, or any number of other offenses listed in the Class Statutes on the bulletin board.

She appointed me a lawyer, which scared me to death at first, but after that first halting presentation before a jury, which, to my amazement, returned a verdict in my favor, I quickly began to gain confidence. It turned out there was no real trick to winning cases in our court; it was hard to produce actual witnesses to cheating or spitball shooting, because during tests the "witnesses" were pretty well occupied in concentrating, or cheating, themselves, and a veteran spitball shooter could get off a shot with one hand from under a desk with a fairly high degree of accuracy. Also, after the first week or so in our small democracy it was hard to pick a jury that didn't contain a few grateful criminals I had defended in the past. Our court had a ring of authenticity to it, too, which also worked to the defendant's advantage, in that the most damning evidence never carried as much weight as a good show.

Despite her position on the bench, Gwen could bring charges too, and her cases were the most ticklish to handle, but to our surprise, no one was more delighted than she was when a defendant was acquitted that she knew for a fact was guilty! This was American jurisprudence at its best, she said; it proved that everyone had an equal chance under the law, whether he was guilty or not. To us lawyers and criminals this was only right and proper, but it brought Nancy Buckhorn, the Methodist minister's daughter and our class prosecutor, close to tears. She and Gwen had to have several consultations.

Time after time Gwen demonstrated her complete and absolute faith in the system; she stuck to her guns and left discipline entirely up to the court no matter what, even when it became obvious that things were getting out of hand. As for the class, we were convinced that self-government was a wonderful thing indeed. By the approach of spring we were doing anything we wanted in class; cheating was rampant, spitballs and erasers showered the air, and students wandered in and out of class at will. I enjoyed the respect of my classmates that I had never had before, policemen were getting extra desserts at lunch, and it was virtually impossible to convict anyone on any charge whatsoever: all in all we were enjoying about as corrupt and lawless a society as could be imagined anywhere.

Swish.

The sound came from somewhere behind me, beyond the hedge. I paid little attention to it, and went back to sipping iced tea and reading my *Captain Marvel*.

It was Saturday, and one of the first days of reliable warmth. Spring in Quarrytown, that high in the foothills, was always an uncertain thing. The sun had been standing out brightly for weeks, and looked inviting enough through the windows, but when school let out, those who broke for the buses with their coats under their arms and sweaters knotted around their waists were likely as not soon wearing them on their shivering backs.

But that day it was warm. Down the road, Wash Fuller's martin gourds hung motionless in the sky, disturbed only by the intermittent landings and departings of martins busily bringing straws for their nests.

Wash's dog, Jincey, could sleep quietly at the step without having to move around the corner every time the wind shifted.

It was quiet in the yard. Insects worked in the scuppernong arbor and buzzed among the fruit trees, and beyond, to the left of the house, old Aaron Tim clucked softly to his brown, bony-shouldered mule as they broke ground for Mrs. Bell's garden.

It was decidedly spring.

I began to drowse and the print started running together. Then, from over the hedge there came a light slap, as of someone swatting an insect, followed by another swish of cloth on cloth, and I realized someone was in the hammock. Mr. Woodall often sunned himself there as soon as the weather permitted, but I knew he was inside listening to a ball game. You could hear the radio a block away.

"Damnit!" There was an angrier slap, a rustle of the hammock, and Gwen came around the hedge, dressed in white short shorts and a halter. "Oh . . . well, hello!" She watched me a moment, tucking in the ends of a towel she had wound into a turban. "I didn't know anyone was back here."

"I . . . I was just sitting here, reading." I felt the need to explain somehow, about being there. She had that look in her face.

A slow smile spread over her face. "It's all right," she said. "I'm flattered."

"Huh?"

"Don't be ashamed, Earl, it's perfectly normal at your age." She stepped closer and looked down at my comic book, standing so close I was aware of the tiny beads of perspiration on her long, shapely legs. "Back to your old habits, I see. Doesn't your aunt care about your reading those things?"

"Not when they don't cost anything. I traded this one off Fred Wygart, who gets 'em free at his daddy's drugstore."

She sat down beside me and took a cigarette from a blue case and lit it with a matching lighter. "I don't

142

know why I keep trying, I really don't. I beat my brains out, and I-just-can-not-get-through!"

"I'm sorry."

"Ah, I'm just upset about that civics class thing, I guess. I had another conference with Mr. Guest yesterday, and as of Monday, our court is permanently adjourned and I'm back to teaching the Constitution . . . the Bill of Rights . . . de-dah, de-dah, de-dah . . ."

"Oh, that's too bad."

"Well, school will be out soon. Maybe next year will be better. There's one happy note, at least. Thelma Martin's just discovered she's pregnant and she's arranged for me to take over as drama coach next year. Thank God and George Martin for that!" She turned and looked at me, blinking her eyes slowly, thinking.

"I can't act," I said quickly. "I couldn't even remember the lines! Miss Esther sends me to the store for two things, she's got to write 'em down, and, and clumsy? I can't even walk across a room without knocking things over . . ."

"Oh, stop it, Earl. What's the matter with you anyway? You have got to be the strangest kid I have ever come across. It's like pulling teeth to draw you out of yourself, and yet when I forced you into that lawyer part, you came on like gangbusters! You've got to learn to assert yourself, have a little confidence, or you're never going to have any friends."

"I've got friends," I said.

"Well, I've never seen them. You skulk around that school like you're afraid somebody's going to say 'boo' to you. Don't you have any special friends you hang around with?"

"Sure, there's Em, Tio, the shop boys . . ."

"Not these colored people, for heaven's sake. I mean white friends, outside of this—niggertown. You've gone to school all these years, surely you've developed a few white friends along the way."

"Yeah, but when school let out they went uptown and I came back to the Ape Yard."

"But there must have been class parties, little dances and hayrides and things."

It was hard to explain. "Oh, sure but, well, they all *knew* each other, they went to church together, they invited each other to join clubs, their folks went out together. Nobody knew me, they didn't know my folks, and when I came around it was always said, 'oh.' I guess I just got tired of that 'oh.' "

"Well, you can't bury yourself down here for the rest of your life, even Jayell has finally realized that. At some time, you've got to come to terms with the real world."

In that moment, for the first time, I think I got an inkling of what was in Gwen's mind, of the way she saw things. "This," I said, waving a hand toward the Ape Yard, "this is not *real* to you?"

She thought about it a moment, and laughed. "You know, now that you mention it, the whole place does have an unreal quality about it: look at your aunt, prodding those old people around like she's going to *make* them live a hundred years; old man Teague and your friend Tio, constantly patching up and slapping paint on that run-down grocery store as though they're going to turn it into a supermarket, and Jayell, creating those splendid little houses—for trash to live in! Even that horrible Indian you tag around after, undoubtedly the most grotesque, worthless caricature of a human being that ever drew breath, and he acts as if he were king of the world! I swear, not one of them has even the faintest grip on reality! Maybe the heat in this depressing hollow and—and the awful fumes from that quarry, do something to the brain after a while. At least there's hope for Jayell, if I can get him out of here in time. And you too, Earl, if you get out of here, and with the right kind of people."

"But I like the people down here. Tio's brighter than I am, at least he makes better grades, and Em —well, he's free and independent, that's his way, but if he liked you, and somebody tried to hurt you, he'd kill 'em, without even thinking about it. Have you got a better friend than that?"

"Earl, you're fantasizing again—and that's exactly what I'm talking about. Listen to me, very shortly

144

you'll be leaving all this. Nature forces change, whether we want it or not. You're growing up now, soon you'll want to move out of this hollow and start a life of your own, meet a girl . . . how about that," she asked, turning to me, "haven't you begun to notice any changes lately?"

I didn't say anything.

She took the towel from her hair and ran it down her legs, wiping off the perspiration. "How about girls, Earl? Surely there's some little girl at school you've taken a shine to by now."

"No."

"Oh, come on, you have begun to notice girls, haven't you? I don't know, you've had such a strange upbringing, it wouldn't surprise me if . . . you do *know* about sex, don't you?"

"Oh, back'ards and forwards!"

"Thank you."

"Huh?"

"My legs," she said, smiling, "you were staring at them."

"Oh, no, ma'am! I . . . I was just . . ."

"And you *were* watching me through the hedge, weren't you?"

I rolled the comic book and set my chin on it.

Her voice was firm. "Now listen to me, Earl, there's nothing wrong with a healthy interest in sex, but there's a great deal wrong with not being honest, with me, and with yourself. Now, you were looking at me, weren't you?"

I closed my eyes and nodded.

"There. And for being honest, and for the compliment to me, I thank you." She looked at me, shaking her head. "Lord, would you be a case study for Dr. Fenworth! He was my professor in Early Childhood Development." Suddenly she stubbed out her cigarette and got to her knees and faced me. "Tell me, what sports do you like. Football? Baseball? Basketball?"

I shook my head to each of them.

"Don't you like sports at all?"

"I like swimming—and Tio and I wrestle a lot."

"Oh, reea-ally!" She studied me closely. "Do you ever . . . ah, *dream* about girls?"

"Not especially."

"Let's analyze some of your dreams. Quick, what did you dream last night?"

"I don't remember."

"Ah, hah. Earl, I can't help you if you won't co-operate. Now, I want you to think carefully before you answer—and trust me. Do you ever dream about boys?"

"Oh, sure, lots of times."

She leaned closely, our noses almost touching. "And what boy do you dream about most?"

"Tio, I guess."

She straightened. "Oh, my God!"

Taking a moment to compose herself, she set her jaw, and said, "Earl, look at my breast!" And to my utter disbelief, she yanked down her halter top.

I broke out in a clammy sweat.

She waited.

I checked the clouds.

"Earl, you've got to try! Look at my breast!"

"Uh, which one?"

"My God you can't even—the left one, then, the left one! Look at it!"

I slowly lowered my eyes.

"Quick," she panted, "what are you thinking?"

"Miss Esther . . ."

"Ah, *hah!*"

"If she caught me at this she'd skin me alive. I've got to go."

She pulled up her halter and placed her hands on my shoulders. "You've got problems, Earl. I tell you what, why don't you and I go on a picnic."

"Do what?"

"Just the two of us, we'll go down to the lake and just sit under the trees and talk. I've got this book . . ."

As I was debating between faking a stroke and making an all-out break for the hedges, the sweet music of salvation touched my ear, the ragged piston bang of Jayell Croom's pickup.

Right away I knew something was up. The truck bed was filled with grinning shop boys. Jojohn waved from the cab. Jayell got out and came limping across the lawn in a new sports coat and tie, stitching with nerves. "Come on," he said, "get in the truck."

"What's all this?"

"I'll show you. Come on."

"But shouldn't I at least get dressed first?"

"Never mind," said Jayell, "get in, get in!"

Em was crawling in the back with the others. They hoisted me over the side.

"What's he want all of us along for?" I asked.

"Must be scared to go it alone," Em said.

"Well, I hope she likes it," said Skeeter. "I ain't goin' through that again!"

We drove out to Marble Park and up past the postage-stamp lawns, heads lifting from putters, from car washings and mowings, Gwen watching but not saying anything, fighting to control her hair. Jayell turned up the final hill and stopped before the house.

It was beautiful, framed there under the trees. Clean, massively built, but light as a song. We waited as Gwen got out and walked around the hood and stood looking at it.

"I came up here at sunrise," Jayell said, "and when I looked at it, I knew I'd done something special. I just walked around and around it. I'd turn away and then try to look at it fresh, and each time it looked new to me. Crazy." He looked at me and grinned. "Not sleeping and eating right, I guess. It's simple, not like anything I've done before—but I've never built anything better. That's me, with love. Boy, you think I'm crazy?"

"Everybody says so."

Jayell laughed. "Let's show her inside."

Gwen moved into the house stiffly, hesitantly. She stopped in the high-ceilinged living room and slid her hand over the marble mantlepiece. "It's beautiful, Jayell," she said, "perfectly beautiful."

But was she just complimenting him? There is a feeling you have when something is shared, a feeling that doesn't need bright smiles and glittering eyes. As yet, that feeling wasn't there.

"We carried them fireplace stones from the Mayhorn plantation," said Skeeter eagerly, "bet there's two ton of rock in there."

"Come sit in this chair," said Carlos, standing behind the brass-studded easy chair. "That's real leather, you know, ain't no vinyl." She sat in the chair, and sprang out with a laugh when it rocked. "I'm not ready for the knitting-needles bit yet, Carlos."

"That door's solid oak," said little Jackie James, "talk about a bother to hang? But, look here, moves like a feather . . ."

"Boys . . ." said Jayell. So we hushed, and followed her through the house, past the effort screaming to be noticed, the thousand small perfections hidden in simplicity, our teeth raw with wanting to speak, eagerly watching her face.

She liked the spacious kitchen, the abundance of cabinets. Perhaps they could hire somebody until she learned to cook. She was as terrible a cook as her mother. We trooped up the carpeted stairs, past the hand-rubbed miles of paneling. Skeeter dragged a rag along his brightly varnished banister rail. She was tickled with the nursery with its miniature furniture, done in blue, but teased Jayell that her family ran to girls. I stood by the crib admiring the dowels in the railings. A pure misery drilling those holes to equal depths. In the guest room even Jayell couldn't resist. He stamped the board planking of the floor, "That's real wooden pegs in there, you know. You don't see that anymore."

"Jayell," she said, "I just can't believe it. It's like a dream . . . like a dream." She was turning, really looking now, as if gradually recovering from shock. "The colors, everything, it's like you looked inside my head and . . ."

"Wait," said Jayell nervously, "wait a minute." And he pushed open the door to the master bedroom.

Gwen entered the room softly, her shoulders close, like a little girl.

If the rest of the house was wrought with meticulous effort and careful attention to Gwen's tastes, this room was Jayell's masterpiece. Gwen stood taking it all in, the gleaming mahogany, the dark beams soaring over the thick, luxurious carpet, the delicate ivory handles and elegant curving mirrors, the paintings, the drapes. It *was* Gwen, even I could see that, as much of her in line, in tone, in texture as can be said of a person in inanimate things. It sparkled around her, the love, the effort, the backbreaking devotion that only Jayell could give so completely, and not leave a trace of himself. She rested a hand on the post of the canopied bed and turned to look at him, her eyes moist, the sunlight striking gold in her hair.

A little electric pulse ran through the crowd in the hall. We were turning, grinning at each other. Jojohn slapped his hands. I wanted to shout! I could have grabbed her and kissed her and danced in the middle of the floor!

Then I caught Jayell's eye. He was smiling at us; he made a small motion with his head. Carlos nudged us, backing into the hall. He pulled the door to and we tiptoed softly down the stairs.

13

THE WEDDING WAS SET FOR THE SEVENTEENTH OF April, and it was to be a church wedding. Jayell wanted a quick civil ceremony, but since Gwen and her mother had conceded to his refusal to have the wedding in Atlanta, he felt he had to give in on that point.

Gwen's mother came to town a week prior to the wedding, and after one visit to the boardinghouse, put up at the Marble City Hotel and took her daughter with her. From the time she arrived, Mrs. Burns was completely in charge of the wedding plans. She was a butterfly general, flitting about, spluttering over this, swooping down on that, teary-eyed and always looking at the point of collapse, but always perfectly in command. On her arrival, Jayell disappeared, and stayed gone until the day of the wedding.

Gwen's father showed up the morning of the wedding with a sizable delegation of relatives. A tall man with Gwen's coloring and close-set eyes, he stood about smiling nervously through his horn-rimmed glasses, trying to keep out of the way, and looking as though he would like to become part of the furniture until the whole affair was over. Seeing his discomfort, Mr. Rampey and Mr. Burroughs took him around the church for a pass of the bottle and became his constant companions for the duration. Gwen's younger brother, Larry, a pre-med student at Emory, whom she had insisted be best man, blew into town around noon in a Thunderbird convertible emblazoned with fraternity decals and immediately made it clear that he preferred his own company to anyone else's. He stood apart twirling the wedding band on his little finger, a ring Gwen had allowed her mother to select in Atlanta, and watched the boarders troop by with a bemused expression as though he were cataloguing a parade of diseases.

The little Episcopal church was filled to overflowing. The whole boardinghouse had turned out for it. Funerals were old hat to our crowd, but a wedding fetched the lot. Miss Esther brought some of her church friends. Even Mr. Teague dressed up and came. We loaded up the groom's side of the aisle and the boarders out-cried the blood kin.

The Hendersons from Marble Park were there, plus many of Gwen's friends on the faculty at Quarrytown High, including Thelma Martin and her husband, George. "If somebody's getting Jayell Crooms to the altar," he was saying, "I don't want to miss it."

There was an uncommonly long wait, it seemed to

me, in getting the proceedings started. Chafing in the hard collar of a new white shirt, I sat next to a window, which was closed, as they all were, lest a breeze disturb some of Mrs. Burns's decorations, I suppose. The new sports coat Miss Esther bought me was stiflingly hot, which wasn't surprising. It was a hundred percent wool. But it was on sale.

After a while I became aware of a mild commotion in the church foyer. Nothing much, a very subdued wandering in and out, and whispering, the way it might be when a theater is afire and they're trying to decide how best to break it to the people. The minister went out. Then Mrs. Burns.

Then a very peculiar thing happened. The church windows began rising and falling. Starting at the rear, on our side, and moving up the length of the church, one after another would rise an inch or two, just enough to let the sunlight shine under the stained glass onto the startled people in the pews, then abruptly drop shut again.

When the window beside me went up the mystery was solved. It was Em Jojohn opening them from the outside, in search of me. As soon as his bloodshot eyes found me, relief flooded his face. He slapped a finger to his lips and frantically motioned me outside, and slammed down the window with such a loud bang the organist stopped playing.

"Said what?" shouted Mr. Woodall into the silence. The others fell to shushing him, but their whisperings only served to confuse him more, until the poor man was in such a state of agitation that Mrs. Bell and Mr. Jurgen had to lead him outside. I seized the opportunity and ducked out the side exit by the choir loft.

Jayell's pickup was outside, all decked out for the honeymoon, and Em beside it, dancing with excitement. Carlos steadied himself drunkenly at the wheel.

"What is it? What's wrong?"

Em formed his mouth to speak, but stopped, looking over my head, stark terror climbing in his eyes. I looked back, and saw that he had good reason.

It was Miss Esther coming down the sidewalk, marching as if to war.

She shouldered me aside and hung one of her wrath-of-hell stares on Jojohn. "Two seconds, mister!" she cried.

"It's old Jaybird," Em rumbled piteously, "he's down at Dirsey's, been there all night, says he ain't *studyin'* gettin' marr'ed!"

There was a very dark thunderhead that built over that brightly lit afternoon sidewalk, darkening us all in its shadow, centered directly over the top of Miss Esther's head. I was aware of it, and Em rolled his eyes aloft as if he could actually see it. Carlos sat quivering, more sober now than the Episcopal minister.

She looked from Em to Carlos. "Are you listening to me?"

They were.

"You climb in that truck, you go and get Mr. Jayell Crooms and have him at this church, in his wedding clothes, in twenty minutes flat—or you-will-wish-you-had-*never* been born!"

It was not a time to dawdle. Em hit the truck bed in a single bound and I snagged the tailgate and managed to climb aboard as Carlos was clawing away. The frightened boy squalled rubber two blocks up the street before he could get the truck into second gear. We cleared all four wheels on the railroad ramp, landed on the Ape Yard road, and careened down the hollow throwing gravel and scattering dogs, chickens and people, with Em standing at the windshield trying to spare what lives he could by shouting them out of the way. Tio saw us coming barely in time to run his fully loaded delivery bike into the creek.

Squealing to a momentary halt at the shop, Carlos ducked in and scooped up an armload of the formal wear Jayell had rented and threw it to me on his way back out. Miraculously, the whole outfit was there except for the cuff links, studs and one shoe.

We found Jayell leaning precariously on Dirsey's bar with one leg wrapped around the stool, a glass in one hand, a near-empty bottle in the other, from which he was studiously pouring whiskey on his wrist. The place was littered with empty bottles and full celebrants, sleeping peacefully where they fell. Dirsey patiently wiped a glass.

As we burst through the door Jayell turned groggily and pointed with the bottle. "I tole you . . . I ain't goin' . . ."

Before he could finish he was on his way out, Em's arms locked around his chest and Carlos carrying his feet.

Word apparently had spread, because on the return trip up the hollow, a crowd was ready and waiting. They lined the roads and hills, and cheered wildly as the truck came roaring by. Tio, standing beside his dripping bike, held up soaked tatters of what were once bags of groceries and shook them at us as we passed. I couldn't hear him, but his lips read: You-gonna-pay-for-this!

Bucketing back over the railroad, Carlos cut hard by the water department, taking the most direct route back to the church, even though it took us straight through the center of town. We shot across Main Street and into the square, scattering people in the crosswalks, with Jayell floundering in the back as Em and I stripped him down and stuffed him into his wedding clothes.

"I can't do it, Em!" Jayell sobbed drunkenly, "I can't!"

"I know, boy, but Miss Esther *said!*"

We had him clothed down to the missing shoe when Carlos ran up the sidewalk at the church. Miss Esther stood glowering from the steps, fist on her hip, pocketbook in her business hand.

"We done it," said Jojohn proudly, lowering Jayell to where Carlos could steady him. "Keep a hand on him, now." Jayell blinked about at those around him, his feet groping for moving earth.

Miss Esther came and stood before him. "Jayell, I feel like taking a stick of stovewood to you."

Jayell got her in focus, and slowly lowered his head.

"He'll start cryin' again," warned Em.

Gwen's mother was white. The minister stepped forward. "I'll explain there has been an unavoidable delay, and we'll reschedule for tomorrow."

Jayell's head came up sharply. "What?" Getting his bearings, he leaned forward, Em and Carlos still clinging, and pointed a finger in the minister's face. "What reschedule for tomorrow? The wedding's today, ain't it? These folks came from At-*lanta!* To see a *wedding!* You can't keep *Atlanta* folks waiting—for a *wedding!*" He nodded, pleased with himself. He had settled everything.

"Oh, my Lord, what shall we do?" wept Gwen's mother.

Jayell smiled benevolently at her, weaving in his crumpled clothes.

"Ma'am," said Em, removing his hat, "at least today's he's this far, and he's willin'. Knowin' this boy, I wouldn't take no chance on tomorra."

Jayell nodded again, and wiped his nose with a hanging cuff.

Miss Esther sighed and turned to Gwen's mother. "There's more'n a grain of truth to that. Seems to me you better go with what you got."

Mrs. Burns consulted briefly with her husband, whose only response was a shrug, and with the minister. Finally she said in a hard voice, one that reminded me of Gwen's that morning in the hall, "Well, I don't care. Whatever happens, my daughter deserves it. She deserves it. I tried to tell her. I just thank God we're not in Atlanta!"

"Amen!" said Jayell, and pulled away from Carlos to climb the steps. But he had trouble negotiating them, and Gwen's brother stepped up to take his arm. Jayell whirled around on him. "Put your hands on me, Larry, and I'll knock you on your ass!"

"Jaaayell!" barked Miss Esther.

"Well, I didn't want him for a best man anyway! The groom's supposed to pick the best man, ain't he? And I don't want *him* for my best man . . ." He pointed into the crowd below. "I want—I want Carlos!"

154

In the moment of stunned silence that followed he leaned down and clapped the startled black boy on the shoulder. "I want Carlos. He's the—best man I know."

There was tension in the air you could taste. The minister began anxiously clearing his throat.

"Jayell," said Miss Esther, "this has been enough for one day."

And to everyone's surprise, especially Em, Carlos and me, Jayell stared right back at her, and his voice was almost sober. "It's the most important day of my life, Miss Esther. I don't want that punk to stand up with me. I want my friends. I want it to be special."

And Miss Esther understood. Through the drunkenness, the disheveled appearance, the childlike petulance, she understood that it was a special day for him, simply more than he could handle.

"Well this," she said, "is just going too far. You're only half of all this, Jayell. You've got to remember—only half."

He considered, wobbling uncertainly on the step as he looked about. "Em, then. I want Em for my best man."

Miss Esther looked at Gwen's mother. "I don't care!" said the other woman with a quivering shake of her head. "I don't care!"

We had all started into the church when Jayell, primed by that victory, played his last card. Faking a stumble, he cried, "I can't make it! Carlos, come here!" and before anyone could react he reached down and hauled Carlos up the steps. "Em, you keep hold of that side, Carlos, get this one. Hurt my foot!" he called to the others. "Got to have my boy here help me. Hold that door there, son," he told the usher. "Atta boy." And before he could be stopped he was dragging the two of them through the foyer and down the bright blue carpeted aisle.

The service was strained, but beautiful, and if I had thought the boarders were crying before, at the first chord of the wedding march they showed that they had only been priming themselves. Before the ceremony was half over they had used up every Kleenex and pocket handkerchief in the pew. Miss Esther, prepared as usual for all contingencies, sat dry-eyed, one ear cocked to the proceedings, casually tearing off and passing along sheets of toilet paper she had wadded in her pocketbook.

I have to admit, it finally got to me too. Whether it was the decorations, the music and the flowers and the romantic atmosphere, seeing Jayell down there looking as helpless as all grooms look at the altar, or the knowledge that Gwen was moving out of the house, I don't know, but it was all I could do to keep from choking up.

Gwen almost choked too, when she appeared in the aisle and saw the rumpled condition Jayell was in, and Em and Carlos looking sheepishly at her on either side of him. But aside from that initial jerk of surprise, she never showed it; she gritted down and kept coming. Knowing Jayell, I guess she expected that the wedding might be different in some way.

Jayell looked hung out and dried. He stood stolidly through the rites, haltingly murmuring his vows, with the toes of his stockinged foot laid over the one with the shoe.

There was one awkward moment with the ring, a little chicanery I don't think anyone else caught, but which I recognized as pure Jayell, having his wish at last.

Em had stood listening intently for his cue, the ring handed to him by Gwen's brother clutched tightly in his fist, and when the minister called for it to be placed on the prayer book he shoveled it out on his glistening palm. But at that moment Jayell's elbow bumped Em's, and the ring dropped to the floor.

Instantly Jayell bent to retrieve it, and in a moment of apparent confusion, turned and shoved the ring on Carlos. The startled youth returned it to the prayer book with the speed with which he might have hand-fed a moccasin.

The minister took it to the altar for the blessing.

Jayell turned to Carlos and smiled.

As soon as they were pronounced man and wife, Jayell flipped up Gwen's veil and kissed her, and started hauling her down the aisle. Mrs. Burns caught up with them at the door, and amid the confusion of congratulating boarders, Em and Carlos breaking for sunlight and small boys throwing rice, she remembered them about the reception.

"You go right ahead and have it, darling," shouted Jayell.

"It's all right, Mother," said Gwen, catching at her gown as Jayell dragged her down the steps.

But as Jayell reached sunshine and fresh air, all the strain, exhaustion and booze seemed to hit him at once. He wavered unsteadily, recovered, pulled Gwen toward the truck.

"Jayell," cried George Martin, "you're taking my car," which sat all decorated at the curb.

"It's all right, Mother," said Gwen vacantly, and I realized the poor girl was feeling the strain too.

Jayell pulled at her, staggered again, and went down flat on the sidewalk.

Em hurriedly lifted him and stretched him out in the back of the truck, from which he raised himself momentarily in the shower of rice and yelled, "Carlos, get us out of here!" before collapsing again. Poor terrified Carlos obediently jumped behind the wheel and fired the engine.

"Y' ain't got your bride!" screamed Em, and quickly hoisted the girl and dumped her in the battered cab beside Carlos. Fighting her gown and veil with a fist full of flowers, Gwen finally got rid of the bouquet by flinging it in a high backward arc.

Gwen's mother stood on the steps sobbing hysterically, aimlessly shoving her husband's arm back and forth. Mr. Burns, well braced by Burroughs and Rampey, simply stood smiling as his daughter was driven away to her honeymoon in a truck with her groom passed out in the back.

Carlos, a wrung-out case of nerves, with a white girl in a bridal gown beside him, clutched the wheel and drove carefully this time, with such depth of concentration that I don't think he took note of it when he cut too short at the corner and pulled the front fender off of Larry Burns's Thunderbird.

BOOK TWO

14

ONE OF THE FINEST THINGS TO DO ON A DULL SUNDAY
afternoon was to go inner-tubing on the Little Iron
River, and the Sunday following Jayell's wedding
seemed perfect. The day had all the markings: the
heat, the sluggish stirrings, the musty smell, like yesterday called back for another shift. By midmorning
even the clouds seemed to knock off and head home,
dragging their shadows over the clothesline. When I
went down after breakfast to wake Jojohn, he rubbed
his soles on the blanket, scratched the insides of his
thighs, opened one eye and hung a string of pro-
fanity across a full minute. It was just that kind of a
day.

So, with nothing ahead more promising than a
snake handler with cottonmouths everybody *knew*
were defanged coming to Lamb of God Pentecostal
that night, we decided to pick up Tio and have a
day's run on the river. It would be good for Tio, too,
we figured. Despite his and Em's nagging, Mr. Teague
still hadn't come around to the notion of investing
his small savings in a complete remodeling job and
giving the supermarket a run for its money, and the
store had continued to lose business.

There was more in store for us that day than we
imagined. Indeed, the world I had known was about
to start coming apart at the seams. But at that mo-

ment, the only thought in our heads was to try and get around the corner of Sunday.

Starting eight miles up at Shady Point, where an obliging pulpwood cutter let us off, we shucked our clothes, shoved off in the inner tubes Em had rescued from a construction site, and spent the afternoon drifting home.

That part of the river is gone today, the miles of fertile bottomland engulfed by the backwaters of the great Oconostee dam, and of course the speedboats would make it unsafe for tubing. But that summer of 1953 was a different world in many ways, and there was a Little Iron River to go tubing on.

I was trailing a fishing line as usual, though I snagged and lost more hooks than I ever caught fish. Once I hooked something really big, a catfish, Em said, since nothing else grew that big in the river, and I quickly discovered that a skinny boy in an inner tube is in a poor bargaining position with a fish of any size. We had a circular good time for several minutes until I capsized against a log. Em carried on so he nearly upset his cooler of beer, and Tio, naked except for his hat, laughed so hard he slipped down through his inner tube and nearly drowned.

After we had been on the water about an hour the sky began to darken and it came up a shower, a brief summer spill that hung like a curtain over the river. As the chill set in we slid off the tubes and floated alongside.

"Done this with a girl one time," called Em.

"Done what, Em?" said Tio, kicking closer and holding on tight to his hat.

"Went swimmin' in the rain. Purty little gal that lived down the road from us." He hung his elbows over the side of his inner tube, in a soft mood, a wistful look on his face. "God, she was a fine little gal."

"Were you in love with her?" I asked.

"In a way, I reckon I was. But that was when I was young and didn't know nothin'."

"How come you didn't marry her?" said Tio.

"She was white," he said.

"Somehow, Jojohn," I said, "I can't see that stopping you."

Em paddled along with one hand, the rain draining down his face. "Like I said, I was young, and didn't know nothin'."

"Maybe it ain't too late," said Tio, seizing on it, "I'll bet you—I'll bet you she ain't married to this day. She lives alone, and clerks in a store, and goes home every night and sets by herself. And she's got this big old clawed-up tomcat that reminds her of you, and she just sets and looks at him. Why, I'll bet if you went back there today . . ."

Em said, "Shut up, Tio. I can't hear the rain."

We drifted along for a while in the cold gray splashing, moving slowly, without purpose, flowing where the river took us.

Finally I said, "Are you still in love with her?"

"Sometimes," he answered, "when I need her."

"What do you mean by that?"

"Love is a thing to take out when you need it, then put it away someplace. Nobody could stand it all the time."

"Jayell could, he's *got* to have it all the time."

"Jayell don't understand what it's all about. That's why he's in the shape he's in. Fools let it lead 'em around by the nose, like they do everything else."

"You mean to say you don't wish you'd married that girl, so she could be with you now?"

"If we'd got married, that'd have been one life. This one's another. That's all."

"But what's the use of loving somebody," I said, "if you can't have that somebody with you?"

Em pulled his hair out of his face. "Earl, all that's between a man and a woman is the same that's between two cats, or a couple of them fish down there. It's just nature sayin', 'Get in there and replace yourself, bring on some more of your kind before you die!' Love is a thing in your mind. But," he said, "you get attached to anybody or anything in this world, and you're askin' for trouble. What if the person you love happens to be the wrong color, or you get separated for some reason; what if they marry somebody else, or they die? What are you going to do, let it tear you apart, and lay back and waller and cry!"

He tapped his skull. "This is where you live, where all the things that matter are stored, where nobody can't get at 'em. You keep squared away up here, you're all right, it don't matter what goes on outside.

"So, they come to take away a love you got—they can't do it, any more'n they can take your good times. It's closed off, safe and warm, and whenever you need it, it's there. It's the only place it ever was anyway."

"You make it sound like going to the cupboard for a biscuit," Tio said.

Em rested a cheek on his hand and looked at him. "I wonder what Teague'd give me to drown you."

"That girl, is she with you now, Em, right this minute?"

Em nodded.

"What's it like, Em? What's it like?"

The rain was slackening off, falling to a scattered pelting across the water. Em lowered his chin on the tube.

"Sssh . . . look," he said, "listen."

From the shivering cold and chaotic gray splashing we drifted into the first shafts of sunlight breaking through the trees, soft dazzling strokes of warmth, dappling, sparkling on the water, the noise subsiding to the last pitting droplets from the overhanging leaves. And clearing before us again, the old beauty of the earth, comforting, familiar, yet fresh, emerging ever new, as always, from each shower. The trees, washed of their dust to deeper greens, lifted their branches lightly in the afterbreeze. Birds darted out, flicking, fussing at the wet and slowly the woods revived with its million throbbings of insects. Under the patching sunshadows the river flowed quietly again.

Coming to the most deserted part of the river, the

163

whine of saws began to reach us. We heaved ourselves into the inner tubes. Em pulled closer his cooler of beer. We would soon be passing Doc Bobo's sawmill. Time for caution.

Bobo ran the mill with black convict labor he bought from the county prison camp. It was not an uncommon practice, the so-called "work-release" programs, in which the most trusted convicts were allowed outside to work for private individuals for a small wage. But Bobo housed and fed his gang in his own enclosures at the mill. He took the worst lot, the hard cases, the troublemakers, and what wages there were went to the camp warden. It was a good arrangement. The county looked the other way.

As we drew nearer the Negro convicts straightened from their work to look. We must have been a peculiar sight to them, free as chips, floating along the river. Heads matted with sawdust, they stood watching with dripping faces until a scowling black guard, a "dog boy" in the characteristic snappy clothes and metal-studded leather belt, fired his shotgun in the air. A warning to them, and us. They bent again to their work, the logs racked forth, the great saw screaming in the river-bottom heat of the quiet Sunday afternoon. From wire pens on the other side of the mill came the barking of the bulldogs Bobo bred for his fights.

Farther down we spotted a big convict working on the bank, a great broad-shouldered giant with a hideous scar that ran from his scalp down across one clouded eye. He saw us and stopped and leaned on his ax. Em lazily paddled closer, appearing to doze, but keeping a sharp eye out. When he was within range, he pulled two bottles of beer from the cooler and sent them arcing toward the bank. The Negro nodded slowly and smiled.

Cloudeye Pollock was boss con at the mill. He had once saved Em's life when Em first hit town, ran afoul of the law and pulled a six-month sentence there. Em had quickly run afoul of the dog boys too, and landed in solitary confiement.

164

". . . throwed me in this twenty-foot hole in the ground, and said they's going to let me starve. Liked to done it too. There was water down there, if you could drink it, but it was even too deep to find worms you could dig out of the bank. Well, sir, after I don't know how long, weeks, whatever, when I was figurin' that was about it, old Cloudeye killed a bull-dog and dropped him down to me one night. It was tough as shoe leather, but it kept me alive till they decided to let me out of there."

We lazed along through the afternoon, all three half asleep by the time we made the final mile before home. As we drifted around the bend at Castle's mill, I became dimly aware of singing. Far off, but coming closer. I was just too groggy to care. Suddenly Em's voice shook me wide awake.

"Great God A'mighty!"

Rehobath Pentecostal was situated near the river at that point, and as I looked up I saw upwards of a hundred people filing down the hill toward the water.

"It's a blessed baptizin'!" said Tio, and the three of us began frantically back-slapping and hauling on the cord of the clothes bucket. But in our furor the line got loose and the tube carrying the bucket drifted away. Thrashing and bumping against each other, we eddied farther out into the swifter current, and soon we were so far out in the middle of the river there was danger of being seen. We reversed ourselves and struck hard for the cover of the bank.

The singing was growing louder, and it seemed certain the three of us, naked, would coast directly into their midst. There was a fallen tree that stretched out from the bank and lay half submerged in the water, and the preacher and the initiates were gathering behind it in the milder current. We could hear the preacher's voice coaxing his flock out into the stream. We slipped into the water, and clinging to the tubes, and steering and ruddering as best we could without splashing, drifted in among the opposite branches. It was too late to try and climb out; with the crowds just yards away and children romp-

165

ing about there was no way to sneak up the bank and into the trees without being seen.

We watched as the baptismal candidates filed along the other side of the tree, pulling themselves through the waist-deep water by groping the branches. A pair of deacons brought up the rear, steadying between them an enormous middle-aged lady who was obviously terrified of the water. They inched along, the two men speaking soothingly as she jerked and splashed, punching down her cotton dress and grabbing back at her supporters. Tio snickered and Em gripped him still.

"Don't you worry, sister Alford," the pastor was saying, "they won't let you slip." He went back to help them calm her down. "Look now, see, it's only waist deep, and this is as far as we're going. Now, we'll just take you first and get it all over with."

"What? Oh, no! I just couldn't, brother Reese. Let me wait till last! I'll be all right if you'll just let me rest a minute!"

"Very well, sister," said the reverend soothingly, "you just wait here and we'll show you there's nothing to worry about."

The preacher took the first man and folded his arms on his chest, and the service began. "I baptize thee, Walter Ethridge, in the name of the Father, and of the Son, and of the Holy Ghost," and he leaned the man down and quickly brought him up. "There, you see how easy it is, sister Alford?" But from the look on her face, sister Alford was growing even more frantic as the water swirled around her. The preacher continued, and finally they were all in a state of grace except sister Alford, who was in a state of near hysteria: "I just can't, brother Reese! I just can't put my head under that water!"

"Now, sister, you're not going to make us send you over to the Methodists, are you?" There were chuckles among the deacons. "Just close your eyes and it'll be over in a minute." But when he tried to position her, sister Alford went rigid. He couldn't budge her. "If you'll give me a hand, brother Smith, brother Wig-

166

gins . . ." They came and stood by her side as the preacher prayed, and then they tried to immerse her. They might as well have tried to duck the rock of Gibraltar. She was fixed. They leaned and pulled. Sister Alford stood. Another brother came over and the four of them tried to wrestle her down. Tio put his mouth under the water and bubbles started coming up.

Two other men splashed down into the river and added their efforts. Brother Smith was lifting himself on her shoulders and brother Wiggins struggled to trip her; all to no avail. They could have built a bridge on her. Laughter was breaking out along the bank.

Suddenly sister Alford lost her balance, just enough to startle her out of her trance, and with a screech she threw off her attackers and bolted, tripped, and went under the surface, and somehow in her flailings managed to become ensnared in the submerged branches of the tree. The preacher and the brothers clambered over each other, grabbing for the thrashing feet.

"My God," muttered Em, "she'll bring the whole crowd down here! Let's try to push her out!" He slipped under the water, and I followed him, with Tio, clamping a hand on his hat, right behind. We groped along through the branches until we found her, wedged in the limbs, eyes locked open and staring.

She stared at us through the sunstreaked water, hanging before her in all our naked glory.

Em smiled.

Tio lifted his hat.

At that sister Alford freed herself.

As we surfaced she was erupting on the other side of the tree in a violence of churning water. She whooshed straight up, bellowing at the top of her voice and plowing down deacons as she made for the bank. The others dived aside as she thundered by them in a storm of white cotton and foaming spray. The crowd on the bank cleared a path for her, and she charged through them and up the river road, honking and slinging water like a great white goose, until we lost sight of her through the woods.

Through the silence came brother Reese's voice. "Praise God!" he shouted. "Sister Alford has seen Je-sus!"

And the river bottom resounded with hallelujahs.

Luck was with us, and we found our bucket of clothes eddying against a hummock of trash about a mile farther down the river. We pulled out and dressed at the trestle below the Ape Yard, and stumbled up the railroad, worn out and ravenous. Tio offered to feed us, but we said we'd take a chance on leftovers at home and came on up the hill.

As we cleared the patch of woods above the garage I felt a mild twinge of alarm.

Dr. Breisner's car was parked in the driveway. He made regular visits to the boardinghouse, but a Sunday visit was out of the ordinary. Then, as we neared the yard Mrs. Porter suddenly burst onto the porch, veins standing in her neck, and stopped me cold.

"Be brave, boy! Be brave! It's your Aunt Esther—Lord God, honey, she's dying!"

15

I FELL AGAINST THE DOOR, BREATHING HARD. MISS Esther was sitting up in bed buttoning her gown. Dr. Breisner stood beside her in his baggy seersucker suit, shaking down what looked to be, in my excitement, a large black thermometer, but turned out to be his fountain pen. His heavy brows knitted in concentration as he tried to get it to write. Miss Esther was staring at me.

"Mr. Whitaker, what is this commotion?"

I tried to get my legs to stop quaking. "They said—what is it? How is she, doctor?"

Miss Esther snorted. "You might as well talk to that wall. Doctors don't talk, they just like to poke and feel."

Dr. Breisner tried a few marks on a prescription blank, tore it off and stared at his nib. "Heart," he said.

"What?" Miss Esther was leaning half off her bed. "Speak up, Huff, I can't hear you."

"Heart attack," he said, "plain, old-fashioned heart attack."

Miss Esther's spine stiffened. "Heart attack! Why there's never been heart trouble in my family! My daddy lived to be ninety-two and worked like a horse till the day he died. The Whitaker tickers are sound as a dollar!"

"Be that as it may . . ."

"It was the Cahills ran to bad hearts . . . look at Wylie!"

"I know about Wylie, but the fact remains . . ."

"Cancer . . . ! Now there was three or four took cancer. But not heart trouble!"

"I don't care about that . . ."

"Did you check for cancer? Maybe it was cancer and looked like heart trouble."

"Damnit all, Esther, will you shut up a minute!" Dr. Breisner leaned over her as though he might strike her if she interrupted again. "It's your *heart!* And besides that you've got high blood pressure, and the last thing you need is to have me shouting at you!"

Dr. Breisner sat on the edge of the bed. *"I've* got high blood pressure. I don't need the shouting either." He turned to her. "Now, listen to me." Dr. Breisner knew he had to be simple and direct, else he would be there all night. "That spell this afternoon was serious, and I think you've had these before." He held up a hand to shush her. "Never mind, I'm not interested. The fact is, you've had enough. Your chasing around days are over. You run up those stairs one more time, you lift anything heavier than a chamberpot, and you're going to be looking at Jesus. That's as plain as I can put it into words."

Miss Esther pinched her lips. "Well, that just about makes me out to be an invalid; is that what you're saying, doctor?"

Dr. Breisner was serious. "You ought to be in a hospital right now. At any rate, you can't stay here. You keep running after these old folks and one day—" He snapped his fingers.

"Can't stay here! Can't—well, just where do you think I can go? Tell me that!"

"You've got a boy up in North Carolina . . ."

"Pffft!"

"Either that, or the county home."

Miss Esther looked at him. "Huff, you're serious about that thing, ain't you?"

Dr. Breisner didn't answer. He wrote out two prescriptions, tore them off and handed them to me. "I'll drop you by the drugstore. I want her started on these tonight."

"How much longer do you give me, doctor?"

"You take your medicine, stop playing mother hen, and stay off those stairs, and I'll get you married again."

"Well," she said, "if all I got to worry about is heart trouble, I'll count on it. Hah! Hoo—what say, *doctor?*"

Dr. Breisner bit the edge of a smile and picked up his bag. As we came out on the porch she threw open the upstairs window. "I'll count on it for sure! Don't forget your bill now, Huff, I want to pay for this visit! Hah!"

"Yeah, yeah, yeah." Dr. Breisner was stepping over missing planks in the steps.

When I got back from the drugstore she was downstairs repeating it for the others, embellishing, talking a mile a minute, rocking and harking in the best of spirits; any traces of fear or anxiety were hidden in the vagaries of those incessant vocal thrashings, buried under that rock-hard surface of humor.

Miss Esther followed the doctor's orders for the whole of two days, then she was up again and running, chenille housecoat flying, supervising a complete housecleaning, leaf-raking, hedge-trimming. And she even had Em clean and paint the gutters, and repair the steps. We worried, the boarders pleaded, all to no avail. I was puzzled. I had seen the boarders do that: take an almost childish delight in defying the doctor, whispering behind their hands that they hadn't been taking that new prescription. But for Miss Esther it was completely out of character. True, she wouldn't want the doctor to *know* she was taking his advice, but she would. She was too sensible.

Then, as I watched her moving among the boarders, it hit me for the first time, and hard, a thing that had never occurred to me would happen.

Miss Esther, too, was getting old.

"Em, I'm worried."

"Hell, that old woman will be around to supervise *all* our funerals."

"She's not herself, I can tell."

"Seems more herself than ever, if you ask me," he said, leaning the ladder against the house.

"And she's up to something, I can't figure out what, but she's got something cooking."

"She's always up to sump'n. Time she ain't, that's when you want to worry."

"No, I mean something serious. A couple of times I've caught her on the telephone late at night, and she ran off, acted real funny about it. One time she was talking to the operator, like it was long distance."

"Yeah?" That got Em's interest. The two absolutely unjustifiable extravagances in Miss Esther's household were steak and long-distance phone calls.

One Friday morning, three weeks after her attack, I was making the rounds with the bell when Miss Esther called me into her room. She was sitting up in bed, looking tired, drawn, as though she hadn't slept. Only her voice had the old brusqueness and strength.

"Well, it's all settled. Vance will be here Thursday."

"Ma'am?"

"Going to North Carolina, you and me. Stay with

Van and Lucille. They've got a big place outside of Durham, plenty of room. How about that, hah?"

"We're—leaving here?" I felt my blood pounding, a distant feeling. Unreal.

"I didn't want to say anything till it was all settled. But it ain't no percentage laying around here. If I got to lay back, I'll lay back on Mr. Vance. He's got it coming, the hateful thing."

"But, you don't have to do that. We'll take care of you."

"Who? These old folks? Pshaw! Can't hardly take care of themselves. No, sir, there ain't no invalids in this house. I never let 'em lay down on me, and I ain't going to show 'em how." She took off her glasses and looked at me. "How long you been with me, boy?"

"Eight . . ." I cleared my throat, "eight years."

"Hmh," she nodded. "Purt near raised you, didn't I, young 'un? We purt near got it done. Well, there's sump'n you better understand. Vance ain't too happy about assumin' responsibility for you, so you'll have to watch your p's and q's up there. The hateful rascal. We never did have much of a family. Like old man Burroughs says, relatives are generally people you wouldn't be seen with if you wasn't kin to 'em. Don't lay too much store by family. I laid too much store by family and look where it got me: married to Wylie Cahill and dragged to this hell hole a virgin and a bride."

"Then what you want to move in with Vance for?"

"To collect, that's what for! That scoundrel owes me! I tried to help him—give, give, give, and all he ever done for me was kill off Wylie, and that was unintentional. Well, it's Mr. Vance's turn to do some giving, and old mama's going to collect." She tapped her chest. "My ticker's punched."

"What about the boarders?" I said. "What's going to happen to them?"

Miss Esther polished her glasses. "I don't know. I've done all I could. They just got to take over from here." She was holding it in with that iron control, dealing with facts, not emotion. "I never let 'em quit up to

172

now. I can't do no more. Tell 'em I want to see 'em in the parlor after breakfast."

She sat looking out of the window.

"I'm not hungry. I'll stay with you a while."

"There's a place waiting for you at the table, mister!"

16

VANCE AND LUCILLE CAHILL ARRIVED ON THURSDAY morning in a new station wagon with the eleven-year-old twins, Victor and Vanessa, asleep on a mattress in the back, and towing an aged bird dog in a U-Haul trailer. "Spider goes ever'where with us," chuckled Vance proudly, lifting the bruised animal down.

Vance was approaching forty now, with bulging neck and a thick stomach and a sweaty, blond crew-cut. The twins were perfect miniatures of their father. The girl climbed out crossly, rubbing sleep drool off her wrist and complaining about the heat, and her brother clambered straight up the steps, brushing aside his grandmother's arms, shouting that he had to "tee-tee." Their mother, a frail listless woman with a per-petual headaches, stood waving in their commotion without interest, as though birthing this pair had sim-ply shucked her. Introduced to me, she gave a cordial wince of pain and sought the nearest chair.

Vance's greeting to his mother dwelled mainly on his surprise at how much weight she had put on. She returned the compliment, introduced him around, and spent the rest of the evening in her room pack-ing while Farette fed us supper. Afterwards, when the boarders had escaped to their rooms, Vance sat at the table moodily watching Farette and me clear away the dishes while Victor and Vanessa pulled things from the kitchen cabinets, chased each other around the room and wrestled under the table. Finally he called me into the dining room. He sat propped on his elbow, rubbing his hands thoughtfully.

"How old are you now, boy?"

"Fourteen."

Vance shook his head. "What kind of work can you get at fourteen?" He fingered a beet pickle out of the jar and rolled it in his jaw.

"I'm tall, I'd probably pass for much older."

He looked me over. "Nah, never do it. Damn, oughta be sump'n—what are you doin' now? You're doin' sump'n to help pay your keep here, ain't you?"

"Well, I do chores . . ."

"I mean payin' work, boy! How about a paper route? Ain't you even got a paper route?"

"I've tried. There's a waiting list."

"I've never heard of such a thing!"

"It's a small town, a small paper."

Vance eyed me suspiciously. "Well, by God, you c'n bet I'll find you sump'n!" He wiped his fingers on the mouth of the beet jar and dried them in his pocket. "You'll not lay off and grow fat at my house and not turn a hand." Further discussion was made impossible at that point by Victor and Vanessa, who were trying to pull the cat from behind the refrigerator with a coat hanger. "Off to bed, everybody," ordered Vance.

I slept on the extra bed in Mr. Jurgen's room, as Victor claimed my room for himself. He didn't sleep much, though; I could hear him most of the night searching through my closet and dresser.

In fact, hardly anyone slept that night. To a stranger first coming, it might have gone unnoticed, but if you live for a while in a house of old people, you become attuned to certain shadings of solitude, levels of quiet. You find that there is a difference between the silence of sulking and the silence filled with grief, or the silence of someone merely listening to the softening of a day. You learn the peaks of smaller joys. Come the first bloom of an African violet, the arrival of a photograph of a new grandson, a call to the telephone after a long Sunday's wait, the reaction was small perhaps—the quick whisper of slippers on the carpet, a tap on a door, a soft murmuring—but under it all an exuberance that rang through the house.

And that night, with its muted stirrings: a restless toss of bedsprings, a window sliding open, the jerk of the bathroom light chain, the intensity was there. The house was as charged as a summer storm.

Mr. Jurgen turned over in his bed. I was afraid my own tossing had kept him awake, and braced for his griping.

Instead, he said, softly, "I can't sleep."

"Sir?" Mr. Jurgen had never before spoken to me in a tone softer than a sharp reprimand.

He didn't speak again right away. He lay on his side, looking over the end of his pillow. Finally, he said, "I don't know what's going to become of us."

I sat up in bed. I couldn't believe it! My old enemy, Mr. Jurgen. I got out of bed and went and stood beside him.

"Are you scared, Mr. Jurgen?"

He didn't answer.

"Mr. Jurgen," I said, "are you scared?"

He lay looking up at me from the cold square of moonlight, his hands knotted on top of the covers.

I leaned over him.

"Don't you be scared, Mr. Jurgen," I said angrily. "Don't you do that to me! I was scared one time. I lay in that room over there scared to death through many a night, and all you done was complain about my crying. Now don't you make me care about your being scared. It ain't right. It ain't fair. I don't care what happens to you! I don't care if they take you to the county home and lock you away for good and nobody ever comes to see you again! You don't *deserve* nothing better, you hear me? You don't deserve nothing better, you sorry old . . ."

Suddenly he jerked upright and slapped me across the face. "Get away from me!" he shouted. "If you're going to stay in my room you get back in that bed and keep your impudent mouth shut, you hear me?

I hope—I hope that son of hers puts you in the reformatory where you belong!" And he whirled over in bed and snatched the covers over his ears.

I went back to my bed, my face hot and stinging. That's better, Mr. Jurgen, I thought. Much better. Hate me, but don't make me cry with you. Don't make me cry with you. I couldn't stand that just now.

17

THE VANCE CAHILLS WERE IN TOWN ONLY THROUGH the weekend, the time required to "get Miss Esther's affairs in order," which meant placing the house with a realtor and crating up the things that Lucille liked, and those that Miss Esther absolutely refused to part with, for shipment to North Carolina.

On Sunday afternoon Mr. J. J. Bearden of Bearden Real Estate assembled everyone in the living room. Mr. Bearden was a humble, hunch-shouldered man with a confidential air who leaned close when he talked and breathed on you like a dentist. He greeted each of the boarders in turn, and waited until they were settled. As he was about to start, the front door opened and Mr. Teague came into the parlor, followed by Tio, who took a seat with Em and me on the hall stairs. Mr. Teague made his way to a chair, nodding to everyone, and sat slowly rubbing his knees, watching Victor and Vanessa shove each other off the coffee table. Miss Esther stayed in her room.

"Ah, what a terrible, terrible time," said Mr. Bearden, licking his long front teeth. "I've been a friend of Wylie and Esther Cahill since the day they came to this town, and I can't tell you what sadness it brings me to conduct the business at hand." Mr. Bearden said that a buyer for the property had already been found, and he was happy to assure everyone that the

176

house would continue just like Miss Esther had wanted, as a home for all of her old friends for as long as they wished to stay. The boarders were visibly relieved.

"However," continued Mr. Bearden, "the new owner finds it necessary to make a slight increase in the rate you are now paying."

"How slight?" Mr. Jurgen wanted to know.

"Ten dollars a month."

"Ten dollars!" cried Mrs. Porter.

"Esther Cahill," Mr. Bearden said hastily, "is, as you all know, a most generous woman, but we must remember that to the new owner this is strictly a business enterprise, with certain obvious risks. The house is already in an advanced state of decay, and to assume the liability for boarders of advanced age and physical disability living here . . ."

"Who's disabled!" roared Mr. Burroughs, getting to his feet.

"We're not disabled," echoed Mrs. Cline.

"Yes, well . . . nevertheless . . ." Mr. Bearden had to step over Victor and Vanessa, who were wrestling at his feet.

"But we can't afford ten dollars more a month," protested Mrs. Porter.

"I'm very sorry," said Mr. Bearden, "there's nothing I can do."

"Why the very . . . !" Mr. Burroughs was interrupted by Victor and Vanessa tumbling against his legs. He whirled on Lucille. "Madam, if you don't get a hand on these disgusting look-alikes, I'm gonna *stomp* 'em into *one obedient child!*"

Lucille immediately scurried to collar her children and bustled them off to the kitchen. Vance sat glowering, but said nothing.

"Please," said Mr. Bearden, "there's really no point in discussing it further. The decision is final."

Mr. Rampey spoke up. "Who is this new owner, we'll have a talk with him."

"For reasons of his own he has asked to remain anonymous," said Mr. Bearden. "Anyway, I'm sure it would be useless to bargain. He and I have agreed that it would be impossible to operate the house profitably at the current rate. It's simply a matter of dollars and cents. Now, Farette has agreed to stay on as cook and housekeeper, and Mr. Jojohn"—he looked around until he found Em on the stairs—"Mr. Jojohn, you may continue to stay in that garage on the property, and take your meals at the house, and you will be paid ten dollars a month to continue in charge of general maintenance . . . but for that additional salary we must be assured of a little more regularity from you. You must agree to stay on the premises year round and not go rambling off when the mood strikes you."

Em got down from the stairs and ambled into the living room and looked down at the realtor. "Horse face, you couldn't buy my regularity for ten *thousand* dollars a month. If the deal I had with the old woman ain't good enough for you and your boss I'll leave tonight. Fact, it's gettin' to be too much of a strain anyhow. Place is so old and wore out it takes twelve hours a day now to keep the pipes from comin' apart and steps from fallin' in an killin' somebody. Might pay us both if you just got somebody else to keep the place up, wash the windows, rake the yards, clean the gutters, fix busted furniture, unstop the drains . . ."

"Now, now, Mr. Jojohn . . . I'm sure we can come to terms suitable . . ."

"I'll tell you what *I'll* do," said Em. "I'll stay in the loft until I get tired of stayin' there. If these folks wants a job done here and there, and I feel up to it, I'll do it. I don't want no meals, and I don't want a dime from you nor that son of a bitch—pardon me, ladies—that was ashamed to show his face here tonight. Them's *my* terms, and until somebody comes down to that loft to throw me out, I'll figure they're agreeable to all sides."

Em started to put on his hat and stopped at the sound of sniffling coming from the corner. It was Mrs.

Metcalf. She looked up, dabbing at her nose with a handkerchief.

The Indian bent down to her. "You scared, little lady?"

She went on sniffling, looking up at him like a frightened little girl, wadding the handkerchief to her mouth.

Em frowned. "There's a mean old woman upstairs," he said. "She'd raise holy hell if she knowed you's down here carryin' on thataway."

Mrs. Metcalf smiled, a little laugh broke through the sob.

Em turned around to those in the parlor. "She put in a lot o' time on you people. You was her family, more of her family than her own, and she took a lot of pride in you. Now, if you got notions that you ain't people no more, if you don't think you'll have the gumption to put on your clothes and feed yourselves when she's gone, and you're gonna go to pieces and start actin' like a bunch of damn fools, I'd appreciate it if you'd just pack your bags and call your young'uns to come get you! And I wish you'd do it tonight and be gone 'fore she comes down in the mornin'. I got a lot o' respect for that old woman, and I'd hate to see her shamed thataway!"

He stopped for a moment, looking at me and at Tio, then abruptly jammed his hat on his head and stalked out into the afternoon.

In the redness of the late afternoon sun I took a last walk through the Ape Yard. I walked along the hogback hills, through the glowing fingers that probed the shadows of the hollow, breaking a weed, smelling it, looking again at the store, stopping to remember that place in the river. It was a dismal place, after all; what could there be of gullies and shanties and vine-covered trees to carry away? There would be other sandy creeks, other gulley fortresses, other banks to slide on to the river.

I crossed the hollow and walked up into the town, circling the square, and along the closed stores, look-

179

ing for someone to say goodbye to. I had spent most of my life in the town, shouldn't there be someone to let know I was leaving? Gwen had said she would arrange things at school, but wouldn't there be another person who, after a week or so, would say, "Whatever happened to old Earl Whitaker? Where has he gone?" If I died there would be someone to say that, wouldn't there?

Wouldn't there?

I stood on the square and gazed along the rows of empty storefronts. Overhead the automatic streetlights were fading on, rising to the darkness as the sun comes to morning, lighting whoever may be standing there, casting the same light when he is gone.

There was a vagrant sitting on a park bench nearby. A man with a curl of red hair stuck to his pasty white forehead. He sat with one shoe off pulling a sock luxuriously through his toes, his yellowed eyes watching me.

I turned and walked away.

Late in the night, after hours of walking, I found myself back in the Ape Yard, in front of the Starlite Café in Cabbage Alley. The Starlite was run by Gus Mayfair, who was a porter at the Marble City Hotel uptown until the new manager fired him for drinking. I stopped and tapped on the glass. Gus came from behind the counter with a rag in his hand and squinted through the window, and unlocked the door. "Just closing up," he said.

"I, uh—I was just leaving town and thought I'd get one more of your good hamburgers, Gus."

"I done turned off the grill," he said. Gus was sleepy and didn't like working at the café anyway. Gus had enjoyed working at the hotel, where he got to wear a uniform and rich white people tipped him and joked with him. But the new manager had let him go. It had been all right with the old manager if he took a drink on the job; the old manager drank himself, and surprised a maid in one of the rooms now and then. But the new manager had let Gus go, even though he only took an occasional drink.

"That's okay," I said, "maybe I'll stop by the bus station diner."

Gus waited with the key in the lock. There was a long crack across the glass door where a drunk had tried to kick it in and Gus had reinforced the crack with a spine and ribs of tape.

"I'm going up to North Carolina," I said. "I don't guess I'll be coming back."

"Yeah—well, good luck to you."

"Right," I said. "Well, goodbye, Gus."

The door closed and a moment later the neon sign went out and bugs plunged and dived and fluttered about helplessly in the dark.

I climbed the hills to the garage and I knew, long before I was close enough to look for a light, that there would be none.

There was no need to strike a light, I knew every splinter of the place. Finding Em's cot, I tumbled on it and lay in the dark and listened to the high whine of the gulley crickets and the muffled, faraway drone of the Ape Yard. The loft, still smelling of warm daydust, cracked and popped as the old garage settled itself in the cooling air of the night.

18

BY NOON THE NEXT DAY THE MOVING VAN HAD LEFT, the station wagon was loaded, and the hired ambulance had arrived for Miss Esther. Vance had howled in protest over the extravagance until a hurried call to the insurance agent reassured him that it was covered by her major medical. But when the men arrived with a stretcher she shooed them out of her room and came down carrying her bag. She further flabbergasted her son by ordering one of the attendants into the back and crawling in beside the driver. "But, Mama," spluttered Vance, "what's the good of having an ambulance if you're going to ride up front?"

"I'll lay down if I get tired," she said. "First I want to see how this gentleman drives. You all up there"— she adjusted her hat and looked along the line of boarders at the porch balustrade—"you better write to me, now." There were to be no hand-wringing goodbyes, she had made sure of that. She was up before daylight, visiting each of them in their rooms. Now she just looked at them, her old soldiers lined stiffly at the rail, and they at her, etching in, I supposed, those last details of face and feature, the turn of a mouth, the slope of a shoulder, as I had painted in my trees, my bend in the river. When at last she was done, Miss Esther nodded, cranked up her window and ordered her driver on.

The boarders turned and filed past me into the house, still dry-eyed, though Mrs. Metcalf was straining hard, and as they passed, each one touched me in a brief goodbye, a squeeze of the arm, a clap on the head, and walked on, none of us trying to speak in a moment too tight, too full for the rattle of empty words.

Vance worked my suitcase under the straps of the luggage carrier, and I crawled into the station wagon between the twins, each of whom had claimed family rights to a window seat. Vance and Lucille were making a last check of the house when suddenly Victor rolled down the window and yelled:

"You get out of this yard, nigger!"

Tio leaned his bike against the steps and came over to the car. Victor shook his fist in Tio's face. "You want to fight, nigger?"

"Be still," I said, "he's a friend of mine."

Tio handed me a sack through the window. "Mr. Teague sent you some apples."

"Don't you touch this car," warned Victor. Vanessa giggled.

"Tell him thank you for me."

Tio nodded. He tried to say something else but kept getting interrupted by Victor, who had devised a new game. Watching Tio closely, he carefully managed to keep his head in our line of sight. Tio moved around to the back window and lifted his voice. "You seen Em?"

"No, I was about to ask you . . ."

Tio shook his head. He looked at me and shrugged.

"Well, when you see him, tell him . . ." Tio had to cup his ear, Victor and Vanessa were rapping their knuckles on the glass, making faces at him.

"Tell him what . . .?" Tio was straining to hear.

"Nothing," I said. "Never mind."

Tio adjusted his hat. The nervous tic was starting under his eye. The twins had their faces pressed against the back window, their tongues madly licking the glass. "Well, if I don't see you again"—he looked down at the noses pressed flat, the pink tongues lapping large wet circles—"take care." And, snatching a brick out of the flower bed, he slammed it against the window with such a bone-jarring smack that both twins' foreheads bounced off the glass. They thrashed about in the seat with such howls that eventually Vance ran waddling out of the house, but by that time Tio was pedaling far down the street.

Finally we got under way. The car rolled north through the scrub pine and rabbit country, swaying heavily in the dips and turns, the U-Haul tugging on the bumper. Vance cursed under his breath as his push-button settings failed to turn up any country music stations. He fiddled with the dial. Lucille sat tense and silent, one hand covering her eyes, cringing as far as she could from the blaring speaker.

The air in the back was stifling. The twins twisted the knobs of the window handles and eyed me maliciously, the sweat standing out on their fat faces. It was as if they could see their odors attacking me.

I knew they were sizing me up, resenting this in-

183

trusion into their family, and unsure yet as to how to turn it to their own advantage. As we rode I stopped feeling sorry for poor Spider cramped in the over-loaded U-Haul. He had by far the better deal.

We crossed Savannah River into South Carolina. Vance, having found his blue-grass, now puffed his cigar contentedly, his wrist hung over the wheel, snapping his fingers to Flatt and Scruggs.

Presently the disc jockey, an energetic teenager, segued a chattering teletype over his music and fear-lessly attempted a news cast, forcing his voice down an octave for the occasion.

"Repeating an earlier news bulletin—the Supreme Court ruled today that the states of the nation do not have the right to separate Negro and white pupils in different public schools. By a unanimous 9 to 0 vote, the High Court held that such segregation of the races is unconstitutional."

"What! Good God-a-mighty!" Vance lunged forward and whipped up the volume. "Quiet, everybody!"

"The most violent reaction came from Georgia Governor Herman Talmadge, who had repeatedly vowed that there will never be mixed schools while he is governor. In a prepared statement the governor said, and I quote, 'The United States Supreme Court by its decision today has reduced our Constitution to a mere scrap of paper. It (the court) has blatantly ignored all law and precedent and usurped from the Congress and the people the power to amend the Constitution and from the Congress the authority to make the laws of the land.' Governor James F. Byrnes of South Carolina, a former Supreme Court justice, said because it has been held many times the separate-but-equal doctrine, and I quote again, 'was not viola-tive of the Constitution, I am shocked to learn that the Court has reversed itself.' For further develop-ments, stay tuned to—" The announcer gave the sta-tion's call letters, the time, and played a jingle that launched the next half-hour of his show.

"By damn, did you hear that?" Vance was purple. "Have they gone slap crazy? Did he say *all* the schools, or *when* they had to be mixed? Did you hear him say when?" Lucille shook her head, or perhaps she only trembled.

"I'm gonna stop and call that station," said Vance. "That kid didn't give enough to tell what the hell's going on!"

"Oh, Van," whined Lucille, "let's please don't stop. We'll find out when we get home. I want to get on home."

"No, sir!" bellowed Vance, rising to the hint of opposition. "I'm gonna get the straight dope, and while I'm at it I might just give 'em a little hell for lettin' a damn kid give out such an important item as that." Vance hooked an elbow over the back of the seat and addressed himself to me, glancing only occasionally at the road. "You take, I don't care who it is, when they get on the radio or the TV they got a responsibility to the public, and when they screw up I for one let 'em know about it! I call up the stations around home all the time. There was one last week, had a preacher on that didn't know as much about the Bible as that kid there"—indicating Vanessa, who, looking faint, had her nose pressed to a private half-inch crack in the glass—"and there he was spoutin' off about the Garden of Eden bein' a symbol, and all that stuff. You know, college preacher. Well, I got the station manager on the phone and didn't I tell him a thing! He was real nice about it. Damn, there oughta be a gas station around here somewhere. You seen one, honey?"

Lucille shook her head, or trembled, again.

Vance grinned in the mirror. "You can't fool me about my Bible," he continued. "I keep up with my preaching. I've heard the best of 'em. I used to like Billy Graham till he got surrounded by all them sharkskin suits. I still like Oral Roberts, though, he's all right. I seen him in person once," Vance bragged, "he healed a pregnant woman."

Lucille raised her head and looked at him. "She had a crippled laig," she explained.

"Yeah. Well, when old Oral got done with her she

185

didn't have it. She just throwed down her crutches and danced up and down that aisle. They had to carry her out of there."

"On account of she was so happy," appended Lucille.

"Right. Hey, look, there's a station just over that next rise. Anybody got to go?"

Vance pulled in to the side of the station and went in to the pay phone. Victor and Vanessa grabbed the paddle-key from the attendant and raced around the corner to the ladies' room, their mother tottering along behind with a bottle of Lysol, calling for them to wait.

I pushed open the door and jumped out and stood leaning on the burning car in the clean, fresh air. Vance's back was to me. He gestured wildly to the party on the phone.

There was no time for reasoning. Sometimes desperation relieves us of that civilized faculty and throws us directly on our instincts, where things get done. And in that moment I acted on instinct as surely, as unhesitatingly as if Jojohn had been shouting in my ear. I clawed my suitcase out of the luggage carrier and broke for the nearby woods as hard as my feet could run.

At the edge of the trees I threw my bag over a barbed-wire fence and dived after it and rolled in the grass like a dog. Families, like houses, sometimes have a distinctive smell, and theirs was clinging to me like pond scum.

After a while they reassembled at the car and noticed my absence.

Vance went to the men's room and came back shaking his head. They held a conference. Vance honked the horn a few times, then circled the station calling me and looked into the men's room again. Then Victor noticed my suitcase missing. He and Vanessa ran out and looked up and down the highway and Vance went back to question the station attendant. There was an anxious moment when it occurred to me that he might call the police, but presently he came stomping back to the car, ordered them all in, and a mo-

186

ment later the station wagon was bumping out onto the highway.

I stood up from behind the fence and watched it grow small in the distance, the white moon faces of Victor and Vanessa still looking out the back window. A cool breeze washed through the pasture, bringing the sweet smell of the grass and trees. The sun burned cleanly through the sweep of the land. I stood at the edge of the trees and said goodbye to the last remnants of that strange institution: my family. I supposed it would be the last I would see of Miss Esther, and I would miss her. I knew for a fact it was the last I would see of the Vance Cahills.

And, as it turned out later, it was the last I was to see of my bone-handled pocketknife that cousin Victor had seen me packing, and so admired.

I spent the rest of the day and part of the night hitchhiking my way back home, finally catching a ride the last leg from Little Holland with a man who worked a coffee route. It was against company rules to pick up hitchhikers, he said, but I had an honest face. He was so friendly it flashed through my mind that I might have found myself another sharpshooter. But I was wrong, and later felt ashamed about it. He was just a nice man who wanted to do me a favor. We chatted along and he told me about his hobby, which was making piggy banks out of discarded coffee cans. He let me have one for half price.

Coming across the railroad trestle by moonlight, shaking a pebble in the coffee-can bank, and catching sight of the boardinghouse with its hall light burning, it was as though I had been away a thousand years.

I ran through the front door and climbed through the house, shouting everyone awake. "Mr. Rampey! Mr. Burroughs! Mrs. Bell! I'm home . . . Mrs. Cline!" They piled into the hall in their nightclothes, shouting, grabbing me, calling to wake the others. It was a carrying on sufficient to rouse the neighborhood. They were all asking questions at once, interrupting each other, re-asking things I'd just answered, Mr. Rampey loudly echoing every word for Mr. Woodall. "To the dinin' room!" shouted Farette, elbowing her way through, "I swear to goodness!"

When we were finally settled in the dining room, I had to start all over. Farette got her stove fired up and put the coffee pot on, dashing to the door every two minutes to catch what she could.

When I was all done, and every minor point covered to everyone's satisfaction, they all sat quietly, mulling over this new turn of events. "Well," said Mrs. Porter, patting my hand, "we'll write Esther and tell her not to worry about a thing. We'll take good care of you. You're our little boy now."

I put down my cup. "I've been thinking about that," I said. "I thought about it all the way home. I just turned fourteen. I'm not anybody's little boy anymore. And I sure can't ask you to keep me."

"What?" she said.

"Why that's nonsense," said Mrs. Metcalf.

"Hey, sport," said Mr. Rampey, "you don't have to worry . . ."

"No, I mean it." I cleared my throat and tried to sound as mature, as deliberate as I could. "I appreciate everything you've done for me, you and Miss Esther. But it's time I was on my own. It's going to be hard enough on you as it is, and now that they've upped your rent . . ."

"By God!" snorted Mr. Burroughs, "first we're disabled—now we're paupers!"

"Mr. Burroughs, I mean no disrespect, but I can't be a burden any longer, not to you or anybody. Let's face it, we're all on our own now. Can I do less than you're doing?"

"But where will you stay?" asked Mrs. Bell.

"I'll move out in the garage loft with Em, if he comes back, that is."

Farette spoke from the door. "You'll get a fever in that place!"

The others started in with their protests. I got up and walked to the door. "Please understand, my mind's made up. I've got to do it. I've got to try."

They were silent for a while. They looked at each other anxiously, each waiting for the other to speak.

Finally Mrs. Metcalf said, "You *would* come to us if you needed anything . . . ?"

"If I need you, I promise. And please don't tell Miss Esther, it would only worry her more."

I started out.

"Boy . . . !" Mr. Burroughs got up and came to the door, his long fingers closing tightly on my arm. "You do what you want to do," he said, "but you get in trouble, you need anything, and you don't come to us—I'll take a stick to you."

"Yes, sir."

In dead seriousness, he leaned close and confided, "You can trust us. We're not family."

"Yes, Mr. Burroughs."

As I passed by Farette at the stove, her cordy little hand reached out and snagged my belt. "You still comin' for yo' meals, I expect."

"No, Farette, don't you see, it would be pointless if I did that."

She turned back to the stove. "Do what you want, then. Make no difference to me."

I started to leave, then stopped, and reached over and kissed her quickly on the cheek. She stiffened, but quickly busied herself again at the stove. I picked up my suitcase and walked out of the kitchen, stepping carefully over the roses.

19

I AWOKE THE NEXT MORNING IN A NEW WORLD. IT was raining, and water leaked through a crack beside the window and splattered on the sill. It took several moments to realize where I was, and then I lay on Em's cot listening to the rain drumming and fighting the empty feeling inside me. I pulled the footlocker up to the window and sat looking up through the trees toward the boardinghouse. It sat still and gray in the rain, the warmth, the look of life still lingering. It wouldn't be for long, I thought, without Miss Esther. I stood up and shoved the footlocker back in place. Enough, she would have said. There wasn't time for that. There were too many things to sort out. Too much to be done. One step at a time, Mr. Whitaker. Just one single step at a time.

When the rain let up I bounded out of the loft and went looking for Tio. And once out again and moving, I felt better. I broke into a run, skimming along the familiar ridges. At last I spotted him struggling along Cabbage Alley, his basket loaded and a kerosene can on the handlebars with an Irish potato plugging the spout.

With a shout and a running dive off a high yard I caught him around the neck and we, the bike and the groceries went piling into the gutter. The hollering and wrestling brought out the neighborhood dogs, and they danced around the mud puddles rejoicing with us until one of them found a broken package of bologna and led the others away.

Finally Tio shoved me away. "Hey man! What's the matter with you? Help me get this stuff!" and he scrambled to replug the pouring kerosene. I tried to help him, but I couldn't. All I could do was sit in the mud and laugh. A woman came around the corner leading a little girl in pigtails and stopped and stared at my condition. That was even funnier. I jumped up and started grabbing canned goods and shoving them in her arms. She hurriedly dragged the child away. I couldn't stop laughing. I was drunk, and could not be responsible.

"All right," Tio said firmly, "now get a hold of yourself. What you doin' back here?"

I told him, as best I could, about the break from the Cahills, about leaving the boardinghouse.

"I'm a man," I said.

"Yeah. Right. Now get your head about you. You

190

hungry? You had anything to eat?" I shook my head and Tio unwound a can of Vienna sausage. I wolfed it down, along with a wedge of cheese. "Where you gon' live now?"

"In the loft, I guess. Where's Jojohn, have you seen him?"

"Some of 'em said he was hittin' the joints down river toward Cedar Crossing. Said they seen him in Birdsong's the other night, tyin' on a drunk that'd put all his others in the shade."

"Birdsong's? I heard the sheriff had closed him down."

"The sheriff's always closin' him down. But somehow he gets open again. You goin' after Jojohn?"

"No, I don't think so," I said.

Tio looked at me. "How come?"

"I don't know. I've just got this feeling . . . No, if he's still around, and he wants to come home, let him. If not, well, that's okay too."

Tio shrugged. "Suit yourself." He kicked up the stand and got on his bike.

"Hey," I said, "let's go take a dip in the river."

"What? I got work to do, I ain't got no time to go swimmin'!"

"Aw, come on, Tio, just one . . ."

"And you ain't neither! You got to start figurin' how you gon' live now your aunt's gone! Where you gon' eat? You thought about that?"

"Aw, Tio . . ."

"Naw, man, you got to think about them things. You're on your own now, you got responsibilities."

"Tomorrow!—I'll work it all out tomorrow."

"Tomorrow! You don't even know where you gon' eat tonight! You talkin' 'bout bein' a man—you're more like a newborn baby! Now you get that playin' out your head and start tendin' to business."

"Well, I don't *know* how to—I don't know where to start!"

"That's what I figured. All right, you start with Jay-ell. He just back from his honeymoon, maybe he's got some work you can do. And school! Tomorrow

191

mornin' you get yourself up there and get checked back in that school 'fore you lose a whole year."

"Oh! Yeah, hey, guess what I heard on the radio . . . !"

"Tonight I'll bring you sump'n to eat," he continued, "enough to last you a couple of days anyway, in case Jojohn ain't back before then. And if he's gone for good, well, we'll just have to work sump'n out. But right now you get down to Jayell's and see about that job." He shoved off and pedaled down the street. "It's close to dinnertime, he ought to be around the shop now. Get goin', man. You're grown now. No more good times."

"The school," I yelled after him, "didn't you hear? We may be goin' together. They've passed a law!"

Tio threw up a hand, but I knew he didn't hear me. He was pushing away hard, his whole body pumping on the strokes.

I found Jayell sitting in his truck behind the shop, lunching on a can of tomatoes. "Where the hell did you come from?" he said.

I explained that I couldn't be a burden on the Cahills anymore and had decided to come back, and wondered if he had any work for me.

Jayell rummaged in his pocket. "Hell, I'll spot you some money, Early boy."

"I didn't come begging," I said. "I come looking for work."

Jayell looked at me. "Well, things are about as bad for me as they can get right now, Earl. That damned house of Gwen's has just about put me under; drained off most everything I had in the bank, I'm behind on two loans now, and business is about as bad as I've ever seen it. I've got one house under way right now, and after that—I don't know what we'll do." Jayell shook his head. "And to have to take time off for a honeymoon!"

"Well, look, I don't want to put you out. I know I'm not too good at building, and if you don't need any help right now . . ."

"Help, sure I need help," he said quickly. "I need

192

all the help I can get! You feel like doing some painting?"

I was confused, as I usually ended up when I tried to follow Jayell's thinking. "But I thought you said . . ."

"Kid, you want to talk or you want to work? I asked you about the painting."

"Sure, I like to paint . . ."

"Okay, then, get in. You can free up Skeeter so he can get back to the shop. He hates a paintbrush anyway. You're slow but you're careful, and that's what counts." Jayell tossed away the empty tomato can and cranked the truck. "Come on—you going? Get in, get in!"

The house was for a young black quarry worker named Ruben Johnson who had just moved down from Salisbury. Jayell was building him a drum-shaped two-bedroom on telephone poles sunk in the marsh of Fletcher Bottom. The house stood about twelve feet from the ground with a walkway running to the bank of the street. Skeeter gladly turned over his paintbrush and I took his place on the ladder.

How fast things had settled back down, I thought. Here I was an orphan one day, with no place to go, and a working man the next, with a full-time job and a place to live. Who needed more than that? Maybe a painter was what I was cut out to be. Certainly I was no good at carpentry, and the thought of a quarry gave me the shivers. Even Jayell said I was a good painter. Well, he came as close to saying that as Jayell could get to a compliment. Maybe I'd have my own van truck some day—and hire a couple of helpers! The only drawback I could see was I hadn't any experience with liquor. Well, I'd just have to learn the trade a step at a time.

Around six o'clock, when the sun was slanting over the rim of the Ape Yard and we were racing to finish against the oncoming dark, one of the boys on the roof said something and pointed. I looked down and saw a car pulling to a stop under the chinaberry trees.

It was a dark green Lincoln Continental.

Doc Bobo and Clyde Fay got out and stepped quickly along the planking, followed by a little man who hurried along behind them clutching a shirt pocket bulging with ball-point pens. I recognized him as the man who had been selling the cheap, pre-fabricated little homes around town.

"Who's building this house?" demanded Doc Bobo.

One of the boys pointed to Jayell on the roof. Doc Bobo lifted his hat to shade his eyes. "I'm told you're building this house for Ruben Johnson," he said.

Jayell pulled a shingle into place. "That's right. Why?"

"There must be some mistake," said the salesman. "He told me when he got ready for a house he was gonna let me build it for him."

"Oh? First I heard about it." He looked at the man. "You got a contract?"

"He was to sign today," said the salesman. "We was just out looking for him."

"Well, he must have changed his mind," said Jayell.

"He can't do that," said Doc Bobo. "We had an agreement. I was to co-sign his note."

"The bank said he didn't need a co-signer. And I guess he figured he could do without your kickback and this guy's rate of interest."

"We had an agreement," repeated Doc Bobo angrily, "and it still stands. Ruben Johnson wouldn't do this to me—he's indebted to me at the present time."

"I suspect a lot of people are. That has nothing to do with me. I'm just building a house."

Doc Bobo looked over the house, the movable walkway that was built on the order of a drawbridge. Ruben's young wife especially liked the drawbridge, Jayell said. When it was raised the house was safely isolated above the ground. Ruben moonlighted nights at the mill. "We don't need your peculiar structures in the Ape Yard, Mr. Crooms. You make my people look ridiculous. A house on stilts! Who wants a thing like that?"

"Anybody in this bottom would be glad to have it when that creek backs up next spring. And talk about peculiar structures!" Jayell stood up and pointed. "From here I can see a whole hillside of what I'd call very peculiar structures: roofs caving in, rotted porches, falling pillars—there's one without even a door, just a burlap curtain! You own some downright strange-looking houses yourself, Doc! Besides, my houses never seemed to bother you until that prefab crook started coming around with his kickbacks. Why don't you quit sniffing the air for a new scheme and stick to what you're good at—burying people."

Doc Bobo tugged on his hat and looked about the job. He walked over to the nearest group of shop boys and said something to them. They immediately dropped their tools and walked off the job. Jayell stepped to the edge of the roof and shook his hammer. "Quitting time is five o'clock!" They quickened their pace down the red clay road. Doc Bobo turned to the others, and one by one they followed. Jayell whirled on Bobo in a rage. "You son of a bitch!" He flung down a handful of roofing tacks and sprang for the ladder.

A moment later I heard Jayell yell.

Positioned against a circular roof, the ladder was not secure enough to bear Jayell's weight thrown on it in a fit of anger. Once it started sliding there was nothing to grab hold of. Jayell came off the front of the house kicking away to jump free, but the momentum carried him and the ladder down an embankment into a pile of lumber and vines.

"Get to him! Get to him!" cried Bobo.

When we reached him he was pushing up on his elbow, blood streaming down his face. Doc Bobo tried to get an arm under his back.

"No!" gasped Jayell, "the leg, goddamnit, the leg!"

Then I saw the bone, white as a chicken's bone, sticking out above his sock. His foot was wedged under some timbers and I tried frantically to pull them away. Clyde Fay bent silently to his work, lifting away the heavy timbers with ease.

Jayell was a long time coming out from under the

anesthetic. Gwen put her hand on his forehead. "How do you feel, darling?" she said softly.

"Fine," he said groggily. After repeated efforts at shaking himself awake, he looked down at the leg. "Did they leave it on—or is that a dummy cast to cheer me up?"

"*Sssh,* just rest now."

"Give me a cigarette."

"You don't need a cigarette just now. Would you like some water?"

"How's a cigarette going to hurt my goddamned leg? Give me a cigarette!"

Gwen groped nervously in her bag. She lit the smoke and Jayell took a deep drag. "Thank God it was the good leg," he said sardonically, "would'a been a shame to bust up the one with all those rods and pins in it. They spent a lot of time rebuilding that baby. Got a whole erector set in there. Hey! Maybe they shortened this one to match! Earl, get my rule!"

"*Sssh,* Jayell, please . . ."

"But I might not have a limp anymore . . ."

"Jayell, stop it!"

"Stop! Hell, I am stopped, woman. If there's anything I am at this moment, it's *stopped!*"

Gwen fumbled for the buzzer. A nurse put her head in the door. "He needs something," Gwen said. The nurse nodded and disappeared.

"You bet I need something," Jayell said. "Early, you think you can find me a jar of stumphole?"

"You'd better go," said Gwen. It was more than a request.

"Go to Dirsey, boy, tell him I want the rottenest stuff he's got!"

"It's all right, darling," Gwen said soothingly, "it's going to be all right now. Everything's going to be just fine."

20

THAT NIGHT TIO CAME STRUGGLING UP THE GULLEY with a slab of fatback, some flour wrapped in newspaper, and a small jar of molasses. We fried the fatback and crumbled molasses in it and I sopped it with shards of the hoecake he made in the skillet.

"Did you go by the hospital?" I asked.

'Yeah."

"How is he?"

"I didn't get to talk to him. They said he got to raisin' so much hell the doctor had to knock him out again."

"Boy, what a mess," I said.

"That house for Ruben Johnson was the only one he had too, and now with him laid up in the hospital . . . Hey! I wonder if we could finish that house! I could round up Skeeter and Carlos and the shop boys and . . ."

Tio held up his hand, listening. He got up and went to the window and then I heard it too, the sound of a siren turning in by the fairgrounds.

"Well, you can forget that idea," Tio said.

It was a fire truck, roaring down the hollow toward a red glow over Fletcher Bottom.

Tio shook his head. "I'll bet everywhere that Bobo steps, he kills the grass."

I sat down at the table. "What's coming next . . ."

"I don't guess you've heard from Jojohn. Well, don't you worry, old papa Tio won't let you starve."

And he kept his word. Every night he came with sardines, a few sprouting potatoes, pigs knuckles, salt mackerel, and even a porkchop when he could snitch it. We both felt bad stealing from Mr. Teague, until we hit on the idea that Tio was just opening a secret account for me. We would keep a careful tally of everything he brought, and I would pay for it as soon as I was able. That relieved both our consciences, and when the stealing switched to simple debt, Tio started stealing a better class of goods.

But other problems began cropping up, things I'd never thought about before, such as laundry. At the boardinghouse my dirty clothes had always disappeared magically and turned up clean in the drawers. Now they just piled up in the corner and lay there. I tried putting them in the washtub and stomping around on them while I bathed, and tying bricks in the legs of my jeans to pull out the wrinkles while they hung from the limbs to dry. That worked fairly well for the jeans, but my shirts were stopping people on the street.

Gwen finally called me aside one day at school. "Earl," she said, "you've got to *do* something!"

Finally Tio brought me an old iron without a cord he had traded off of somebody, and I heated it on the stove and destroyed my one white shirt with it.

It was the infernal bleaching. I remembered Farette putting in Clorox with the whites, and I did that. What I didn't remember was the careful rinsing, and made do with a swish and a wring. When I put the iron to it, it developed large brown holes and the collar came loose at one end.

"For God's sake," cried Tio, "get what clothes you got left and let's take 'em to Grandma Tyne!"

"What'll I pay her with?"

"We'll think of something. But you go through another washday, you gon' be naked!"

Grandma Tyne was a knotty little black woman in a red-roofed house on the river with somebody's wash always drying on the porch rail. As usual she was on the back porch prodding in her old wringer machine with a boiled white stick, suds and bluing soaking through the floor boards and foaming off into the garden.

"Got your list of what you want from the store this week, Grandma?" Tio asked.

198

Grandma Tyne poked a ballooning overalls pocket under the rinse water and pursed her lips. "Better bring me some flour, a bag of dry beans—don't matter what kind—navy's all right. Need a can'a lard, some Peach snuff . . ."

"Wait a minute." Tio took his pencil out of his pocket and rummaged in her safe until he found a piece of paper bag. He looked in the oven and got us each a sausage biscuit from the pan she always kept there, and sat down at the table. "Wish you'd make a list," he said.

Grandma Tyne rapped the suds off her stick and stuck it carefully between the rafters. "You learn me to write, Mr. Smarty Britches, and I will."

He clamped the sausage biscuit between his teeth and noted down the items as she called them off. When he was done he folded the paper and stuck it in his pocket. "Want to pay a little sump'n on your account this week?"

"Don't you come at me with none o' your mess, boy. Ain't I keepin' up that bill with y'all's washin'?"

Tio winked at me. "Not with me keepin' the books nowadays. You just keep gettin' further and further behind."

"Shoot!" Grandma stabbed in her machine. "If I could buy you for what you're worth and sell you for what you *think* you're worth, I'd be done retired!"

"Listen at that," Tio said, "and me comin' here bringin' her another customer. Earl's by hisself now, Grandma, and if he keeps washin' his clothes hisself he's gon' to have to put 'em in a bag to hang 'em up."

"Sho', I'll do your wash, honey," she said. "That them there? Bring 'em hyeah."

"I haven't got any money, Grandma," I said. "Maybe I could do some chores or something?"

"Just run 'em in with ours and we'll put it on the groceries," Tio said.

"Sho—sho—that'll be fine," she said, "and I can always use a little coal. You get you a bucket and look along the tracks where the coal cars unload," she told me, "and pick me up a little coal from time to time."

"I'll do that," I said.

"Lawd," she said, "I wish ever'body could make do without money. But the light comp'ny and that insurance—they want the *money*. Doc Bobo says he can't carry me another week. Got to get that up somewhere. I dunno where."

"Can't carry you for what?" I asked.

"My burial insurance, honey," she said proudly.

"You've got burial insurance with Doc Bobo?"

"One thousand dollars' worth. Ain't lettin' the county put me in no hole out yonder behind the prison camp where nobody can't find my grave. Gon' have me a nice funeral, with flowers—just lots of flowers."

"You ready?" Tio said to me. I sopped the last smear of sausage grease off the oilcloth and folded the remains of the biscuit into my mouth. "You be sure and make that payment now, Grandma," he said, " 'cause me and Doc Bobo done got it figured that when you kick off I'm gonna hide the body and we gon' split the thousand dollars."

He made a jump for the porch but she caught him behind the neck with a sopping shirt, and circled down the hill in a crazy dance, laughing and shaking his collar.

Still, I had to have money, and the next day after school I started combing the town for work. It was to be one of the bitterest experiences of my life.

The classified ads turned up nothing, as did the state employment office. I went to Bobo's mill, to the quarries, the sheds, the gas stations, and found everywhere that the state was protecting me from serious employment because of my age.

After trying all the stores at Galaxy Plaza, I started on the north side of the square and made a canvass of the entire town: the hardware store, poolroom, department stores, the bank, the dry cleaning plant, the drugstore, the bottling plant—even the fire station and courthouse. I walked in every place that had a public entrance, and asked if they had any kind of a job for a boy. Some were polite and took up time, others simply shook their heads or waved me away. There was an ad in the window of the new bowling alley for a pin boy, but when I applied, the manager took me aside and explained that what he needed was another colored boy.

At the telephone office I thought I was on to something. A lady in cat-eye glasses with pearly rims handed me an application form and questioned me lengthily about my possibilities as a lineman. It went on and on, and I grew more excited by the minute—then the lady broke. There was other laughter, and then I saw a group of linemen crowded in the door of the day room, spilling their coffee. A secretary put her head down on her desk.

In the circus, I'm told, chimps have an instinctive hatred for the exaggerated smiles of clowns, and will attack on sight. For me, it's those cat-eye glasses with the pearly rims. I've never been able to overcome it.

Panic was beginning to set in. I saw the boarders from time to time; Mrs. Bell had come down to show me a letter from Miss Esther, raising general hell about my defection and demanding to know how I was getting on, but I always put up a big front and tried not to let any of them discover the truth. Tio continued to drop off food, but I saw less and less of him as he and Mr. Teague became engaged in a massive remodeling of the store. Mr. Teague had finally given in, and they were going to turn it into a regular supermarket, Tio said. He was scouting the Valley Farm store like an enemy agent, noting every facet of its operation.

Finally I decided to go and have a talk with Jayell, who had been moved back to the house in Marble Park. Admittedly, he was a poor prospect for practical advice, but he was the only one I had. I waited until an afternoon when I knew Gwen was at a faculty meeting, so that at least I could avoid seeing her. One of the reasons I had taken Tio's advice and reported back to school so promptly, even though it was going to be out in a couple of weeks, was because I wanted to finish the eighth grade and get shed of that woman altogether.

"Well, come in! Come in!"

Jayell was sitting at the fireplace, cracking pecans on the hearth with his cast. He racked around in his chair to look at me with bleary eyes, and went back to shelling nuts. I knew it was useless. Jayell's spirit had been at low ebb ever since the accident. The bank had repossessed some of his equipment, refusing even to talk to him about an extension. They were living on Gwen's salary, which was barely enough to meet household expenses and the mortgage payments on the lot, and now had somehow to cope with the enormous medical bills. Jayell had bought accident insurance, he was certain of it; and sure enough, the box under his bed turned up policies protecting him against just about every possible catastrophe that could befall a man, but the half-dozen that still happened to be in force were all life insurance policies.

The man from Smithbilt homes had stopped by several times to renew his offer of work when Jayell was able to get about again, and Gwen frankly saw no other way out. Jayell refused to talk about it—or anything else, for that matter. He sat brooding in the house at Marble Park, except for those times Carlos and Skeeter would come and lift him into the truck and take him to Dirsey's to get blind, falling-down drunk. He wasn't even drawing anymore.

Jayell sighed and threw a handful of shells into the fireplace. "Everything can go to hell overnight, can't it, Early boy?" He raised his head and looked at me. "How old are you now?"

"Fourteen."

He thought about it. "Well, you got a hard row to hoe, but you'll get by. I was fifteen when I got fed up with the old man and left home. You're young, and you're a little backward, but you'll come out of that. The thing you got to remember now is that you've got all the responsibilities of an adult, but none of the rights. Legally, you can't get credit, sign a contract, or even rent a post office box. People may do business with you, but if they cheat you there's nothing you can do about it, because no paper you sign will be legal. And they *will* cheat you, believe me, they'll overcharge you, they'll outbargain you, they'll take every advantage your lack of experience gives 'em, 'cause that's the way business operates, and it makes no allowance for age. In business as in everything else in this lovely world, the weak and the helpless are eaten first. Above all," he said emphatically, "don't you get in trouble of any kind. Don't even let the law know you're alive."

"Why?"

" 'Cause for you, even hookey from school is a crime that can get you sent up. It makes people nervous to see a kid running around loose, and any chance they get, they'll put you away. Stay low, stay quiet, be respectful but firm where money is concerned, and when you get the short end, consider it tuition and try not to repeat the course. Anything else I can do to cheer you up?"

"Not unless you can tell me where I can find a job."

Jayell brought down the heel of his cast too hard and bent over, picking meat from among the shell fragments.

"You're asking the wrong person. I couldn't even get a job as a nutcracker. No, Earl, you've got it all against you," he said bitterly, "you're not even old enough to get married, so you could live off your wife."

"Jayell, what about you, you given up your dream? You not going to build anymore?"

Jayell gritted his teeth. "Dreams," he said, "are for fools. Gotta keep remembering that. Have it, taste it, and let it go. To expect it to last is only to invite hell on earth."

"I don't understand."

"When you've lived long enough, you will. Jojohn," he nodded. "He knows what it's all about. He keeps it all in his head, where it belongs. Wouldn't see him go building no houses!"

"But—I thought it was Jojohn who told you to build 'em . . ."

"Oh, he did. But it was a suggestion of the moment, don't you see? Jojohn lives for the moment he's in, and lets the rest slide by. Hell, it wouldn't occur to him to worry about the future! He said build 'em; it didn't bother him whether the dream would last. It's fools like me who try for permanence. Jojohn's always gone before the echoes die!"

"Echoes . . . ?"

Jayell sat up in his chair, his hooded eyes burning. "Earl, man is a freak in this world. Look at all the other animals—those dumb, plodding creatures, every damned one as much a part of the total order as the seasons. They reproduce, they die, and that's that. No hope of heaven. No sad songs. That's how we should be.

"Only in man something went wrong. We understand more than we should, we have wills, we have imaginations and, God save us, fantasies of love and joy, knowing—*knowing* that every bit of it ends when our bones are put in the earth! Don't you see how much it's against the Divine grain, the natural order of things? It's like there was some huge mistake!

"But, of course, I know there hasn't been any mistake. So, so you know what I think?" Jayell hunched forward, scruffing his chair on the floor. "I have this notion that maybe this world is the hell of the angels. That maybe we're creatures with angels exiled in our souls, banished to this godawful existence, howling in despair . . ."

"Jayell, I came here to feel better . . . I don't need to hear anything like . . ."

". . . and all those beautiful dreams we have are only the ravings of those angels, their screams in our animal minds."

I jumped to my feet. "I'm not gonna stay and listen to such nonsense as that . . . I never heard such as that in any church *I* ever went to! And you call yourself a religious man!"

"Earl, hasn't it been the dream of religious man for all time—to release the angel in his soul when he dies —and know real peace, at last?"

"I don't know how you can believe such a thing."

Jayell sighed. He leaned his head back against the cushion of faded, multicolored squares spelling out his initials that his mother had made, and that he had brought up from the shop. "It's only a thought and, oh Lordy, I hope I'm wrong. But that's the trouble with an honest mind," he said sadly, "it takes you so many places you don't want to go."

I rushed out and left him there. On the porch I saw a blue car coasting to a stop on the dirt road in the woods next to the house. Phaedra Boggs got out. She called out to me, saying something I didn't bother to hear. She stood watching me as I crossed the yard and broke into a run down the road.

I walked the streets and around the square, Jayell's words pounding, the feeling of desperation building. The summer streets were filled with young people. They sat on fenders at the drugstore and shouted to those passing in hot rods, they sprang along twirling tennis rackets, bicycled past with bathing suits on their handlebars on their way to the city pool. Not a worry in the world, performing to the hilt their role in the golden, carefree pageant that youth was supposed to be.

And here I was, moving through them without so much as drawing a glance, heading back for the Ape Yard, where I was, in truth, as much a stranger.

I lay on the cot in the loft, hours passed, it began to grow dark. A hot metallic taste burned at the back of my throat. Was I ready to take responsibility for this creature named Earl Whitaker, to do his thinking for him?

In our readings on the porch, Gwen had quoted a writer named Steinbeck as saying a boy gets to be a man when a man is needed.

A man was needed now, desperately needed. But it was so hard to give up being a boy. I wanted so much to stay a little longer in that golden time.

I lay on the cot in the fading light and begged for it as a dying man must beg for moments of life.

Then, ominously, something started to happen.

The subtle nausea. The light throwing faint, wavering shades of green. The old symptoms of that night at Miss Esther's when things had become more than I could stand, and I had to go to the hospital. From out of the wood's drone I heard the mumbling voice of Dr. Breisner . . .

"No!" I screamed. It *could not* happen again!

Suddenly I was on my feet, throwing everything I could lift at the walls, screaming at the top of my voice. I kicked over the cot, the footlocker—the frustration turning to anger, feeding on itself. I knocked down the makeshift ironing plank and swept everything from the shelves. I smashed the tin stove apart and fell on it, kicking and beating it into a twisted mass of metal.

It was dark. I stood in the wreckage of the loft, sweat pouring off of me. I wiped it away and turned and saw in the mirror a pale figure with blood on its face. My hands were bleeding. I threw open the door and sprang down the steps and raced out across the sedgefield.

Down below the field stood the dark wall of the woods, waiting. I couldn't stop. I wouldn't let myself stop. The old terror swelled up in me, I felt a hush, things were gathering, watching. Something skittered through the underbrush, something that couldn't contain itself, dancing with maniacal glee. Limbs waved as they scampered aloft. The woods loomed above me, stretching its darkened maw. I threw myself forward into it. I ran off that moonlit field and into the woods, and all the breath I had left came out in one hoarse, throat-scalding cry.

I thrashed through the underbrush like a demon hound, incoherent sounds ripping out of me, searching them out among the shadows, charging bushes where things might hide, falling and rolling and getting up to charge again. I fought through the night of the woods, screaming out to them, laughing, mocking. I fell into a gulley and, kicking through briars and entangling vines, I clambered down its length until it opened out on flat ground. I ran around trees, clapping my hands, shouting, barking, howling with triumphant glee.

I stumbled out into another field, and below me, the walls of the old swimming quarry shone gray in the moonlight, the great hole black and foreboding. And I was running toward it.

There was a dizziness, my legs grew numb . . .

". . . when you're the most scared, Early boy . . ."

I hit the edge running, and dived.

There was a long, terrifying moment of weightlessness, of floating stomach and flashing granite walls, the shock of contact and then the surfacing in the streaming cold, my own jubilant cries mingling with the echoes of splashing water ringing off the darkened walls. I threw back my head and fought the water with furious strokes, the night clouds rolling overhead. At the other end of the quarry I pulled out and lay on a ledge, exhausted.

Gasping for breath, I let them wash over me, the old dark visions, the uncertain, unnamed feelings I had so persistently pushed away.

I would have no more of fear. No more of the old, vague terrors that had haunted me so long. If those unseen monsters stood at the edge of the woods I would welcome their faces now, to have a chance with my hands at their throats. Fear was a twisted disease of childhood, to have and be rid of, like the mumps. I would not carry it any longer.

And if adulthood was another nightmare of the unseen, unknown, with no certainty out there but death, so be it. I would live on the moment, like Jojohn. I would belong to me.

I arose and started for home, slopping soaking wet through the once forbidding, reaching, night woods, slapping at the leaves.

Cornering by the Simmons place, I heard a dog barking. Vicious. Frantic. The squeaking of wire.

Then I saw the other large figure at the fence, waving his arms and howling back at the dog.

21

"LEAVE ME ALONE! GET AWAY, YOU HEAR ME? GET your hands off me!" In the garage, I wrestled him into the makeshift bathroom, dodging his flailing elbows. He fell heavily against the tin wall, shooting out cracks in the enamel, and he glared at me through a grotesque black mask of shoe polish. "What did you come back for?"

"I might ask you the same thing." I tried to unbutton his shirt and he pushed me away. I slapped his hands aside and he pushed me away again, then ripped off his shirt in drunken disgust and threw it at me. He slid to the floor and sat there, wheezing, his shoulders jerking in a turbulent rhythm. The flesh sagged heavily on his massive chest.

"I ain't lookin' after you. Don't come expectin' me to . . ."

"Who the hell asked you to look after me! I don't need you, I came back here to live, and it didn't matter to me if I never saw your ugly face again!"

I soaked the torn shirt in a bucket and dusted it with washing powder and scrubbed his face. He grumbled and turned aside, and I jerked him back by the hair and bore down harder. He watched me through slitted eyes turning red from the strong soap.

"Damned ole animal," I said, "who could think they *ever* had a need of *you*." When his face had come through the shoe polish and there remained only the black lines in the creases of his skin, I emptied the bucket of water over his head. He sat

208

glowering as it matted his hair and ran in dirty rivulets down his chest, soaking the floor and pouring off onto the dirt floor of the garage. "Ain't you something, laying out in those river joints like an old dog, lettin' people play tricks on you and make a fool of you, and then come back here talking about me needing *you* to look after *me!* Let me tell you something, Jojohn, I'd spend the rest of my life on my knees begging crumbs at Vance Cahill's table before I'd ask a minute of your time! I don't need you for anything, and I don't expect ever *to* need you for anything; so far as I'm concerned you can crawl back down that river and stay gone!"

I threw the bucket against the wall and left the room.

Tio came with a bag of groceries; he looked at the demolished loft but said nothing, knowing after a while Em was back. Em came staggering up the steps. He sat at the table in drunken silence while I ate supper. After a while he started munching on the Mary Jane candy Tio had brought. He sat glumly chewing, wrappers and all, spitting an occasional piece of paper from his teeth. I ignored him.

Finally Tio started unwrapping them for him. "Well, I'd a swore we'd seen the last of you," he said.

Em sat staring ahead. "Ain't no use," he said.

"In what?"

"Tryin'."

Tio looked at me. "Tryin' what?"

Em was silent for a moment. Finally he sighed. "Pore little puppy."

"Puppy?" Tio looked from Em to me. "What puppy?"

Em's voice began to quiver. "Little beagle puppy I found on the highway yesterday. He'd been run over, and there he was, draggin' hisself along on his little front legs." Em rubbed his nose. "I didn't know what to do for him—he was tryin' so hard—didn't know what'd happened to him. Should'a put him outa his misery. Knowed I should. But I couldn't bring my-

209

self. I said, 'Little dog, ain't no use in you and me tryin' . . .'" His voice broke.

"Then what happened?" Tio said.

"Nothin'," Em sniffed. "I just stood over him so he wouldn't git hit again." He shook his head sadly. "Took more'n an hour for him to die."

"And you just stood there in the middle of the road," I said.

"Shoulda put him out of his misery," Em said again. "I've drowned cats. Once when the mama bitch died I had to shotgun a whole pile of puppies. But this time, I just couldn't do it. I don't know what's happenin' to me." He choked up. The tears rolled down his cheeks.

Tio picked up a piece of candy and stuck it in his jaw. "So you just stood there in the middle of the road, with the cars going by, and grieved over the dog."

"Over him, and me," Em gasped. " 'Cause it could have been me. Someday I'll die like that, with nobody around to grieve. So I grieved for him and me, both of us tryin' to get along down the road, and gettin' hit by sump'n too big to understand, and we don't know why."

Tio looked at Em and me. He shook his head and unwrapped another Mary Jane. "Beats all," he said, "settin' here grievin' his own death."

Em grabbed the candy from Tio's hand. "YOU DON'T KNOW NOTHIN' AND YOU NEVER WILL, SO WHAT YOU DOIN' COMIN' AROUND BOTHERIN' A BEREAVED PERSON AND EATIN' UP HIS MARY JANES! GET THE HELL OUTA HERE!"

Em went to the sink and picked up the water bucket and poured it over his face and head. He tilted his head back, drinking the last of the water. He slammed down the empty bucket and something caught his eye. He leaned forward and looked into the piece of broken mirror on the wall. "What happened h'yere?" He pulled at the blackened lines around his eyes.

"Somebody painted your face with shoe polish," I said.

"THEY DONE WHAT!"

"You must have passed out at one of those joints on the river. Probably Birdsong's. When are you going to learn to stay out of those trashy places." They were always playing tricks on Em at Birdsong's. They never could decide whether he was black or not. I wished many times the sheriff could close that gambling-moonshine joint for good.

Em's chest heaved with building anger. "Birdsong's." He gritted his teeth in a bitter grin. "That's what I needed."

Tio turned to leave. "I'll see you later."

"Where you goin'?" Em demanded.

"Home."

"Naw," said Em, jamming his hat on his head and grabbing Tio by the arm, "you come with me," and he hauled him out of the door.

Birdsong's, a small shack of a fish camp that stood on wooden pilings over the water, was just peaking to the midnight business as we came down the river road. The wooded parking lot was jammed with cars, and several outboards were tied up at the dock. Lew Birdsong was sitting at a game of poker when Em heaved in at the door. Someone at the bar called out, "Hey, Chief Blackface is back among us!" And laughter swelled around the room.

Em seized Tio by the collar and marched him up to Birdsong's table. "You see this here, Birdsong? This is a nigger—what you tried to make me appear like. He is what he is, and I am what I am, and it's important to both of us that you know the difference."

"Do your war dance for him, Indian!" The fellow on Birdsong's left gathered a handful of beer bottles and shoved them across the table.

Lew Birdsong grinned and leaned back to scratch his chest. "Well, you got to understand, we didn't have no red shoe polish. 'Course, if we'd knowed you was coming back we'd of made an effort to get

211

some." That was followed by another round of laughter.

"Do your war dance, go on, show 'em," insisted the other fellow. He shoved the bottles again and one tipped over, pouring beer down the Indian's leg.

Em looked down at the puddle of foam dripping off the toe of his boot. "Uh-huh," he mumbled deep down, and grabbing the man by the neck, he plucked him from the chair. Back-stepping quickly toward the door, he gave a sideways turn and the man went over the porch rail with a startled yell that ended with a splash in the river.

Men were pushing up from everywhere. Em stood laughing, smacking his palm with his fist. Two men came at him and he wiped them down with a chair. Then he was at Birdsong's table, and as they started to rise he bounced them away from his fists as though he was shooting pool. The proprietor went down flat, and cold. I grabbed for Tio and we dived under a table. Somebody stepped on my hand and Tio helped me kick him off. It was a running jumble of legs and breaking furniture and the Indian's laughter. Somebody went through a window.

A lot of the customers were clearing out. I heard cars and outboards cranking. Birdsong's was not popular with the law. But there were others, Birdsong's regulars, who ran liquor for him, who were obliged to stay and put up a show. They circled and clubbed at the Indian, tried to get behind him. One of them did and got hurled headlong into the bar. A man wrapped himself around Em's legs, trying to trip him up; Em gripped the man's head between his knees while he knocked two more away, then freed the fellow's head with a piledriver fist. The bartender, a short, stocky fellow, ran down the counter and jumped on Em's shoulders and lifted a bat. Em laughed and dived headfirst into the wall, and came up unencumbered.

Tio couldn't stand it any longer. He ducked behind the bar and dealt a man a glancing blow to the head with a bottle. The man swore and gave chase and Tio crawled into a lower cabinet. But the man got it open and as he was dragging Tio out by the heels I tackled him from the rear. He turned in a rage and, grabbing me by the shirt, was lifting his fist when Tio's foot rose hard between his legs. The man froze in pain.

"Heah now!" Em had seen the man ready to strike and reached and snatched him across the counter, but when he saw the pale face before him and the man hanging limp with pain, he dropped him to the floor in puzzlement.

Em shook his head and downed a swallow from one of the bottles on the counter. "Damndest thing I ever saw."

The floor was piled with bodies. Some crawled in pain. A skinny backwoodsman sat holding the two halves of his broken false teeth. They were new. You could tell.

"All right, git moving now." Em walked around the room, shaking them awake, prodding the crawlers with his foot. "Clear out or drown."

"Come on, Em, let's get out of here," I said.

"Ain't done yit," said Em. "Come on, git up there, now!" He began dragging the crumpled forms out the door.

"Em, what are you doing?"

"I'm sick and tired of this place. Ever' time I've come here they've cheated me, ridiculed me, and served me bad liquor. I'm fed up."

When the last of them were dumped in the parking lot, Em rummaged around in the shed and came out with an ax.

"Em, are you crazy?" I tried to get it away from him but he brushed me aside. The man Em had thrown in the river was crawling up the bank, dripping. Em stepped on him on his way to the shack.

Tio and I watched in disbelief as he climbed down to the boat dock and started chopping away at the pilings. He worked through the first line, then crawled in a skiff and pushed under the shack, and, wedging himself steady with a brace of oars, set to work on the others. The flimsy building began to settle down over him.

"Em, get out from under there!"

When the building began to lean down toward the water he came pushing out, climbed the bank, and ran out onto the porch and jumped up and down, furious at its slowness. "Slide, damn you, slide!"

With a popping of joists the old shack shifted, the porch was almost touching the water. "Get off there, Em!" He lumbered along the porch, jumping, grabbing supports and leaning out over the water, shouting at it to move. When the boat dock was under water he lunged up the boardwalk, found a timber, and jammed it under the upper side of the house and got his shoulder under it. The Indian's moans piercing the night, inch by inch the building tilted, lower and lower, until the current got a grip on the porch.

There was an enormous crash and slide of furniture and glass falling about inside. Then a rush of water and a sigh as the shack slid off the bank. It bobbed there in the stream, a big black thing of peculiar shape, shifting, twisting a little downstream, leaving stubs of pillars where it sat; power lines snapped and lay on the ground.

Cars were cranking and driving away. Lew Birdsong sat propped on his hands, looking dazedly around. He was still sitting that way, looking around for his fish camp, when we lost sight of him through the trees.

22

FEELING BETTER, EM DECIDED HE WANTED A BATH, and sat by the well singing softly to himself. I poured bucket after bucket of water over him and told him all that had happened, the cigarette in his mouth washing apart until only a strip of paper lay on his lip. He sat smiling and humming that wordless song as he watched the dawn drift in from the woods.

"Not a thing to worry about," he said, pulling on his clothes. "We'll make out just fine. Damn, I'm hungry!"

He walked up to pay his respects to the boarders (returning with a lard pail filled with hot food), and went out to see Jayell, and spent the next few days cleaning attics, basements, and doing whatever odd jobs he could turn up while I was in school.

One day a lady whose Florida room he helped redo gave him an aquarium of tropical fish, with which he was delighted. He set it in the window and showed me how the sun striking the corner of the tank just right threw a lavish spectrum of colors across the wall.

But all my arguing couldn't save the fish. He fried them up crispy brown and ate them on Ritz crackers.

Pets? You got to feed and look after?

Not for him!

I don't know what he told the boarders about our condition when he went up there to see them that first day home—he swore he told them nothing—but he must have done some very broad hinting, because pretty soon they started having Mr. Teague, Tio, Em and me up to the house for Saturday night suppers. "To help keep the food bill equal to what we're being charged for!" said Mrs. Porter.

And, they said, they wanted a chance to pump Mr. Teague in detail about all that was going on at the store.

The boarders themselves, surprisingly, were doing remarkably well. Far from the collapse of spirit I expected when Miss Esther left, there was an activity around the house I had never seen before. They all turned out for yard work now, even Mr. Jurgen. The women were busy making quilts; they were doing some babysitting for members of Pinnacle church. Mr. Rampey and Mr. Woodall ventured down to help Wash Fuller overhaul his Plymouth. And they were all trooping off to Sunday services together—even Mr. Burroughs.

Those Saturday night suppers were among the best times I ever had, a riot of reminiscing, with each of them outdoing the other in telling tall tales, often, as was their custom, with two or three of them going at it at the same time.

And it was the first of these get-togethers that brought Farette's situation into the open at the boardinghouse and forced the boarders to face it, and make a decision. And having done that, they laid the groundwork for what came later.

Farette was about the same age as the boarders, and although she protected her position as official cook and housekeeper with a sharp tongue and a watchful eye, over the years, the work had plainly become too much for her to do alone, and it had become natural for Miss Esther and the others to help out in the kitchen at mealtimes and wash the dishes afterward, to take turns with the washing and ironing and general cleaning.

In short, Farette had become just one more old person living in the house—except for two notable differences. One was that she still attended Free Rent A.M.E. church in the hollow while the others walked uptown—which I never thought much about; A.M.E. was closer, and Em and I preferred it to Pinnacle Baptist ourselves. The other, to which I had given a great deal of thought over the years, was that while I was confined to the thunder and roar of mealtimes in the dining room, Farette got to eat by herself in the serenity of the kitchen.

That privacy, our invitations to supper cost her.

Tio and I were sitting on the front porch that first night, flipping a little mumbley peg with our knives and listening to the men's voices in the living room as we waited for supper, and when those wonderful words, "Y'all 'bout ready?" came from the dining room in Farette's clarion voice, there was a general scramble in that direction.

As we passed through the dining room Mr. Teague

tutned to Tio for clarification on a point he was making to Mr. Rampey.

"The way we arranged the shelves and the meat cases, how much floor space was it that we added to the store?"

"A hundred and twenty square feet," said Tio.

"A hundred and twenty square feet," said Mr. Teague proudly.

"Plus that don't count the extra shelves we built up front," said Tio, "and when you figure we pyramid the canned goods now like *they* do, two four-foot squares—and that's extra, that was just walkin' space before, let's see that comes to . . ."

During this time they had walked into the dining room where the others were already taking their usual places, and Tio, calculating rapidly on his fingers, sat down opposite Mr. Teague, just as he was accustomed to doing at home. "In all it comes to two hundred and thirty-eight . . ."

Tio came to in the hush.

What had stopped the talk was Farette, who, leaning over the table to set down the gravy boat, stood frozen, staring at him. Then the others turned to look, and Tio, his eyes widening in horror, scrambled to his feet.

Up to that moment, no one had given a thought to Tio's presence, and now everyone was as dumbfounded as Tio himself, who, unable to move or think, stood gripping the back of his chair.

It was awful. No one could think what to do.

And it was into that desperate silence that Mr. Burroughs, late to the table as usual, came harrumphing and clearing his throat from the bathroom.

He swung through the door and stopped, focusing on what all the quiet was about. And when he perceived it he stood surveying it, the way he might a stalled car, his white moustache working. He looked at Tio. He looked at Farette.

At last he stepped forward, lowered his long arms until his knuckles rested on the table, and roared:

"Oh-what-the-hell . . . !"

It was as though he had cut the strings on a lot of balloons; all the tension at once rose to laughter. Mr. Rampey and Mrs. Bell grabbed Tio and pulled him into his chair.

"Farette!" cried Mrs. Metcalf, and she and Mrs. Porter and Mr. Burroughs all grabbed the frightened little woman at once. Mrs. Cline tottered to the kitchen for her plate.

Laughing with the others at her discomfort, I jumped up and ran for an extra chair. When she was finally seated, I leaned across to her and said, "You didn't think you'd get away with it forever, did you?"

But she was up to it. She carefully removed and folded her apron in her lap and, sitting stiff as a ramrod, pinched her lips and looked slowly around at all the grinning faces.

Finally she snapped, "Well? Ain't nobody at this table gon' ax a *blessin'!*"

But we couldn't live on that one meal a week. We cast about for every possible source of earning money.

In the back of a magazine I found an offer to become solvent in my spare time by selling religious mottoes. It struck me that I could do worse than throwing in with Providence on a get-rich scheme, as there was bound to be a little supernatural help in the selling of such a product. I would even tithe a tenth of the profits as an added guarantee. I had heard positive-thinking businessmen testify at Pinnacle Baptist that they owed their entire success to the practice.

The mottoes were verses of Scripture written in glitter on an electric blue background that sold for a quarter apiece. Sure enough, Providence held up its end of the deal. They sold like hotcakes, especially in the Ape Yard. In fact, I was surprised to find that the poorest shanties housed the best prospects. When they were all sold I had collected a little over eight dollars, and a blue coating on my fingers that would take time to wear off. But then I found myself in a moral dilemma. With the money before me on the cot, I thought less and less of the tithing. It seemed a

218

reckless commitment to a "silent partner" who had remained altogether too silent when the doors were slamming. I stewed about it. I even offered Him a chance to speak up, right then and there, and clear away my doubts once and for all. It's not often a person gets to pray while holding the trump card, and it gave me a glorious sense of power. All right, I said, stay silent this time and it's going to cost you something. I waited, but He didn't take the bait. Still, I was uneasy. Then I hit on what seemed to me a brilliant solution: I simply opened an account with Providence as I had with Mr. Teague!

In the end I kept the company's share too.

I got several threatening letters about an inspector-somebody who was in my area and would see that I got prosecuted to the fullest extent of the law if I didn't remit the company's money at once. But having brazenly put the Lord on the cuff, I wasn't about to be intimidated by some mail-order house in New Jersey.

With my new wealth I paid three dollars on account to Tio, bought a new pair of tennis shoes, chipped in on another second-hand trash burner to replace the one I'd smashed ("What in the world happened up here?" Em had asked. "I got mad," I said. "Well, next time you feel a mad comin' on, holler, so I can guy off the building!"), treated Em to a Saturday at the picture show with a box of chocolate-covered cherries, and brought home milkshakes for breakfast. The next morning I was still sick from the candy, and endured Em's snickers as I poured the curdled milkshakes out the window.

That was foolish, I thought. I would have to guard against such childish splurges in the future. Suddenly I became very fearful for our money, and insisted that we keep it in a safe place. There was an old birdhouse on a pole mounted to the side of the garage. I worked it loose from its U-clamps and pulled it into the loft. Prying off the top of the birdhouse, I found that my coffee-can bank would just fit snugly inside. I put our money in it, replaced the top, and slid the pole back in the clamps. The birds would have to look to themselves.

Flushed with the success of the motto business, I next sent off for garden seeds to sell, failing to note that agriculture, unlike religion, is seasonal, and most people already had gardens producing. After a few days I shelved my sales kit and gave up.

Then Em saw it, and I wished many times over I had burned it.

"That's what we ought to do," he cried, "plant us a late vegetable garden! Lord, how long has it been since I've tasted fresh vegetables right out of the ground!"

I'd seen it happen many times. Once a person becomes overpowered by the ancient longing to put seeds in the ground, he can no longer be dealt with as a rational human being. He is a person obsessed. You can kill him, but you can't talk him out of it. He will find soil to plant in if he has to haul it; he will plant on solid rock, in clayey yards, on rooftops, in windowboxes, in cans, in paper cups, wherever a seed can put down roots and push a bud into the sun. I'd known people who would change their religion before they would see a spring come without breaking ground.

It is a curious malady, and can strike suddenly and without warning, even after, as in Em's case, lying dormant for many years. The old lust came up in him that night, and the next morning before daybreak there he was out beside the garage ripping with a pick, dropping great clots of grass, the "hah! hah!" of his breath matching the slamming strokes.

I trudged along behind him with a shovel, breaking up clods without enthusiasm, something telling me that I was in for a trying time.

"Dig deep, boy, them roots gotta have room to grow!" When the ground was broken he sifted it, worried, and grabbed a sack from the garage and headed for the woods. "We gotta get some woods dirt to mix in."

"You're gonna haul more dirt? We got a whole

planet under there! What do we need more dirt for?"

"Shut up and come on!" he explained.

After the area had been crawled over and picked free of every sprig it housed, Em permitted the planting to begin—and was even more impossible about that. If a package said three seeds to the hill, he put in five, just to be safe. I stuck the onion bulbs in too deep; he yelled I was choking them, and fell on his knees and brushed away dirt as though they were, indeed, gasping for air. I tried planting the tomato plants in their paper pulp cups, as the roots were already growing through, and got damned for being the ignorantest fool, by far, he ever met. "Just stand over there," he huffed in exasperation, "you're gonna mess up in spite a *all* I can do!" So I took to the shade, gratefully, picked my blisters and let him go.

And he kept at it, from morning till night.

"It's a nice garden, a fine garden," I ventured after a few days. "I hope Mrs. Bell doesn't come down to retrieve a few of the tools you've stolen from her and see it, because I'm sure the shock and envy would be more than the poor woman could stand. But, Em, until that plot of ground actually starts growing something, we got to figure some way to put some food on the table."

Em stood leaning on his rake.

"I been thinkin' about it!" He spied a caterpillar trespassing out of the grass toward his garden and leaned down to free it of its troubles. "Doin' this kind of work clears a man's head so he *can* think! Ain't a thing to worry about, boy. You get out of school tomorrow; the next day we'll just head for Cooper Corner."

23

COOPER CORNER WAS A SHADED, WINDSWEPT CORNER up near the fairgrounds, the gathering place for day laborers from the Ape Yard. We settled ourselves under the umbrella oak and waited, and for a while it seemed no one else was coming. Then, with the first gray tinting of the air they began emerging from the shadows of the hollow. They drifted up the winding paths and settled around us with a rustle of crusted work clothes, the soft scrapings of leather. They all looked tired and sleepy, and smelled of the sweat of yesterdays in the sun.

"Good mornin'," bellowed Em cheerfully. Most of them knew him and returned the greeting with easy familiarity. Old Aaron Tim, twisting wax from his ears with a matchstick and spreading it on his dried, cracked lips, shook his head and chuckled. "Come to do a little work, Em?"

"*We* come to work, me and this grown man h'yere," said Em, and went over to engage the younger boys in a game of searching for echoes, their voices bouncing back from the darkened hollow.

They were an elite corps, those morning hopefuls of Cooper Corner. They came each morning, sometimes whole families, and sat on the roots of the massive oak, on the curb, on the ground, and waited, sometimes all day. They came to pick cotton, to pull corn, to bale hay. They were there to spread asphalt, to dig ditches, to move furniture, to lay pipe and tend yard. They strung fences, killed hogs, trimmed trees; they cleaned basements, unloaded freight cars, and climbed shivering cold from their drafty shacks to fire the furnaces for the waking town. Whatever work there was, they were there to do it, their one goal each day: to put something on the table that night.

With the grown ones came the young apprentices, some barely walking, to learn a trade in which there was no promotion, and the pay was always the least they would take.

After a while a pickup puttered to the curb with milk cans rattling in the back. A farmer in a sun helmet bawled out, "Need two hands to roof a barn."

None of the black people moved, apparently in deference to us, who were first. Em looked about, and seeing this, stood up and dusted his pants. The farmer looked us over.

"What'chall doin' out here?"

"Lookin' for work," Em said.

"Bet. I can get some of these niggers to work cheaper."

"Then get 'em," Em said, "but don't go trying to bluff me down on price before we've even talked work."

"Well, I suppose it wouldn't hurt to have a big 'un like you handling that tin. Get in." He looked at me. "Don't need no kids."

"He goes where I go. He works like a man, and if he falls behind I'll catch him up."

The farmer shifted gears. "I'll take your word on that." Em and I climbed in the back of the truck, but as we started off Em banged on the roof of the cab. The farmer slammed on the brakes. "You never said what you was payin'."

"Seventy-five cents an hour for you, fifty for the kid."

"That the goin' rate?" Em called to the crowd. Someone down front nodded. Em shook his head and settled himself in the truck. "Drive on," he said.

The farmer, whose name was Hutchinson, ran a small dairy five miles out the Calhoun Falls highway. Four men were already at work, hammering down the corrugated sheathing on a new milking barn. Fat, white-faced cattle grazed below an enormous poultry house where hundreds of leghorns clucked and shuffled behind the latticed walls. Over the hill came the deep-throated throb of a tractor.

Our job was to haul the roofing from stacks by the farmhouse and drag it up swaying ladders to the men on the roof. Hutchinson furnished no gloves, and in minutes the skin was fuzzed between our thumbs and forefingers and angry red cracks opened in our hands. Hutchinson stayed with us the whole time, shouting instructions to the carpenters and stamping about impatiently as we worked the tin up the ladders. He seemed to grow more agitated with each trip I made up the hill.

"You said he could do a man's work," he shouted up at Em.

"He is doing a man's work," Em shot back. "You're judgin' him by me, and I'm doin' the work of four men. Now, stand clear of this ladder before you get your head split open." There was laughter from the other side of the roof. Hutchinson blew his nose furiously on the ground.

By twelve o'clock the job was finished and the carpenters went home. He hadn't *said* it was a full day's work he was offering, but he hadn't said otherwise either. Nevertheless, I was glad it was over. Em and I stood waiting at the pumphouse for our pay while Hutchinson busied himself in the house. It finally occurred to us, from the sounds coming from the kitchen, that he was having his dinner. He kept us waiting for over an hour. At last he came shuffling across the yard, his face sour with the prospect of paying out money. "Let's see now," he said, thumbing through his time book.

"Six twenty-five," Em said.

Hutchinson's head jerked up. "What?"

"Five hours, at seventy-five for me, fifty for the boy."

"You started at eight o'clock! I looked at my watch the minute we drove in the yard."

"I seen you did, so I checked it too. It was a little before seven."

"I'll be damned!" shouted Hutchinson. "You ain't

comin on my place and skinnin' me, you goddamned—
gypsy or whatever you are! Here's five dollars, and
that's twice what you're worth, the both of you!"

Em was trembling, his breath growing erratic.

I stepped in front of him and took the money.

"Em," I spoke quickly, keeping my voice down,
"I know you want to hit him, but if you hit him
right now you'll kill him, and they'll put you away
and I don't need you put away. I need you with me
right now. And besides, it wouldn't be worth gettin'
put away for killing the likes of him. A lyin', cheatin',
robbin' son of a bitch like him. But he needs hittin',
somebody ought to hit him, but not somebody that'll
kill him, so I guess it ought to be me!" And with
that I turned and smacked the startled farmer as hard
as I could across the mouth.

He staggered back a few steps and touched his
bleeding lip in amazement. Em was even more amazed,
so much so he forgot his anger. "Well, I'll be damned,"
he said. Hutchinson, a little pale under his whiskers,
lost no time retreating to the house. "I'll be damned,"
Em said. He said it over and over as we walked back
to town, looking at me from time to time, his dark
eyes shining with pride.

"He done what?" laughed Jayell that night at Dirsey's, and as Em told it again he broke up, pounding
his casted leg on the floor.

"Said, 'Don't *you* hit him, Em, you'll get us in
trouble.' Then—*whap!* right in the chops. Surprised
me more'n it did old man Hutchinson!" Em doubled
over with laughter.

Jayell fought down a coughing fit and ordered more
beers. "He's Esther's blood all right," said Dirsey. "By
the way, what you hear from her lately?"

"We got a letter here from her yesterday," I said.
I fished it out of my pocket. "And there's something
in it about you, Dirsey."

"Yeah," said Em, "read him that part."

"It's at the bottom, but I'll come to it," I said.

"Got to do things in order, of course," Em said. "He's her blood," he said, nodding.

"Ssh, Em," said Jayell.

I read:

"*Dear Everybody, Farette and Earl,*

Rec. your letter Mrs. Bell, and so glad to hear. Hope this finds you all well. I am about to get over the summer cold I had—from the change of climate I guess and am ready to go again. It is awful hot here now. I was surprised at it being this hot in North Carolina, but Vance laughed at me and said N.C. and Georgia wasn't that far apart in their weather. I guess I just forgot. It's been so long. Well I'm really glad to hear Earl is getting along well. I could still skin him for running off like that, but if he wants to stay on a while I guess it's all right. I know you all will look after him. Any expense he causes you now, you send me the bill and I'll see Vance pays it. We'll see if he laughs about that. Ha! ha! Must close now as Lucille is not feeling well and I have to fix dinner for the twins. Oh, and I was really tickled about that good for nothing Jojohn planting him a garden. I never thought I'd see the day he'd raise anything besides h——. Anyhow, anything that may keep him from spending so much time at that sorry Dirsey's can't do him anything but good. Pls. keep well and write soon.

Love to all, Esther."

"Can't do him anything but good!" laughed Dirsey, relishing it. "Oh, there ain't but one of Miss Esther. I remember the night she come down here after Wylie. Come through that door hotter'n a two-dollar pistol and, brothers, I mean she lit'ally cleaned house! Grabbed that deer up there"—Dirsey turned and pointed over the bar to the buck's head, which had one antler broken off—"I had it hanging over by the door then, and she commenced to swing it this-away —like a sickle, don't you know—and didn't she have

226

those gentlemen climbin' the walls! In two minutes flat there wasn't a bottle left standing nor a customer on the place but Wylie, and she left here behind him —goosin' him with that damned horn! He told me she probed him all the way home!"

Dirsey leaned on the bar until the laugher subsided. "Yessir, that Esther was sump'n else. I'm gonna miss her. I guess the old folks miss her too. What's become of them now?"

"They're stayin' on at the house," said Em. "The son of a bitch that bought the place has upped the rent on 'em, but they're toughin' it out as best they can."

"The hell you say—upped the rent! Who bought it?"

"Who the hell knows," said Jayell. "One or another of them blue-blood bastards that owns every other square inch of this town! You know how they do, buy up little bits and pieces of property here and there on the quiet until they get a big enough chunk to put up a big business or development and turn a whopping profit. Did you know they bought the Blue Light quarry property off an old colored woman for fifty dollars an acre?"

Dirsey whistled softly. "And how many million has it turned over?"

"It'll never change," said Jayell. "Pretty soon there'll be twelve of 'em ownin' the world and chargin' the rest of us rent. Hell, I expect Luther Pierce to sell that shop property out from under me any day."

"Speakin' of which, Jaybird," said Em, "when you gonna get that place cranked up again? Me and the boy here could use some work."

Jayell twisted his beer on the counter. "I don't know, Em. Don't look like I ever will. Right now I couldn't get financin' to build a doghouse. Got to do something, though, and soon."

"Listen at him poor-mouth," said Dirsey, "Mr. Marble Park. Talk about your blue-bloods . . ."

Jayell slammed down his beer. "Goddamnit, don't talk to me about that place! I wish I had never heard that name! Them and their dinner parties and their damned bridge games. You know what my wife had me doin' yesterday . . . addressin' envelopes beggin' money for the Community Chest! And us sittin' up there eatin' tuna fish sandwiches. And I done it! That's what stumps me. I done it! God-a-mighty-damn!"

"Well, that job with Smithbilt's still open, ain't it?" said Em. "You can get around well enough to do that."

"Yeah—yeah, Smithbilt. Jesus, if I had this past year to do over again . . ." Jayell gritted his teeth. "You know, I'll wonder until the day I die if that damned Fay didn't push that ladder out from under me. I wouldn't put it past that Bobo one minute."

Dirsey shook his head. "One of these days somebody's gonna kill that son of a bitch."

"Won't be a day too soon," muttered Em.

Dirsey looked at him. "I'm surprised you and him ain't crossed paths somewhere already."

Em shook his head. "He leaves me alone. I leave him alone."

"Well," said Dirsey, "Mr. Bobo's time might not be long off, the way things are goin'. Lots of folks stirred up about that Supreme Court thing. Did you know there's talk around town about organizin' a Klan?"

"Shoot," said Jayell, wiping his mouth, "that won't bother the Fathers. They'll keep a lid on things. Just gives 'em a new bogeyman."

"Fathers?" said Dirsey. "Who're you talking about, Jayell?"

"The Southern Fathers!" said Jayell, getting into his preaching voice again. "That same land-owning, mill-owning little intermarried club of blue-bloods I was talking about before. Those almighty bastards and their watchdog politicians who've always run the South like it was their own private plantation, that's who I'm talking about!"

Dirsey eyed the number of bottles Em was absently forming into a circle on the bar. "Yeah, well, tell you what, Jayell, you've had a bad time . . . why don't you go on home and get some sleep and . . ."

But Jayell was just warming to his subject. He

propped his elbow on the bar and wavered a finger at Dirsey. "Didn't you go hear Senator Broward's speech at the auditorium last night? 'Never!' he said. 'No, sir, not a thing to worry about, go back to work, go back to sleep; it's just another bogeyman, and we'll protect you. The structure is intact.'" Jayell's shoulders tightened in a futile gesture. "Don't you see, the Fathers have always ruled the South like it was a dull child, a child taught to work for nothing and want little. And to be controlled, a child's got to know the bogeyman! And they give us the bogeymen, don't they? Over the years, they've played the campaign trails with a trunkful of costumes, but there's two of them—a little frayed from use—that still remain as favorites. They never fail to fetch the crowd: the Federal Government, that old enemy on the Potomac whose sworn purpose is to bleed to death and gobble up the South, and that Dark Lurking Menace in the Ape Yards."

Jayell drained his bottle and set it down. Conversation had stopped at Dirsey's; other customers had turned and were listening. "And now they've got the bogeyman for the fifties, haven't they, and he's special, made-to-order, a perfect combination of the other two!" Jayell leaned forward, his face darkened to a sinister scowl. "A nine-headed monster in the black judicial robes of the highest Court!

"But," he said, leaning back, eyes bulging, "like the Senator said, there's not a thing to worry about. They haven't even set a date for compliance—why there's years and years of political maneuvering ahead! And as everybody knows, in the fine art of delaying progress, Southern politicians are recognized masters!"

"Progress?" said a man down the bar. "You call mixing the schools progress?"

"Hey, come on, Jayell," said Dirsey under his breath, eyeing the others, "hold it down a little bit, will you."

But Jayell, heartened by the challenge to his opinion, turned and regarded the man solemnly. He slowly slid down off the stool.

"Jayell . . ." Dirsey moved after him down the bar,

shrugging to the other man about Jayell's condition. "Em!" he called, jerking his head rapidly.

Jayell limped up to the man, who readied himself. But Jayell only stood looking at him. He turned to the others and raised his arms in benediction. "No worry, my children," he said soothingly. "Go back to sleep. This is the New South, not the old. The Fathers want no disruption in the industrial generation. Not now, just when things are booming! Go back to sleep, and be glad this is the twentieth century and not the nineteenth, when the Fathers' needs were different, and they cried alarm! And you, my gentle brothers, were called upon to lead us into the nation's bloodiest war."

At Dirsey's frantic urging, Em finally sighed and shuffled down the bar and lifted Jayell under his arm. "Pore little fool. Ain't never had no sense. Never will have none." I held the door open for them.

Dirsey, greatly relieved, was wiping the bar. "Next time you write your Aunt Esther, you tell her hello for me, son, you'll do that for me, won't you?" he called. "Tell her old Dirsey sends his love."

I waved and let the door go.

24

As the days went by at Cooper Corner we learned not to be so quick to step forward, and when men of Hutchinson's reputation came we watched the black people for the hesitation, the polite mutterings of work already promised, and let their trucks go by. It was good to be out early again and working. We bolted a quick breakfast at the bus station, the only place open at that time of the morning, and raced each other to the corner, shouting to hear our voices bounce off the darkened buildings.

But it was a summer of mercilessly hard work. I crawled for miles through fields dragging baskets and sacks; I unloaded truckloads of feed and fertilizer, stacked thousands of bricks. I stood all day in sweltering woods cutting pulpwood and slapping mosquitoes, rocking a cross-cut saw in the endless monotony that blurs the hours and makes the mind go wandering for beautiful things. And later, watched red cracks open in my hands from wrenching corn from withered stalks and shoveling it about in cribs of black dust that left my lungs aching for days after.

Em kept after me, goading, pushing, yelling when he caught me hopefully watching a dark cloud on the horizon that might rain us out. " 'Course it's hard work. Ever' child ought to be made to do work he hates to do, so he'll want to get out and find sump'n better!"

The pleasures were simple: the taste of water at three o'clock in the afternoon, the soothing massage of a vibrating truck bed on aching thighs, calluses that came to toughen split and bleeding flesh.

I felt myself perceptibly aging that summer, work will age you as surely as time. I got up slower and sighed like the men when I sat down. But there was a hardening too, and that felt good. My hands were like bark when I washed. There were no new muscles that I could see, but I was lean and tough and didn't tire as easily, and, best of all, my left arm was becoming almost as strong as my right.

To Em, life was singing again. He had work he could throw himself into, he had money for Dirsey's and Deva's, and above all, he had his garden.

He was out there every morning before I was awake, and as soon in the evening as he could get home, hoeing, fertilizing, suckering, stringing bean runners, hauling water from the well and talking to the vegetables. And let a bug be caught sunning itself on one of Em's leaves, or a worm be found with its head in one of his tomatoes, and the next instant the poor creature was headed toward oblivion under

231

the dancing boots of the incoherently screaming Indian.

"Boy, look at this! Just look at this!"

Em worried and fretted along the line of overripe tomatoes on the sills; he picked up cucumbers, squash, bell peppers, clucking like a mother hen over her eggs, running his fingers over withering skins. Peas lay wilting in the sink.

The garden, such a nuisance in the planting, now presented us with another problem.

Overabundance.

I was sick of vegetables. I never wanted to see another vegetable, and still that garden produced.

"Why don't you throw them out? Give them away!"

"What! Precious as vegetables are? Do you know what prices they're bringin' these days?"

"Well, I'll tell you this, I'm not eatin' another vegetable for breakfast!"

"What we need is an icebox!" Em pushed back his hat, thinking. "You know what? Tio said they throwed out that old drink box when they was redoin' the store."

"I know. I wish they hadn't done that."

"I'll bet you it's still around somewhere, and that'd make a perfect icebox! Let's go take a look!"

We walked down the woods to the newly renovated store.

It hardly looked like the same place. Tio had repainted it, inside and out, with bright red trim and put new green vegetable bins out front. There was a new sign over the door, and the gas pumps, painted blue and silver, stood in the yard like a pair of admirals.

Tio stood under the awning in a bright new apron with his name hand-inked on the pocket. We politely stopped to check for improvements that needed praising. I wanted that icebox as bad as Em at that point, and Tio in a sulk would get us nowhere. "I don't believe I've seen that before," I said eagerly, pointing to the flashing red light in the peanut-parching machine.

232

"Kind of catches your eye, don't it?" acknowledged Tio.

"Bright as a blessed rainbow," said Em, looking over the store. "It just don't look like the same place."

"We're gonna show 'em," said Tio. "We're gonna show 'em good."

"Don't knows I'd a picked that color, though," said Em, looking at the nervous orange of the kerosene pump. "Most kerosene pumps I've seen were green."

"That makes our different, then, don't it?" said Tio.

"I kind of like it," I said, cutting an eye at Em. "What more natural way to advertise kerosene than to paint it the color of fire?"

Jojohn, having realized his error, smiled with relief. "Ah, boy, you got a head on your shoulders."

"Come look inside!" Tio said.

The entire store had been scrubbed and rearranged. The shelves sported a new coat of white, and the floor boards were so clean they looked boiled. The counters were freshly topped with bright linoleum, and squares of it marched away up the stairs. Mr. Teague, in a new bow tie, fidgeted and turned in the checkout cubicle like a cat trying to get comfortable in a corner. "Tio will have to find what you need," he called out, "I don't know where nothing is anymore!"

"That's what the signs is for," said Tio. He lowered his voice. "Hardest part of all was to get him to go self-service. Mr. Teague still thinks you got to run and wait on folks. Here, wait up, Em, get you a shopping cart." He snatched a flimsy contraption away from the wall.

"We don't need a shopping . . ." Em stopped and stared at it. "That looks like a baby carriage."

Tio grinned. "That's what it was before I made it over. It's a pistol, ain't it?"

"Look," said Em, "what we came about is, I figured we could make an icebox out of that old drink box y'all throwed out. Is it still around?"

"Yeah, it's out back there." He led us out into the weeds behind the store and pulled aside a piece of rotted plywood. "I hated to see it go; it was one of our main attractions. The new box don't freeze drinks yet, but I'm working on it."

We dragged the box back to the front of the store and lifted the lid. It had a fist-size hole in the bottom and the sheathing was rusted loose, but the insulated box inside seemed solid enough. Tio had salvaged the frame and motor for possible use elsewhere.

"Made to order," said Em, and sent Tio back for his tools. Mr. Teague came out complaining of the slowest business day he'd seen in months, and sat on the bench under the awning to watch. "Gonna make an icebox outa that, are you? Tio's about ruined the new box trying to make it freeze drinks like that one did. Fool froze up and busted a whole case of drinks last week." Mr. Teague looked from Em to me. "Whole damn case of drinks . . ."

Em chiseled and hacksawed the box in half along its belly, even with the bottom of the insulated box inside. What was left was half a drink box with a lid, and an outer skirt of sheathing. "There we are, boy. We take and bury it in a corner of the garage where it's dark and cool, drop in a block of ice now and then, and we got the best icebox anywhere around. It's even got its own hole for drainage."

"Em," said Tio, "you're a wonder."

"Come on, let's get this thing up the hill," I said, "before that vegetable garden eats the garage."

"Customer!" cried Tio. He dropped his end and bounded toward a pickup pulling up to the tanks. "Yessir, Mr. Mangum, fill 'er up?" I was surprised to see Paulie Mangum stopping there. Mr. Teague had long since cut off his credit. Paulie lived in the next house down the road from the store and was the only person I ever heard Miss Esther call white trash. No one knew what he did for a living. For recreation he beat his wife.

Paulie answered Tio by first telling him to get his goddamned foot off his running board, then he handed him a piece of paper and jerked a thumb at Mr.

Teague, and scratched off out of the yard. Tio came back reading the leaflet.

"What is it, Tio?" called Mr. Teague.

"Just a revival," said Tio without looking up.

The old man shook his head. "Paulie Mangum handin' out revival notices. I've lived too long."

Tio returned to where we were standing and handed the paper to me. It said:

KNIGHTS OF THE KU KLUX KLAN

Will present a program
August 22nd
8:30 P.M.

Four miles south on Hwy. 93
at Otis Barton's auction barn.
All concerned white citizens
are invited to

COME HEAR THE TRUTH
Featuring the Rev. Haskell Spann
of Clingham, Georgia

Free transportation will be
provided.

I had heard about the Klan, of course, but their activities had always been confined to a time before I was born. I was surprised they still existed, especially here in Quarrytown.

"Come on," said Em, "let's get this icebox home."

"The twenty-second—that's today," said Tio. "The meeting's tonight! Hey, you want to go?"

"To a Klan meetin'?"

"Why not? They sent us an invitation, didn't they?"

"Heck, yeah, why not? Hey, Em, you wanta come?" Em, out of patience, was hoisting the drink box on his back. "Fine lotta help you are," he grumbled.

"Do you want to go with us tonight?" I repeated.

"Hell no," he said, "I'm goin' to church!"

"Church!"

Mr. Teague was off the bench like a shot. He stood

on the sidewalk, mouth agape, blinking, and I realized that Em had just exposed Tio's latest business-improving scheme.

"Merciful God, that's what's wrong! *Tio, we're open on Sunday!*"

25

THE NIGHT WAS AGLOW BEHIND BARTON'S AUCTION barn. The song was "The Old Rugged Cross." And so strange to be crawling toward it through the weeds, toward that comforting old hymn trembling with fear, as though a monster might be calling in your mother's voice.

There were about a hundred people in the pasture, leaning against their vehicles, standing, squatting, singing, while a huge cross lapped its fire in the wind. On a flatbed truck a half-dozen men sat in metal folding chairs. They all wore white sheets and pointed hats, some trimmed in red, some in blue. A couple had brought their families, also in costume, the children, replicas of their fathers, playing around the truck in their own little sheets and caps. When the singing was finished the people waited silently, watching the great cross billow and roar and consume itself in black-orange flames.

I knew most of the people there, a number of whom had been forced out of the Ape Yard by the influx of blacks. Paulie Mangum was there, of course, and Pete Stokes, the deputy sheriff, and Vince Dupree, who ran the upholstery shop. Rudy and Randy Owens stood by their respective trucks, not talking to each other, of course. The brothers ran competitive gas stations and hadn't spoken to each other since World War Two. Something to do with a prostitute in Germany. The only one of the Klansmen on the

truck that I recognized right off was Rudy Alf Newton, a house painter who hadn't painted anything in
recent memory but the front window of the finance
company that had repossessed his car. One Saturday
night in the picture show Alf awoke suddenly from
a drunken nap and began firing a pistol at the villain
on the screen. He hadn't been off the road more than
a month.

One of the Klansmen stood up and stepped to the
edge of the truck. Then I recognized Otis Barton.
He flipped a hand out of a floppy sleeve and adjusted his glasses, and for me the spell was broken.
I had to suppress a laugh. On Otis the pointed hat
looked like a dunce cap.

"Friends," he said gravely, "you all know why we're
here. You've heard the news. We've never had trouble with the niggers in Pollard County. We've treated
'em right and they've stayed where they belong. But
they've been active. They've been pushing. Eisen-
hower's screwed up the army to where a man can't
serve his country without living with 'em, and now
the Su-preme Court wants to put 'em in the schools
with our kids!"

Otis waited for the murmur to subside. "Now, many
of you heard Senator Broward when he was in town
a couple weeks ago; said wasn't anything to worry
about, but some of us feel it's time to get organized
and be ready to meet this thing head on. The Klan's
not been too active in recent years, but it's gettin'
active now, and I feel it's time to organize a klavern
here in Quarrytown. These gentlemen on the platform
here are members of the Clingham, Georgia, Klan.
I want you to listen to what they've got to say, and
then walk up here and meet us man to man, and tell
us where you stand on this thing." Otis patted his
chest, fumbling for an opening, and finding none,
turned away and, somewhat self-consciously, pulled up
his gown. He extracted a piece of paper and read the
introduction: "The featured speaker tonight is an ordained man of God, and a respected member of his
community. He is pastor of the Logan branch Church

237

of God of Clingham, Georgia, a Mason, Oddfellow, Woodman of the World, and Kludd of the Clingham Klan. I want you to make welcome, the Reverend Haskell Spann!"

Otis stepped back clapping loudly and the crowd half-heartedly took up the applause, clapping stiff-armed below the belt as country people do. The Reverend Spann was a tall, heavy man with craggy cheeks and broad, thick hands. He might have been a carpenter or a bricklayer, and probably was. I knew the man well from my experiences in backwoods churches. I was all ready for his trancelike, swaying shout-preaching, "Love-ah, God-ah, repent-ah," but when he started preaching, it was a different kind of sermon. This man was preaching hate.

Pure hate. It was the blood of every thought, every word. And as they listened, the men on the ground slowly, one by one, as though touched by some faint electric pulse, moved off the fenders and raised out of their squats and stood at attention, scarcely breathing. The man was not easy with his tongue; the words faltered and sentences broke off in the bell-tolling chant of his ranting. But the hate was there, eloquently there, and the people on the ground responded. Something ominous pervaded that gathering; it was as strong in the air as the black pine smoke that settled from the whipping flames. Hatred that night became a tangible thing.

"The nigger has got to be dealt with!" he roared, leaning a trembling finger into the light, "before he mongrelizes our race, and his ordained curse marks the skin of your own grandchildren!"

Amen, brother . . . !"

Tio and I nearly jumped out of our skins. Doc Bobo and Clyde Fay stepped out of the shadows not five yards to the right of us.

Without hesitation they made their way toward the truck. Stunned, the townspeople let them through. The Reverend Spann, a gesture frozen in air, at last found his voice.

"By the Lord Jesus . . . *coons!"*

Doc Bobo continued along, nodding and bowing his way through.

The minister whirled around. "Albert! Raeford! Are you gon' just set there?" Instantly, Alf Newton jumped off the truck and came running. The other two Klansmen clambered down after him, one of them clutching a tire iron. Scooping up a rock, Alf darted through the crowd toward Bobo; he was drawing up sideways, already into his swing, when Clyde Fay stepped forward and shot a fist to his jaw that dropped him in his sheet like a sack of flour. The next man doubled over with a boot in his groin, and the third was drawing back with the tire iron when his head suddenly snapped from under his hat with the force of the big Negro's fist. Alf Newton rolled to his feet and charged. Fay reached down and lifted him off the ground and stood looking at him, their eyes level.

Alf Newton screamed in fury, "Lemme go, nigger, I'll kill you!" He squirmed and yelled over his shoulder, "Y'all come on here!"

"Hold on there!" shouted Otis Barton. He turned to Reverend Spann. "That's Bobo, the one I told you about. Y'all hold up . . . listen, I think it's all right, we ought to let him . . . let 'em through there, let 'em come on through."

Doc Bobo touched Fay's arm and Fay lowered the little red-faced Klansman to the ground. Bobo stepped forward, smiling politely, and climbed the steps to the truck. The Reverend Spann was plainly perplexed; it was obvious he was not accustomed to having black people appear at Klan meetings, let alone come up to speak, but he didn't know what to do about it either. He looked to the local folks, but they were doing nothing. In fact, some of them looked eager to hear what the black man was going to say. The minister had no choice but to step aside, although his look told the crowd he considered it highly irregular.

Doc Bobo waited, in that curious attitude of authority and humility he carried off so well, until the men on the platform reclaimed their chairs. But when he turned and faced the crowd, there was iron in his voice. "As your humble servant these thirty-odd years, I come to ask the reason for this gathering to-night, to learn what has been done to merit your distrust. Has any black man used the wrong rest-room in Pollard County, sat on the wrong stool at a café, touched the wrong water fountain, conducted himself in any manner whatever to warrant your anger? If so, give me his name," he said, pointing. "*Give me his name* . . . and he'll not see the sunrise tomorrow!"

Doc Bobo paused to run his gaze along every face in the crowd. "My friends, we are well aware of your concern in light of recent events, but you must know that your concern is but one-tenth of ours. We, who ask nothing but to offer you our good and faithful service as we have served your fathers and grand-fathers, we pray, gentlemen, that you will not, at this most crucial time in our relations, allow a wedge of suspicion to be driven betweeen us.

"Is this a time for disruption? New industries are coming to this region, new textile and chemical con-cerns are locating around us, as the honorable Senator Broward has pointed out, to bolster our own magnifi-cent granite industry. There is talk of a hydroelectric dam to be built at Oconostee, with limitless economic possibilities for both our peoples, for federal jobs, gentlemen, and a boost to our local economy that will be felt in every business. Will we show a face of dissension? A community in racial turmoil? Or will we agree that *peace* is the common goal of both our races?" And here Doc Bobo emphasized his point: "*Peace as we have known it in this town?*"

He paused to let it sink in.

"You know me," he said softly, "you know what I stand for. Do you really feel a need for vigilantes? Is that the message we want sent from our town?

"Let us hold our fears to the light. The Supreme Court, by some vague reasoning known only to itself, has decreed that separate schools is unconstitutional. They have set no date, so, as the good Senator said, having made this gesture to the new liberal element

240

that now controls our government, like as not they will forget the matter and turn their attention to other, more meaningful business. At any rate, as the Senator also pointed out, there is such a thing as states' rights, and we are fortunate enough to have people in Congress well equipped to look after our interests. Therefore, gentlemen, I trust you will forget this matter and turn your attention to other and more important affairs, such as the big centennial we have to celebrate this coming year, the first hundred years of our granite industry. You gentlemen of the Klan," he said, turning, "you come down to the Ape Yard, then, and we'll give you some barbecue that'll melt in your mouth!"

There was a loosening among the crowd. Even the Klansmen were chuckling their relief. "As for you, my friends and neighbors"—Doc Bobo struck a wide-eyed, comic pose—"you keep yo' eye on de Supreme Co't. Ah'll take keer o' de Ape Yah'd!"

Caught by the sudden switch, a favorite trick of Bobo's at the civic clubs, the crowd roared its approval, bursting into enthusiastic applause. Doc Bobo quickly stepped down from the truck and made his way through the crowd, nodding to acquaintances, shaking hands, as he and Fay made their way across the pasture to the woods.

I felt it was time for us to be getting away from there, but when I moved Tio gripped my arm. He pointed with his chin. Then I saw them, black men, about a dozen of them, guns drawn, melting back into the trees.

We gave them plenty of time to clear the woods before we started crawling out.

saying neither, let me catch that. [illegible] he was a true
[illegible] and I was relegated to manning the great [illegible]
and with no parts. [illegible] in from time to those
[illegible] [illegible] on the [illegible]

26

WITH THE COMING OF FALL, WORK GOT SCARCER AT
the Corner. There was never enough to go around, and
by unspoken agreement Em and I sat still with the
other younger men until those with children had
found work, and then the elderly. Often as not, that
was all there was, and we returned home with nothing
but hope for the next day. Finally school started and
I was limited to whatever I could find in the afternoons. Most often I found nothing but Em sitting
under the oak, still waiting. At last we gave up the
Corner for good and left the others, the regulars, the
eternal hopefuls, waiting under the fall clouds as cold
and gray as road-bank snow, talking of trivial things
in their jumbled jargon. The sleepy, waiting families.
Old Aaron Tim with twine in his shoes idling under
the umbrella oak. Small boys shouting for echoes.

I stood on the curb a long time.

If I was to continue going to school, something had
to be done. I was wearing my last pair of pants. The
only other good pair I had, the corduroys, had caught
on a hacksaw blade stuck under the siding of the garage and been ripped open to the knee.

I stood, looking up and down the street, trying to
get up my courage.

The Good Samaritan Center was a combined effort of the local churches that collected clothing
and other discards to be sold cheaply or given away
to the needy. Pinnacle Baptist was one of its chief
supporters. Miss Esther had collected a box every
Christmas. After all those boxes I had delivered to
the Center for Miss Esther, it didn't seem like charity
to ask for one pair of school-grade pants.

It still didn't seem so to me, and I had given it a lot

of thought since my and Em's argument about it the night before. In a roundabout way I had mentioned the possibility of the Center, and Em frowned and shook his head. It was a hypocritical position, I thought, but he was adamant. I was not to go begging.

But apparently it was all right to go to school in rags.

Em couldn't be expected to understand, so I had to make up my own mind. And I had. As soon as he lay down for his nap I had slipped away.

And now that I'd come this far, I told myself, I had to go through with it.

After a last check of the streets for someone who might recognize me, I shoved open the door and marched in.

And all the confidence I had mustered promptly went to shreds under the eyes of the charity ladies. Middle-aged, wealthy, dressed in the best from Atlanta's fashion houses, they were two bright Easter eggs among the pile of rags. One was sitting in a lawn chair knitting, talking to another standing at the counter. The one at the counter glanced up, then finished what she was saying before turning to me, smoothing her hips. "Yes?"

"I'd like a pair of pants, please."

"Oh?" She lifted an eyebrow at the knitter and spread her virgin white hands on the counter. "And who might you be?"

"Earl Whitaker. I'll take anything at all," I said, then added, "My aunt used to give a lot."

"Couldn't your parents come in with you?"

"No, ma'am."

The knitter stood up to have a better look at me. She squinted through her tinted glasses. They exchanged looks.

"Are you from around here?" said the first one.

"Maybe he's from out in the country," said the knitter. "Are you from out in the country?"

"No, ma'am—I just need one pair—for school. I could pay you something . . ."

"Well, no, it's for charity. That's what the Center

243

is for—for charity, but we don't usually give out to children. Now, if your mother's ashamed to come in . . ."

I wasn't going to make it. Fear you can fight against, shout down with anger. But not shame. There is no defense against shame. "Never mind," I said, "I don't need them."

I turned around and came face to face with Em Jojohn, staring through the glass.

The door banged open and there he stood, in as grand a rage as I had ever seen. "What the hell are you doin' here!" he roared. "Didn't you hear what I told you?"

"I don't give a damn what you told me!" I shouted back at him.

I wanted to get away and hide. I started by him and he grabbed my arm and flung me back.

"You don't beg!"

"You don't tell me what to do! Get out of my way!"

The charity ladies moved farther down the counter. One of them glanced at the telephone.

"Who are you to talk anyway? The first time I ever saw you, you was begging!"

"I beg!" he shouted furiously. "I do anything I want to! *You don't beg!*" And with that he grabbed me by the nape of the neck and literally threw me out into the street.

I scrambled to my feet and charged him, dimly aware of people stopping to look, of the ladies cowering at the door. He grabbed my shirt and snatched me into the alley.

"I'll kill you, Jojohn! So help me God, I'll kill you!" I twisted and managed to land a solid kick into him. He howled in pain and slammed me up against the brick wall. "I ain't never put a hand to you yet, boy . . . !"

I caught him hard on the chin. He shook it off and I caught him from the other side. He growled and stepped back, and I went headfirst into a pile of crates.

He dragged me out by the heels and shook me

violently until I thought my neck would snap, and then he shoved his face close to mine.

"Look at you! See what it done to you! I can beg 'cause the sons a bitches owes me! It don't shame me. But look at you! Don't you *never* do nothin' that shames you!" And he flung me over his shoulder and carried me, fighting and kicking and yelling with every ounce of strength I had, out through the block of stores, along the warehouses, across the railroad and down into the Ape Yard.

He strode down the middle of the road, cars slowing and moving around us, people leaning out to stare. I continued to fight him, shouting myself hoarse with every cuss word I knew, until finally, striding across the iron bridge of Twig Creek, he growled with exasperation and heaved me over the rail.

I surfaced gasping in the freezing cold water to fling a final set of epithets after him as he continued up the road, muttering and slinging his arms.

We went back to scouting up odd jobs around town, which wasn't much but a little yard work here and there, and helping a couple of the warehouses with their fall inventories. Tio offered to reopen my account at the store but I turned him down. It was too much of a strain getting the other one paid off. Besides, I told him, trying not to gag on the words, we had a few shelves of Em's vegetables that the boarders had canned for him.

The boarders were still doing well, and still having us up for supper, but there was a growing concern among all of us during that time, and from a source none of us would have expected. It was the tone of the letters coming from North Carolina, a tone that was anything but like Miss Esther. The boarders wrote to her faithfully once a week, and under their prodding I managed to get off a note to her now and then —mostly the "I'm fine, how are you?" variety—but the sporadic responses we got back were becoming less inquiring about what was going on around the house, the neighborhood; they dropped their advice about cleaning and canning, their raucous anecdotes, and were centering more and more on the small, confined world in which Miss Esther now found herself, becoming ever more morose with each writing.

The boarders were down at the store one Friday afternoon when I came in, and Mrs. Bell was just finishing reading the latest one to Mr. Teague:

". . . took us all out to supper at a restaurant last night. It was good to be out for a change, but I couldn't enjoy it. He fussed the whole time. He sent his dinner back three times. I told him he better not send it back anymore or they might spit in it or something. Lucille got upset about that and we had to leave.

"They haven't talked to me all day. I don't care.

"It sure is pretty out the window. I always did like the fall. It always made me want to be up and about doing things. But I just don't have the energy I used to. The doctor says I'm sleeping too much.

"I guess I'm just catching up on all I lost with you all. ha.

"Must close now, it's getting harder to see to write. It comes on me sometimes. It must be this new medicine, I think I may be allergic to it.

Love to all, Esther."

Mrs. Bell tucked the letter back in its envelope and handed it to me.

"It just don't sound like Esther," said Mrs. Porter. "She's not happy up there."

"Well, of course she ain't happy," said Mr. Rampey. "Would you be, locked in with that tribe?"

"Esther's very strong," said Mrs. Bell. "I'm sure her son is caring for her the best he can."

"Oh, for God's sake," snapped Mr. Jurgen, jerking open the drink cooler, "that son of hers couldn't properly care for a hog! Would you like a drink, Lester?"

"Not out of there," said Mr. Rampey.

"I'd like a Dr. Pepper, please," said Mrs. Metcalf. "You know," she said, "maybe she is allergic to her medicine . . ."

Mr. Burroughs pulled out a Pepsi and held it aloft. "What happened to that box that used to freeze 'em?" he wanted to know.

"I wish we'd never let her go," said Mrs. Cline. "We could have taken care of her."

"Come in, Theron, come in," called Mr. Teague over the register. Theron Walsh, the young black man who read meters for the power company in the Ape Yard, came in the store. "What can I do for you?"

"Mr. Teague, I come to see can I use your telephone. They want me to call the po-lice down there."

"Police? Where, down where? Who wants you to call?"

"The welfare lady, down at Miz Lampham's, lady lives down in the bottom. She's been sick lately and now she's in there and the do' locked and the welfare lady say we better get the po-lice. She said would I come up and call."

Mr. Teague came out from beind the counter. "I'll go see about her. Tio!"

"I'll come too, you might need some help," said Mr. Burroughs.

"Yeah," said Mr. Rampey. "Woody, *hey Woody!*" Mr. Woodhall dropped his Nehi on the floor. "Come on," said Mr. Rampey, motioning. Mr. Jurgen was already holding the door.

"You ladies take care of the store," said Mr. Teague.

"But," protested Mrs. Metcalf, "we don't know . . ."

"Prices are stamped on most everything," said Mr. Teague. "If it ain't, charge whatever seems fair. Go right in, go right in," he said to two black women coming in, "you'll be more'n taken care of."

The Lampham woman had been in the hollow less than a year. She lived alone in a shack in Fletcher Bottom. When we arrived there was already a small crowd milling about the yard. A couple of young boys clung to the window sill, trying to peer in.

The young white woman from the welfare depart-

247

ment was on the porch. "We can see her in bed in there," she said. "Where are the police?"

"Never mind the police," said Mr. Teague, making his way stiffly up the steps. "How long since anybody's checked on her?"

"The neighbors say she hasn't been seen for two or three days. One of my clients called the office."

"I thought she was on the welfare. Ain't you been keepin' a check on her?"

"Well, now," the woman corrected him, "she's not on welfare . . ."

"But she signed up better 'n four months ago," said Mr. Teague. "She told me so herself."

"She did fill out an application, but it was incomplete so it was never processed."

"What!"

"The medical history was incomplete. It was sent over to the Senior Citizens Visiting Committee to have someone call on her to check it out, but . . ."

"God almighty damn," muttered Mr. Burroughs.

"Listen, we're overworked as it is . . ." Mr. Teague was already trying the door. "Wait, now, don't you think we ought to call . . ."

"Stand aside there, Alvah!" Mr. Burroughs strode briskly across the porch and his size-thirteen brogan landed beside the flimsy doorknob. The door banged opened and Mr. Teague marched into the house.

The skeletal old black woman raised herself feebly and groped on the night table for her glasses. Mr. Teague went straight to her bedside and bent down to look in her face. "It's Alvah Teague, what's wrong with you, Ruby?"

She wet her lips and tried to speak.

"How long since you seen the doctor?"

"Who—who is it?" She was frightened and confused.

Mr. Teague walked to the door. "Anybody know her people?"

A woman stepped forward. "She got a boy down in Columbus, Mist' Teague. He were due to be sent overseas."

248

Mr. Teague put his hands on his hips, blinking, thinking. He looked up at Mr. Burroughs. The other man looked down at the woman and slowly wiped his mouth. "Ramp!"

He reached down and snatched back the sheets, exposing legs as small as a child's. Mr. Rampey knelt on the other side of the bed and they lifted her carefully and made their way out through the crowd.

Mr. Rampey looked up at the welfare lady. "How come you people can take such good care of them that *don't* need it."

With the help of Jurgen and Woodall, they eased themselves and the Lampham woman on the truck bed and sat cradling her in their arms. Tio adjusted the bricks under the seat and got back behind the wheel. "Easy now, boy," said Mr. Teague, "watch them ruts."

Dr. Breisner pronounced it pneumonia, with complications. "And with the malnutrition . . . hell." He gave her a shot and sent Tio to the drugstore with two prescriptions. "I don't give her the night, though."

"Shouldn't she be in the hospital?" asked Mr. Porter.

Dr. Breisner sighed. "Hell, I wouldn't even move her again. They'll just kill her up there. Let her sleep."

Out in the hall Dr. Breisner said, "Well, Horace, looks like you've got another guest," and, with a sardonic smile added, "I didn't know you were taking in the black ones now."

Mr. Burroughs looked in at the women slowly gathering their rockers about the bed. Two of them were fixing a tent. Farette came in with a steaming kettle.

"Is she black, Huff?" He shook his head. "Well, you know, when you get our age it's hard to tell."

They walked together down the stairs. "Well, anyhow," said Dr. Breisner, "this one won't be with you too long."

"Aw, hell, that's what you've promised all the rest of us at one time or another, and we'll be around to take you in. By the way, how your boys doin', Huff?"

"Doin' fine. The oldest one, Henry, just made captain; he and Mary are still in Pensacola. Tad finished up his doctorate this fall at the university, and of course Joseph is still in high school."

Surprised, Mr. Burroughs said, "I didn't know Tad was gonna make a doctor too."

"Hell, not a real doctor. A Ph.D., in history, for Christ's sake. Fact, he's been in and out of town all summer doing work on his dissertation."

"On his what?"

"He's doing his final project for his degree on Pollard County history." Dr. Breisner shook his head. "Gotta hand it to him, though, he pulled one off there. He got a two-thousand-dollar grant from the Pollard Centennial Commission to do a pamphlet on the history of the granite industry here, you know, the hundred years since the Poncini brothers, and the promise of a five-hundred-dollar bonus if he locates the Robinson grave . . . he's spend most of his time this summer on that."

"Hell, they've dug up half the Johns property lookin' for that scutter and they ain't found him yet."

"Yeah, but Tad says he's on to something they don't know about. He's got this theory. Anyway, he says come centennial time in January he'll be ready to spring old Easter Robinson once and for all."

"Well," said Mr. Burroughs, "still and all, the town would do better with another real doctor than a dead Civil War bandit. Want a little something, Huff?"

Dr. Breisner shook his head, but Mr. Rampey was already at his elbow twisting a cork. The doctor took a long swallow and came up wet-eyed. "Damn, Ramp, that's awful! Where you buyin' it now?"

"Travis Turner, and I believe the son of a bitch is cutting it with Clorox."

"Pour it out. That damn stuff'll eat out your stomach."

"Well, if that damn Baptist courthouse gang wouldn't keep the county voted dry . . ."

"I've got a bottle of good stuff in the car. Come with me, boy, and I'll send it in. Keep an eye on the old woman, Horace. I'll stop by in the morning—if I don't hear from you before then."

"She'll be here," said Mr. Burroughs. He leaned against the porch post. "That crowd upstairs won't let her go."

27

FINALLY, WE GOT A BREAK. JAYELL, NO LONGER ABLE to bear watching Gwen leave the house for work, and apparently having drunk his melancholic self-pity to the dregs, came tearing out of convalescence and took the job with Smithbilt Homes. They had no major projects going in Quarrytown at the time, only an occasional house or two contracted by individuals, but on those Jayell gave Em, the shop boys and me every hour of work he could. His new income also enabled him to reopen the shop for repairs and cabinet work.

Jayell's first assignment was the bogging Abbeville development, where his first action was to cut the work force by half. He reorganized the teams of heavy-equipment operators, carpenters, masons, electricians and painters and put them on strictly scheduled plans, would not tolerate the slightest holdup or delay, and unleashed his maniacal wrath on any supplier with a late delivery. Within a couple of weeks the project was not only moving again but ahead of schedule, with a precision and attention to quality construction that made even the FHA inspectors shake their heads. Several of Smithbilt's board members flew up from Miami to inspect the job. They had long luncheons with Jayell, and took back some of his designs.

Gwen was ecstatic. She and Jayell had been invited to join the country club. She was having her
genealogy traced with an eye toward the DAR. She
began giving lavish parties—lavish by Jayell's standards
anyway. Jayell's idea of a big get-together was to bring
his television set and a washtub of iced beer down
to the shop for himself, Em, Skeeter and Carlos to
watch Tech stomp Georgia. Gwen had him start a
swimming pool in the backyard like the Hendersons'
("Now? In September?"), and for his birthday surprised him with the announcement that with her
first paycheck of the school year she had made a
down payment on a lot at Lake Lorraine.

It seemed Jayell was being ensconced at last in
what he called that "nouveau middle class."

"Great God in heaven!" he moaned over the din of
a Dirsey's Saturday night. "You know what I did last
night? I played mahjong! Mah-damn-shong! Can you
believe it? With Herbie Craft and his wife, for pete's
sake. A lousy vice-president of First National Bank, a
high-class loan shark, and she's treating the bastard
like royalty. "Dear," she says—says 'you know Mr.
Craft.' and I say, 'Sure I know him. He repossessed
my mama's first refrigerator!' *Hooo*—you should have
seen his face!" Jayell took a long draught of beer
and sleeved his mouth. "And you know where she is
tonight? She's at the armory practicin' a play for that
Little Theater she helped organize. Yessir, she's in
her black toreadors and a little yellow blouse pulled
up and tied up to here, and she's prancing around
that stage and gettin' kissed by Wendell Hines! And
you know sump'n else?" Jayell's eyes narrowed
menacingly. "When it opens, I'll have to go and
watch him do it, and *applaud* the son of a bitch!"

There was silence at the bar. They all sympathized
with him. It threw a pall on the place.

"Kee-rist," muttered a truck driver from New Jersey, and ordered fresh beers all around.

"Kee-rist," echoed Em, and reached for his.

Gwen had grown increasingly cool to me, even at

school, and avoided Em altogether. The shop boys, being black, posed no social threat to her. But Em and I were different, and I could tell she never knew quite what to do about us.

Then, a few days after that night at Dirsey's, she managed that final break between Jayell and the Ape Yard. A minor happenstance gave her the opportunity and she seized on it, and Em and I were ordered away for good.

Em and I were helping Jayell pour cement for the swimming pool. The missionary board was meeting at Gwen's house that day, so we had strict instructions to keep outside, which we did, except for slipping into the kitchen for water, since the plumbers working on the pool had turned off the outside spigot. Soon after the guests arrived I stepped in for a drink, and since it was the day after the Little Theater opening, they were taking time before the meeting to congraulate Gwen on the play, which she had not only played a leading role in but also directed. Sissy Davis, the mayor's sister, was reading the review in the *Star*:

> ". . . and certain to be nominated for the Quarry-town Little Theater's first Oscar is a delightful newcomer to our community, Gwendolyn Burns Crooms. Mrs. Crooms, a member of the Quarry-town High Faculty (where she assumed the duties of drama coach from the capable hands of Thelma Martin, who is on leave of absence this year), was a prime mover this summer in the establishment of the Little Theater, and proved last night that she is not only a capable director but a splendid actress as well. She was utterly delight-ful as the vampish ex-wife, Clara, and literally threw herself into the role.
>
> "Frivolous, witty and charming, her face often conveyed more than words, and even the lift of an eyebrow could be devastating. She was completely believable as the cunning Clara, struggling to win back her ex-husband's affections. Estelle

Watson, as the best friend, apparently had some difficulty in getting her lines across to the audience, but Wendell Hines and Carl Lee Wyche were perfect as the boisterous army buddies, Pit Stop and Ed, and kept the audience in gales of laughter. Technical director Lorne Suggs' inspired stage setting provided a worthy frame for this top drawer production, written by our own Hal T. Whitmire of the Star *staff. The play will run two more nights, Friday and Saturday, with an 8:30 P.M. curtain time. Tickets are one dollar—fifty cents for students—and may be purchased at the door, or at the* Star *office."*

"Well!" Sissy Davis put down the paper and looked around the room. "It seems we have a celebrity in our midst today!" The ladies put down their Sanka for a burst of applause.

"Oh, really," fluttered Gwen, "the cast, the crew, they were all just so marvelous to work with. And with their help I have to say it was as good as anything I've seen in Atlanta." The ladies put down their cups for another round of applause. "We're off to an excellent start," she continued, "and with the continued support of the community, and the talents of people like Lorne Suggs, we just can't help but have the finest Little Theater in Georgia." That brought applause for Hilda Suggs, the director's wife, to be passed on to her husband. "Now, really," said Gwen, "we should get on with our meeting. I'm sure Reverend March has other commitments."

The ladies dutifully put away their cake and coffee and the minister led into a discussion of the church's sponsored missionary, one Reverend Pritchard, who was toiling among some natives in New Guinea. I was about to slip back out to work, but became so engrossed in the trials of the missionary, outlined in a letter which the pastor read aloud, that I couldn't tear myself away.

It seemed the Reverend Pritchard was working with

a stone-age tribe that hadn't the foggiest notion of any kind of civilization, and were the stubbornest lot, he believed, to whom anyone had ever tried to bring the Lord. And the Reverend was up to his elbows. They hadn't any more care for religion than a bunch of hogs, he said, and thought services at chapel nothing more than a grand time for settling intervillage squabbles. A man couldn't shut his eyes in prayer for fear of getting brained by his neighbor. He was at his wit's end. His wife had made some progress in curtailing fornication in the schoolhouse this year, but for his part, he could see little hope for elevating this lot to salvation while they were still killing one another at vespers. He closed with a request for the congregation's prayers, and a couple more gross of brassieres. It seemed the men of the village, in a childish display of jealousy, wouldn't let their wives wear them unless they had them too. The Reverend also needed another shipment of Testaments and toilet paper, but asked that they be packed separately this time, as the savages still hadn't learned the difference.

"Huh!" rumbled a voice through the quiet. "Seems to me your Reverend needs to get off his knees and spray that crowd with bird shot!" Everyone looked up as Em Jojohn loped in and hung his bulk on the mantel. "Forgo your Testaments and send him a good twelve-gauge, that's what's needed to fetch that bunch."

Gwen looked about frantically. Her eyes fell on me. I shrugged and waggled my water glass, disclaiming any responsibility. "This is Mr. Jojohn," she said uncomfortably, "he's helping my husband in the yard."

"Funny thing about religion, Reverend," Em studied his cigarette and flicked an ash in the vase. "It don't seem worthwhile to transplant it when it springs up so natural by itself. Take the case of Waldo Payne."

"I—I'm afraid I don't see your point," said the minister.

"The point? Why, the point is simple." Em paced the hearth, warming to his talk, a rambling monologue that I knew would lead nowhere and accomplish nothing but to get him out of the sun for a few minutes.

"There was this fellow named Waldo Payne I used to tie steel with. Wild'un, they called him. He was a wild'un too. Come out of Cumberland Gap. A real scrapper, I mean into sump'n *all* the time! Seems like it didn't come a Monday the job super wasn't down at the jail bailin' Waldo out of one scrape or another. But a worker? You never seen the beat. Come hot weather or cold, there wasn't a rod buster on the job could come anywhere near him for layin' in steel. Take a day it's a hundred in the shade and everybody else is eatin' salt tablets and suckin' the water can, old Wild'un's in the steel pile hollerin', 'Where's them number elebens!' Put him on a sewage tank with two other guys and big horizontals going up, and you never see Waldo on the lighter end. No sir, he's in the middle with the curve and the weight, and workin' the others to keep up with him too. He'd lay them big bars acrost his knees and climb that tank like a monkey, with the others just a scramblin', 'cause you see, once the middle got higher than the ends, the weight was throwed on them! Then before they got their wall belts hitched good, old Waldo'd have his saddle ties on and was back down at the steel pile, hollerin' 'Gimme them number elebens.' "

Em shook his head and chuckled and drained somebody's coffee cup, and continued before Gwen could interrupt. "One day, up in Virginia, we was pouring this dam. Waldo was handling the concrete bucket. They was pouring through a chute in the river and lettin' the concrete set up under water. Well, nobody knows how it happened; wasn't carelessness 'cause Jimmy Leggett was the crane operator, and Jimmy Leggett could take a drag line and pick your hat off the ground, but somehow Waldo got bumped with the concrete bucket, and down the chute he went."

"Oh." Sissy Davis put a hand to her mouth. "How awful!"

Em lit a cigarette and took his time. Gwen sat staring at the floor.

"Well?" said another lady. "Did they get him out?"

"Get him out? From under forty foot of water with three yards of concrete on him? How were they gonna get him out of that?"

"Then what did they do?"

"Why, the only thing they could do—they started pouring concrete again."

"On top of him?" asked the minister incredulously.

Em grimaced and rubbed his neck impatiently. "Well, there wasn't no way to pour *around* him, was there? 'Sides, if they stopped, and let the concrete set up, there'd be a seam, a weak place. Naw, when the super come running and was told what happened, he just told 'em to get on with it, and went for the sheriff."

"What a terrible tragedy," said Sissy Davis.

"Not altogether," said Em. "Waldo's wife was compensated, and folks said she seemed a lot happier with the insurance money than she'd ever been with Wild'un. As for him, well, he lived like he wanted and got buried in style. What more could any man want? Think about it, the whole Emalette River dam for a vault! Ain't a pharaoh or emperor ever had a tomb that'd stand up to Waldo Payne's."

Something was worrying the preacher. He just couldn't leave it alone. "I still fail to see the relevance of that to our discussion of religion."

"Coming to that, Reverend." Em pointed to Gwen's coffee cup. "You through with that?" She nodded without lifting her head, and he picked it up and drained it. "Well, when the dam was near completion the super had a big stone vase fitted into the side, just below the guard rail, to put flowers in. Some of Wild'un's pals requested it, in a kind of memorial. And when the job was finished one of the local churches took it up, and put in flowers for Wild'un regular. Then, as time went on, strangers got to dropping in change to help pay for the flowers, thinking it was some kind of shrine or something. Then young folks got to courting up there, and throwing in pennies to make wishes and stuff. Well, before long word got around among the hill people that the dam had healing powers, and a faith healer got to holding revivals up there, and before you knew it, it got to be such a hazard with the crowds holding up traffic and the faithful falling in the river that the law stepped in and had the vase knocked off. They even had to put up a watchman's booth to keep traffic moving until things quieted down again; which it did even'chally, though some said the watchman took money from hard believers for a long time after. But, as I said, it did quiet down even'chally and things got back to normal."

The preacher waited, but it became obvious the Indian was through. He pressed his thumbs to his temples. "I'm afraid, Mr.—ah, Jojohn, I still don't see your point."

"You don't." Em shrugged his shoulders in exasperation. "Well, that's all for me, then," he said, heading for the hall, "for I can't make it no plainer."

I shook my head. He had done it again. His purpose accomplished, cool, refreshed, leaving behind confusion. On another occasion, for another crowd, he might have delivered up his story on sweet Sally Flagg, who took on Fort Bragg.

Later, I kind of wished he'd done it that time.

Because, as I said, the whole thing backfired anyway. When the guests had gone Gwen came out to where we were screeding cement and told Jayell in no uncertain terms she didn't want us back there anymore.

"Aw, honey, come on . . ."

"I mean it, Jayell!" she said, tossing her hair in fury. "That is absolutely the last straw!"

Jayell stood meekly, caught in a moment of Jayell weakness and confusion, looking for a way out.

"I didn't mean no harm . . ." Em began, and she whirled on him.

"Shut up, you—you filthy animal! You are absolutely the most—grotesque excuse for a human being I have ever met. Why don't you take that trashy kid and stay in that slimy Ape Yard where you belong!"

Jayell dropped his screed board. "Gwen, for pete's sake!"

"Jayell," said Em, "if you don't slap hell out'n her now, I might just do it for you."

"Come on, Em," I said, "let's go." I took his arm, but he wouldn't budge. He stood staring at her.

Jayell came between them, nervously rubbing his hands on his thighs. "Look fellas, she's upset. She'll cool off and . . ."

Em, trembling, turned down to me. "Well, trash, what we goin' to do now? Can't neither one of us hit her 'cause she's a woman. I reckon', Jayell, that don't leave nobody but you." And he swung a fist under Jayell's chin that lifted him off the ground. Gwen screamed and ran to him.

Jayell sat dazed, looking around, more puzzled than anything.

"You're a damn fool, Jay," Em said, "and fools are entitled to make mistakes. But anybody that makes a mistake and thinks he's got to live with it is a bigger fool than I care to be associated with."

"Heyyy . . ." Jayell pulled himself up and stood leaning on Gwen. "Hey look, fellas, we'll—get together later, huh?"

Em stopped and turned around. "You better see about gettin' yourself together," he said.

We returned to the Ape Yard, and to hunting for odd jobs again, as Em would no longer even tolerate the mention of Jayell's name.

I didn't see Jayell again for more than a month, until the night I thought the devil was trying to run me down on a motorcycle.

28

FALL HAD DRIED FAST INTO A RATTLING, BROWN October. It was Halloween night. The streets were filled with little trick-or-treaters in dime-store masks, pouring past the store—where Mr. Teague and Tio had laid in an extra supply of candy for them—and on up the hill to the boardinghouse. The boarders had pushed Ruby Lampham's bed against the upstairs window and gathered round to watch Mr. Burroughs and Mr. Rampey, in sheets and horrible "dough-faces," leap out of the hedges and scare hell out of the kids.

It was freezing cold, and I was coming home from the picture show at a brisk half-trot, hands pocketed and shoulders hunched against the wind. It had been a triple horror feature, with two free passes to everyone who could sit through all three shows, and I couldn't pass that up. Em could. He sat home with the footlocker leaned against the door and the lamp turned up full wick.

Passing the courthouse, I heard a cherrybomb go off, and two boys came across the square with a policeman hot behind them, holding his flapping holster and hollering for them to stop. There would be the usual vandalism: broken windows and sugared gas tanks. A few roughnecks to be claimed at the police station in the morning. A warning editorial.

I stopped at Bullard's bicycle shop to read the signatures on his window. Old man Bullard's plate-glass window had survived generations of Halloweens through an unspoken agreement with the town's youngsters. While other merchants grumbled and swore at the graffiti they found on their windows, Mr. Bullard provided soap chips on his sill, and left the scribblings up, the clean ones anyway, until the next rain washed them away. Gradually the slogans were replaced by signatures, and it became a ritual; kids came from across town, from the Ape Yard, to sign Mr. Bullard's window. The names changed as generations grew up and moved away, most never to be heard from again, nor have their names appear in public again; but for that one brief time between Halloween and rain they stood on Bullard's window in downtown Quarrytown for all the world to see. I scribbled my name in a small space in the lower corner and stood back to look at it, wondering how long it would be before the next rain.

Then, with a curious sensation building inside me, I reached down with my sleeve and rubbed it out. I wouldn't leave myself at the whim of any rain, and my name, after all, belonged to me. I puzzled over it for a moment, surprised at my own reaction, then decided I didn't really care why I had done it. I had done a lot of things lately that I couldn't really explain; I was acting more from feeling now than from thought, and was more comfortable than I had been in a long time. I shrugged and turned away, then came back and pocketed a few soap chips from the ledge. We were running low.

Crossing over the railroad ramp to start down into the Ape Yard, I thought I heard something, and stopped and turned my ear to the wind. There was nothing. The yellow lights glowed along the hollow. Perhaps it was the wind blowing out of the Ape Yard.

Then I heard it again. Sirens. From the rear, far off beyond the warehouses. Then another sound came to me, a ripping motor, behind the warehouses and closing fast. It grew louder and louder until suddenly a motorcycle burst from between the buildings. It turned hard onto Railroad Street with skidding wheels and came blasting straight up the ramp. I dived and rolled down the embankment as it shot by me, bucketed over the railroad tracks, and went dipping down into the Ape Yard. I scrambled to my feet to catch sight of it, to be sure of what I had seen. Sure enough, the driver was dressed head to foot in a glowing red devil's costume!

The sirens came howling out of the buildings and police cars roared over the railroad tracks and went after him, their red lights whipping the darkness. But I knew they would never catch him. The devil was already out of sight, running without lights, and the Ape Yard paths led a dozen ways up into the hills.

I continued on my way, and as I drew close to Twig Creek I could see they had already lost him. The patrol cars were cruising, red lights topping a rise and descending, the sirens still. At the iron bridge at the bottom of the hollow a police car pulled up beside me and stopped.

"What you doing down here, boy?"

"Going home—I'm taking a short cut."

"Where you been?"

"To the picture show."

"You see a motorcycle come by here?"

"One passed me up at the railroad, but I ain't seen him since."

The policeman turned and repeated it for his partner. "Well, you get on home. Got no business down here this time of night."

"Yes, sir."

They drove off, and I stood stock still. I was looking straight at the devil.

He was lying in the shallow creek, pinned on his back under his motorcycle and struggling to keep his head above water.

I jumped off the bridge and splashed through the freezing current. The rider was clutching a rock and trying to kick off the bike, gasping and sucking for breath in the clinging hood. I ripped it off, and when I saw the face, the devil himself would have been less of a shock.

"Phaedra Boggs!"

"The rear wheel, damnit, try and lift it up!"

I tried. It wouldn't budge. It was the largest motorcycle I had ever seen, and it was jammed solid. She put a foot against it and we both strained. I knelt in the water and tried to dig under it, and felt it wedged so tightly in the rocks I knew we would never get it off. "I've got to get help," I said. "Can you hold on?"

"Hurry," she said, "hurry."

I splashed up the bank, my mind racing. The nearest place was Dirsey's. I ran down the hill and crossed over two streets to the back road that led to the river. I burst in, and the first person I saw, morosely draped on the bar, was Jayell Crooms.

"Jayell! Come quick, it's Phaedra!"

"What?" He blinked at me. "What is it, boy?"

"Phaedra Boggs, she's going to drown!"

The truck screeched to a halt on the bridge and Jayell and I hit the water together. Phaedra was almost under, but fighting, throwing her head, cursing and spewing water and holding on like a demon. Jayell dived under and wrapped his arms around the rear wheel and groaned with the effort and the pain he must have felt in his leg. Still he strained, backing and digging in the bottom. I grabbed on and tried to help him twist it, still to no avail. Roaring with frustration, Jayell heaved and struggled, then suddenly slipped and fell, but the weight and twisting motion loosened it from its bind. We grabbed it again, and with Phaedra pushing hard with her free foot, we finally wrenched it away. Jayell got an arm under her back and lifted her up, and they stood clinging to each other.

Shivering, Phaedra said, "Damned pot-holedy bridge."

"Can you walk?"

"Yeah, but take it slow."

We made our way to the bank. They were both limping so badly I had to pull them out. Jayell sat Phaedra on the running board and painfully knelt to feel her ankle. "I don't think it's broke," she said. "Probably just sprained." He ripped open the satiny pants leg and exposed a gaping cut across her calf. He tore a bandage off his shirt and tied it up. "We'd better get you to a doctor," he said.

"For a little cut? Naw, just get me home." She hugged herself, her whole body was shaking.

I saw a red light cruising along the ridge. "You better take that costume off," I said.

"Never mind that, let's get out of here."

We drove along the creek road past the last row of houses and the smelly Poncini quarry, then Jayell turned up through the pine thicket toward the cemetery. At the edge of the sedgefield Phaedra ordered him to stop. "I can make it the rest of the way on foot. Don't want to risk waking Mama."

But she was limping so bad she had to stop and rest on the first tombstone. Jayell got out and went to help her, but he was in as bad shape as she was. "If you two come rustling and scraping out of the cemetery that way you're just going to get yourselves shot," I said.

I got between them and Jayell clapped me on the head. "Early boy, where'd we be without you?"

The Boggs house was dark except for the light from the livingroom shade. "What about your old man?" said Jayell.

Phaedra gritted her teeth. "No worry, tonight's his night with his woman in Little Holland. Just go slow and don't make noise."

The back door was unlocked. Phaedra eased it open and listened, and the three of us, trembling and breathing heavily from near exhaustion, felt our way painfully down the hall to Phaedra's bedroom.

Once inside, Phaedra's grip loosened, and she slid unconscious to the floor.

"Wouldn't you know," gasped Jayell, "she'd pull a stunt like that. Give me a hand."

Together we lifted her onto the bed. I straightened her legs and got her shoes off. Jayell unzipped the clammy costume, and when I looked around I saw why she had been reluctant to take it off at the creek. She wasn't wearing anything underneath. Jayell pulled it off and she lay glistening in the moonlight.

She was a gloriously beautiful girl.

He found some dry clothing and began drying her

off, dabbing the wadded clothing over her body and gently wiping the creek mud from her hair. Her eyes came open and she lay watching him, an amused expression on her face. "Having a good time, Jack?"

Jayell stopped and looked at her.

She pulled herself up and leaned against the headboard. "Hand me a cigarette, will you, sport?"

I fumbled for the pack on the bedside table. She steadied my hand with the match. She took a deep drag and exhaled, watching Jayell, the cigarette held stiffly in quivering china fingers. It was so strange: old rough-edged, beautiful Phaedra, eyes crinkling with genuine warmth, so soft and helpless-looking, and yet so tenderly strong.

And so completely naked.

"We bet—" I cleared my throat, "we better be going."

"Yeah," said Jayell. He turned to leave but her hand closed firmly on his wrist.

"No, don't go," she said. "I didn't leave you in your convalescence."

Then my memory flashed back to the time I saw Phaedra drive up through the woods the day I was leaving Jayell's house. With all else that had happened that day I had completely washed it out of my mind.

Jayell stopped, listening to the sounds of the house. "Her light is on," he whispered.

"It's always on." Suddenly she stubbed out the cigarette. "Stay with me, Jack."

"I don't think . . ." Her hands were sliding down his stomach, stroking, caressing. "Phaedra, for God's sake!" Those expert fingers were inside his thighs, rubbing, working. She was unbuttoning his shirt.

"Jayell," I said, shifting from one foot to the other, "don't you think . . ." He tried to pull away and she threw an arm around his neck and pulled him down, her mouth devouring his face. She was on her knees, squirming against him, the strong muscles of her back tensing as she crushed her breasts against his chest. She was licking his eyes, his ear, his neck. Slowly his arms encircled her.

265

"Hey, now, y'all get ahold of yourselves!"

Abruptly she turned and pushed him down on the pillows and knelt above him, tugging at his trousers. She ripped them open and her lips and tongue were moving again, her golden hair brushing his stomach. Jayell trembled violently, making sounds in his throat. The room was reeling. I couldn't breathe. My legs were paralyzed. "For God's sake!" I gasped, backing away. I turned and jerked open the door, and stopped. Suddenly I was alert to something else. In the cold air of the hall the night came crashing into place, the senses rushing together and warning.

The odor hit me first. A dark, rotting smell. Then I heard the sound, the soft whisper of something sliding along the floor.

I bounded back to the bed. "Jayell! Phaedra!" They were enveloped in each other in a raging heat, in the violence of each other. Phaedra's eyes were tightly shut. She moved with the rhythm of breezes, unconscious, celebrating the act in its purely animal essence, suspended, lost in the moment of her most natural self.

"All right," I cried, dancing in slopping wet shoes, "Just stay here, then!" I tried the window. I jerked and tugged but it was warped and swollen with the rain. "Oh, Lord," I muttered. "Oh, Lord in heaven." I bolted for the door and jerked it open.

There in the darkness sat a subhuman thing. And it was staring at me. The hollowed eyes shone with fury.

"*Eeeeee!*" The stringy blonde hair, half eaten away by a crust of scabs, shook with the arc of the bony fist that buried itself in my stomach.

I doubled over, numb with white-hot pain, and felt a grip in my hair. I was on my knees, trying to pull away, trying to crawl, but it hung to me like a monkey, skittering with demonic glee, nails digging into my scalp, suffocating me in its smell. The knees on the floor made the sounds of bones.

Suddenly there was a shadow bending by me, strong white arms, and struggling, protests and whinings. Phaedra straightened with a figure in her arms, no larger than a child, and hurriedly limped for the door. I heard their voices in the hall, Phaedra's gentle, coaxing, and the other, garrulous, phlegm-chested, stabbing with bitter invective. "Rotten! Leave me to die . . . filthy bitch!"

"It's all right, Mama, it's all right. Come on now, back to bed. I'll get your medicine . . ."

". . . got in there? Hah? Marvin! Marvin . . ."

"Papa's asleep. *Ssssh,* now, Mama, it's all right."

"Let me die . . . oh, sweet Jesus, please let me die!"

Jayell was clawing for his clothes. He bundled them in his arms and we scrambled out the hall, off the porch, and hit the ground running. Well into the cemetery, he danced on the freezing sand and pulled them on. "You *are* crazy," I said shakily, "crazy as everybody says. What is wrong with you, Jayell?"

He was sniffing, looking around for a shoe. "Leave me alone. Leave me alone." He rounded the tombstones, holding his aching leg, looking for the shoe.

"How could you leave her? She's in love with you, can't you see that?"

He gritted his teeth and made a sound like a wounded cat, a cry of shivering agony over the tombstones. I followed him limping across the stony ground. He was hugging himself, hobbling away from the piercing cries of the house. "I tried," he said in a choking voice, "I begged her! She wouldn't leave, I couldn't get her away from—that *thing* in there! And there was Gwen—straight up, clean, feeling nothing. Oh, Goddamn! Goddamn! Goddamn! Why has it *all* got to be this way?"

We rounded the curve through the sedgefield, Jayell limping and sobbing, absently looking along the roadside for his shoe, moving away from the dismal house, standing quiet now, all dark and gray but for that dim, eternal glow that shone from the living-room shades.

Em sat watching the night. He said nothing as I

pulled off my sopping clothes and climbed into bed. He poured another glass of whiskey from the fruit jar he held on his lap and took a long swallow, his eyes fixed on me.

"What you seen tonight?"

"Just ghosts and goblins, Em, ghosts and goblins." I studied the big U.S. on the army blanket.

"What'd you do, fall in the river?"

I turned and looked at him. He wasn't drunk.

"You saw us go through the field, didn't you?"

"It was a matter of time."

I sat up in bed. "You knew they'd been seein' each other while he was laid up, didn't you?"

"I know lots of things," he said, the expression unchanging in his eyes.

"Jayell wanted to marry Phaedra. She turned *him* down, did you know that? She turned him down because of her mother. Seems like everybody is strapped in one way or another, don't it." I shivered, and lay down and cocooned myself in the blanket lest I catch cold from the wet. "I saw her mother tonight," I said. "You never know what's in the next house, do you, Em?"

Em sat drinking quietly, watcing the night. He was sitting that way, his breath singing softly, when I finally drifted off to sleep.

29

WHEN TIO FOUND OUT ABOUT THE MOTORCYCLE HE was beside himself. "That's an old Harley 80 stroker!" he cried as Em lifted it out of the water. "She'll bust the road wide open!"

"Won't be bustin' nothin' anymore," observed Em, watching the mud and water drip. "Front tire's gone,

268

frame twisted. You got a piece of junk there's what you got."

Tio was all over it, squatting, feeling, testing, pulling. "You don't know what you're talkin' about, man; we take her apart and clean her up, touch up a little here and there, this mama bird'll totally fly!"

We dragged it back to the garage and Tio cleared a space and began overhauling operations immediately. He spread one of Mr. Teague's best bedsheets on the dirt floor, and in no time it was covered with rods, tubes, bearings, pistons, springs, gaskets and metal entrails of every shape and size. I was amazed at how many parts a motorcycle could be broken into, and still Tio was taking parts out of parts. I was surprised when he set the wheels aside without removing the spokes. Then he started removing the spokes.

"I can't stand here and watch this slaughter," said Em, and wandered off to get a beer.

Later that afternoon, when I was in the loft fixing supper, I heard a slight noise, like coals falling in the heater. At first I thought nothing of it, thinking it was Tio down below. Then I heard it again, a scraping, and coming not from below, but from the shed side of the garage, and I turned in time to see a blue-jeaned leg come over the window sill. Phaedra Boggs lifted herself easily through the opening and dropped Jayell's missing shoe on the floor.

"Hi, sport," she said, smiling.

"Well, hello," I said. "You know, there's a door over on the other side."

"Yeah, I know," she said, tugging at her sweatshirt. "I didn't want to be seen from the house. You can't see this side from up there."

"I didn't know you could see *any* side from your place." That was a revelation. I had always thought the garage was completely secluded. She went to the window and pointed. "Up through there, see that little patch of white? That's the corner of my bedroom. You can see the whole place from up there. I used to watch you and the Indian sleeping on the roof in the summer—that looked like fun—and a couple of times I saw you coming up from the shower. Hah! You're blushing!" Her eyes twinkled mischievously. "Aw, don't worry, Early boy, you got nothing big enough to be seen from that distance."

I shoved a pot to the back of the stove and she broke up, doubling over, the laughter coming in deep, rich waves. After a moment, she said, "Seriously, I came to thank you, Earl, boy. You pulled me out of a grand mess last night."

"Yeah, well, I thought I was saving the devil. If I'd known it was you I might have let you drown. Want some coffee?"

"I'd love some. Here, I'll fix it. Sit down."

I lifted myself on the sill. "What were they after you for anyway?"

Phaedra shrugged. "Speeding, the costume—who knows. The highway patrol got in behind me about ten miles out, and I guess they radioed ahead because the city boys had a roadblock waiting at Four Forks. It was close gettin' there for a while."

'Where were you coming from?"

"Fraternity-house party in Athens. Vince Oliver took me over. But the games got childish so Sally grabbed her clothes and came home. The devil suit was the nearest thing handy."

"How did you come by the bike?"

"Some jerk stopped and offered me a lift home, but it turned out it was his home he had in mind, so I unloaded him at a red light and came on."

"It's downstairs, by the way. What you want us to do with it?"

"Keep it, sell it for junk—who cares."

"Won't he come looking for it?"

"Nah, the creep never even asked where I lived. He got a couple of free feels, consider it paid for." Phaedra winked, without humor. "You got to hold yourself high."

"Phaedra, why do you treat yourself like a whore?"

Phaedra looked at me, the old hard glint in her eye. "All women are whores, Early boy. Only the prices vary."

There were footsteps on the stairs. Uneven steps. Phaedra lifted her head and looked at me. Neither of us had to guess who it was. Jayell knocked the mud off his boots and opened the door. He saw Phaedra and stopped.

"Don't panic, Jack." Phaedra was amused at his discomfort. "I just came to deliver your shoe. There's lipstick on the toe, but I don't think your wife will notice."

Jayell grinned and pulled up a chair. "Anybody ever tell you you're a smartass?"

She chuckled. "All the time, Jack, all the time."

"Before you two get any notions of starting up where you left off last night," I said, "I want to warn you, me and Em run a Christian loft."

Jayell began pulling cockleburs out of his cuff. "Then, how about some of that coffee?"

"It's Jojohn's," Phaedra warned. "Tastes like hot tar with chicory in it. Got another cup, Earl?"

"You'll have to get a jelly glass."

"Where is Em?" said Jayell. "I got a load of concrete blocks to get off before dark."

"He's due back for supper any minute."

"How are things at Smithbilt?" asked Phaedra.

"Repetitive." Jayell took his coffee and blew on it. He looked around the loft. "Well, how do you like living with Jojohn?"

"Beats sleeping in a ditch," I said, "but not much."

Jayell thumped the thin flooring with his boot and ran his eyes along the studded walls. "Remind me to put you some plywood on these walls—at least keep the wind out." He spied my spider web in the corner and lifted his cap to swipe at it. I caught him just in time to save it.

"That's my project for biology class," I said. "I've got to take him to school next week."

"Growing your own spider, huh? Hell, I'll bet there's enough of 'em around the old shop by now to supply the whole school. I'm in the wrong business." He scraped his chair around and studied it. The black and yellow spider sat at the top of the web, no doubt studying Jayell in return. "What kind is it?"

"Regular old garden spider," I said.

Phaedra leaned down. *Epeira gemma.*

"Oh, well, yeah, 'course you'd have the proper insect name . . ."

"Spiders aren't insects," she said, sipping her coffee. "Arachnids."

"What's this little lump here?" Jayell pointed to a silky sac near the center of the web.

"That's a fly he caught. You must have scared him off his dinner."

"Nah, he's canning that one for later—see how he's got it all wrapped up? Couldn't eat it like that."

"They don't eat 'em," I said, "they just suck out the juice. Spiders are on a liquid diet."

"Yeah?"

"Tha-a-at's right," said Phaedra. She put her head down close to his. "Catches him . . . binds him up . . . and sucks-the-poor-bastard-dry."

Jayell turned and looked in her eyes. She was watching him closely. He glanced back at the hapless creature in his silken coffin—then suddenly shoved back his chair and pulled on his cap. "Well, I can't wait around all day. Tell Em I'll catch him another time."

At that moment there were other footsteps on the stairs. Heavier ones. Em and Jayell almost collided in the door.

"Hyeah, now—I didn't know we had comp'ny."

"Just leavin'," said Jayell, edging by, "talk to you later."

"What about the blocks?" I said.

"Too dark now, I'll load 'em off in the morning." Jayell brushed by Em and went stumping unevenly down the stairs.

"Who bit his tail?" said Em.

"Ah, he's a funny bird," said Phaedra, throwing a leg over the sill. "How you been, Em?"

"Doin' no good a'tall. Hey, you ain't leavin' too!"

"Yeah, runnin' late." She leaned over and flicked a

hand through my hair. "Thanks again, Early boy."
And she dropped down onto the shed.

"Damn," mused Em, "I show up and they go out
the doors and winders. Looks like I'd get used to it
sometimes." He went to the kitchen shelf and took
down his candy jar. "Old Tio still at it down there?"

"Yeah—don't get in that candy now, I'm just about to
fix supper. You made us miss a job, you know. Where
have you been?"

"Some of us went down't the funeral home to see
Ruben Johnson—one Jayell tried to build that house
for last summer? Somebody done a job on him with
a knife. *Whew!* Wadn't hardly enough left to recognize."

The words went through me like a chill.

Ruben Johnson had disappeared after the incident
over the house. The night of the fire his wife and
baby were picked up by dog boys and moved into the
upper floor of the funeral home. Doc Bobo was "looking after them," it was said, until Ruben came back.

Apparently, Ruben Johnson had finally come back.

I looked at Em. His eyes were flat, unrevealing.
He chewed nonchalantly on his candy.

Tio was back at dawn the next morning, and every
day thereafter we were awakened at first light by the
sounds of banging metal. He worked until school
time, then returned in the afternoons as soon as he
could get away from the store. The thing became an
obsession with him, afternoons became too short,
and soon he was working into the night. He barged
through the trap door during supper, snatched the
oil lamp off the table and descended without a word.
"If he ain't done soon," said Em, dragging the table
into the moonlight, "I'm going to have to kill him."

Finally the bike was cleaned and ready to be reassembled, and at that point my usefulness, as scant
as it had been before, dropped to absolute zero. In
my hands, none of the parts fit back together. Tio
was building assemblages like clockwork, but for me
even obvious pieces wouldn't mate, nuts liked to cross-
thread on me. If I reached for a hammer to tap a

piece into compliance, he was instantly beside me saying, "Here, let me catch that." Soon he was doing it all, and I was relegated to manning the grease gun and washing parts. Em looked in from time to time, snorted, and went on his way.

At last the bike was reassembled except for the front wheel, which had suffered the most extensive damage. The tire was ripped open and the rim bent beyond repair. An afternoon's search through the weeds of Bledsoe's junk yard turned up a useable replacement, and Bledsoe made us a good deal on a tire with a lingering of tread and only the tiniest cracks of dry rot. The wheel was smaller than the original and gave the bike a slight forward pitch, which presented no real problem until the bike was brought to a stop. Then it had a tendency to throw the rider over the handlebars. When it was finished, gassed, and waxed to a mirror shine, we wheeled it out into the pasture and Tio hollered Em out of his nap.

"Well," said Em, looking at the torn fender and jagged hole in the muffler, "you got it all back together, but I can't says that's much of an improvement."

"She's old and she's been treated rough," said Tio, "but she's still got a lot of romp in her." He threw a leg over the seat and rocked down on the starter. The old bike quivered, but sat. Again he tried, and again the machine managed to calm itself. Em pushed back his hat and grinned. Tio jiggled a spark-plug wire, worked the gas, and rocked down hard. There was a violent awakening, a breath of indecision, then the motor caught, lunged hysterically for several moments, then settled into a loping, clattering idle. Em Jojohn yelled and clapped his hands.

Grinning with excitement, Tio wiped his hands and worked the throttle until the old engine was revved into a state of shuddering fenders, then lifted his foot and went blasting across the pasture. Halfway across he got it under control, chugged two laps around the bumpy pasture, and finally came coasting back, beaming in triumph and kicking down the stand.

"You see that?" he yelled. "She wanted to run right out from under me! I'm tellin' you, this here could be the hottest thing on the road!"

"She's already that," said Em, touching the engine, "and she ain't more'n cranked up good."

"Give me a turn," I yelled. Tio quickly explained the brakes and twist-grip throttle, and Em steadied the heavy bike while I got aboard. A moment later I was bumping over the grass in utter disbelief, exhilarating in the swish of the wind and the strange new feeling of power in hand. I slowly circled the field, bouncing with excitement and waving to the cows, who stood watching from the safety of the woods. "Unbelievable!" was all I could say on returning. "It's just absolutely unbelievable!"

When I dismounted Tio was trying to talk Em into taking a turn. The Indian was aghast. "You remind me of a damn fool," he said.

"Ain't nothing to it," said Tio, "you can do it if Earl can. Look, here's your throttle . . ."

Em backed away, shaking his head. "Anybody'd set two gallons of gas afire and get straddle of it ain't right in his head."

"Then I'll drive," said Tio. "Get on behind me and I'll show you how easy it is."

"Go on, Em, let him take you for a turn." Em got interested in the clouds and Tio and I waited, steeped in that ruthless determination to share an experience. Seeing that we weren't going to back down, and too proud to walk away himself, Em realized finally that he was caught. After several silent moments of shooting glances at the bike, at us, and back at the clouds, he abruptly flung himself on the seat and wrapped his arms around Tio's waist.

"Slack off," Tio protested, "you're cuttin' off my wind!"

After some more shuffling and resettling, getting his feet placed just right and battening down his hat, Em was ready. Tio kicked off and the overloaded bike went laboring over the hill. On the first return Em looked over and managed a tentative smile, but

275

maintained a grip that had Tio mouth-breathing. One more lap and Tio dismounted, gasping. "You can handle it now," he wheezed, and stretched himself on the grass.

Em eased cautiously forward and gave the seat a couple of test bounces. He looked uncertainly at me.

"Go ahead, Em, you can do it."

A study in concentration, he pushed off, wobbled a few yards, and fell on his side.

"You got to keep it balanced," said Tio as we righted him, "like on a bicycle."

"I can do it. I can do it."

Em mounted and tried again. "More speed!" yelled Tio. "More speed!" Em twisted the throttle and the bike blasted into a smoother path. "That's it! That's the way!" Em wavered uncertainly around the hill, and when he emerged on the north side still in control, we cheered and clapped our hands. Em flashed a broad smile and flapped his elbows with exhilaration, which, with a twist-grip throttle, was a decided mistake.

Under the sudden surge of gasoline, the engine sputtered, caught and leaped ahead in a smoky, blue roar.

We watched helplessly as the Indian streaked across the mud flat, jumped a gully, narrowly missed the pear tree, hit a log and went all heels and elbows into a pile of dry branches. When we got to him he was thrashing out, cursing majestically, blood beading in white scratches on his face and neck. Tio got to the whirling bike and shut it down.

"Leave 'er alone!" roared Jojohn, ripping branches from his collar. "Get your hands off her!"

"Aw, come on, Em, you gave it a good ride," said Tio.

"Yeah," I said, "ain't no use killing yourself."

Shoving us aside, Em furiously lifted the offending machine, carried it to a level place, and slammed it down on its devilish wheels. Flinging himself once more in the saddle, he commanded, "Fire her up again!"

"Em, you're gonna tear it up," moaned Tio.

"I'm gonna ride her," Em reasoned, "or I'm gonna wrap her around that goddamned tree!" He shoved his Vaseline jar at me. "Hold my matches."

Tio sighed and rocked down the starter, and Indian and bike went to war again. Tio and I sat down on the log to wait.

Around the pasture they dipped and climbed. Em held the throttle at exact dead level, puttering smoothly across the grassy flat, circling the upper end in precisely the same tracks, chugging businesslike along the edge of the woods.

Growing bored with watching him, Tio and I played mumbley-peg on a log. We wrestled awhile. We played Tarzan in the pear tree and saw who could hang one-armed the longest. Tio found an interesting bug and we toyed with it for a good half-hour until, without warning, the bug lifted wings we didn't know it had and flew away.

"You reckon he just don't know how to shut it down and is too proud to say so?" Tio wondered.

"No," I said, watching him go by, "Em's found a new world, and he's trying to come to terms with it. I wouldn't count too much on gettin' your bike back."

"Aw," said Tio, finally, turning for home, "Mr. Teague'd never let me keep it anyway."

I leaned against the pear tree and after a while began to doze. The sinking sun turned the Georgia hills to burnished copper. Crickets called to the approaching dark.

Round and round went the Indian, locked into his route like a carnival pony, elbows rigid, his face fixed in wonderment, leaning gently into the turns.

Tio forgave the loss of the bike; in fact, within a week he was hot on the idea that what it needed was a cart, and was hard at work building that. Jayell helped him with the design and supplied tubing and lumber, and Em and I helped him scour Bledsoe's and the foundry for angle braces and wheels. It was a dandy; lightweight, maneuverable, and capable of carrying the three of us without strain. Em painted it yellow and drove it around to all his river haunts, showing it off, bragging about it. He never came to trust it entirely, and remained a frightened driver, but he got where he wanted to go, and after two or three weeks could even bring it to a halt without going over the handlebars.

30

"DAMNIT, HOLD STILL!"

"You cut me!" I jumped off the stool and rubbed my stinging neck. My hand came away with blood on it. "Look at that! Would you just look at that?"

"Jes' a little nick. Set down." Em grabbed my arm and pulled me back on the stool. "Never heard such carryin' on over a little scratch."

"I'll probably get blood poisoning. Whoever heard of cuttin' hair with hedge shears anyway?"

"Seventy-five cents for a barber—ain't no sense in it. Tilt your head so I can wipe it off."

"Don't use that towel, it's dirty. Get the yellow one."

Em flipped the towel back over the rafter and pulled down the clean one. "The way you wash clothes, it's hard to tell."

"Well, if you got any complaints, the washtub's on the wall and the rub board right beside it."

"I got no complaints."

"And the next time you polish your boots I wish you'd use a newspaper. Look at that floor."

Work had been scarce, and it was cold; the thermometer hung at twelve degrees and the wind howled up out of the Ape Yard in gusts that lifted tin and sent a bird side-stepping to get his balance. And worst of all, it was Christmas. That whiplash frenzy of joy that cracked at the end of each dying year was flying upon us again.

Holidays always seemed forced on us somehow, as though they originated elsewhere and the Ape Yard only imitated, without knowing why. It was as if an order came down saying, "All right, Ape Yard, it's Valentine's Day. Never mind how you feel, it's the *calendar day* for you to LOVE! Swap those cutout hearts. Christmas! Christmas . . . Savior's birthday—no, it's not actually His birthday, but it's the day we've set aside for it, now stir yourselves! New Year's! Happy New Year Everybody . . . !"

During the two weeks before Christmas, Em and I had combed the town for work, but despite the commercial frenzy of the season, jobs were not easy to find. They were snapped up by vacationing students to buy their sweethearts ID bracelets and hi-fi albums. We helped Triangle Hardware relocate in a new building, cleaned bricks at a burned-out service station, and for three days I filled in for an ailing soda jerk at Saxon's pharmacy. Em was almost relieved when he was laid off from the job on the coal truck. Wasn't his kind of dirt, he said.

Christmas Eve the town lay exhausted. Last-minute shoppers combed the stores under the weary eyes of clock-watcing clerks. At the clubs and halls white jacketed Negroes trayed drinks to those already too drunk to heed the combos' call to dance. The firemen's wreaths hung from lampposts with the same air of loss and desolation as the peeling Nativity scene propped on the courthouse lawn, while around town, church choirs hopefully primed their "Messiahs." On Rock Crusher Road hotblooded virgins wallowed in bushes of crinolines to consummate new "steadies," sealed with mustard-seed lockets and St. Christopher medals. Young married couples, tired, broke but happy, cruised the streets listening to carols and showing their children the Christmas lights. And along the Ape Yard, children lay dreaming of leather cowboy suits and dolls that walked and talked and all the beautiful toys that wheeled and flashed, while their mothers

279

filled shoe boxes with fruit and bulk candy and cardboard games, and shame-drunken fathers spat in the grate.

The field behind the garage was beautiful: the night blue-cold clear, and the grass still shimmering from a trace of snow in the morning. While Em cut my hair I soaked my thumb in a cup of cold water. I was going to lose my nail, it was already darkening, but the throbbing was slowing and numbness overtaking the pain. Despite the accident I felt lucky to have gotten the two days' work at the water department sorting pipe fittings for inventory. The pay was good, a dollar an hour, and nobody ever rushed anybody at the water department. I should have watched Ronnie with that box of ells, though, I know he was clumsy. Ronnie was the city manager's son, home from college for the holidays, who worked with one hand and fondled a white pipe with the other.

"Finger still hurtin'?"

"It's all right."

Em dusted baking soda down my neck and I got down to brush out the hair. I didn't want to look in the mirror.

"*Mehhhrry Chris-mus!* Ho-Ho-Hoooo! *Meh-rry! Mehrry . . . !*" Tio bounced through the door in a cotton beard, clutching an enormous bulge under his jacket.

"Now ain't that a sight," said Em, "a pregnant black Santa Claus."

Tio sat on the footlocker and crossed his legs. "Go ahead and laugh and have your simple-minded fun, while I set here and decide whether I'm gonna get up and leave, or, in the spirit of the season, take pity on them that don't know no better"—he unzipped his jacket and pulled out a jar of purplish liquid—"and allow you to share my Christmas cheer."

Instantly sobered, Em leaned down and inspected the jar. "Where in this world," he whispered reverently, "did you find muskydine wine?"

"Somebody left off two gallons at the store. Mr.

Teague went to bed with the other jar a little while ago."

There was a hurried scramble for glasses and I got my first taste of homemade wine. It was something of a disappointment, strong and acrid and not at all the mellow flavor I expected. "You got to develop a taste for it," said Em, refilling his glass, "just sip along and let it get to know you."

Tio belched and waggled his glass. "Spare me a little more, then. Me and that stuff's ole friends already."

Em grudgingly complied, but held on to the jar. We talked along and sipped wine for a while. At least I sipped, Tio and Em were guzzling. When an hour or so had passed, and the wine slowed its descent in the jar, Em suddenly looked around and said, "Damn, I'm starved. When we gonna eat, Earl?"

"Yes, sir, food. Coming right up." I got up and looked in the cupboard. "What would you like, some canned spaghetti?"

"Oh, my Lord."

"I could reheat the pig's feet and okra."

"Not for me."

"How about if I fry up some fatback?"

"Boy, you're gonna fry my stomach to death."

"Well, that's it, unless you want to go down to the café."

"How much we got in the birdhouse?"

I shook my head, remembering. "Not enough to go to the café."

Em groaned and stretched himself on the cot. "Here it is Christmas Eve. Tomorra everybody in this town will be havin' ham and tur-key, with dres-sin', cranberry sauce, hot biscuits, giblet gravy, and here we are—what y'all going to have, Tio?"

"Mr. Teague generally fixes a chicken, unless he sells 'em all."

"Chicken! You hear that, boy? How long since we had a piece of chicken?"

"Not since that last Sunday at Miss Esther's, I guess."

Suddenly Em sat up. He looked at me, as though trying to remember something. Then he was up, stomping into his boots. "By God, we're gonna have us a chicken!"

"How?"

"You remember that old bastard with the dairy farm that done us out that money? He had a whole house full of chickens."

"You ain't thinkin' . . ."

"The hell I ain't!"

Tio was on his feet immediately, glassy-eyed and erupting with questions.

"Need some wire," Em said, "straight baling wire. Ought to be some down in the shed, that and a long stick of some kind." Tio found the wire and Em pulled the handle out of a broken hoe. He tied the wire to one end of the hoe handle, ran it through a nail bent to form a loop, and back along the handle to the other end, where he wrapped it around his hand. He made a loop with the wire, snapped it shut on the chair post a couple of times to test it out, and turned and grinned at us. "Get out the bike," he said.

Following Em's plan, we came in behind the Hutchinson farm from the Calhoun Falls highway. We left the bike in the woods and approached from the south end, jumping the frozen drainage ditch and working our way along the fence. Crouching low and keeping a careful watch on the farmhouse, we dodged from building to building until we reached the equipment shed below the poultry house. "Might as well settle down here till he goes to bed," said Em. At the top of the hill the farmhouse sat in shaded darkness except for a light in the kitchen.

Em unscrewed the wine jar and took a long sip. He offered it to me. "I believe I've had enough," I said. I didn't know if it was the excitement or what, but I felt a little queasy from what I had drunk already.

"I'll take another sniff," volunteered Tio.

"You done 'bout sniffed yourself silly," said Em. "And for God's sake, *take off that beard!*"

282

"*Ssssh!* Both of you! You want to wake the whole place?" It had started out a dark night, but a wind came up and the clabbery cloud cover started to drift; the new top of the dairy barn shone silvery in the moonlight. After a while I saw the kitchen light go out; a moment later a colored glow flooded the shrubbery under the living-room window. I swore under my breath and crawled back to where Em and Tio were swapping the jar. "Fine bunch of thieves we are. Boy, we sure can pick our nights."

"What's wrong?" said Em.

"It's Christmas Eve, remember? They'll be up half the night fixing Santa Claus!"

"No," Em said, shaking his head, "he's got no family."

"How do you know that?"

"You can always see signs of kids around a place, if there is any kids, and the day he kept us waitin' out by the pumphouse I seen him in the kitchen fixin' his own dinner. Wouldn't have been fixin' his own dinner if he had a wife, would he?"

"You amaze me," Tio said.

"Well, then he's fixing Santa Claus for himself," I said. "I just saw Christmas tree lights come on."

"Yeah?" Em crawled forward and looked out. "That's queer, he ain't the type to do that."

"Did you know he thought Em was a gypsy?" I said.

Tio sniggered and Em shushed him. "We better go see," he said. "That don't fit at all."

"All three of us?" I asked. "Hadn't just one ought to go?"

"Nah, we ought to stay together. If one goes, and it's clear, he's got to come all the way back past the poultry house to get the others, and then go back up there. No sense in spreadin' ourselves all over the farm carryin' messages, is it? Tio, damnit, stop suckin' on that jar!" He snatched it from him, finished it off in a few heavy swallows, and tossed it away.

"That'll remove the temptation," I said.

Tio started to snigger again, got caught in a pro-

tracted belch, and sat on the ground trying to un-
strangle himself.

"I'll just swear," said Em, yanking off the cotton
beard and pounding his back.

When Tio could breathe again we got on all fours
and set off through the weeds, Em leading the way
and me bringing up the rear, with Tio managing along
in the middle in a listing, sideways crawl. I began to
grow more and more uneasy.

There was no warning bark from the house, but
we weren't really worried about that anyway. Hutchinson wasn't the type to feed scraps to a dog that
could be fattening up his hogs. We reached the corner of the house and pulled Tio to his feet and moved
cautiously along to the living-room window. Em removed his hat and edged out past the window until
the tinted light slid over one eye.

That eye squinted to accustom itself to the light,
flew open in surprise, blinked a couple of times, and
then the other eye came out to join it. They both
stood transfixed.

The thin-limbed cedar tree stood blinking in the
corner casting its brilliant patterns over the room in
electric celebration; on the ceiling, the walls, the
room's drab, slip-covered furniture—and on the naked
white figures writhing joyously on the floor. Their
heads were toward us, Mr. Hutchinson's face buried
in her shoulder and his bald spot waving like a tiny
moon in the semidarkness. The woman's center-ridged
forehead and the waves of thick red hair spilled over
the sateen pillow were unmistakable. It was Eva Flynn
from Mae's Truck Stop.

Tio squinched his eyes and the cackle started to
build in his throat. Em clamped a hand over his mouth
and lifted him away by his britches. I raced behind
them across the backyard and down the hill, Tio's feet
kicking the air and his breath spluttering between the
Indian's fingers. When we were safely below the barn
the three of us collapsed in the weeds, holding our
faces and kicking in helpless agony. It was one of
those uncontrollable, side-aching times, when it really
hurt and we couldn't stop. And no sooner would we

begin to get control when one would snort and set the others off again.

"Well, boys," said Em, pulling himself weakly to his knees and speaking gruffly, "we better get them chickens . . ." he tried, and couldn't resist it, "while the rooster's occupied!"

"Yaaaaaaagh," gurgled Tio, and Em collapsed on his face again.

It seemed we were doomed to spend the rest of the night floundering in the weeds of Hutchinson's pasture.

When there was absolutely no breath left, not a kink in an internal organ, we dragged ourselves to our feet, not daring to even look at each other, and stumbled off toward the poultry house.

Tio and I watched through the slatted walls while Em lifted the latch and eased inside with the chicken catcher. He stood a moment to get his bearings, then carefully made his way along the rows of ghostly white chickens. A hen clucked and stood up and Em froze. After a while she settled back down.

Selecting a plump pullet on the bottom row, Em eased out the wire loop. Tio and I stopped breathing. The wire was invisible in the dark, all I could see was the hoe handle inching toward her head. Suddenly the noose snapped shut. Em jerked her to the ground and put a foot on her to stop the fluttering. That was all. It was so quick and quiet there was hardly a stir among her sleeping sisters. *"Ssssew!"* Tio shook his head in inebriated admiration.

Em loosened the snare and the chicken lay dead, her wings spreading slowly away from her body. He quickly caught two more the same way, and handed them through the door. I put them into the sack. "Better get one more," he said. He was starting back for it when Tio gave a *"Pssst!"* through the crack. He kept going *"pssst"* until Em came over.

"Let me get the last 'un," he said.

"You ain't in no shape," Em whispered.

"Aw man, ain't I been watchin' you do it? Come

285

on, lemme get one. Ain't no use to you havin' all the fun."

Em sighed. "Come quiet, then."

Tio groped through the door and got a grip on the catcher, and Em steadied him up and pointed him toward the chickens. "Em, are you crazy?" I whispered. Em put his finger to his lips and grinned.

Tio weaved away toward the roosts. Two old hens on the bottom pole stood up, heads cocking, and watched his approach with interest. Tio drew up before them, readied himself, and, after considerable fumbling, the wire loop lifted out, wavered uncertainly over their heads, and slowly settled on the one on the right. The hen watched it descend toward her, then at the last moment flicked her head and the loop slid down her wing. Em covered his mouth and turned away.

Tio grinned sheepishly. He tugged at his hat and tried again. Out of patience, the hen hopped to the ground and trotted away under the roost. Tio stared after her. The action seemed completely to confuse him. He turned to Em for guidance. But Em was unable to offer it; he was clinging helplessly to a roof pole, his hat cocked in the air and shaking violently.

Tio propped himself drunkenly on the catcher and considered the situation. He bent down and looked under the roost, then back at Jojohn. Finally, he took the course of action that must have seemed most obvious to him at the time. He got down on his knees and crawled under the roost poles after her.

When I finally got Em's attention and frantically pointed out what was happening, Em quickly tiptoed to the end of the roost and bent down. "Tio!" he cried in a hoarse whisper. "You damn idiot, come outa there!"

At that moment I heard the noose squeak shut—on the infuriated chicken's leg, it turned out.

With the first screech from under the roost, the entire leghorn population lifted into the air in one thundering, fluttering, ear-splitting cloud, exposing Tio standing between the roost poles, gamely hang-

286

ing onto his plunging prey. The air was full of chickens; they banged against the walls, the ceiling, the doors, perching momentarily on rafters, only to get bumped off by incoming flights; they surged between the roosts in foaming currents and leap-frogged each other high into the air, shooting off showers of feathers. Em had given up trying to reach Tio and was wildly flailing his way toward the door.

The back porch light came on. A bulb lit up by the pumphouse.

I ran to the door and jerked it open, unable to hear my own voice yelling, but the open door gave the boiling poultry a square of moonlight to aim for and out they came, spilling over me and pouring off down the hillside in a squawking, raging white flood.

The first shotgun blast clanged across the poultry house roof and sprayed against the milking barn.

At that point Em gave up trying for the door and came through the wall in a shower of splintering lath.

He found Tio and pulled him out, still clutching the catcher and the flouncing chicken. I had a good head start on them, but at the silo Jojohn passed me, hat in hand and a firm grip on Tio's collar, knees pumping high and grunting with pounding breaths as he ran.

"Uh-huh! Uh-huh! Uh-huh! Uh-huh!"

The second shot rang out and I felt the sack jump in my hand, and realized for the first time I was still carrying the other chickens.

I jumped the ditch and dived into the cart with Tio as Em was turning out on the creek road. We followed the back roads for several miles before swinging back onto the highway, but even then we were sure every pair of headlights we saw was either Hutchinson or the sheriff, and stopped and pulled the bike into the bushes.

But eventually we grew confident and relaxed. Em peppered along toward home and I sat watching the pavement glide from under my feet. Tio was already asleep with his head on the sack.

As we crossed the river bridge at the lower end of

the Ape Yard, Em cut his speed and yelled back over his shoulder, "You feel like dressin' these things?"

"What do you mean?"

Up the slope to the right glowed the lights of the Rainbow Supper Club. "Man, I'm just about whupped," he said.

"Me too," I said. It was well after midnight.

"I sure don't feel like dressin' these things."

"Well, somebody's got to, if you want your chicken dinner tomorrow." I might have known you'd put it off on me, I thought. But then as we drew nearer to the supper club, a smoky aroma cut the air, and I got the drift of his meaning.

"I can't wait for no tomorra, I'm 'bout to perish. What say we swap 'em off for some of old Bubba's barbeque!"

"After all that trouble for a chicken dinner?"

"Aw, them old birds are prob'ly tough anyhow." He was already turning off on the supper-club road. "How we gonna bake no chicken in the first place—ain't even got no oven! Talkin' 'bout fixin' chicken, and ain't even got no oven."

"You've got a point there."

"We don't even know nothing 'bout cookin' chicken."

"Right again, Em."

"But old Bubba sure knows how to cook barbeque."

That was true. Bubba White's Rainbow Supper Club, a barnlike structure converted from an old flour mill on the river, was almost as famous for its barbeque as for the murders that took place there. Bubba White was a stump of a man with the benevolent face of a black Santa Claus, and a violent temper. He had been brought up on a number of charges, and once in a while, when the public outcry became loud enough, his place was raided and padlocked. But within a few months the Rainbow was back in business, the cellar restocked with bootleg whiskey, and convicts from the county stockade waiting Bubba's tables.

Bubba White was Doc Bobo's brother-in-law.

Em coasted around the parked cars to the kitchen. He knocked, but the noise from the jukebox drowned him out. He knocked again, and this time the door bucked on its hinges. Bubba himself peered out of the smoking kitchen, his maroon tie tucked in his belt, sweat glistening on his bald head and curling his collar. He recognized Em and grinned, "Hey, what say, what say."

Em held up the chickens. The ragged wing flopped open. "Bubba, we got some nice pullets here. How 'bout a trade for some of that good barbecue?"

Bubba White sucked his teeth and leaned out and looked around the yard. He saw me trying to rouse Tio and glanced back suspiciously at Em. "It's all right," said Em, "just a couple boys I brought along to help me catch 'em."

Bubba looked at the chickens, hanging lifeless in Em's big fists. "How long them chickens been dead, man?"

"Not more'n a hour. They're still warm, feel 'em."

Bubba felt the corpses carefully. "This 'un looks like it's been run over."

"That one got caught in a shotgun blast"—an explanation that lifted Bubba's eyebrows—"but these others ain't got a bruise on 'em."

When Bubba had finished his examination, he turned and held out the birds to a broad-hipped woman who was working a barbecue fork between the black iron doors. "Take these chickens, Etta, and fix these boys sump'n to eat." He picked up a bottle from the cabinet. "Want a little sump'n, Em?"

"Better not," said Em, "I had some wine awhile ago and it don't do me to mix it."

Bubba chuckled. "Still got that tejus stomach, huh?"

"Raw as a whore at camp meetin'," said Em, rubbing his middle. "Sometimes I think the linin' gone."

Bubba's head jerked in silent laughter. He opened the door to the main dining room and pointed up to the balcony. "You all go up and get a seat. Send your food right up." He beckoned to a waiter.

Em leaned over and tapped the cook on the shoulder. "Put lots'a hot sauce on mine, Etta."

The waiter led us through the dancers moving slowly among the wood supports that ran up to the heavy-beamed mill roof. At the tables around the main floor couples ate and laughed and held one another in the shadowy flicker of candles, soft in the mood of sex and food in the room where their ancestors had labored in slavery, lulled by the electric robot sitting in the corner, neon bubbles coursing its veins, singing in the voice of Muddy Waters.

We followed the young waiter up the stairs to the balcony, where he placed us at a table overlooking the river. The place was so warm the windows were left open, and a cold breeze mixed with the hot, rich odors that drifted up from the kitchen. We sat watching the dancers until the waiter returned with smoking plates of minced pork and french fries and passed around frozen mugs of root beer.

It was as though I had never tasted food before. We sat eating in perfect contentment.

Outside, the river trees shivered as a black wind brought a mist of sleet, the pellets shooting by the millions through the tavern-lit leaves to do a silvery dance among the darkened roofs.

Pungent barbecue steamed into the air to mingle with our frozen breaths, washed down with burning swallows from the dark mugs numb in our hands. I looked up from the red candle flickering on the table.

"Merry Christmas," I said.

Em nodded and winked. "Merry Christmas."

"Merry Christmas," I said.

Tio, glassy-eyed, his mouth crammed full, lifted his battered hat.

"Mnm-ynnuh," he said.

And it was. The best I could ever remember.

BOOK THREE

31

IT WAS THE FIRST SATURDAY IN THE NEW YEAR, Poncini Day, the official opening of the six-month-long centennial observance, and a thundering, hell-springing day in Quarrytown. Mayor Crowler had made a proclamation speech from the courthouse steps. Poncini Park, a network of sidewalks and benches crisscrossing two acres of azaleas behind Galaxy Plaza, had been dedicated.

The streets were jammed with people vying for bargains at the Poncini Day sales, people in newly sprouting beards, in derby hats and string ties and homemade grandma dresses; not altogether authentic, maybe, but *Old Timey*.

A square dance was in progress in Allie Shafer's car lot, under a big banner proclaiming Centennial-Sell-Out-Time. Somehow a couple of the Cohen boys had just beat out the favored Amborsini twins in a Poncini Brothers look-alike contest on the square, and some perfectly authentic native tongue was flying among the older Italians.

The Jaycees sold hot dogs. The high-school band seranaded from the courthouse lawn. Buggies and wagons snarled downtown traffic.

A frightened horse bolted and ran in the front door of the Marble City Hotel, trapping the woman driver under the canopy. They finally had to unhitch the horse and lead him through the lobby and out the back and lifted the hysterical driver through a slit in the canvas.

On our way home, Em and I fell in with a crowd in the back of the county library setting out to find the grave of Easter Robinson. Tad Breisner, the doctor's son, was there, along with a half-dozen other historians and archeologists from the university in Athens with their charts and documents, arguing and comparing records with members of the Pollard Historical Society and its visibly upset president, Odetta Woolsen, while the Presbyterian minister tried to placate them. Auxiliary ladies in heavy skirts passed out hot coffee and Tad Breisner's pamphlets.

Mrs. Woolsen had been upset ever since those pamphlets first appeared.

Easter Robinson, a "brass-ankle," half-Indian, half-Negro, was a tall, dashing figure and the central character in much of the foothills folklore. With a band of outlaws and army deserters he had pursued a lucrative career of plunder and murder back and forth across Georgia and South Carolina from 1854 until 1862, until he happened along up the Little Iron River and came to a mysterious end at Colonel David Johns's estate.

The official version of the cutthroat's demise, as set forth in the journal of the Reverend Josiah Whittier, the historical society's founder, held that Robinson had been shot by the valiant Mrs. Johns as he and his gang battered the door of the mansion in the colonel's absence. The historical society had enshrined Mrs. Johns's birthplace on the Atlanta highway and turned the mansion into the Martha Pickner Johns Memorial Library.

Now Tad Breisner had come along with his pamphlets, replete with laboriously detailed research, and even photostated copies of letters in Mrs. Johns's hand, giving horrifying credence for the first time to that other, darker version of the story.

That account, previously dismissed as salacious slave

293

gossip, held that Robinson was, in fact, no stranger to the Johns residence during periods of the colonel's absence, and met his death climbing out of the upstairs bedroom window one night when one of the female servants, a new girl and unfamiliar with the custom of the place, brained him with a stick of stovewood. Mrs. Johns, the account went on, had Robinson buried in a Johns family vault below the slave quarters, and later had the errant girl flogged and sent to Savannah.

At any rate, notorious as he was, Easter Robinson had brought a glimmer of fame to Pollard County, and all sides were determined to resurrect and claim him during the centennial year. Tad Breisner, with his team of experts from the university and the services of surveyors and earth-moving equipment donated by the granite association, had sworn to bring him to light before the week was out. The assemblage set off from the rear of the mansion, following a dry creek bed through the fields toward the east end of the Johns property, drawing ever closer to the lip of the Ape Yard. Here the discussion grew heated indeed.

"This simply cannot be," said Mrs. Woolsen. "The easternmost boundary of the Johns estate followed the southerly turn of the creek. It's right here in Reverend Whittier's Journal." Mrs. Woolsen, having authored two books on Pollard County history herself, was not accustomed to having her sources questioned.

Tad Breisner tapped a roll of Xeroxed maps. "These plats are from the capital archives, and they coincide perfectly with the courthouse records. It must be remembered that Reverend Whittier chronicled more from popular belief than fact, and his tracts were appended to a historical account drawn a good deal from memory late in life." He opened a leather-bound tome on his knee. "Now, the one point on which all sources agree is that Robinson was buried below the slave quarters, by the creek that, in its southeasterly turn, formed the northeast corner of the Johns property. But since we're fairly sure of the boundary markers at the front of the estate, it's back here that the total acreage is being short-changed. And it's this creek bed that's causing the problem. Now, what everybody's failed to take into account is that on a plateau like this, a shallow creek tends to meander to a considerable extent. And in the past hundred years, this creek did in fact cut over and join Twig Creek, cutting short the Johns property. But before the construction in the hollow, it flowed along this depression a couple of hundred yards farther northeast before it turned. Let's proceed on that assumption for the time being at least." And off they trekked again, the men shedding their frock coats in the bright afternoon sunshine, the ladies snatching their dresses through the briars. Em shared his hip pint with a perspiring bulldozer operator and made a friend who gave us a ride.

No little curiosity was aroused in the Ape Yard by the procession marching down the slopes, and soon its number was enlarged by several dozen black faces as it filed along the hillside shacks. "It cannot be," protested Mrs. Woolsen, "it simply can*not* be here!" When we reached the last surveyor's pole, Tad Breisner called a halt. We were on the weedy apron of eroded land directly between the garage and Mr. Teague's grocery.

Tio came skipping across the rocks. "What's happenin', man?"

"Easter Robinson's grave, it's right around here somewhere!"

"Shoooeeee!" Tio said. We had played Easter Robinson all up and down those hills.

There was a conference among the Athenians; a consultation of maps, comparison of figures and notation of topography, and a final stretching of tapes. At last Tad Breisner stepped forth and pointed to a rectangle cornered by stakes. "It is the opinion of my colleagues and myself that the grave is within that perimeter. Dr. Spetchen here estimates a ten-to twelve-foot overburden accumulation due to erosion since that time, which would have covered many topographical features and altered bench marks, of course, but we are all agreed that this was the former bed of the creek. That being true, and all other calculations being correct, this should be the true northeast corner shown on the original deed."

This announcement was met with great excitement by the crowd, which by this time had grown to at least a hundred. Mayor Crowler wanted to know whose property it was that held this singular honor. Somebody called out that it was Mr. Teague's.

"No it ain't," said Mr. Teague from the other side of the creek, "my property stops right here. That used to belong to the Cahills. I don't know . . ."

"It's mine," said a voice, and Doc Harley Bobo stepped through the crowd. "I purchased it when Mrs. Cahill left town."

Em smiled down at me. "Meet your new landlord . . . Mr. No-Face."

Mayor Crowler explained the mission of the expedition and asked permission to dig for remains, laying on heavily for civic pride and historical significance.

Tad Breisner explained, "Being pressed for time and funds, our plan is to do a quick excavation and sift for artifacts. I have good reason to believe," and here he slipped a glance at Mrs. Woolsen, "that he was buried in a vault. If not, this clay may have preserved some of the bones, or at any rate there may be a sword, pistol, buckle or some other article of hardware."

"Hey, Doc," called Mr. Teague, "you ain't gonna let 'em set up no toll-payin' shrine back here, are you?"

"Oh, good heavens, no," said Mrs. Woolsen, eyeing the black children crowding dangerously close to her skirts. "The remains would be placed in the county museum."

Doc Bobo, hat in hand, smiling broadly as Flake Webster roved about with his camera, said, "It would be my honor to have you dig here. In fact, if you could use some additional help . . ."

Tad Breisner gave the signal and the bulldozers dropped their blades and began rolling up topsoil.

"Just see they fill every shovelful back in," said Mr. Teague, turning back for the store. "This county's too full of holes as it is."

Work commenced through the afternoon, the dozers scraping up soil for a front-end loader, which in turn dumped it through a slanted iron framework to separate out rocks and break up larger chunks of clay; and from there, the cloddy earth was shoveled through wire screens to be raked and sifted by hand.

By sundown, when Tad Breisner called a halt for the day, the excavation had produced a rusted roll of wire, a hubcap, several fence posts, and a basket full of broken jars, but no sign of Easter Robinson. When work resumed the following morning, the lemonade ladies didn't return, nor did Mrs. Woolsen. Em Jojohn displayed a similar lack of interest, much to the regret of the equipment operators who kept asking about him. The Ape Yard children were there in full force, much to the aggrievement of Tad, who had spent the preceding day passing judgment on whether each of the dozens of peculiar stones they found was or was not an arrowhead.

Shortly after noon there was a commotion in the pit.

The bulldozers were down about twenty feet and could go no deeper. What had at first been thought to be a slab, or a fragment of a shelf, continued to grow larger as more dozers came to push earth away. The tracks slipped across a floor of solid rock.

Pink rock, sparkling and glistening in the sun.

Mr. Thurston, of Blue Light Monuments, climbed down to inspect it. "It's marble, all right!" he said excitedly. "Push out a little more there!" The dozers moved back in, racking and spinning until an area of several hundred feet lay exposed. Other granite men came down.

"The finest grade of pink marble I've ever seen in this part of the country," said Wilbur Taylor of the Three Angels sheds. "Wouldn't expect to see that kind of stuff this side of Salisbury."

"Could be just a shelf," said another.

"Well, sure, you'd need a core sample," said Mr. Thurston, "but look"—he waved a hand over the rosy expanse—"you ever see a surface that big with as few flaws?"

The men shook their heads in admission that they hadn't.

"Hey! Over here—over here!" A bulldozer operator in the north corner of the excavation was standing up, waving his arms. He pointed to a large block of earth, which at first glance looked like a clay-caked boulder, tilted on the corner of his blade. The Athenians fell over each other getting to it and dropped to their knees, clawing at it with eager fingers.

A rusted metal corner appeared through the clay. "Hold it," cried Tad Breisner. He ordered everyone away and with the help of Dr. Spetchen and a couple of their colleagues carefully wrapped the entire block in protective tarpaulins. A truck was hastily summoned, it was lifted aboard, and they rode with it up the hollow, shouting caution to the driver, hugging their find.

Word came back a few days later, in a front-page article in the *Star*. It was Robinson's remains, all right, those of a large person, measuring to a height of six-feet-four, with a fractured skull, and they were encased in a heavy bronze vault bearing the Johns family coat-of-arms.

Odetta Woolsen was not available for comment, but within a week the historical society had withdrawn its fund for the support and maintenance of Martha Johns's birthplace, and a petition was before the county commission to change the name of the county library.

32

TIO WALKED BACK AND FORTH, CALCULATING. EM
and I sat shelling peanuts, watching him deliberate.
The principle was sound, we all agreed on that. By
rights the automatic potato bin should work like a
charm.

The manager of the Valley Farm store had grown
so accustomed to seeing Tio hanging around studying
his operations that he took the boy aside to give him
advice from time to time. Always keeping your shelves
and bins stocked was basic, he said; customers never
liked to buy the last few items of anything. In shoe
stores, he pointed out, didn't they always bring you
shoes to try on from somewhere in the back? It was
because that vast display you saw along the walls was
mostly empty boxes!

And there never was a more faithful disciple. Tio
stuffed paper in the bottoms of half-empty hampers.
He sawed shelves in half lengthwise, shortening their
depth so that it took only half the stock to keep them
looking full.

But that was simple. Practical. What Tio craved was
automation. So when he spotted the tray bin at the
new cafeteria in Galaxy Plaza, the idea set him on fire.
He rushed back to Mr. Teague's and immediately
began construction on the world's first automatic, self-
adjusting sweet potato bin.

The principle of the tray bin was elementary enough:
by the use of springs or counterweights down in the
bin, the load was shifted higher each time a tray was
removed from the stack, bringing the next tray level
with the top of the bin. You never knew how many
trays were left until you lifted the last one out.

If it worked with trays, it ought to work with sweet

potatoes, Tio said. He fitted heavy springs in the wooden potato bin and covered them with a loose plywood bottom. As the potatoes were removed, lightening the load, the potatoes would rise, keeping the bin looking full.

Tio hoisted hampers of potatoes to test their weight. He put a foot in the bin and felt the tension of the springs. Finally, he was satisfied. "Okay, Em, climb in the bin and mash that plywood bottom all the way down."

It seemed more sensible to me to check the tension by just pouring in the potatoes, and letting them depress the springs gradually. But when I ventured that suggestion, I only drew the creator's wrath.

"You, who can't even build yourself a decent ironin' board, knows all about such things, I reckon, and can say how it ought to be done. Em, climb in that bin."

Em smilingly obliged, and when the platform was depressed Tio wedged a peg through a knothole to hold it down.

"Em, don't you think he ought to . . ."

Em put a finger to his lips and closed his eyes.

When the bottom was secured Em stepped out and started helping Tio fill the bin, emptying hamper after hamper. I walked outside for another bag of peanuts.

As I was closing the lid of the roasting machine a blur of motion caught my eye up the road, descending from toward the fairgrounds.

I stood on Mr. Teague's steps and watched it coming, an aged yellow school bus, careening down the road like a runaway rollercoaster car. It rattled across the bridge and with a screech of brakes turned into the curve up to Mr. Teague's, looking for sure as though it wouldn't make it, but miraculously it did, sliding to a catty-cornered halt inches away from the gas pumps and skirting pea gravel across the front of the store.

"Merciful God, let me off!" a voice cried, and a moment later the boarders were pouring out the door.

"I didn't do so bad for a first time," said Mr. Rampey, sliding out of the driver's seat. "Thought I done pretty good, didn't you, Lucia?"

Mr. Teague, brought out by the commotion, stood in amazement as the old people got their legs steady under them, tugging at garments.

"What do you think of it, Alvah?" said Mr. Rampey. "We got transportation now." He turned to Tio. "Fill 'er up, boy."

"We got a coffin, is what we got," said Mrs. Porter, helping Ruby Lampham down. "He might as well drive us right on to the cemetery."

"Where'd you get that thing," said Mr. Teague.

"Picked it up down at Bledsoe's," said Mr. Burroughs, "we'll need it in our business."

"He was going' to scrap it for parts," said Mr. Rampey.

"Business, what business?" asked Mr. Teague.

"We paid too much for it," sniffed Mr. Jurgen.

"I need a drink, Alvah," said Mr. Burroughs, lunging for the store, "like I never needed one before."

"We can go on and buy the groceries while we're here, can't we?" said Mrs. Metcalf.

"We buy the groceries on Friday," said Farette.

"I'd like a cold drink too," said Mrs. Cline as they crowded into the store.

"I don't mean that," said Mr. Burroughs, waving his away, "I need a real drink! Where's your bottle, Alvah?"

"I could stand a nip myself," said Mr. Rampey.

"Not you, for heaven's sake!" cried Mr. Burroughs.

Mr. Teague brought a bottle from upstairs and gave it to Mr. Burroughs. "Now what's this about a business?"

When Mr. Burroughs' eyes horizoned again he let out a long sigh and leaned on the register.

"Would anyone like one of these oatmeal cakes?" asked Mrs. Bell. "Maybe we should take some with us."

"Mr. Burroughs . . ." It was Mrs Porter, waving a bottle of white powder. "Dr. Sweete's foot powders," she chirped. "You'll want to get a good soak now."

"Lord God, woman, we've got no time to be thinkin' about foot soaking! We've got business to tend."

"What business?" screamed Mr. Teague.

Mr. Woodall started and turned around. "Business?"

Mr. Burroughs' eyes lit eagerly. "Antiques, Alvah! Bric-a-brac for the centennial folks. Got the idea from the way the ladies' quilts are bein' snapped up. You knew they were making quilts, didn't you? Well, the other day Doris Walker came to pick one up—you know her, wife of Haley Walker runs the tractor place —and she had this cousin with her from out of Four Forks, and she decided she wanted one too. Well, I got to guyin' the ladies a little, and I told 'em—told the cousin, that is—that quilt she wanted would cost her ten dollars extra, 'cause a little blue swatch of cloth in it had come from a coat that belonged to one of the original Poncini brothers! Told her, 'Oh, yeah, my folks knew 'em well. Had 'em over for supper many a time. They was a little peculiar, to be sure, but fine I-talian people!' Well, sir, I want you to know she grabbed that quilt out of my hands before I could say P-turkey, and there I stood with a handful of money! I was goin' to hand it back, don't you know, but Rampey hauled me out of the room. Well, we talked it over, and struck the notion that there was a lot of old-timey stuff layin' around the children's attics—if the scoundrels ain't thrown it away, that is, and we thought we'd just go fetch it out and sell it!"

Mr. Jurgen broke in, "Some of it we might have to make out to be a little older than it is, if you know what I mean."

Mr. Burroughs leaned close. "Uh—that business about the Poncini brothers' coat"—he winked—"the ladies don't have to know about that."

Mrs. Metcalf came up. "If we're going to that supper we'd better hurry."

"Supper?" said Mr. Teague.

"The First Methodist is having a supper on the ground," said Mr. Burroughs. "There's a lot of them going on right now too, and you know, when we eat out, we dock the landlord!"

"Liable to be a customer or two there too," said Mr. Jurgen, "so we brought along a few quilts just in case."

"All right everybody!" shouted Mr. Burroughs, and the boarders began making their way out of the store.

On his way out Mr. Rampey handed Mr. Teague a half-eaten candy bar. "Can't eat this Baby Ruth, Alvah, there's a little speck of something there . . ."

They all boarded the bus again, and with a grind of gears it wobbled down into the road, stopped, backed up, choked, started again, and finally went moaning up the hollow.

Mr. Teague was about to start up the stairs, for a nap probably, when Tio suddenly remembered his potato bin.

"Hey, Mr. Teague," he said triumphantly, "look at this!" And he reached down and yanked out the peg.

Well, that bin erupted like a volcano.

It rained sweet potatoes for a full five minutes. I dived under a counter and Em crouched in the corner, shielding himself as best he could with one of the hamper lids. Mr. Teague, caught in the middle of the maelstrom, lurched about the floor beseeching God and protecting his head with his arms.

As the storm abated he stumbled about wild-eyed, starting and flinching as the last of the potatoes, bottles and cans rolled off the shelves and thunked to the floor, and when at last he found Tio he stared at him in utter amazement.

"Merciful God," he cried, *"how did you manage to blow up the yams!"*

I was drawn up under the counter beating the floor, trying to get my breath. Em stood in the corner and held his sides and just hooted, gasped and hooted.

After a while I became aware that our laughter was being joined by others, and when I could, I put my head out. I stopped laughing.

It was Doc Bobo, Mr. William Thurston of Blue Light Monuments, president of the granite association, and Mayor Walter Crowler himself.

"It seems we're in the midst of a celebration, Alvah," said the granite man as they came into the store.

303

Mr. Teague climbed on his stool behind the register and wiped his twitching head with a towel. "Lord God, I don't know. If gunpowder wasn't so high . . ."

"You know the mayor, Bobo . . ."

The mayor put out his hand. "Hello, Alvah, how've you been?"

"Damn, Walter, two visits in two weeks, and usually you don't even come down at election time."

Mr. Thurston cleared his throat. "Well, we got the core sample reports, and they're even better than we expected." He walked around, taking in the store. "Mind you, I'm not saying it's the find of the century, it's only construction-grade marble, and old blue-gray's been our bread and butter a long time, but there's a market for it, and we think there's enough there to justify a small quarry. It's not a shallow shelf, the cores showed that, but of course they mightn't have showed the flaws either. There's considerable overburden to contend with, plus the store and a number of those shacks that would have to be cleared away, and, of course, more tests would have to be run before any definite propositions could be made, but . . ."

"Wait a minute," said Mr. Teague, dropping the towel, "am I to understand you want to tear down my store—to dig a granite quarry?"

Mr. Thurston was surprised. "I thought that's what we were talking about—that's why we've been cutting core samples . . ."

"I didn't authorize nobody to be cuttin' core samples on my land!"

"Not on your land, on Doc Bobo's across the creek. We've had the equipment back there all week . . ."

"I never paid no attention. I thought they was fillin' in that hole. I didn't know you was lookin' to dig another one!"

"Well, the point is, the rock was located on Doc Bobo's land, but a quarry would take up this whole area, including the store property. I thought you'd be pleased . . ."

"No, sir, my property ain't for sale!"

"Well, sale—lease, or whatever, what I'm trying to make you understand, Alvah . . ."

"What I'm trying to make you understand, Billy Thurston, is there ain't going to be no uprootin' of my place of business to dig for tombstones!"

"You're not serious."

"The hell he ain't," said Tio.

"The hell I ain't," echoed Mr. Teague, then whirled on the boy. "If you don't gather up them taters I'll put you on the chain gang!"

"Mister Teague," said Doc Bobo, "perhaps you don't understand. I own most of the property in question, but Mr. Thurston and other members of the granite industry have expressed a genuine interest in helping get a quarry started down here. They have made a most generous offer of a corporate enterprise, with their backing, equipment, expertise . . . a most lucrative proposition. Now, I own most of the property, but it is impossible to sink a quarry without your co-operation, and that of the other people who own lots adjacent to it. You, of course, own the largest share, next to me. The others have already expressed an interest in selling their bits and pieces to turn a nice profit, why not you, who stands to gain the most of all?"

"Because," said Mr. Teague, "I'm in the grocery business. I've been in the grocery business for fifty-two years, and I've no interest in going into the granite business and digging another blasted rectum in the earth!"

"Alvah," said the mayor, "as you know, this is a one-industry town. We need every source of supply if we expect to survive. This could affect the progress of the entire community."

"Progress!" snorted Mr. Teague. "You come down to this slum and talk to me about progress. If you'd been down here to pave a street or dig a sewer line in the past forty years you might have found your precious rock in time to do us all some good. You're too late, Mayor. Don't expect me to concern myself with this town's progress. I never gave a damn for the

305

granite business. To have the curse of being born in a place that can't produce nothing but rocks! I'd rather be from the blessed manure capital! And you want me to give up my place of business so you can dig more tombstones!"

"But look what we're offering you," said Mr. Thurston, "a chance to get out of this hollow—this slum, as you called it—and spend the rest of your life in comfort. Look around you, Alvah, you call this a business? In another five years the chains will have closed your doors!"

"In another five years, the Lord willing, they'll have closed my coffin! What can you offer me, seventy-three years old, a trip around the world? A big house in Marble Park and hobnob rights with you and that country-club gang? It's too late for me to leave this hollow. I've spent my life down here. I've got a place to live, work to do, and folks that holds me with some respect. What can you offer me to beat that?"

"Mr. Teague," said the mayor, speaking more formally, more earnestly now, "let me be quite candid with you. Confidentially, I didn't want to go into this aspect of it just now, but as you know, we're observing the hundredth anniversary of our little granite industry this year. Statewide attention is being focused on us. And at the big windup celebration in June we will have dignitaries here from the state capital and from Washington, the governor, congressmen. And Senator Broward is bringing some important people from Washington to look at the Oconostee dam. There could be national publicity. As you may have heard, we're under consideration for a federally subsidized housing project to replace many of the substandard dwellings that will be flooded by the dam. I think you'll agree this is the time to put our best foot forward. And given the present conditions, we believe it would be an excellent thing for us to be able to announce the first black member of the granite association, to show ourselves as a community of stability, working together for the benefit of all our

306

people. We are all eager to extend ourselves toward that effort."

Mr. Teague was silent. And moving in on that silence, Doc Bobo said, "In short, speaking bluntly, Mr. Teague, this is important not only to me, but to other people, in high political circles. Take that housing project; when the government appropriates money for black people, they like to see a black face or two on the committees. That's the look of the times, if you know what I mean. And that situation with the schools. Everybody wants that kept quiet, but the word is this thing is just getting started, and there's people who want reliable black folks in high places when they really start pushing, people who can be trusted. This granite association thing could be the perfect springboard to political appointments, where in the coming years I could be of invaluable service to our district. That's why it's so important that this opportunity not be allowed to pass.

"And of course," he said, "I would appeal to you on behalf of your good colored friends and customers around you, for what they stand to gain in the sale of their property, and the new jobs a quarry down here would provide. It's not often such a financial opportunity as this comes to the Ape Yard."

"Gentlemen," said Mr. Teague, "I don't care if you put Bobo in a position to siphon off every federal dollar they pour in here, with government subsidies or whatever. You can make him *president* of the granite association. Run him for Congress! But you ain't going to do it by tearin' down my store.

"And don't you talk to me about opportunities for black folks, Bobo. I been feedin' the ones you're lettin' starve. Raise that mill above slave wages and then come talk to me." He shook his head. "I know about how you get folks to sell property, and I know, and they know, that once you and the granite people get done tradin' 'em around, you'll end up with whatever profits there is, and all they'll get is another hole in the ground to work in that freezes in the winter and hits a hundred and twenty degrees in the summer.

307

So don't talk to me about opportunities for black folks, Doc. I don't see no opportunity in it for nobody but you . . . and you ain't been black for thirty years."

The three men looked at each other. The mayor turned and stalked angrily out of the store. After a moment, the others followed him.

Tio could barely suppress his jubilation until they were out of earshot. "Did you hear that old man?" he cried. "Did you hear what he laid on those guys!"

"Tio-o-o!"

"Gittin' 'em, Mr. Teague . . . gatherin' 'em up right now!"

33

NOTHING MORE WAS HEARD FROM THE MAYOR OR THE granite association, but the very next day Doc Bobo began quietly buying the property around Mr. Teague. One by one the shacks were emptied, their occupants relocated in the cheap prefab little houses that began springing up along the south side of the hollow.

"Let him clean 'em all out," said Mr. Teague, "till I'm the only one left over here, just help to see the store better."

To the great relief of the boarders and myself, who had been on edge ever since we learned that our new landlord was Doc Bobo, Mr. J. J. Bearden came by the next day to tell us that for the time being at least, the boardinghouse property was in no danger. It was that area below Sunflower Street, including the Teague property, that was under primary consideration. Should the quarry operations expand to require more ground later on . . . well, we would take that as it came. Thet would be months, anyway, perhaps years.

"If he's countin' on Teague to sell," said Mr. Burroughs, "he better figure longer than that!"

"Well," said Mrs. Bell, "it was nice of him to send us word so soon anyway."

"He didn't want you to worry a minute," said Mr. Bearden, bowing his way off the porch.

"Hey, J.J.," Mr. Rampey called, "How come Bobo was so shy about lettin' us know he'd bought the place?"

Mr. Bearden came back to the steps. "Well, confidentially," he said, "he didn't quite know how you folks might feel renting from . . . ah, him. You know how it is."

"Yeah," said Mr. Rampey.

"He's asked me to make every effort to see that you feel—comfortable here."

"We'd feel a lot more comfortable if he hadn't upped the rent," said Mr. Jurgen.

Mr. Bearden turned toward his car and stopped, remembering something. "Oh, yes"—he was looking at Ruby Lampham—"I don't quite understand . . ."

"About our extra cook?" said Mr. Burroughs. "Don't worry, J.J., she won't cost you a cent."

"Oh, well . . ."

"Slave labor, tell Bobo. He'll like that."

"Yes, well . . . whatever." Mr. Bearden worked the door open and climbed in his car. "If you need anything now, just call . . ." He was backing out the drive.

"We're still gonna dock him when we eat out!" Mr. Jurgen yelled.

It was true, Doc Bobo had always walked very gingerly around white people. I remembered the time Miss Esther had Em destroy Bobo's shack across the road where the Kitchens woman lived and he'd never said a word. And he obviously knew that I was back and living in the garage with Em, and no mention had been made of it.

Remembering suddenly that we would continue to have that place in the woods to live, I rushed uptown to break the good news to Em.

Em was more interested in his game of pool.

He took his time, carefully lining up his shot, slowly

stroking the cue through his fingers. He shot, and scratched.

The stranger across the table laughed. "That's the one, big feller, you just set my supper on the stove." The stranger, a stringy country fellow in white shirt, khaki pants and a cowboy hat, leaned across the table and easily sank the shot. Em got another beer and stood by swigging and scowling as the other man continued to sink balls as though he knew secret ridges in the table.

"There you are, I've been looking for you two everywhere." It was Jayell, sweaty and grimy, his denim jacket covered with rock dust. "Em, I'm building a retaining wall around the yard. You and Earl want to help me haul some rock?"

Em smiled. "The missus got you buildin' her a wall now, has she?"

The sarcasm didn't go unnoticed, but Jayell brushed it off. "Up there you got to have one, or the whole damned yard washes away. What do you say?"

"I don't know," said Em, scratching his head, "little woman told me not to come about the place anymore."

"Well, you won't . . . we'll be out at the . . . look, damnit, I don't need your mouth, I need your back. You don't want the work, say so!"

Em patiently chalked his cue, studying the game. "Sure, we want the work, Jayell, just let me finish up here."

The door opened and Walt Moody came in, vacant grin fixed, oblivious to the heat. He touched Em's elbow. "You like fried chicken?" Em nodded, intent on the game. "Ain't the gravy good?" Walt Moody paused, expectant, but when he got no further response he moved on to the next man and repeated the questions. A player sliding his cue waited until Walt was out of the way. He continued around the room, repeating his questions to everyone, then went out the door.

Walt Moody never said anything else. His two eternal questions got him a free meal at the drugstore, an occasional beer, a bed for the night at the

310

police station. Some years back someone noticed that Walt greeted women more often than he did men, and they sent him off for an operation. After that the town rested easier, and highschool girls stopped to chat with Walt on the street. He had a permanent seat on the cheerleaders' bench at ball games. I could hear him out on the street now, stopping the giggling Pierce sisters.

"What's the matter with him?" asked the stranger across the table.

"Nothing," said Em, "he's just ahead of his time," and laid a quarter against the stranger's try for the side pocket.

The stranger sank the shot.

"Well, that does it," I said. "That cleans us out."

"Ain't no way to beat him," said Em. "You know why, Early boy? 'Cause that country boy is a pool hustler. Yessir, one of your regular circuit-ridin', shuck-the-local-folks pool hustlers. Ain't that right, country boy? Got your Cadillac parked across town?"

The lanky stranger grinned and racked his cue. "If you can't afford the game, don't play it."

"Oh, I can afford the game," Em said, "if I know who I'm up against. Kind of nettles me, though, to be led in blind."

"You pay as you go in this world, friend." The stranger pushed back his hat and stuck his hands in his pockets. "It just costs some more than others."

Suddenly Em's hand slapped down on the stranger's pocket, gripping the hand inside. "Don't move too quick now, country boy, or I'm gonna keep squeezin' until I hear some finger bones snap." The stranger relaxed, watching the Indian. Em smiled, and with a sudden jerk ripped away the pocket and half the man's trouser leg, and stood clutching his hand, which held a small caliber pistol. "I guessed it was a pistol you had in there," said Em proudly, "and it's a good thing I guessed correct, ain't it? 'Cause if I'd been wrong and you was just playin' with yourself, you'd be in *tar*-uble pain right now—wouldn't you, country boy?"

311

The hustler blanched at the notion.

Em tossed the pistol aside and pressed the man down on the table. "You got a tossin' coin?" he asked me.

I shook my head.

"Maybe he'll let us borry one, then. You got a quarter we can borry, country boy? I'm gonna let the boy toss. Heads I break your arms, tails I don't. Let the boy borry a quarter."

His eyes bulging under the Indian's grip on his collar, the man felt in his pocket and dropped a quarter in my palm with trembling fingers.

Em looked at it and frowned. "Don't believe I'd let him toss with that one if I's you. Looks like to me it's dead sure to come up heads. If I's you I'd let him try another one." The man got the point and dug out another, and another, until Em nodded. I had eight dollars in quarters. The amount Em had lost. I tossed the coin and Em said, "What is it?"

The hustler studied my face intently. I smiled at him. "Tails."

"Well, that's all for me, then. I'm whupped." Em hauled the man up and slapped his shoulder. "By damn, country boy, there just ain't no way to beat you a'tall!"

The hustler made for the door and we watched him clear the traffic and go flopping-britched across the square.

Jayell pulled himself off of the stool. "For Christ's sake, can we go haul some rock now?"

We loaded the truck from a slag pile at one of the quarries. Skeeter and Carlos were there, along with several of the old shop boys. One of them had brought a sack of cold baked sweet potatoes and salted cracklings, and we spent a convivial afternoon hoisting rock and listening to Em's rambling stories. For a while it was like old times. When the truck was loaded Em, who had been carrying on over how Carlos had grown into such a husky young man, and going out of his way to compliment him on the weight he could lift, began to hint that maybe he was ready to do the sledgehammer trick. The trick consisted of gripping the handle in one hand, arm extended, and lowering the sledgehammer toward one's face until it touched the forehead, then lifting it up again. I never saw anyone who could do it but Em, but Carlos, bloated with praise, had to give it a try. Sure enough, he knocked himself cockeyed. Skeeter laughed until he had to sit down.

"All right," said Jayell, "let's get rolling."

When we drove into Marble Park and came in view of Jayell's place, we noticed people gathering in the yard. Gwen was on the steps, engaged in animated conversation with a group of neighbors.

"Oh, my God," said Jayell, "what now?"

As soon as the truck stopped she came running.

"Jay," she said ominously, "we had a near disaster this afternoon."

"What happened?" Jayell climbed out and glanced around the group.

"That limb," she said, pointing, "came *that* close to killing little Harvey Henderson." A giant branch from the dead oak tree that bordered the Henderson property lay at the foot of the tree. "There was no wind or anything; it just broke and fell, right where he had been playing not two minues before!"

"I'd just called him in," interjected Eleanor Henderson, the type who received providential nudgings. "I don't know why—I was watching from the kitchen window, and I had this *feeling*, something just *told* me." She raised her voice to accommodate the new arrivals. "And no sooner had he got in the house than I heard this awful crash! *Ka-womp!* Lord, I thought the roof was coming in!"

They gathered around the great elbow lying on the ground. It was as big around as a man, gray and warty with age. The lawn was littered with bark and twigs shattered from its brittle branches. Gwen was pale. "Jayell, you've been promising to have that tree cut down."

"I know, I know, and I will."

"Well, it would be nice to have it done before it kills somebody."

Jayell bent and put a chip in his mouth. "Yes, and I will have it done, Gwen."

Harold Henderson tried to cut the awkwardness. "There's a tree company in town, Jayell . . ."

"I've tried them," said Jayell, "they're tied up with the telephone company."

Another neighbor spoke up. "How about that colored fella that takes care of your place, Judge?"

All eyes swung to Judge Strickland. He puckered his lips on his pipe and considered it, and shook his head. "He hasn't the experience nor the help for a job like that."

"He's got his boy that works with him."

The judge was mildly irritated; he was not accustomed to having his judgment questioned. "No, I wouldn't risk it. Old man like that—if they did some damage, or one of them got hurt, you could have quite a legal tangle on your hands. No, I wouldn't recommend that at all."

Heads nodded to the wisdom of that, and the yard fell to pondering again.

Then came a voice like a thunderclap.

"Well, damned if this don't beat all *I* ever saw!"

The group broke open and there was Jojohn, hands on his hips, shaking his head in disgust. "Here we got a dozen grown men aworryin' and a-frettin' over one old tree. Why come *we* don't cut her down?"

Harold Henderson was the first to recover. "It's not that simple," he said. "Felling trees is tricky business."

"Tricky, hell, you chop her through the trunk and the top'll hit the ground. I've seen it happen dozens of times. Jayell, you've cleared land, cut pulpwood . . . what's the matter with you?"

"The houses are pretty close, Em, and one that tall ought to be topped out. You'd need safety belts . . . saws . . ."

"Hellfire, all you got to do is run some guy lines, chop 'er on the yea side, and lay 'er down right across the yard; it's a clear fall straight to the woods!"

314

There was an awkward silence, some of the people were clearly offended by this outburst from the sweaty laborer. Women folded their arms and drifted away. Gwen's eyes were blazing. "Jayell, this is getting us nowhere," she said between gritted teeth.

"Look," said Jayell, "we'll talk about it later." He turned to the Hendersons. "Harold, Eleanor, I'm sorry about what happened. I'll have it taken care of right away."

"Well," said Eleanor Henderson, "in the meantime I think you ought to put up a fence or something to keep little children away from that thing."

"I will, Eleanor, I'll do that." They left towing little Harvey, and the others moved away to their own yards. Gwen turned and marched briskly to the house. "That's it for today, fellas," Jayell said to the shop boys. "We'll get a fresh start Monday."

"Tomorrow's Saturday," I said, "we could come back then."

Jayell sighed. "We're supposed to go up to the Hendersons' hunting lodge this weekend."

Em was yanking the bike from under the carport. "Anybody that's goin' with me better come on!"

Em ranted and fumed the rest of the day, and that night there was no peace in the house. He ate little and griped about everything. There were no clean towels. The tea had soured. There was too much mayonnaise in the cole slaw, bones in the salmon croquettes. Down the road, Wash Fuller had gone off and left Jincey in heat and a pack of dogs was tearing down the porch. Up and down, he paced, up and down.

I knelt by the footlocker trying to iron, my knees aching, sweat dripping, the towels under the shirt riding up, riding up.

"Damn fool!" he stormed. "S'all he ever was, all he'll ever be!"

I tried again for the yoke. There was no way to get a good even stroke without the iron bumping into a locker hinge.

"Well, I ain't gonna get mixed up in it. Don't want no part of it. He made his bed . . ."

"Em, if you make me burn this thing . . ." I set my jaw and tried again. Now it was the damned buttons getting caught.

". . . gets moved up yonder where he don't belong —gets so stropped in he can't cut down a goddamned tree, it ain't no skin off mine!"

"Okay, you made your point . . ."

"What the hell do I care, huh? Anybody lets theirselves get tied up in sump'n where they got no business—they deserve what they get!"

"Em, if you don't . . ."

"Hell, naw, I ain't gonna stew over it, let him sweat, let him rot! I don't care. I don't look out for nobody but *me!*"

I slammed down the iron as hard as I could. "For God's sake, will you shut up or get the hell out of here!"

In a burst of fury he kicked the cot over against the wall and grabbed his hat.

Thank God, I thought. When he was like that he was insufferable. Drunk, I could handle him. Sick, I could handle him. But that gripe-gripe-gripe, I never could stand it.

He was stopped at the door. I could feel him standing there.

I kept ironing. I wasn't going to ease the situation. A fine thing, I thought, if he couldn't hold a mad till he got out the door.

Then Em's voice came low and tentative, soothing. "Lord sakes, honey . . . come in, come in."

I looked around, and slowly got to my feet.

It was Phaedra Boggs, standing in the doorway in a dazzling white party dress. Her face was drawn, tears glistened softly on her cheeks. She looked as though she had been crying a long time. She took the chair Em pulled out for her and sat there. Phaedra Boggs, with the look of a lost and frightened child.

There were stains across the front of her dress. Brown stains, like I got in the summer from cradling

316

wood, and for one confused moment I wondered why Phaedra would be toting wood in a new white dress.

Then I caught the smell.

"We need help, Em," she said choking. "Papa's in no shape . . ." She broke down, sobbing uncontrollably.

The Indian knelt beside her and cradled her to him, clumsily patting her shoulder.

34

MRS. BOGGS'S FUNERAL WAS HELD SUNDAY AFTERnoon, a simple graveside service. Reverend Reese of Rehobath Pentecostal officiated. He didn't know the Boggses, but Em pressed five dollars in his hand and he came. Phaedra stood with an arm linked in her father's. Marvin Boggs, a scrawny little man with a brown suit coat over his overalls, stood rubbing his stringy hair in his eyes as he cried. There were just the three of us, besides the preacher. Em didn't come, as I knew he probably wouldn't. He hold the preacher I would show him the way and disappeared.

When the service was over I waited until Phaedra led her father away, and then I broke and came across the ridge running as hard as I could, ripping off the coat and tie and feeling the wind in my face. The ceremony had been more of an ordeal than I had expected. As I stood at the graveside, the memory of the other funeral, the one with the two coffins, had come flashing back, with edges of the howling dream.

I would not put myself through that again. The next funeral I attended would be my own.

I could scarcely breathe.

I slowed to a stop and found myself on the main street of the Ape Yard. People were staring. All right! I told myself, what's the sense bringing up old trou-

317

bles. I deliberately waited until the pounding in my ears subsided, then, slinging my coat and tie over my back, I began slowly to stroll up the road toward Teague's store.

It was the Ape Yard, after all. It was Sunday. The weather was warm. Children ran by rolling hoops.

There was Tio—the store sneaked open on the Sabbath again.

Life!

"Ay, Lord!" I swung into the store.

"Well, would you ever looka yonder, Mr. Teague, it's one of our favorite customers! Yes, sir, sump'n we can help you with?" Good old Tio. He knew, of course, and had wanted to come, but he also knew it was better if he didn't. So he was ready with the next best thing.

"Give me a pound of cheese," I said.

"Pound of cheese for the man!" Tio cut it out of the hoop. "How about some nice goose eggs to go with it? We got fresh ones in today, but ain't nobody buyin' 'em. Probably have to mark 'em down."

Mr. Teague was giving him a hard look.

"No, we got plenty of eggs. Thought I'd get a couple of those fried pies and melt some cheese over them for dessert tonight."

"Peach or apple?" Tio asked, picking over the bakery rack. "Better take apple. Peach don't look too good."

"Apple's fine," I said.

"This one's mashed. Half price on this mashed pie, Mr. Teague?"

The old man looked over and nodded. "Half price —half price," and he went back to his paper.

"How many you say you wanted?"

"Two."

Tio mashed another one. "There you are. Anything else?"

"No, and don't bother to put them in a bag. I gotta run. Em'll be grumbling for his supper."

"Ain't no use to hurry on his account," Tio said, "he ain't home."

"How do you know?"

"I saw him a little while ago, headin' out toward Marble Park."

"Marble Park? Are you sure?"

" 'Course I'm sure. Had a cartload of ropes and things. Skeeter and Carlos was with him. I hollered at him but I guess he didn't hear me . . ."

I batted through the screen door and tore up the alley behind the store, scaring a drunk facing the wall who looked down at his pants and yelled something after me.

Marble Park was resting in its Sunday quiet, the lawns all tended and its residents on the golf course or at the lake. The hacking sounds reached me long before I climbed the upper street and came in sight of Jayell's yard. I ran into the yard holding my sides and stopped, trying to get my breath. Em looked around and saw me and grinned, and went back to swinging his ax.

"Em, have you lost your mind?"

"Boy, you're a born worrier, you know that?" He threw himself into his swing.

Overhead, from the top of the tree, a network of heavy ropes stretched away in all directions, to the trunks of neighboring trees, to the carport, the stone mailbox mount, a fire hydrant, a telephone pole across the street. The topmost rope ran through a block and tackle anchored to a magnolia in the Hendersons' yard, to Carlos, standing nearby. Another traveled through another pulley system and was held by Skeeter, who waved sheepishly from the upstairs bedroom window.

"Did you have to get them mixed up in it?"

"They wanted to come, and I needed the help," Em leaned on his ax and flipped a bead of sweat off his nose. "You know what time it is?"

"No. Em, they're gonna put us under the jail, you know that, don't you? We'll never see daylight again."

"Rest easy, Early boy, I know what I'm about."

"Where did you get all this gear?"

319

"I borried it."

"From where?"

"Where they're puttin' up the new water tower."

"We'll never see daylight again."

"I'll have it back before they know it's gone."

"Aw, Em, why didn't you stay home—I brought you cheese and everything."

"Born worrier," he said, shaking his head. "Now, stand back out of my swing." The hacking continued, Em throwing his whole body into it, thick slabs of wood flying steadily from the wedge-shaped wound in the tree.

Half an hour, an hour dragged by, and then I realized something funny was going on. For no good reason Em had stopped working. The tree was hardly more than notched when he ceased his energetic chopping and began puttering around, sizing up the tree, checking tension on the lines. Another half-hour went by. Skeeter sat in the upstairs window, his line dangling loosely in his hand. Carlos dawdled in the shadow of the magnolia.

Suddenly Em, standing at the edge of the yard smoking, making a lame pretense at surveying the job, threw down his cigarette and ran for his ax. Then I saw the Hendersons' station wagon pulling into the entrance to Marble Park. When they drove up with screeching brakes and slamming doors, Em was furiously hacking again.

Gwen was gasping with rage, "You have no right . . . who told you . . ." Jayell limped up, neighbors came running.

Em looked genuinely confused and disappointed. "I was going to surprise you," he said.

"Surprise us!" she shrieked. "You raving maniac! Of all the unmitigated . . . you!" She aimed a trembling finger at Skeeter. "You get out of my bedroom!"

"Now, just hold on," said Em, "ain't nothing to make a fuss about."

"Somebody do something!" cried Gwen. "Harold, your house is in jeopardy too!" Galvanized into action by her panic, Harold Henderson ran to one of the

320

guy ropes. Em latched a hand on his shoulder and tumbled him to the ground.

"Now, ever'body just hold on!" The people stopped and backed away. "Jayell, come over here!" Jayell obediently limped up to him, and Em looked down and spoke carefully, deliberately, in a voice low enough so that the others couldn't hear. "Phaedra Boggs's mama. She's dead."

Jayell looked up at him. He stood so for several moments, his eyes flickering as he studied the Indian's face.

"Now, I want you to listen to me. See up there"—he pointed to the top of the tree—"look there—and there, see what I done? Got sustainers there, there and there, and the topmost lines with the main tension is run through them block and tackles the boys are holdin'. They can lift an automobile apiece with them rigs. Now, look at the way she's notched, big broad notch, okay?

"So, if you keep your guy lines taut, and throw most of the pull to Skeeter, there ain't but one way she can fall"—he pointed his arm, palm-bladed—"shoop! Right between the carport and the road. But," he said, watching Jayell intently, "you'll want to be careful, 'cause if you let them guy lines there and there get slack on you, and Carlos lays back on his rope too hard . . ." he slowly swung his stiffened arm toward the house, "then you better get Skeeter out of there."

Em handed the ax to Jayell and walked to the edge of the yard.

Jayell said nothing. He stood squinting into the sun. Then he drifted along the yard, surveying the situation, calculating angles. He rubbed his hand over his mouth.

A breeze caught the top branches and the big tree groaned. A hush fell over the yard. "Tighten up there, Skeet," ordered Em, and in the upstairs window the boy set his foot against the sill and leaned. "Everybody clear out of here." The people didn't have to be told twice. They were all crossing the road into Judge Strickland's yard. All except Gwen, who stood in a kind of trance.

Jayell turned and looked at Jojohn, and in that brief, savage glance of joy there was for an instant the old, other Jayell—the idiot—looking out of his eyes.

I heard a loud crack and a man in a baseball cap ticked with fishhooks jerked off his sunglasses and pointed. "There's a crack starting, Jayell!"

Instantly Jayell was in charge. He ran to the window and shouted up at Skeeter. "Throw me down that line and get out of there." Skeeter hesitated and looked at Em. "Do what I tell you!" Skeeter tossed him the line and jumped to the stoop and dropped to the ground. "Em, untie the one on the mailbox."

"I wouldn't do that, Jayell."

"Don't argue with me; from now on this is mine, you hear me? Everybody, do exactly what I say!" Jayell picked up Skeeter's line and backed off with the heavy rope braced across his back. "Earl, untie the one on the hydrant, then Em, you break loose those other two." We jumped to obey his orders. I was certain then of what he was up to. Em was swaying, singing softly to himself.

"All right, Carlos, from now on it's going to be you and me. When I tell you, you turn loose and run like hell, you hear me?" Carlos nodded, blowing with the strain. "The one in the road now, Earl, hurry!"

I ran to the one anchored to the telephone pole and grappled with the knot; it was already drawing, spitting fibers. Suddenly it snapped and lashed across the yard, sending ropes whirling in the pulleys.

"Now, Carlos! Let her *g-o-o-o!*"

Carlos threw down his line and streaked for the road. Jayell lay down on his line, churning the ground with his heels.

A loud, steady popping filled the air. The gigantic tree listed, then stood motionless for a breath, defying gravity, as though held by ancient roots in the wind. Then with a shift on its severed trunk, a shudder that traveled up its branches like a wind of shock, the great oak twisted and began its slow, floating fall toward the earth.

Gwen's face was clouding, darkening to scream, when Jayell grabbed her arm and dragged her out of the yard.

The great trunk knifed through the roof and main bearing wall with an explosion of timbers, the upper floors gave way, adding to the distortion of weight, and the entire house crumbled inward with a convulsive spasm of heaving walls and splintering windows.

The neighborhood was deathly quiet. There was no movement but for the Indian turning slowly in the road, mumbling his rumbling chant.

"Uh-huh. Uh-huh. Uh-huh."

Jayell climbed up the sloping trunk and looked down into the devastated rooms, an insane smile jerking at the corners of his mouth. "Broke its back," he said, "just busted it all to hell." I edged up for a look. It was like something out of a nightmare. Parts of the roof still hanging sloped crazily inward, and shingles and bits of plaster littered the rug. The glass china cabinet was crushed flat, pictures and lamps lay on the floor, furniture and appliances stood out from the walls, overturned, smashed, covered with debris. Water spouted from the upstairs bathroom.

Jayell stood up and addressed the crowd. "Well, that's it folks. The show's over. I don't know what to tell you about the mortgage, Harry, you'll have to get with Charley of Insurance. Oh, and tell Christine we won't be over for bridge Tuesday. Wendell of Good Works, I'm afraid I'll have to withdraw from your Rabies Immunization Drive, and I will no longer canvass for the Community Chest. Eleanor and Harold, I hereby resign from the Marble Park Recreation Association; you can have the boat, the fishing gear, and anybody who can get to the closet can have the golf clubs. You can dig up those blue-ribbon roses and take 'em home if you like, your honor, they never grew worth a damn for me, even though I gave 'em

323

water purified through my very own kidneys. Em! You son of a bitch!"

He bounded down the tree. Em backed away, then broke and ran. Jayell chased him across the yard, lunged and tumbled him to the ground, Em uncertain at first, fighting him off. Then they were both laughing, pummeling each other, rolling in the road.

Eleanor Henderson led Gwen away. Someone was fanning a lady on the grass.

Jayell leaped on the bike and romped the starter. "Come on here, we got drinking to do!" Em grabbed his hat and tumbled in the cart and the two of them went careening over the hill and out the winding streets of Marble Park.

Gwen stayed with the Hendersons for two days, under the care of Dr. Breisner, and then packed a suitcase and left for Atlanta.

35

It was more than two weeks before Em and Jayell were heard from again. One Thursday, at suppertime, Em came wandering up the steps. Alone.

And to all questions about Jayell, or where they had been, he would only close one eye and answer, "Shhhhhhhh."

Phaedra Boggs must have been keeping a close watch on our place from her house, because Em was hardly in the door and scratching around for his supper before she came bounding in behind him.

"Where's Jayell?" she panted breathlessly.

Em casually rummaged in the ice bucket and filled his tea glass.

"Well—what did you do with him!"

"Done nothing with him," Em said. " 'Course, the blue boys up in Carolina, now they done sump'n with him." He made a to-do over selecting a piece of ice.

Phaedra snatched the glass from his hand and hurled it out the window. "I'm in no mood for you, Indian!"

"Ain't nothin' serious, fer God's sake! We was at a dance up in Greenville and he got in a scrape over some little tow-headed gal and they locked him up, that's all."

"And you just went off and left him?"

"Well, he hadn't no more use for me, had he? Wasn't no point in goin' to jail with him. So when the cops come, I climbed out of there. 'Sides, what are you pityin' him for? He's gettin' his three squares a day, and here I can't finish one meal without somebody throwin' my tea glass out the winder!"

"Three squares a—how long has he been locked up?"

"Oh, three, four days, I forget. I ain't been eatin' regular. South Carolina's hard on the stomach. What they need over there . . ."

"Why didn't you come and tell somebody!"

"Well, I hung around—tried to make bail—get the damages took keer of. But the bondsman couldn't get hold of his wife, and I couldn't make 'em understand about his house gettin' mashed, and him bein' a little tore up over that, and back and forth, and oh—it was a general mess. I'll tell you—till finally they just told me to be gone from there." Em shook his head sadly. "It's always like that with me. I just was tellin' the boy here . . ."

The screen door banged shut and Phaedra was squeaking the stairs.

"I tried to get him to bail hisself out," Em continued to me, "he had the money. But the truth is, old Jayell just didn't want to come home." He poked through the dirty dishes in the sink, looking for a glass. " 'Course, I figures if the right one was to go after him . . ." He cocked his head to listen as the bike cranked and roared out of the garage. "I swear boy, there ain't another clean glass on the place. If you ain't gonna wash dishes but oncet a week you can just get up here and rinse me out that mayonnaise jar!"

The next day Phaedra brought Jayell home, home being the abandoned shop on the edge of Twig Creek. Em had rousted the shop boys and we spent all morning cleaning it up. There wasn't much in the way of furnishings, but they didn't seem to care. If ever there were two people who didn't care about anything but each other, it was Phaedra and Jayell.

When Mr. Wyche of Smithbilt Homes learned of Jayell's return, he came down to the shop, and he and Jayell talked a long time. Jayell never moved from the steps, never raised his voice. And he let his former employer walk away with his golden future as though he might have been an itinerant pot salesman.

Mr. Burroughs and Mr. Rampey rattled into the yard and unloaded quilts and canned goods from the bus. "Since you're living in sin the ladies didn't feel it altogether proper to come themselves," Mr. Burroughs explained with a chuckle. "Talkin' about propriety—and them up there eatin' with niggers." Phaedra nearly fell off the steps.

"Which reminds me," Mr. Rampey said. "Farette's expectin' y'all for Sunday dinner."

Skeeter's mother brought down two dresses she had made for Phaedra, and the other shop boys' families contributed an assortment of kitchenware and whatever they could spare from their pantries. Those moving across the hollow dropped off odds and ends they said they couldn't use anymore. People stopped in every day to shake Jayell's hand, to leave a little something, or in one way or another make them feel welcome, and let Jayell know they were glad he was home.

Jayell and Phaedra rarely went out. Sometimes I would see them, returning from a late afternoon walk along the river, stopping to chat with an old man on a porch, and once at a fire in the yard at dusk frying cracklins and baking sweet potatoes Tio had brought, and calling in children from the street. Em and I stopped by from time to time, and one night the four of us piled in Jayell's truck with a crock of buttermilk

326

and a couple of shoeboxes of fresh fried doughnuts and went to a country music show at the fairgrounds.

But mostly we left them alone.

It was more than a month before Gwen returned. She had written several times, but I doubt that she ever received a reply. I was sling-blading the early crop of weeds off of the creek bank the afternoon her car screeched to a stop in front of the shop.

Phaedra met her at the door.

"He's not here," she said. "Why don't you just go away somewhere."

"So, this is his new arrangement! They told me Thoreau had returned to Walden, but it seems they left out something."

"Don't try to talk over my head, you overeducated, ill-tempered bitch. Just get the hell away from here."

Gwen folded her arms. "Oh, yes, I think I see it all quite clearly now. The realization is somewhat late in coming, but blinding in its clarity. Enter the little blonde gutter slut, Rebecca of the Ape Yard, and new light shines on our troubled hearth."

"Aw, flush it," said Phaedra. "If you had any real sense you wouldn't have to spout that bookish doubletalk all the time. But I'll tell you something we can both understand: you don't deserve Jayell Crooms and I'm taking him away from you. It's as simple as that."

"Oh, really? Can you be that sure of yourself—an ignorant, back-lot brat with nothing going for you but a good body?"

Phaedra put her hands on her hips. "A girl with a good body's always sure of herself. It's your big-brained broads with the butter-bean asses that's got to worry. Maybe that don't make book sense, but as you get old, you look around and see who's havin' the best time."

"I learned long ago not to try and argue with stupidity," said Gwen. She started to turn away, and Phaedra suddenly stepped out the door and grabbed her arm and spun her around.

"I hate your guts," she said evenly, "so I'm gonna tell you something. You didn't lose Jayell. You never had him. You're no different than those ladies who bring Christmas baskets to the Ape Yard so they can get a peek inside the shacks. Jayell was a novelty to you, a wild thing you had to prune, cultivate, put in a hothouse and make it grow your way. Well, Jayell Crooms sucks his beauty from want, from barrenness, from need. Ape Yard mud nourished him. Struggle makes him grow. You and Marble Park were smothering him."

Gwen looked at her. She started to say something, but couldn't—the thoughts changing. Perplexed, she drew herself up. "I've had about enough of this. Tell my husband that if he has anything further to say to me, I can be reached at my father's."

"I'll tell him nothing," said Phaedra. "You got anything to say to Jayell, write him a note. And you better be sure and sign it. Another night with me and he may not remember your name."

Gwen shouldered her bag and surveyed the scene around her, the girl, the weathered shop, the wind picking leaves in the yard. Squirrels darted among the creek trees, making question marks with their tails. She turned on her heel and walked back to the car. One of Quarrytown's better days, I told myself, watching her go.

36

THE STRAGGLING EXODUS CONTINUED FROM THE LITTLE tin-roofed houses on the sloping acreage surrounding Teague's store. Once, sometimes twice a week one of the poor black families could be seen loading their belongings into a pickup or one of the trucks from Bobo's mill and descending the winding dirt road to the raw, hastily constructed little shacks on the south side of the hollow, many of them merely shells, still unfinished on the inside when their occupants moved in.

"I don't like it," said Em, as we stopped to watch Speck Turner, the black plumber, loading his household goods into the back of his van. His girlfriend came down the steps lugging a trunk. "I don't like what's brewin' down there."

"From what I hear, them that's got to move don't like it much either," I said.

It was no secret that many of them, especially those who had spent years scraping money from their subsistence-level wages at Bobo's mill to pay off their little clapboard homes, were bitter about being moved to the baking, treeless red ridges of the opposite slope, to become renters again. Bobo was selling no more Ape Yard property. There were grumblings. But in the end they sold and moved. No one said no to Doc Bobo.

"What you movin' away for, Byrd?" Mr. Teague asked a retired mill foreman who had lived down the road from him for more than twenty years.

The elderly black man bit off a plug of Brown Mule and looked away. "Doc Bobo made me a good price." He hesitated. There was something else. Finally he fumbled out his stringy wallet. 'Better pay up my bill while I'm here."

"In the middle of the month? Hellfire, you ain't movin' out of the state, you know. Come on back over when you get your pension check."

The other man looked at the floor. "I don't 'spect I be comin' back," he said. "You unnerstan'."

Mr. Teague understood. And as the days went by, he became aware with growing alarm that it was to be the same with the others. Business slowed to a trickle.

There was one other white man with a vested interest, and that was Paulie Mangum, who lived in the decrepit mill shanty next door. And, of course, he was champing at the bit to sell. "Damnit all, Alvah, I got fifty by a hunerd foot on that rock. Wasn't worth a tinker's damn before, but you know what he's offered me for it?"

"Probably a lot more'n he's offered the others," said Mr. Teague.

"But he says it ain't worthwhile to buy ours unless you sell, too. Now, you know I can't pass up the chance to get out of here! Tell you what, you match his offer and I'll sell to you. Druther, in fact, than to that nigger."

"I wouldn't want your property even if I had the money, which I don't. And I sure couldn't match his offer 'cause bein' the only other white man, naturally you'd get a blowed-up figure to help put the pressure on me. So you make a few dollars on the sale—at the same time everybody else stands to lose—includin' me. Bring me one witness to say you're worth it, you drunken lint head, and I'll make the deal!"

"That's spite talk," said Paulie, " 'cause you and me's had words from time to time; I'm talkin' business here, Alvah."

"I'm talkin' business! My business! One I've spent fifty years buildin' up. The question is whether I'm to give up my business so another man can make a profit. His is big business, mine is small, does that mean I have less rights? The chains ain't done it, neither is Bobo and the tombstone people—nobody's going to eat me up!" Mr. Teague pulled a bill off the spike. "Now, unless you want to catch a little sump'n on your account, we got no further *business* to talk about."

One afternoon when Em and I arrived at the shop on a supper invitation from Phaedra, who had turned out to be a surprisingly good cook (by our standards anyway), we watched Jayell maneuver his truck past an overloaded jalopy on the Twig Creek bridge.

"Jesus," he said, alighting in the yard, "have you been up to see those rat traps they're moving into? The damn lumber's so green the studs are already warping! And you know what they're getting for

330

those things? Hear this now—a two-bedroom, unfinished on the inside . . ." Jayell stopped and swung around at the sound of a car turning off the main road and pulling up before the shop building.

Mr. J. J. Bearden of Bearden Real Estate smiled and bowed his way to the steps. "Lord, I never saw so much activity down here, thought I'd never get through that traffic. Evenin', Jayell, evenin'—evenin'."

"Well, goddam, J. J., what brings you to niggertown?"

"Oh, I'm telling you I've been so busy! Never been run so in my life. Textile people—been showing houses till my legs are run *off!* Two more mills opening up over in Lennox County, and we're just gettin' the spillover; they're goin' crazy over there! Twelve hundred new families in the next six months, can you believe that? You can get twenty thousand dollars for a chicken coop these days!"

"That's what I hear," said Jayell, his eye wandering along the distant ridge.

"Well, to business, to business. Oh! Good evenin', ma'am!" He whipped off his hat as Phaedra appeared in the door with a basket of wet clothes under her arm. She nodded and walked on by to the clothesline. "Well, Jayell, I—uh, thought this was your shop . . . uh, I didn't know you had this—well, what I mean . . ."

"J. J., what the hell's on your mind?"

Mr. Bearden popped a mint into his mouth and twitched his nose nervously. "Yes, ah, well the fact is, Jayell—I'm afraid you're going to have to move out of here."

"What?" Jayell jumped to his feet.

Mr. Bearden fumbled in his pocket for a paper. "No later than the first of the month. As you know, Harley Bobo wants to clear this side of the . . ."

"What the hell are you talking about? I rent this place from Luther Pierce!"

"That's right . . . until yesterday, but you see, Bobo bought the place from Luther yesterday."

"For Christ's sake! This is half a mile from where he wants to start that quarry!"

"I know, Jayell, but that's what he wants. Now look, this is a delicate situation, that's why he hired me to handle it instead of coming himself. Bobo doesn't want any trouble, no hard feelings, that's important—most important, he said. If a month wouldn't be enough time . . ."

"Bearden, what the hell's goin' on around here?"

The realtor crunched his mint. He stuck his hands in his pockets. He took them out again. "I don't know, Jayell, I just don't know. I'm not involved in it, understand, my agency's not, I mean; my fee just calls for me to clear this place, settle up with Mangum up here, and—uh"—his nervousness compounded as he swung a look at Em and me—"to—ah, order demolition on the Cahill house. You two will have to move out of that garage, of course; he wants that pulled down too."

I was thunderstruck. "But why? You told us . . ."

Mr. Bearden shrugged. "For some reason he wants all white people moved out of the hollow."

Now Em stood up, his head crowding under the eave. "Is that son of a bitch *calling me white!*"

"Oh, no! Not—it's just that, well, you're—not—black, I suppose . . . listen—" Mr. Bearden was backing toward his car. "I've got to be going. If you'd care to take it up with him, I'd say you have a point, a very good point, but . . . well"—he fumbled his key in the switch and cranked the car—"I'm sure I've done what's required on my part. White—black—I'm in the real estate business, for goodness' sake!" He curled his fingers at Phaedra and drove away.

Nobody spoke. The sun was sliding beyond the west rim of the hollow. A truck had blown a tire down on the road, and the black family was patiently pulling their shabby belongings off the rear. Traffic was backing up in the narrow dirt street.

37

THE BOARDERS SAT IN THE YELLOW LIGHT OF THE parlor lamps as Mr. Bearden talked, motionless, like waxen figures, staring at the floor.

Mr. Bearden took his hat from the hatrack. "You may have all the time you need and, of course, I stand ready to help with arrangements in any way I can. My card is on the mantel. Please do feel free to call."

Finally, after he had gone, Mrs. Metcalf sighed and leaned forward. "Well, that's it, then, isn't it? That's the end of the boardinghouse."

"By God," mumbled Mr. Burroughs, "throwed out of one house, now throwed out of the other."

Mrs. Cline was close to tears. "I ain't going to live with my daughter, that's all I can say."

"Well," snapped Mr. Jurgen, "it don't seem like you got much choice in the matter."

"I have too! I just won't go, that's all!"

Mrs. Porter's fingers trembled as she twisted her handkerchief. "The Lord will provide. If we'll only just put our trust in the Lord . . ."

"Well, He ain't done much providin' so far!" said Mr. Rampey.

"Lester Rampey, there's no call to blaspheme . . ."

"Now, let's don't start bickering!" cried Mr. Burroughs, "we'll be back in that quick enough!"

"Yes, please," said Mrs. Bell, "let's please not do that now . . ."

They fell silent again. I looked at Em, who sat straddling a chair in the corner, slowly twisting a beer in his hands. He blinked uncertainly at me for a moment, and looked away.

We sat in the yellow silence.

333

I don't know how long, maybe five minutes, perhaps ten—it could have been half an hour. But somewhere in the ringing silence another noise came intruding, the climbing road of a tattered muffler, intermingled with distant cries.

Lights flashed across the window shades, a door slammed, there were footsteps on the porch, and in a moment Jayell burst in from the hallway with Phaedra by the hand. He stood surveying the startled boarders, his eyes blazing.

"Get up from there, you damned old corncobs, we're gonna build us a house!"

They sat staring at him. Mr. Burroughs leaned forward on his cane, as if he hadn't heard right.

"Jayell," said Mrs. Porter, "what's come over you?"

Jayell pounced on her and dragged her out of her chair and whirled her around the room. "Good sense, finally, old sweetheart," he shouted. "Hoo-*hoooo!* If you were only a drinkin' woman . . ."

"He's drunk," sniffed Mrs. Cline. "Don't pay any attention to him."

"Miss Boggs," said Mrs. Metcalf, "what do you mean lettin' him . . ."

"Honey, he ain't had a drop," said Phaedra.

Jayell stopped and clapped his hands. "Listen to me, listen now. I got ten acres of Waugh land right over yonder on Wolf Mountain, and there's a mountain of salvage lumber in the weeds around my shop, enough to build three or four houses! Let 'em take this place, and the garage, and my shop. Let 'em take apart every piece, nail 'em end to end, and shove 'em up old Bobo's . . ."

"The Lord sakes!" Mrs. Porter cried. "You ain't serious."

"Boy, are you sure?" said Mr. Rampey excitedly. "Are you sure there's enough . . ."

Jayell whirled and grabbed Phaedra by the shoulders. "Gonna build this girl a castle, a thing that'll float in the air!"

Phaedra nodded, laughing her deep throaty laugh. "A castle out of scrap, Jack, a castle out of scrap."

Jayell turned to Em and me. "And even a loft for the rats!"

"Now, wait a minute," said Mr. Jurgen, squirming forward on the sofa, "you mean to tell us you can build houses, enough to hold this bunch out of nothing but the piles of scrap under them rotted tarpaulins down on the creek? I ain't no builder, and even I can see the foolishness of that."

Jayell stopped. The others turned to stare.

"You got plumbing fixtures, wiring, lighting fixtures? You got paint, you got trim work and hardware, you got window glass, you got masonry for the foundations? You got all that stuff down at your place? I mean, it's one thing to put up one of them little places on the hillsides and out in the woods for a family of three or four, but this is a pretty big crowd you got here. Now, I ain't the one to throw cold water, but I say we got to look careful at every aspect of this . . . 'cause you're a fine boy, Jayell, and I know you mean well, but as everybody here knows, you do tend to get carried away sometimes."

Jayell leaned over him. "Mr. Jurgen," he said softly, "you got a head on your shoulders."

Mr. Jurgen smiled.

"And it's pure *granite!*" shouted Jayell. "Do you think I don't know my business! Of course it's going to take money"—he pulled a piece of paper from his shirt pocket—"but with the materials I've already got, I figure I can do the whole job for less than six thousand dollars."

"Oh," Mr. Jurgen said laughing, bitterly triumphant, "is that all? Why don't you say six million!"

"Jayell, we haven't got that kind of money," said Mr. Rampey.

"Then you'll have to get it up."

"And how do you propose we do that?" said Mrs. Porter.

"It's simple, pool what you got and raise the rest among your children."

Mr. Rampey exhaled slowly. "If you think for one minute they'd give us . . ."

"Give, hell! I ain't talking about giving! I'm talking about a hard business transaction. I'm saying sell your obligations, and buy your freedom!" Jayell looked at the faces hardening around him, turning to disappointment. "Now, wait a minute," he said, "I know you're thinking this is just another lunatic notion, but don't shut me out, listen to me." He went to each of them, pleading, fighting for their attention.

"Look at it this way: say a young couple gets married. Mama and Papa want to be free of them, so they break their backs to set 'em up in their own house. They'll give their last dollar, strip their own house of furniture to do it. They want to be rid of 'em, but they feel guilty about it. All right, same with you. Your young'uns want to be rid of you, so they pay money to keep you here. But they treat you like dirt. Never come to visit, and when they do it's like pullin' teeth till they can get away again. Why? They feel guilty. Anybody who wants freedom feels guilty about it. Now, when they hear this place is closing, they're gonna flat-out panic. They're all worried about you becomin' a burden on 'em in one way or another. As long as they can call this a 'boardinghouse,' it ain't like Mama or Papa is in a nursing home. Now, they either got to put you away, which would make 'em feel guilty, or take you in. You got 'em between the guilt and the freedom. So, you make your move. You put a cash value on that guilt. Make a settlement and turn 'em loose."

"I don't understand it," said Mrs. Metcalf, shaking her head. "I don't understand it at all. But, say, even if they somehow gave us the money to build the house, or they agreed to make the payments for us, what would we live on?"

"Same as old folks always live on! Whatever they can scratch and scrape together. Pool your pensions, your social security, raise you a garden, make your quilts, babysit for people, cash in your burial insurance—what do you care for fancy funerals—it's the life you got left that counts! Die in starvation, maybe, but die independent. Else hush this chatter and go live

336

with your young'uns! Pack for the county home!"

Again the parlor was quiet.

Suddenly Mr. Burroughs was on his feet, choking with laughter. "By God!" he chortled, slapping his hands. "By the living God above!"

"It's crazy," said Mrs. Porter. "I never heard such a crazy thing."

"Crazy is he!" cried Mr. Burroughs, bolting for the hall telephone. "I'll show you how crazy he is when I get through to my loves!" He snatched up the receiver and his long, hammer-blunt fingers fumbled with the dial. "Oh, damn, the man that designed this thing was dreaming of virgins! Missus Bell, be so kind to come twist me out a number!"

Mr. Burroughs put through a call to his eldest son, shouted for a full five minutes, and slammed down the phone. "Hurry now, before they start calling back!" And the others began lining up. One by one they placed their calls, under Mr. Burroughs' prodding and coaxing, and then, with the nervousness of children having just played some monstrous prank, they skittered off to their rooms.

The next morning the boarders' children came off the surrounding hills like warrior ants. The parlor was swarming.

"Mama!" wept Alice Porter. "Have you taken leave of your senses?"

"I've talked to our lawyer," said Henry, the eldest Burroughs. "This time we're going through with it. I'm going to call the state hospital this morning."

"You're mighty right," said his wife, "we've ta'en just about all we can stand. They *all* ought to be declared, Henry."

"No use to just sit and look, Papa," said Marie Rampey, "we know you all got this thing cooked up among you, but you just might as well git it out of your heads right now. What would people say? We'd be the laughingstock!"

But most vociferous of all were the Bell offspring. Mrs. Bell sat clutching her chair arms as they circled, having turns sniping at her. Her son-in-law, Morris,

337

was a junior executive with a monument company. They had a new house in Marble Park with a monogrammed chimney. Matching convertibles. "We oughta left you on the damned farm where you belong," he said. "I told Eva you'd never be nothing but a problem if we brought you to town. Now, if you think I'm going to dish out money for some fool half-baked notion like this, you're crazy, woman!"

"You've paid to keep me here," said Mrs. Bell quietly. "And how much longer will it go on? I don't like being a burden."

"See," said her daughter, "see how she is? You are a burden, Mama, you've never been anything but a burden. Why can't you understand that?"

"She understands it," said Morris. "And you better understand this, woman, we've got a mortgage, we've got kids to school . . ."

"Oh, don't try to reason with her, Morris, she'll just sit there like she always does. I think she should have been in Milledgeville a long time ago. Mama, you've never been anything but an embarrassment to me, with Morris, with everybody. Do you know how hard it was for me to get away from that farm? Do you know what I'm talking about, Mama? Now, I don't deserve to be treated this way, and neither does Morris. We don't deserve this, Mama! *Do you hear me!*"

"*Hear you!*" There was a crash of the coal bucket spinning and Mr. Burroughs grabbed his cane and lurched into the middle of the floor, clutching his bowels and blowing with asthma. Towering over the startled woman, backing her away, he bellowed, "*Hear you?* You're deafening the Chinese! I've never *known* a human capable of such volume. You could shout down a thunderstorm! *Hear you!* Why, there ain't a fleck of paint on a house for miles! You've toppled a bridge somewhere! When you unpucker that volcano of a mouth you split the floors of heaven and ricochet angels off the walls! *Hear you, indeed!* I say bless the planet with a moment of *not* hearing you, and restore to us the whisper of hurricanes! Be still, woman—and *let the earth pass an audible quake!*" . .

338

When she recovered, the Bell daughter dissolved in sniffles and fled to the porch. Livid, Morris came forward to protest, and Mr. Burroughs aimed his nickel-mounted cane at his head. He missed but took down a lamp in the attempt.

Morris went to the porch to console his wife.

But Mr. Burroughs was not through. He rattled open the screen and charged again, and Morris took his wife on to the car. When he saw that the old man still had not given up, but was making heated progress past the flower bed, he cranked up and left. Mr. Burroughs followed them as far as his breath would take him, encouraging their departure with incoherent bellowings, flailing the trunk with his cane.

Presently he returned and burst into the parlor and circled the carpet, red-faced, white moustache working, looking for other takers. There seemed to be none. When his breath came again, he bawled with tremulous finality, *"We are your parents, by god—And we'll have a little respect!* Now, sit down! . . . We have a business proposition!"*

He took his time, carefully outlining the plan as Jayell had proposed it, and filling in the details worked out among the boarders the night before. He sold hard. "When you are young you are under your parents, then you are bound by your children, and when they are gone your parents come in on you again. God, oh, God, when do you ever get free? Well, we're offering you that freedom. We want to break that miserable cycle and take our chances. Is that not worth something? Hell, there's more money than we're asking in the various property you've stolen from us!"

"Well, I'm against it," said the eldest Burroughs son flatly.

Mr. Burroughs leaned over him. "Shut up, Henry! We ain't askin' for a goddamned vote! We're telling you what we're going to do!" Henry started to protest and his father silenced him again. "And don't threaten me with Milledgeville again. You haven't the guts to lock me away. Furthermore, if any of us gets

339

put away, you'll have to put us *all* away. That's our deal. Can you live with that guilt, my darlings?"

Alice Porter blew her nose. "It's like, like you're all going away somewhere to—to die."

"What have we been doing here?" snapped Mrs. Porter. "Quit pumping water, Alice, you'll be free to visit, but on our terms. No more of this family bickering and bossing around. You're going to treat us like people again! I feel good about it, better'n I've felt in a long time."

"All right," said Mr. Burroughs, "down to business. We've got six thousand dollars to raise. Now, Ruby and Farette have no families, so mine will assume their share, say, two thousand dollars for the three of us."

"What?" cried Henry, rising. "Where are we going to get two thousand . . ."

"From the sale of the homeplace you and my other heirs robbed me of," said Mr. Burroughs. "You never did cut the rightful owner in on the proceeds, if you'll remember."

"But, Papa, why should you have to foot the bill for these two?" Henry whined.

"It's my atonement," roared Mr. Burroughs, "for misbehaving in such a manner as to bring you peach-orchard boar-shoats into the world! Now shut up and sit down, Henry, or I'll pack and move in with you tomorrow! Would you like that better, Henry?"

Henry shut up and sat.

"All right, who's next?"

"Well," said Mrs. Cline's daughter, "I'd be glad enough to get Mama out of this hollow. If she wants to move up on the mountain where she'll be more comfortable, I suppose we could help out a little. Though, Lord knows, she's welcome to come and live with us . . ."

"For God's sake, woman, how much?"

"Four"—she glanced at her husband—"say five hundred dollars."

"Why it costs more than that to board her here a year, and you figure your mother to live longer than

340

that, don't you, darling? Remember now, this is a final payment. Make it eight hundred."

"But we don't have that much cash!"

"Then make arrangements with your bank. The Rampeys now, with the fine house in Marble Park."

Around the room the bargaining and pledging continued, the families figuring haltingly among themselves, branching off to other rooms for conferences.

"You're really going out on a limb, Papa," said Henry Burroughs.

"Why not," said the old man, rocking on his heels, "that's where the fruit is."

"You'll never make it work."

"We'll make it work. When one of us dies, we'll bring in some other old codger to take his place. We'll keep it going. That's the trouble with you young people, you got no faith in yourselves."

When the needed sum was met, Mrs. Bell voting a share for her absent daughter and son-in-law, Mr. Burroughs offered his arm to Mrs. Bell. "I believe, madam, it's time for breakfast."

And the other boarders, taking the cue, struggled to their feet and followed them into the hall, jaws set, rheumy eyes glistening, leaving those in the parlor to discover for themselves that they had been dismissed.

Later, when I went down to the garage, I found Em sitting on the comb of the roof, looking off toward the hollow. He sat with one foot drawn up, his head resting on his knee, turning a slice of lemon in his tea glass.

"Well, it's all settled," I said, climbing up beside him, "they got the money."

Em turned and looked at me for a moment.

"Boy," he said, "what you think about you and me just movin' on up the road."

Startled, I looked at him to see if he was serious. He watched me without expression. Dead serious.

"You and me?"

"You and me, just go on over the hill, see what the world's all about."

There it was. As simply as if he had asked me the time. The thing I had daydreamed about for so many years. And, although even as a child I knew I was not allowed to ask for it, I would gladly have given my soul for the offer, and followed him into the mouth of hell.

But now, almost as though it were another voice talking, I heard myself pulling back. "But—where would we go? What would we do?"

"Go any blame place we want to. Do whatever we like."

"Well—I don't know, Em . . ."

"What's the matter? I thought that's what you always wanted."

"Well, it is, or was . . . I just don't know. What about school?"

"School! Let me tell you sump'n, boy. When you're born, you're complete, and don't need nothin' else. After that, any changes you make in yourself you gotta strain and sacrifice. Little piece of you here in exchange for this, little piece there in exchange for that. Lose your sleep stuffin' your head full of books, lose your health makin' a dollar bill, till you end up wise and rich. Then what happens? You die in a pile of clutter, with your head full of clutter. Kinfolks you never liked end up with your possessions and the worms get your cultivated brains. The thing to do is hold down your wants. In tht long run it's less of a strain, and you get to keep more of what you started out with.

"Take me. I come from the largest tribe of Indians east of the Mississippi, and nobody knows their right name, even them. They was speakin' English when the first white man found 'em. They was livin' in houses, hadn't no language of their own, no religion, some had curly hair, some blue eyes. Belonged to no known tribe. They figured we must be Indians, but nobody knowed for sure. So we been called Croatans, the Indians of Robeson County, Cherokee Indians of

Robeson County, and now they call us Lumbees. I never knowed who or what I was for sure. But down home they knowed what we was. We was trash. Nothin'.

"So I said, all right, I ain't Indian, I ain't white, I ain't black. I'll just be Em Jojohn. And I'll be free.

"And so can you be, boy. What's to keep you? You got no family to speak of. There ain't nothin' to hold you in this town. Get out there and get a good grip on yourself before they start moldin' you and shapin' you into what *they* want you to be. You got the rest of your life to go to school. In a couple of years, you get tired of travelin' and you want to go to school, you stop and go to school."

I shook my head. "I don't know, Em. I'll just have to think about it."

He studied me for a moment longer, then, throwing his leg over the comb of the roof, he slid down to the top of the shed, where he turned for a final glance toward the hollow. "You think about it," he called back up to me, and stepped in through the window.

38

THE NEXT MORNING BEFORE LIGHT, EM AND I WERE startled awake by a horrendous ruckus on the stairs. It was Burroughs, Rampey and Jurgen, all decked out in their work clothes, beating on the steps and shouting for us to get a move-on.

"Will you sleep till they pull the place down around you?" hollered Mr. Burroughs.

"Farette's holdin' breakfast, boys," said Mr. Rampey.

After we were stuffed with sausage, grits and eggs until we could hardly walk, we were herded into the bus with the other boarders, and enough box lunches to feed a regiment, and carted off to Jayell's.

Jayell had already recruited his shop boys and was lunging among the piles of salvage lumber that stood in large mounds in the weeds around the shop. He poked through the stacks throwing back tarpaulins, pointing out the materials to be refinished; two-by's, four-by's, oaken beams salvaged from the Mayhorn plantation that burned; pile upon pile of old bits and pieces of churches, country stores, sheds, barns, and houses that had been collected over the years were now passed into the shop by his hustling workers to have nails pulled out, split ends cut off, rough edges planed to the seasoned heart.

The building site Jayell had chosen was a clearing among the oaks and maples on the lower edge of the land deeded to him by Lilly Waugh, just above the rim of the lower end of the Ape Yard where the hogback hills started the steeper incline up Wolf Mountain. The view faced east, away from town, with the Ape Yard on the left, and an access road that was once a pulpwood trail leading up from the Atlanta highway just south of the Little Iron River bridge.

We fell to digging the foundations along Jayell's string markers with picks and shovels, since we had no heavy equipment, and in the rocky hillside it was hard going. From first sweat, which came before the sun was full up, I saw that it was going to be no picnic. In addition to Jayell, we now had the boarders to contend with: Burroughs, Rampey, Jurgen and Woodall flailing wildly with picks and shovels, exhorting everyone to greater efforts, with the women bothering us on every turn with ice water. I was certain we would lose at least three to strokes before noon.

But at sundown they were still hard at it, and when Jayell finally called a halt and the haggard shop boys had drifted away, the boarders had to make a final check for tools left behind; they wanted to know from Jayell how the work had gone that day and what were the plans for tomorrow. And when they finally did pull themselves aboard the bus for the trip home, and lowered themselves stiffly into the seats with fatigue etched deep in their faces, they kept up a running banter with each other and us to cover it.

"I've never done manual labor before," said Mr. Jurgen, who sat primly holding a half jar of ice water between his hands. "I liked it." He turned to Mrs. Bell at the window seat. "It's good being outside, isn't it?"

"And you did well, too," she said.

"I thought I did," he nodded. "I thought I did right well. My father would have been proud of me today." The other voices on the bus gradually died and heads turned as the usually reticent Mr. Jurgen, his eyes fixed on the Ape Yard houses rolling by, babbled on about his past, about his years as a bookkeeper for the Blue Light quarries and how he had risen to the position of office manager with only a high-school education, and how he had hated the work. "I had wanted to work in a dress shop, is what I wanted, but my father would have none of that. He said it wasn't a fit occupation for a man. He was a very strict man, my father, but a wonderful man. A stonecutter. I made a dress for my sister once, and oh, did he hit the ceiling! I always had a flair for women's clothes—I'll bet I could have designed them if I could have got the education." Oblivious to the listening, swaying faces, Mr. Jurgen chatted on, about his life as a boy and how proud his father would have been if he could have seen him with that pick on the mountain today, tiny droplets of translucent, congealing blood inching through the sweat on the side of the cold glass of the ice-water jar he gripped between his hands.

The next morning we hit it early again, and every day thereafter. We got the foundation dug, the floorings down, and soon walls started going up, but the two houses, the larger of which was to be for the boarders with rooms for Em and me on the second floor, were still, to me at least, assuming no recognizable shape. Jayell was framing off into new directions, new dimensions, until even Carlos, the most experienced of the shop boys, was frowning at the plans and shaking his head.

"Never mind," said Jayell, "never mind. Come help me here." And he would put Carlos's hands to some task and rush off to confuse someone else.

"Look at him," said Phaedra, "look at the little rascal go."

After a couple of weeks the construction crew acquired a new member.

"Sure I can use you, Tio," said Jayell, "if you don't mind working cheap. But you sure Mr. Teague can spare you from the store?"

"Ain't nothin' goin' on down there," Tio said. "Ain't nobody but a few old ones left, and them's too sick to get out. Got to do sump'n. We ain't hardly breakin' even."

"Well, you know I can't pay much."

"Anything'll help out. We're scratchin' every nickel we can get. We spent everything we had on the store, and there's bills comin' due."

As activity picked up around the shop and at the site on Wolf Mountain, more boys came to hang around and watch, and, when no one was looking, to take a hand. Carlos had to retrieve his rule from one of them three times in the space of an hour. Mr. Burroughs suffered under the unflinching gaze of another, a solemn-faced twelve-year-old in ragged overalls, until he whacked his finger and turned on the youth with a tirade that almost blasted the boy off the mountain.

Down in the shop Skeeter was complaining of similar problems, he couldn't even get to the lathe, he said; turn around and a stranger was sanding your cabinet door, another was heating glue, and there were two with a basket that tried to catch shavings before they hit the floor, where a third with the broom might get at them.

"All right," said Jayell, when he'd had enough, "if you're going to help, get in here and let's do it right." He organized a crew of the older boys to work with Carlos on the mountain, and another couple of dozen

346

under the supervision of Skeeter and Jackie James in the shop, and appointed the smaller ones independent water contractors. At one point I counted twenty-seven water boys running the routes between the nearest Ape Yard wells and the crews at the shop and on the mountain, which released the women to fix lunches and sell quilts. An unexpected dividend came when an old contractor friend of Jayell's, Werb O'Connell, who did a profitable business in the county despite Smithbilt's competition, dropped by and offered to subcontract his cabinet work to Jayell. "Hell, yes, we can handle it, Werb," Jayell said eagerly, and revamped the shop to accommodate it. By that time the shop force was thinned down to a dozen regulars, hard-working boys who showed real ability, and soon another informal class was in operation: "Don't fight the wood, work with it! Wood butchers . . . you're nothing but a bunch of damned wood butchers!"

One afternoon in a secluded place in the road a black man, strange, yet somehow familiar, waved down the truck. We were alongside him before even Jayell recognized Willie Daniels. The figure slouched in the faded overalls, the thin features under the leather cap had aged far beyond the three years he had been gone.

"Hello, Willie," said Jayell. "Heard you were out, and wondered why you hadn't been around."

Willie tucked his hands behind his bib. He had always been uncomfortable with white people, even Jayell. Jayell let the truck idle.

Two of the original members of Jayell's old shop crew were Willie and Boyce Daniels. They were the kind of twins who were always seen together, each reflecting the other's low-key personality, always smiling shyly somewhere in the background. Both were quiet, polite boys who had never been in any kind of trouble, both honor students at Pelham Grace School. But when the hot-car ring was broken in 1951 and the garage on the river raided, Willie and Boyce were among those named in the indictments. Some said they had incurred Doc Bobo's wrath. Others said they had simply been traded for two who had incurred his favor. Willie had just been paroled on good behavior. Boyce had been killed in prison.

"They say you buildin' ag'in." Willie's gaze was fixed somewhere over the hood of the truck.

"Well, I'm building myself a house, doing a little cabinet work. I can always use another good hand."

Willie nodded. His mouth tightened. He had the same shy manner as before he went to prison, but now there was a dark, disturbed look in his eye. He seemed aware of it, and kept his eyes averted. "You spoze you could help me get a place for Mama? You know, her house is on that lan'."

"I know," Jayell said.

"She got to get off."

Willie's mother was a tall, handsome woman with light brown skin. When her boys were sent to prison, one of the dog boys, "So-So" Clark, moved into the house. So-So was one of Bobo's most trusted lieutenants, whose chief responsibility was control of the gambling on the dog fights, sports, and any other book that was in the Ape Yard. In general, the dog boys had the run of the hollow, taking what they wanted without pay and living where, and with whom, they chose. And to those who pleased them, they were able to extend a certain generosity: clothes, jewelry, a car, or even a little three-room house. Before he died that spring, So-So Clark had arranged cancellation of the mortgage Doc Bobo held on Willie's mother's house.

"Well, damn, that's tough, Willie. But look, those prefabs are not all that bad. Tell you what, when she gets moved in I'll come over and help you finish it out for her, okay?"

Willie looked up, the anger, the bitterness full in his face now. "They give her nothing for it. Just say she got to get out. She signed it over this morning."

Jayell's hands twisted on the wheel. He lit a cigarette with shaking fingers. "I'm sorry, Willie," he said, "I wish I could help you, but I got all I can handle right now. I've got to get my house built. Let me do some

thinking. If I come up with anything I'll let you know."
And he put the truck in gear and drove off, leaving
Willie standing in the road.

We had gone less than a hundred yards when his
foot suddenly stomped the brake so hard Skeeter came
over on top of Phaedra and me.

"For Christ's sake!" he yelled. "I've got ten acres of
land and enough lumber to build three houses! Willie!
Hey, Willie, come on up here!" He slumped back in
the seat shaking his head. "What the hell's wrong with
me?"

Phaedra smiled. "Not a thing, Jack," she said. "Not
a thing in this world."

39

THE DAY WORK BEGAN ON THE DANIELS HOUSE, A LIT-
tle farther up the slope to the right of the other two,
more onlookers drifted up from the Ape Yard. Neighbors came to watch, to roam through the curious
structures and tease Willie Daniels and his mother
about the prospects of living in such a bizarre house.

"Where's the door, Sarah?" one asked Willie's mother. "This it here?"

"Mist' Jayell don't build no doors," said another,
"you got to climb in and out the winders."

"One thing sho', nobody gon' break in on you, Sarah,
less'n they come down the chimbley."

A stocking-capped woman clapped her hands. "Hit
ain't got no chimbley neither!"

Children climbed through the bright colors and
strange geometric shapes, uncertain at first, as though
finding themselves in some fantastic world of adult
play-houses, disturbed, as children are when adults
do outrageous, childlike things. It was a storybook
world that had no relation to the drab, gray existence

of the hollow. But in that environment, spurred by the excitement of the boarders and the bustling energy of the shop boys, old crusts of behavior began to fall away, for both the children and the adults. They began to relax and enjoy it too. They wandered about, touching, marveling, laughing at the antics of Jayell as he sprang from house to house, trying to be everywhere at once, absorbed in one of his all-consuming fevers of creation. They drifted down the mountain and brought back other folks to watch, and at sundown men just getting off work came to see. They were still coming in ones and twos when we finally knocked off for the day.

That night Em Jojohn was even more worried. He didn't like the idea of building the Daniels house. "There's a pot boilin' down there," he said, pointing to the hollow, "and now we done stuck our hand in it." Again he talked about leaving. He got out his canvas traveling bag.

"Em, you're talkin' foolishness! Here things are just startin' to look up for us, and you're wantin' to run off and leave it. That house is going to belong to us just as much as it is the boarders, can't you understand that? For the first time we won't be living off somebody else, we'll have our own place!"

"Well, damn, you sound like you're gettin' ready to retire! I don't know what . . . there's the old folks up there jumpin' aroun' like kids, and you're talkin' like an old man. The whole damn place is goin' crazy!"

And he grew increasingly uneasy during the next two days as more and more people climbed the hogback hills, and the carnival atmosphere increased. He worked methodically, saying little to anyone, snapped back at Jayell's orders and cursed the visitors in his way, and he became even surlier at night. On Friday morning he was reluctant to leave the loft. He fidgeted. He stalled. He didn't feel well. The damned mountain rocks had scratched up his boots. He couldn't find his sock. He fooled around until we missed the boarders' bus, and breakfast, and then yelled, "Well, go on, if you're in such a damned hurry, I'll come on

350

later!" I ran down to the shop and caught Jayell as he was finishing up his instructions to Skeeter and Jackie and the boys there, and rode with him and Phaedra to the job.

When we drove up to the jobsite Jayell took one look and said, "Holy Christ!"

The place was jammed with people. More than a hundred of them stood in the trees. When Jayell stopped, Speck Turner came through the crowd. "Mornin', Jayell."

"Speck, what the hell's goin' on here?"

"Sure some purty houses you got here," the plumber said with a grin.

"Yeah, yeah, what's this all about?"

"Well, we come to talk a little bi'ness. See, me and Loomis and Simon there all gettin' put off in them little shell things up the hollow, and—well, we figured maybe we could work a little deal and get you to build us houses up here like you doin' for Willie."

"Yeah?" Jayell turned to look at Carlos, thinking about it.

"Myself, I could take on the plumbin', see, and we all got the money Bobo give us for our places—I don't know how you pricin' now, or what you want for the lots . . ."

"How many?" said Jayell, trying to figure. "What's all these others here for?"

"They just come to help," said Carlos.

"To help?" said Jayell. "I can't afford a damn army!"

"Said you ain't got to pay 'em nothin'," Carlos added, "ain't nothin' much goin' on at the corner these days." Carlos stepped closer. "Most of these folks from down Fletcher Bottom. They gon' get moved out when the dam gets built."

Jayell looked around at the Ape Yard's most wretched, the ragged day laborers standing in their torn and faded shirts, beltless trousers and flopping brogans.

"Do they know anything about building?"

"No, but they'll do what you tell 'em." Jayell hesi-

351

tated, and Carlos continued. "They wants to help, Jayell, and they ain't got nothin' else to do."

"Well . . ."

"Just one more thing," said Carlos, "like I say, a lot of 'em gon' get washed out when the river rises. If you got enough scrap to put up a couple more little houses . . ."

Jayell stood looking at him. He ran his eyes along the rows of black faces that surrounded him, then turned and looked at Phaedra, still sitting in the truck. She merely returned his gaze, a smile playing at her mouth. Jayell wiped his face. He turned and surveyed his acreage, looking from marker to marker, and up the rocky terrain that climbed sharply from the rear of the three houses already begun.

He opened his mouth to speak to Carlos, and stopped. The crowd was murmuring, shifting.

Then we saw it too. The green car nosing through the trees. In the hush it purred softly along the rows of people, who quickly opened a path before it and watched its glistening body glide past, their faces fixed in the fear and reverence of a pagan people observing the passage of an idol god.

The car moved up to the grassy mound where Jayell stood, and Doc Bobo got out and stood smiling.

"Well, it seems that what I've been hearing was not just idle rumor." He saw Phaedra and immediately took off his hat. "Good morning, ma'am, good morning."

"What do you want, Bobo?" snapped Jayell.

"Why, I just heard that you were building again, Mr. Crooms, and, like these people"—he turned and looked at the faces around him, faces averted now, staring at the ground—"I just *had* to come and see! And they are something, aren't they? Oh, Mr. Crooms, I believe you've outdone yourself this time. Let me see, now, that large one would be for these nice folks from the Cahill place." He turned quickly to the boarders, who stood nearby. "I do hope this regrettable move has not been too disruptive. Mr. Bearden has promised me that he is making every effort to see that you are inconvenienced as little as possible. Now, that one, Mr. Crooms, ah—that house could be for no one but you yourself." He shook his head admiringly. "Indeed, you are a man of unique talents. But that third one, now, who could that one be for?"

There was a pause. Doc Bobo turned around and looked directly at Willie Daniels.

He repeated, pointedly, more in the tone of a command, *"Who is that one for?"*

Willie Daniels licked his lips nervously. He glanced at Jayell. Finally he said softly, "It's mine."

"What's that, Willie?"

The boy cleared his throat. "It's for Mama—and me."

"But Willie, we're going to build you and your mama a house, a pretty house, right up the hollow. You don't need two houses, do you, Willie?"

The young man stood watching the undertaker, his head tilted back, nostrils flaring softly with his breathing.

"Do you, Willie?"

Willie lowered his head. "Naw, suh."

"Of course not." Doc Bobo smiled. He turned to Speck Turner, Simon Jesup and Loomis Freeman. "Anybody else thinking about moving up here with these white folks?"

Wordlessly, the plumber and his friends dropped down into the road and walked away.

"Speck!" Jayell called.

"Anybody else got business on this mountain?"

The people were turning, drifting down the rocky slopes.

Doc Bobo turned to Carlos and the shop boys. "Anybody else?"

And even they, one by one, were laying down their tools, pulling off their nail aprons, climbing down the ladders.

"Oh, Christ," muttered Jayell, watching them. He walked down to the truck and put a hand on one hip and leaned on the fender. Phaedra got out and stood

353

beside him, trembling in anger, glaring at Carlos as he moved by them, his head lowered.

"Go ahead, run, you gutless sons of bitches!"

I felt my heart stop.

It was Tio, standing on the knoll before the Daniels house. He cupped a hand to his mouth. "You heard the man, crawl back in that hole like a bunch of rats! Desert Jayell like you done Mr. Teague. Go on, git in them shacks till the big man comes for some more of your blood!"

Most everyone, including Doc Bobo, was in a state of shock. People had stopped and stood staring, as though having difficulty believing what they had heard.

Doc Bobo stepped up to the boy, who stood defiantly, his chin jutted out. "Why ain't you at the store where you belong?" he said.

"Because there ain't nothin' to do at the store, thanks to you!"

Doc Bobo turned and signaled with his finger. The car door opened and Clyde Fay slid out.

"Why you god—" Jayell's move was cut short by Carlos, who grabbed him and pinned him against the truck. "No, Jayell, please," he said, terrified.

The people fell back as Fay came quickly up the slope, stepping gracefully, almost delicately over the dew-soaked grass, wrapping his wide belt around one hand.

Tio stood where he was, watching him come.

"Stop him!" I screamed. Doc Bobo, who stood only a few yards away, turned around. "Stop him!" And then with the weight in my shaking hand, I remembered I was holding a hammer, and while the undertaker stood looking at me, annoyed at the outburst, I slung the hammer into his face.

He lurched away, grabbing at his nose, and in the next instant I was swatted to the ground like a fly. An iron hand closed on my arm and I was jerked up again so hard my feet cleared the ground. I bumped into somebody who was yelling, and through the soft, cottony throbbings I became aware that Fay was holding both me and Tio.

"Put 'em down!"

The voice was a roll of thunder. Tio stopped struggling, Fay stood watching, alert, heads were turning around to Em Jojohn, who was coming around the corner of the Daniels house. He shuffled heavily down the yard and confronted Doc Bobo and Fay.

"Let 'em go."

"You stay out of this, Jojohn," said Doc Bobo, clutching a handkerchief to his bleeding nose.

"I'll get out of it when you turn loose them boys."

"I have no quarrel with you," said Doc Bobo.

"I got one with you," said Jojohn. "I pulled six months at your sawmill. Your man bought me for fifty cents a day. I've let it go till now, but you move ag'in them boys and I'm gonna start collectin' back wages."

"I got one too!" roared a voice from the rear, and Horace Burroughs was stiffly negotiating the slope. "Count me in there," said Mr. Rampey, hefting a rock, and Jurgen and Woodall were pushing their way through the crowd. Jayell's fist landed beside Carlos' head, staggering him, and he leaped away. Phaedra sprang over the side of the truck.

"Hold on—no!" cried Doc Bobo. He shook Fay's arm to turn us loose and shouldered the giant away. He backed off from the approaching white people. It was obvious this new development had taken him by surprise, and this confrontation was not what he wanted. "Get in the car, Fay, get in the car. Please," he said, holding up his hands, "please, I want no trouble."

The others followed them to the edge of the yard and stopped as he and Fay got in the limousine. "I want no trouble," Doc Bobo repeated anxiously, and slammed the door. Clyde Fay cranked the engine and the people in the trees watched in a trance as the car circled the lumber piles and drove away down the mountain.

Jayell stepped down to Carlos. He was sweating, his eyes wild. "Go get every piece of lumber at the shop, all of it, every scrap you can find!" We need salvage crews!" he shouted at the crowd. "Anybody that's got a vehicle, scour the Ape Yard, spread out around town, along the river, anybody that's got a piece of board he'll part with, an outhouse he ain't using, any piece of lumber you can find along the road, bring it up here! Tio, get in my truck and go find Mr. I. V. Tagg and tell him to come up here, we got a lot of figuring to do." He raised his voice again to the crowd. "I don't know how many we'll be able to build, but we'll do what we can. Come on, fall in here!"

40

THE NEXT MORNING EM REFUSED TO BUDGE FROM the loft. "Stay away from there, boy! We're through with that place, you hear me!"

"Speak for yourself," I said, pulling on my clothes.

"We done crossed Bobo now, can't you get that through your head? We crossed Bobo!"

"And he backed down, didn't he?" I said, feeling extra good about having busted him one.

"He backed down 'cause he's too smart to tangle with white people! But that jus' means he'll start workin' *through* white people to get what he wants. You don't know the power that man's got!"

I stomped into my shoes and headed for the door. Em grabbed me and spun me around. "Is the damned place worth gettin' killed for?"

"Em, all I know is there's sump'n fine happenin' on that mountain. Jayell feels it, the boarders feel it—the whole Ape Yard is alive with it now. And I'm part of it. I'm helping to make it happen! I got a place there. For the first time I got a place! And there ain't no-body, Doc Bobo nor anybody else, goin' to take it away from me. Tio had the guts to stand up to him; he sure ain't throwin' a scare into me!"

"You ain't got a place, boy—come back here—you

356

ain't got a place," he shouted after me, but I was already taking the steps, "any more than me!"

When I got down to the shop I saw that part of what Em had predicted was already happening. The sheriff's car was there, and a truck from the city electric company. The man had disconnected power from the shop. Jayell was arguing violently with the sheriff.

"Jayell, you might as well calm down," Sheriff Carter Middleton was saying. "Doc Bobo owns the place, and he wants the power off, and you out of here—today. What can I say?"

"You can say you're the spineless son of a bitch *I've* always said you were!"

"Jayell . . ."

"I'll build 'em," Jayell shouted, "without power tools! With hand tools—with my goddamned *pocket-knife*—I'm gonna build them houses!"

Sheriff Middleton sighed. He took off his hat and mopped away sweat that came early in the baking slopes of the hollow. "Jayell, I've known you all your life. I knowed your daddy. Hell, how many times have I carried him home when he was drunk to keep from lockin' him up—used to stand there while your mama cried and prayed over him, and helped her put him to bed. You remember that, don't you? Who was it got you off the time you busted in the furniture store, all set to whip Bud Calloway's ass for sayin' sump'n nasty to your mama for bein' behind on her account? I ain't your enemy, Jayell. But you got to understand, we got a touchy situation here. This centennial thing's comin' to a head pretty soon. We're gonna have the big boys here, from Atlanta, from Washington, and everybody's real anxious that everything goes right. I got my orders, loud and clear. We're gonna show 'em a model community. Now, there's folks worried about what's goin' on down here. Old man Teague's bucked up over sellin' that little scrap of land so Bobo can start him a quarry, which the granite people had planned to make a big whoopde-do over, and right in the middle of uneasiness over the school thing, you're gettin' the niggers stirred

357

up down here and movin' 'em out of the hollow. Now, I'd like to know just what the hell you're doin' up on that mountain."

"I'll tell you what I'm doin', Carter, I'm buildin' houses. That's all I'm doin'. Buildin' houses, for me, and as many people as I can move out of this stinkin' hollow."

"You're gonna live up there, with the niggers?"

"I've lived down here with 'em all my life, ain't I! But that was all right wasn't it, as long as we stayed in niggertown, and under Bobo's heel. Well, I got news for you and the city fathers, Carter, me and the niggers are movin' out of niggertown! I'm gonna cover that hillside with houses—Jayell Crooms crazy houses, good, solid little houses that even black people can afford. Gonna make it a showplace of Crooms originals. And when the people passin' that highway see what can be done with scraps and a little imagination, I'm gonna run thieves like Smithbilt out of business! And when those birds from Washington come to talk about building a project for those people gettin' washed out by the dam, I'm gonna show 'em sump'n, I'm gonna have a bunch of 'em already in their own houses, not a damned project, and not at the taxpayers' expense!"

"Christ, Jayell!" said the sheriff. "You really are gonna stir up a hornet's nest. Man, if you go messin' with that deal there *is* gonna be hell to pay!"

"They want a model community," said Jayell, "well, we're gonna show 'em the model community of all time. A community of young, old, black, white and even red if I can get Jojohn to move in. A place for all races, all ages, put together with scraps and sweat and ignorance and hope. A dream village, Carter, think about it!"

The sheriff thought about it. He puffed his cheeks and blew and shook his head. "Jayell, you're a born fool, there's no doubt about it. It's hard to fault you, 'cause I know you mean well, but boy, you're sure headed for trouble. You've always been a wild hair, and folks have put up with that, but they ain't gonna put up with this. There's too much at stake."

Jayell stared at him intently, his fierce blue eyes fixed on the sheriff's face. "You going to close me down, Carter? You going to come in with some kind of injunction and stop me?"

"No, I ain't going to touch you, Jayell, and I'll stand on that. Legally, you're all right. But you know and I know there's other ways, and Bobo knows 'em all, and I warn you, there ain't nobody going to stop him. He's got his own cutthroats, and there's a lot of white people on edge about niggers doin' anything peculiar just now, and he's got influence with them, too. He kept a Klan from startin' up out at Flat Creek, did you know that? He's a devious son of a bitch, and he's smart, and he stands to lose a lot here, and if you cause the boys uptown embarrassment while this centennial thing's goin' on, and keep 'em from settin' Bobo up as their number-one shine boy, they're liable to turn him loose on you." The sheriff got in his car and closed the door. "If that happens, Jayell, you're on your own. My hands are tied. I want you to know that."

"I'll be ready," said Jayell, "and thanks."

"For what?" muttered Phaedra, as the sheriff drove away. "The spineless son of a bitch."

"Aw, honey, Carter's just performing a sheriff's number-one duty—gettin' reelected. Come on, we gotta get moved. We can put up with a couple of rooms until the rest of the house is finished. Skeeter, Jackie, tell the boys to start loadin' the power tools in the truck."

"The tools first, naturally," said Phaedra.

At first only the shop boys and the boarders reappeared at Wolf Mountain. Frightened by the run-in with Bobo, the others, like Em, stayed away. "They'll come around," Jayell said, and went on with the construction as though nothing had happened. After a couple of days without incident, spirits picked up again. Jayell and Phaedra moved into the two enclosed rooms of the strange creation he was building for them, he continued work on the Daniels house, and the boarders began to speculate what final shape their house would take.

On the third day Willie Daniels showed up. He stood silent, watching. "Willie, give Carlos a hand sawing those joists," Jayell said, and kept walking. Willie looked after him, Jayell turned around, walking backward. "And if you lay out drunk again, I'll fire you." Willie grinned, he tugged at his cap and went to work.

Gradually a trickle of onlookers returned. Mostly children at first, then a few mothers who came to get them, and stayed for a few minutes to watch. At the end of the day a worker or two from the mill would come and stand at the edge of the slope and discuss the job among themselves, then drift away to supper. Whenever we had to go down into the hollow, people would turn from their clotheslines, they would stop talking in the picket-fenced yards and watch us pass. They waited. Business went on as usual at the other stores on the Ape Yard main street, but no one came to Teague's grocery. They watched the activity going on at Wolf Mountain, and at Mr. Teague brushing the steps in front of his store, and waited for Doc Bobo's next move.

They didn't have long to wait. The following Monday morning, a beginning workday, there was a disturbance at the edge of the jobsite. Jackie James threw down his board and ran for Jayell. The shop boys were crowding on the other side of the fire where they were boiling coffee, pointing toward an apparition standing in the woods.

"Who is it?" demanded Jayell. "Who's there?"

The tall figure strode down through the tree trunks, dark and dripping from the rain. Lilly Waugh walked straight to the fire and leveled her pistol in Jayell's face.

"Get these niggers off my property!"

"This is not your property, Miss Lilly. We made a trade, remember?"

"I never bargained for niggers on my land!"

"It's my land they're on, and who I bring on my land is my business. There's a mile of woods between here and your house; you won't even know we're here. And I give you my solemn word, nobody will set foot on your property."

She whirled on the shop boys. "Off! Get off or I'll kill ever' one of you." She waved the pistol menacingly and the boys broke and scattered, running for the trees. She stopped beside Tio. "What are you waitin' for, boy?"

"I got hired to do a job, and ain't nobody runnin' me off but the man that hired me."

"Is that so?" she cried, backing away. "Is that so?" She aimed the pistol at him, but Tio didn't budge. Seeing that he would not be frightened, she suddenly turned and pointed the pistol at Jayell. "Then tell him, mister. Two seconds, I'll give you, and then so help me I'll blow your head off!"

His jaw set, Jayell walked around the fire. They stood facing each other, the county's notorious wild ones, staring each other down. "Lilly, you ain't crazy, you're just a scared old woman. But you've been playing that crazy act too long. Now folks believe it. Now, if you was considered sane and shot me, you might be out of jail in a year—Judge Strickland might even shake your hand and call it self-defense. But they couldn't do that for crazy Lilly Waugh. Crazy folks ain't allowed to kill, only the sane ones. They'd put you away, Lilly, you'd spend the rest of your life with the screaming people. Now, I got nothing but respect for a person that's figured a way to keep her pride and privacy and keep folks at a distance, but at this late date don't ruin it. Don't you go gettin' sane, like them. You're too far above that. Put up your gun and go home." Jayell turned and walked toward the house. "All right, I don't pay folks to stand around!"

The boys came edging out of the trees, hesitantly, keeping an eye on the woman. She looked about her, her blue eyes flashing this way and that. "I'll not stand for it," she said angrily, "you wait, you wait and see!"

361

Jayell walked behind an unfinished wall and there was a business-like clatter of boards. Taking the signal, the other boys hurried to their work. Hammering and sawing filled the air. Miss Lilly turned and marched back into the woods.

Jackie James stood up from behind a lumber pile. "Shoot," he said with pride, "Jayell'll show her what *crazy* is!"

41

"GET UP, BOY! SUMP'N'S HAPPENED!" IT WAS EM, standing silhouetted against the predawn blue of the window. When he saw I was awake he stepped through the window onto the roof of the shed. I jumped out of bed and followed him, and we stood looking down into the early shadows of the Ape Yard. I couldn't make out anything unusual; there were a few people moving about, the headlights of cars on their way to the first shift at the mill, kitchen lights burning, the usual early morning stirrings in the hollow.

"I don't see anything. What is it?"

"Ain't right down there," he said, alarm growing in his eyes. "Come on!"

I dressed quickly and we ran down the ridges and along the woods to the road that curved by Teague's store. Then Em put an arm in front of me and pointed.

Then I saw them, white men in old battered cars and trucks, scattered out around the neighborhood. They had parked unobtrusively at different points along the streets, in front of stores, even in people's driveways. They sat quietly in their cars, their lights off.

Em nudged me and we walked along the street toward the store. I could feel their eyes on us as we moved along the darkened street. As we approached a black Chevrolet, the doors opened and two men stepped out.

"Where you goin', big 'un?" one of them asked.

Em stopped. "That some business of yours?"

"I don't believe I'd go around that store if I's you."

"Why?"

"I'd just stay away from there," the man said.

Em lowered his shoulders until he looked the man directly in the eye. "I'm gonna take that as friendly advice, friend. 'Cause, you see, ain't nobody tells me where I can and cannot go, and if I took it as a threat, I'd have to bust ever' bone in your face. I can take it as advice, now, can't I?"

The man looked over at his partner. He swallowed.

"Can't I—please?"

The man nodded.

"Oh, good," said Em. "You got such a pretty face." And he straightened and we continued on our way.

Mr. Teague was alone in the store. He was standing behind the leaning counter in the old part of the store.

"What's happened, Mr. Teague, where's Tio?"

He responded with a grim nod toward the stairs. We raced up the steps to the apartment.

Carlos sat at the kitchen table, perspiration standing on his contorted face. His head was bandaged with a dirty handkerchief. Tio was standing behind him, tight-lipped, peeling Carlos' shirt away from his back. The back of his head and neck were nicked and bleeding, but his back had borne the brunt of the beating. The ragged shirt was matted with pulpy flesh, and as the blood-soaked flannel was pulled away, little lint patches were left standing in the open wounds. Welts stood out like mole burrows across his back. "Doc Bobo," said Tio, "he made the rounds last night. All the shop boys."

"He's next, I told him," said Carlos, shivering as Tio peeled away a swatch of cloth, "I told him he got to git gone!"

363

"Okay," said Em, "that does it. We're gettin' out of here."

Tio didn't answer. He went to the medicine chest and got down a can of yellow salve. Em yanked it out of his hand. "You hear me? We got to get gone!"

Tio snatched his arm away. "Don't tell me what I got to do. I ain't goin' nowhere!"

"The hell you ain't!" Em turned him and shoved him toward the door. "Walk or I'll tote you, but you goin', and now!" He straightened Tio up and dragged him toward the stairs. "Earl, go up and get the bike!"

"It's too late," I said. From the top of the stairs I could see the green hood of the Continental nosing to the curb. We flattened ourselves on the landing as the screen door squeaked open and Doc Bobo's resonant voice came booming into the store.

"Good morning, Mr. Teague!"

Mr. Teague glanced up briefly and went on weighing up cheese. After Doc Bobo came a dozen white men, Paulie Mangum, Otis Barton, and several others I recognized from the Klan gathering at Barton's farm, most of whom had only in recent years moved out of the Ape Yard themselves. They lined up behind Bobo against the opposite wall. There was a shadow movement across the window and Clyde Fay eased himself on his heels by the door. Doc Bobo, his nose heavily bandaged, stepped up to the counter and waited, but Mr. Teague went on with his work, chin up, sighting through his bifocals as he pressed the thin-ground knife through the cheese.

"Ah—if we might have a moment, Mr. Teague."

The old man waited until the scales stopped rolling and wrapped the wedge in brown paper. He peered over his glasses at the crowd. "Well, the word must have got out about my special on turnips!" The men shifted uncomfortably as he met their gaze and nodded in greeting. "Otis, Vern, Alf—ain't seen much of you boys since you moved out of the Yard—where you been keeping yourselves?"

"Mr. Teague," said Doc Bobo, "I'm afraid we're

here on a bit of unpleasant business. Is your delivery boy about?"

"Tio? He's around somewhere, why?"

"We'd like a word with him, if you don't mind."

"Any business you got with him," said Mr. Teague, "you can take up with me."

Doc Bobo looked solemn. "Well, the fact is, Mr. Teague, the boy was involved in a little incident yesterday that's got some folks upset, and they figured it's time one of his own people straightened the boy about a few things. You understand."

"No, ah . . ." Mr. Teague wiped his hands on his apron. "Straighten him out about what?"

"Well, it seems he and some other boys from the Yard was messin' around up at Miss Lilly Waugh's place yesterday, and when she tried to run 'em off they wouldn't leave. She's awful upset about it." Doc Bobo acknowledged the men along the wall. "Naturally, the other folks up that way got a little disturbed too."

"They wasn't messin' around and they wasn't on her property," said Mr. Teague. "They was working for Jayell Crooms, on land she traded to him."

"Mr. Teague, you and I both know that don't make no difference. These are nervous times, times when the least little thing can cause a lot of trouble. She said the Grant boy bucked up real mean, said he threatened her."

"Hell, you all know Lilly Waugh! The woman's liable to say anything. I can't be responsible—"

"Mr. Teague, nobody's blaming you." Doc Bobo leaned in confidentially and spread his manicured hands on the counter. "It's a fine thing you done, taking the boy in and keeping the burden off some poor colored family, and don't think it's not appreciated. If it's anybody's fault, it's mine. I should have seen it coming. The fact is, Mr. Teague, the boy's been living white so long he's just forgot his place. Now, I've been around to see the others, and I can assure you we'll have no more trouble out of them, but it's especially important that we don't overlook the Grant boy. He's coming of age now and it's time to remind him who he is. Time to get that boy off tenderloin and back on pigs' feet and blackeyed peas."

The white men chuckled appreciatively and shifted and spaded their hands in their pockets. Doc Bobo smiled at his joke too, but kept his eyes on Mr. Teague. It saved him his fingers.

With a startled grunt he jerked them away just in time to avoid the cheese knife as it slashed a groove in the counter where they had rested a moment before.

"Take your hat off, nigger."

It was so quiet in the store you could hear the paddle fan rocking softly on its base.

Doc Bobo stood frozen in shock.

Mr. Teague's voice dropped to a raw whisper. "What's the matter with you, boy? What do you mean, layin' your filthy hands on my counter? And standin' here in my store, in front of all these white gentlemen, with your hat still on your *black greasy head!*" The long knife whipped out and Doc Bobo's crisp homburg fluttered to the floor.

"Fay!"

Doc Bobo spoke just in time. Clyde Fay stopped at the end of the counter, only a few feet from Mr. Teague.

I shivered involuntarily. Tio and I looked at each other. It seemed impossible for a man so big to move like that. Like the pictures on movie flip cards, it was as though he was at the door one minute and, in the next instant, at the counter, giving only the illusion of motion.

Mr. Teague cocked his head, birdlike, and studied him a moment, then walked toward him, trailing the knife along the counter. He strained his hooked shoulders to look up into the face that hung above his head. "You going somewhere, boy?" Fay flicked a glance at Bobo. Mr. Teague piped up again, his bald head palsying slightly with rising anger. "You hear me, nigger? What's the matter, thick lips, can't you talk?" Fay towered above him motionless as black marble, his slitted eyes fixed straight ahead. Mr. Teague's lips twisted into a sneer. His voice dropped lower, mimicking, tantalizing. "You black kinky-headed son of a bitch. Lift your hand against me, you outsized jungle monkey. *Come on burr-head!*"

Fay didn't move, but the fury was smoldering in him, pulsing in the muscles of his face. The others sensed it too. It hung in the air like the heavy, rotten odor of death. Only Mr. Teague, perched on the lip of destruction, seemed unconcerned. "Got your hat on too, ain't you? I swear, things is comin' to a state." The knife point drifted slowly upward and tipped Fay's cap from his head. I looked at Tio. His eyes were squeezed shut. "Maybe that fancy coat's too tight. That why you can't answer me, boy?" Mr. Teague sawed a button off Fay's jacket. There was an agonizing moment of silence, and another one rattled to the floor.

Suddenly Doc Bobo was beside them. "Get out of here, Fay." He put a hand on the giant's arm. "Fay! You hear me? Go on, wait outside."

There was a movement of broad shoulders under his jacket; a spring, taut to the breaking point, easing its tension. He retrieved his cap and Doc Bobo's hat and tapped softly across the sloping floor. At the door he turned briefly and glanced at Mr. Teague, then slipped into the sunlight.

"You have made a mistake, Mr. Teague."

Mr. Teague nodded. "A mistake," he said bitterly, "that sums it up. I spent my whole life in a business I never liked, because it was my father's business, and he was proud. That was a mistake.

"And I stayed with it, even when I seen others move away, because I thought people needed me. I thought they were my friends, and a man had an obligation to his friends. I thought they would remember the sick baskets, the bills I let go by when they was out of work, the rationed goods I let 'em have when they'd gambled away their stamp books. In the Depression, grown men stood at this counter and cried like babies, beggin' enough food to stop their kids from eatin' clay, and I gave it to 'em.

"But it was all a mistake. Some of the kids from those families are standin' behind you this minute—lookin' to see blood spilled in my store.

"Finally, when I was old and by myself, there comes a colored woman. She liked to laugh. She made me laugh. She ironed my shirts and put a shine on my floors and made me fried peas and coffee with honey in it. And we'd sit in the afternoon and talk. She was a good woman. It was a good time.

"And when she died I took in her child. I thought I could at least raise him the best I knew how, give him an education—and since I hadn't any family, I figured to leave him the store. Maybe give him an advantage these other poor black kids'd never have.

"But now that all my friends have left me, there won't be nothing to leave him.

"So I see that, too, was a mistake.

"So you go on sucking blood out of misery in the Ape Yard, Doc, but you leave that boy alone. He's all I got left in the world. And don't come draggin' a bunch of white trash in here expectin' to throw a scare into me. I'm too old. I've made too many mistakes, and my life ain't amounted to nothing.

"Get out of my store."

When they had filed out, Mr. Teague crawled weakly onto his stool and wiped his face with his apron.

He looked ready to faint.

42

As soon as the men left, young boys who had been idling at the door went running. In a matter of minutes people were stopping each other in the street, calling up to porches, shouting across the creek.

"Lemme through there, get out of my way!" Em bellowed at those already crowding to the door.

"Where you going, Em?" I said, catching up to him.

"Down the river. Leave me alone."

"When will you be back?" I asked anxiously.

"When I'm drunk enough to stand gettin' killed," he said, and hove down into the road.

The news of Mr. Teague's humiliation of Doc Bobo and his singlehandedly standing off the Flat Creek crowd swept through the Ape Yard with electrifying force, greeted everywhere with shock, disbelief. The story leaped from ridge to ridge, growing in the telling, and the store experienced a sudden upsurge in business. Mr. Teague was in no mood for them, and when they tried to pump him he shrugged them off and went upstairs. When pressed, I related what had happened as accurately as possible, sticking strictly to the facts, not trying to make Mr. Teague out a hero or anything, as I knew he would have wanted.

Tio did the same, I suppose, to the best of his ability. He let it be known that this was a place of business, and he didn't have time to waste with idle rumor-mongers, but as long as bona-fide customers were buying or making token payments on long over-due bills, Tio had a story to tell.

That afternoon people began pouring up the hills to Wolf Mountain. New faces appeared at the jobsite until the crowd numbered in the hundreds.

It was rebellion now, blowing openly through the hollow.

Jayell moved among them, confused, anxious, as happy people babbled at him. "Come to get my house started," shouted Speck Turner, "me and Loomis and Simon . . ."

"I got some money, Mist' Jay," a man covered with rock shed dust was saying, "they puttin' me off my place . . ."

"Shut up! Shut up! I can't think!"

Jayell ran to a pickup truck where a half-dozen men were helping down battered shop boys: Carlos, grinning through his bandages, Skeeter with his foot in a still-moist cast, Jackie James, walking stiffly so as not to move his back and hollering at his mother to leave him alone.

"There's too many!" cried Jayell. "We can't move!"

"Then give 'em sump'n to do," said Carlos. "You organized crews in Abbeville for Smithbilt, you can line these niggers up!"

"We need lumber, scraps of any kind," shouted Jayell. "You there, Loomis, get some people to bring axes and start clearing those trees . . . Carlos, get in that truck I brought up from the shop. Pull out those plans, Skeeter! Get your shop boys over there, never mind . . . trim work, baseboards, start 'em on cabinets . . . we gonna, *listen to me, everybody,* we're gonna need hand tools, anything you got . . ." Jayell turned in circles, shoving aside those in his way. "That's it, we need materials and tools, anything, anything. Now, the rest of you, just move over there until somebody tells you what to do. These fellas in the bandages will be in charge."

Scraps of planking started coming up the slopes, a board from a truck bed, a hog pen. They came with hammers, handsaws, a pound of nails in a rolled paper bag. Through the afternoon and into the next day they kept coming, with jalopies loaded down with lumber, scraps of plywood and tin, rolls of rusted wire, never sure what would be of use to this builder.

Pits were dug for barbecues, trestles laid on saw-

370

horses. They brought messes of vegetables from summer gardens, hams pulled from boxes of salt; iron washpots of stews simmered under the oaks and black women ladled hush-puppy batter in skillets of boiling fat.

The land was cleared, new houses started.

I. V. Tagg sat on a stump with his old hand-cranked comptometer and cranked and figured, signed contracts and notes, and ran cash to the bank and came back to figure again.

"It's chaos!" he cried. "It's madness!"

"I thought this kind of thing was dead and gone," said old man Burroughs, watching people build their neighbors' houses, "and to see it, in this day and time . . ."

Through it all Jayell flapped about like a mad martin, bouncing on ladders, leaping through skeletal walls, shouting orders, measuring, changing plans in mid-construction, running from the woods with his pants at half-mast to scream at the alignment of a roof and dashing back to finish his business.

The struggling laborers mixed mortar with their hands; they held timbers at unaccustomed angles, waiting for the nod; they asked again about this window, the slant of that partition—was this the right mixture of paint? They gathered in silence to watch a plump bob settle, as though on this job even the center of gravity might be different.

The structures climbed through the blistering July heat, forms defying all known symmetry and the common requirements of stress and design. New angles emerged, curving walls, cantilevered porches and steep-winged roofs, domes from which staircases spiraled down to circular rooms.

Jayell's contractor friend, Werb O'Connell, came and stood aghast. Mr. Wyche drove up with a couple of executives of Smithbilt Homes. They wanted to look at Jayell's plans.

"Most of 'em are up here," said Jayell, tapping his head.

371

"I can't tell if it's a lot of little houses, or one big house sprawled out over the mountainside," said Werb O'Connell.

Local architects poked through the houses with levels and rules, they sighted down the hill with instruments. They squatted with sketch pads and tried to pick arguments with Jayell.

"It is what it is!" Jayell said. "For thousands of years man found his shelter in the earth, in trees and caves, gentlemen, the most natural structural environment, and a damned sight better than those boxes we put him in today. A man's environment should free him, not box him in. As Wright said, it's the space that counts, not the walls. Can you beat a tree for living space? Can you sketch a freer, more natural floor plan than a cave? Excuse me."

And as the various houses grew, the master plan emerged, each small building merging into a graceful conformity with the whole. From the foot-thick supports that bit into the hillsides to the free-flowing upper rooms of sunlit airiness, they all swerved and molded together, growing with perfect shape and balance—not imposed upon, but emerging naturally from the existing terrain, their bright colors quilting the summer mountain.

Traffic slowed on the Atlanta highway. People parked and watched from their cars. A retired couple from Florida on their way to see Stone Mountain, which was part of their sightseeing itinerary, stopped and took each other's pictures on each of the porches and turned south again, saying Stone Mountain be damned.

"We're running short of lumber!" Jayell cried. "We've got to have more lumber!"

And the deserted shacks around Teague's property began disintegrating, whole houses disappearing in the night. Word came that there had been rebellious flare-ups at Doc Bobo's sawmill on the Little Iron River, that the convicts were growing careless, letting lumber get away from them.

Each night bundles of lumber came floating down the river, and farther down, along the pulpwood logging trails, pickups and jalopies sat waiting. The next morning fresh stacks of stock sat drying at the jobsite.

At last, the quiet of a Sunday afternoon, when Jayell only allowed work until noon. Mayor Crowler, Mr. William Thurston of Blue Light Monuments, who was also chairman of the centennial commission, and three other board members of the commission drove up to Jayell's new house. Jayell left Phaedra and pushed off the steps and limped down to the car, carrying his Bible in one hand and the bottle of whiskey from which he had been sipping in the other.

"That's quite a combination," said Mayor Crowler, getting out.

"Unbeatable, I've found. One seems to enhance the enjoyment of the other. What can I do for you?"

The men stood looking at the unfinished houses that loomed above them on the craggy mountainside. Seen up close, in detail, the houses looked even more startling than at a distance. "It's like something out of a dream," said Wilbur Taylor, president of the Three Angels sheds.

"It is," said Jayell without inflection.

"Mr. Crooms," said the mayor, "what you're doing here is attracting a great deal of attention, the wrong kind of attention, at the worst possible time. Do you realize that next weekend is the windup of our centennial celebration . . . do you know who will be coming to our town?"

"We're just building houses, Mayor, just building houses."

"A great number of people have put in a great deal of work to see that—"

"There's been a lot of work put in up here, too, Mayor," said Jayell evenly. "There's been people up here that ought to be takin' it easy in a rockin' chair, workin' like I've never seen people work before. Drop by that boardinghouse over yonder . . ."

"You know that's not what I'm talking about," said the mayor curtly, trying to control his anger. "It's down there," he said, pointing to the hollow, "that place is in a turmoil!"

"Because of you and that son of a bitch Bobo! If you'd left old man Teague alone and hadn't shoved people around like a bunch of cattle, this place wouldn't be here, Mayor! You people made this happen, not me!"

"Those people are being provided for. Houses are being built up the hollow . . ."

"You call 'em houses, not me!"

". . . and plans are being made for a project for those displaced by the dam."

"Another Ape Yard, with you and Bobo scoopin' off federal cream! Build all the dams and housing projects you want, Mayor, I'm moving as many as I can up here in the breeze!"

Mr. Thurston broke in. "Your people are stealing lumber now, you know."

"I don't know about that—I got people huntin' scraps all over the country. They could be pullin' it off the courthouse for all I know. You catch 'em, you put 'em in jail."

"We helped you, Jayell," said the mayor. "This whole town helped you. Why won't you help us?"

"But I am helping you! Don't you see! I *am* helping you!"

The mayor sighed. "Well, there's no use belaboring the point. All we ask is that you just stop and let things cool down for a week or so, at least until the centennial festivities are over. While the news media, and the people from the capital and Washington are here, let's just keep our feet on the ground and sit tight. Will you do that for us?"

Jayell's frown turned to a quizzical look, then the wrinkles broke into an unexpected grin. He stood clutching his whiskey and his Bible, he started shaking, looking from one to the other of the surprised faces.

"Mayor, that's the attitude of a man in an outhouse! I can't"—Phaedra started breaking up behind him—"I can't *do* that a *whole week!*"

I started laughing then, at the looks on the men. Phaedra put her hands on her hips and bent over, snorting like a mule; Jayell, laughing at her then, turned and put an arm around her, and the more she laughed, braying and sucking wind, the more tickled he got.

The men started gathering toward the car, watching us like we'd gone insane. Doors slammed, the engine started, and the three of us, beyond control then, sank to the dirt in hysteria, at the foot of the slope of the strange, soaring silhouettes, and laughed and laughed and couldn't stop.

When Wednesday night came with still no sign of Em, I began to get worried, and decided I'd better go looking for him. So Thursday I took off work and spent the day on the bike searching for him along the river. He was in the area; he had been seen at almost every river joint I came to, from Dirsey's all the way up to Shady Point, with stories of drinking bouts that grew rowdier the farther I went. But he was nowhere to be found. It brought to mind one of the rare "Indian" things Em ever said about himself: "If I want to find somebody, there ain't no place he can hide that I can't smell him out; I'll get him if he's a thousand miles away. But if I don't want to *be* found, there ain't nobody can find me."

And it was plain that Em didn't want to be found just now. But he was still around, I was sure of that. It was enough. I turned around and headed home.

Driving back in through Quarrytown I could hear the band practicing in the Granite Bowl behind the courthouse, and when I turned into the square I was amazed at the transformation that had taken place. Banners crossed the streets at every intersection, a wooden reviewing stand was built in front of the courthouse, firemen were hanging pictures of the Poncini brothers from every lamppost. Horses stood hitched to an old mail-delivery wagon on the lawn of the post office; old yellowed maps and photographs of the Poncini quarry in operation were pasted in the window of the *Star*. Out-of-town license plates were everywhere; a traffic cop in a rented turn-of-the-century policeman's uniform did his best to keep cars from running into the mobile unit of an Atlanta television station that was stringing cables across from the reviewing stand and trying to mount a camera on the top of the bank on the corner for the parade. Crowds milled through the granite association's display of early granite-working machinery under a striped tent on the square, along with striated, poor-grade monuments produced by the Poncini quarry. Derby hats, string ties and canes were featured in the windows of every clothing store; newly sprouted beards were in abundance; ladies stood fanning their long skirts in the July heat.

I waved to Mrs. Porter and Mrs. Cline who were selling quilts and "antiques" out of the bus in a vacant lot filled with such hawkers next to Daisy Riley's beauty shop. On a grassy traffic island at the main approach to town from the north side, I passed Miss Minnie Copeland, the spinster music teacher, who sat at a harpsichord wired to a public-address system feeding 1890s tunes into the air. The excitement building toward the impending celebration was roughly equivalent to that of a fireworks display at a carnival during an electric storm.

At Wolf Mountain it was somewhat quieter, but not one degree less intense. The houses grew at a staggering pace. Cars on their way into town were still stopping and turning in to see what was going on. Jayell had to assign the boarders to take turns meeting them at a turnaround place on the access road and explain that this was not a pavilion for the centennial.

Through it all, there was a block in the Ape Yard—the one housing the two-story white building back behind the willows and magnolias with the neon clock sign—that maintained an ominous silence. Bobo's Funeral Home sat quietly in the eye of the storm.

43

FRIDAY NIGHT I WAS ALONE IN THE LOFT EATING supper. It was a beautiful, clear July night. Stars sparkled out the window, through which a cool breeze worried the flame of the lamp on the table.

I would miss the loft. There could be no substitute at Wolf Mountain for its comfort, its smells. I looked around at it, with its splintery ribs, its stains, the empty fish tank, and recalled what it meant to me in those early days in comparison to the boarding-house—that frightening boardinghouse with its strange rooms, its shadows, its curious old faces, the pomp and thunder of Miss Esther . . .

Miss Esther.

I looked at the letter that lay partially unfolded on the table. Mrs. Bell had given it to me that morning. I picked it up and read again the sparse, scrawled sentences:

> . . . another of my spells a week or so back and have been in hosp. since. Doctor says I am doing better. He says that every day so I guess I am. Says I might be able to go home next week. It don't matter to me whether I go back to that house or not . . .

I stiffened, listening.

It wasn't the wind, the sounds of the loft—I sorted through them quickly. It was even, crunching sounds —running feet, coming up the gulley. There were scrapings up the bank, a rattle of brush, then foot-steps on the stairs so heavy the loft felt it, and I knew who it was.

377

Em burst through the door, panting, his eyes wild with fear.

"What is it? Who's after you?"

"Bobo's men! I got word they're searchin' for me along the river!" He jerked down his canvas bag and threw open the footlocker. "I'll grab some clothes. Get the bike started."

I started for the door. "I'll go get Jayell and the others and . . ."

I felt a hand grab my arm and I went spinning to the floor. Em stood over me, jowls quivering.

"I'm done messin' with you! You'll do what I tole you!"

"If you want to go, go!" I shouted at him. "I'm not runnin' anywhere!"

"Then I'm gonna drag you, boy!"

I jumped to my feet. *"I ain't afraid! You hear me? I ain't afraid!"*

"Boy, listen to me. Only damned fools ain't afraid. Right now I'm more scared than I ever been. I don't want to die. You don't begin to care about life till you realize it's got no purpose, then it's everything. And when you ain't part of nothin', when you don't belong nowhere or to nobody and all you got is yourself, when you die it don't mean nothin', the world just comes to an end."

"You talk about not belongin' to nothin'—you got the whole thing started up and soon as trouble comes you want to cut out!"

"Me? I ain't responsible!"

"Yes, you are, and it's time you owned up to it. You're as much a part of it as anybody else, even more. They couldn't have done what they're doin' if it hadn't been for you!"

"I ain't responsible!" he shouted, drawing back as though I'd touched him with fire.

"Whose idea was it to make that tree fall on Jayell's house? If it hadn't been for that he'd never have started those houses. And who was it convinced the old people they could make it after Miss Esther left? Who told Mr. Teague he could take on that chain store? When I could hardly move that arm, who was it wanted to race to the top of a tree? You're responsible, Em Jojohn. *You're responsible for all of us!*"

He stood glaring at me, the fury distilled to two fierce points in his eyes.

"I could cut off my hands," he said quietly, "for the day I pulled you out of that fire."

He turned away, mouth-breathing, trying to control his rage.

"Fire . . . ? Em . . ." I reached to touch him and he slapped my hand away. "Em, what about the fire?"

His voice was rasped with bitterness. "All I ever wanted was to be left alone . . ." He leaned a fist on the table, his breath coming in short, ragged gasps.

It was swirling—the broken pieces, the dream, the monster hands reaching for me . . .

"Em—it was you? You pulled me out of the fire?"

He kept his back to me. After a moment, his head lowered and Em started talking, the words pulsing slowly, as though he bled them.

". . . comin' along the road, and I seen it burnin'. I couldn't get 'em out, wasn't no way I could get 'em out, it was like a tinderbox. They was caught in the bedroom and it was a solid wall of flame. The man tried to get through it and he couldn't . . . the woman was screamin', then I heard you screamin' in the room 'crost the breezeway. I bust in and got you out. I don't know how—the bed was burnin', your clothes was afire. But I got you out. Somehow I got you out."

"And it didn't hit me till I'd got you in the yard and rolled you in the ditch and stood holdin' you while the neighbors come—with you carryin' on out of your head, lookin' at me like I was some demon out of hell, your eyes wild, accusin' me . . . it didn't hit me till then what I'd done.

"I hung around the hospital while they tried to find somebody to take you, watchin' you lay there day after day, starin' at the wall, not talkin', not movin'. The doctor said you'd be all right soon as your arm healed up and you got with your people. But I knew you wouldn't be all right.

"I tried to forget. I done everything to forget. I wished many times I'd just kept walkin' down the road and let you be with your mama and papa. But I didn't. I got in there and pulled you back. And now there was a child that should'a been dead, was probably meant to be dead, a sharecropper's kid that'd never get proper treatment, that nobody'd ever give a damn for, partly crippled, all messed up in your head and not able to get along in the world, and I was the one responsible.

"It hung over me. I couldn't shake it. So when I found out they'd sent you to Georgia, I found myself movin' that way. I said, I'll just have a look at him, see he's gettin' along all right.

"And then I found you—creepin' about the place like a little scared animal, settin' by the drainpipe to pass the night, wakin' up screamin' every time you fell asleep . . ."

The Indian's voice trailed off.

So there it was. My mind was drifting back to the unexplained trips, the ramblings up the road—Em's attempted escapes, from me. Me, the one mistake in his solitary life. I thought of the returnings, the nights of agony, the hatred in his eyes, never suspecting the cause of that agony, the object of that awesome, barely controlled rage . . .

My attention came sharply back to the present. I glanced out the window at the lights glowing in the deceptive peacefulness of the hollow, a sudden panicky feeling welling up in me.

With perfect clarity I saw that in the clash that now was coming, it was Em, the innocent, of no importance to either side, who was most sure to be sacrificed.

And *I* would be responsible.

I had to get him out of there, but alone, on his instincts, where he had the best chance.

I circled the table in front of him fighting to control my voice.

"All right," I said, "you helped me, but you used me too. Now we're even. Go on, get out of here."

Em raised his head and looked at me.

380

"You used me, Em. I told you I didn't need you the last time you came back, but still you kept hanging around. It's because you didn't *want* to go, and I was just an excuse!"

He straightened slowly, the bitter anguish in his face twisting as he struggled for comprehension.

"You slipped up, Em. You got comfortable. It wasn't easy bein' on the road, fightin' the whole world to be your Own Man, was it? But it was easy here in the Ape Yard. You had a place to sleep, you could get fed without too much trouble, nobody to mess with you. You even quit fightin' and scrappin'! How long's it been since you were in a fight anyway? A year? What's the matter, did they wear you down, Em? You lost your nerve? Oh, sure, you stood up to Bobo, with all those white folks backin' you up! But you been hidin' out ever since. You've just plain lost your nerve, haven't you, big 'un? You're afraid to be the old Em anymore!"

He moved, and checked himself. He stood over me, flushed, shaking, his fingers opening, closing. I moved around the table, watching, trying to gauge him.

"So, go on, get out of here, nobody's got you penned up. You know, I used to think that collie dog up the street hated you so much and took on so when you passed because he was behind that fence and he could sense that you were so free. But you're just like him, snarlin' and snappin' and makin' a lot of noise—only for you the gate's been open all the time. So go, if you still got the guts." I grabbed up the canvas bag and flung it into his face. "Go on, you old whipped dog, *tuck your tail between your legs and git!*"

With a roar he suddenly threw the table aside, an unexpected move that cut me off from the door, and came reaching for me, his powerful hands raised, his face hideous. I backed away, looking for an opening, but I was trapped. The dark thing that had tormented him so long was on the surface now, in control and coming for me.

"Easy, man."

Em whirled on the motion and stood crouched.

It was a young black man, in a metal studded belt, sighting down a double-barreled shotgun.

There was another man coming in the door behind him, a short, fat man, with the cherubic features of a black Santa Claus.

"What say, what say," said Bubba White.

Em straightened. The dog boy immediately stepped clear and shouldered his weapon. Both hammers were cocked.

"Easy now, Em," said Bubba White. "Ernie just got that scattergun yesterday, and he's itchin' for a chance to test the pattern."

"What you want, Bubba?"

"Jes' want you to come down to my place. Set down, have a friendly drink."

"Well, like to, Bubba, but I's just tellin' the boy, it's time old Em was easin' up the road."

"Naw . . . ain't no need to rush off now, Em. Time to leave was a week or two ago, before you put your nose in where it didn't belong. Now, folks wants you to stay . . . told me to be sure you did."

"Let him go," I said, "he won't cause you no—"

Bubba White put a hand in my face and shoved me toward the corner. "Stan' over there and keep your mouth shut! And don't bother to run, there's plenty more downstairs." He turned back to Em, and began pulling lengths of chain and padlocks from his coat pockets. "Jes' go down to my place, Em, till this is all over. Don't want you mixin' in where you got no business again."

"Then what?" said Em. He was keeping a worried eye on me.

Very carefully, very slowly, I lifted the chicken catcher from the corner.

"Then we'll see," said Bubba White. He waddled forward, watching Em cautiously. "Now, you jes' put your hands out for me, straight out, and don't do nothin' rambunctious. You gon' do that for me now, ain't you?"

"Uh-huh," said Em.

The wire loop was directly over the dog boy's head. I let it drop, and yanked back as hard as I could as Em dodged aside.

The first blast from the scattergun raked the wall and window, bursting the fish tank, shredding the Lone Ranger poster and blowing the souvenir G-string into flying fuzz. Em's hands hit Bubba White's chest so hard I heard the little fat man's breath lock in his throat. He reeled backward into the dog boy with such force his shoulder went through the flimsy weatherboarding. The second charge triggered and cleaned the lamp off the table and shattered everything on the kitchen shelves.

In the dark and falling glass I heard the trap door thrown open and a flop in the garage below. A moment later the walls shook with the roar of a revving motor.

"Comin' out!" Bubba screamed out the window. "Comin' out!"

There were footsteps running toward the garage, then the sound of doors batting open and the startled cries of men scrambling to get out of the way. From the window I saw the bike tear up the yard toward the boardinghouse. It crashed through the hedge and swerved under the old grape arbor, Jojohn fighting for control. It circled and veered up the driveway toward the street, but it was blocked by cars. Headlights came on, men ran out waving their arms. At the last moment Jojohn braked and the cart came around in a flying skid that sent the men climbing fenders.

Back he came, full throttle, bumping through the backyard and scattering converging shadows. It seemed at the moment that the bike became alive. It was like a skittish, charging animal with a mind of its own, dodging among the fruit trees, careening perilously off the brick borders of flower beds, bucketing over bushes and sending lawn chairs spinning, smashing down rotted clothesline and grape arbor poles—plunging and shying from the frantic hands that grappled for it, and narrowly, sometimes miraculously, avoiding certain disaster, with the helpless, frightened Indian clinging to its back.

Then the bike was turned and heading back toward the garage. He came crashing through the shrubbery and circled in front of the garage. *"Wooooo!"* he sang in the wind. *"Wooooo!"*

Then Bubba's men were running back, closing in on him in a large semicircle, and with a sudden burst of the throttle the Indian swerved down by the garage and went over the edge of the gully.

I jumped out on the shed in time to see him cut hard to hold the slope as he slid down. The bike bottomed, clawed up the other side, then leveled off to the right and went flying, vines and branches ripping. A moment later he burst into the moonlight on the hard-curled mud of the pasture and disappeared into the Ape Yard.

"Let him go!" Bubba White was crying. "Don't go chasin' him. Been too much ruckus already! Get the boy!"

Ernie appeared behind me on the shed and shoved me roughly off into waiting hands below. "Don't you give no more trouble," Bubba said, still wheezing somewhat from the blow to his chest. "I'll slit your throat like a pig."

As they dragged me up to the cars by the boardinghouse I saw why the commotion had failed to bring the boarders. I could see them seated at the dining-room table. A dog boy cradling a gun waved at Bubba and pulled down the shade.

Teague's grocery stood fully lit against only a scattering of yellow lights along the hill. It was deadly quiet, with none of the usual Friday night frolicking. There was no traffic in the streets.

Bubba White led us up the back stairs to the kitchen, where a dog boy let us in. I was shoved through the kitchen to Mr. Teague's front room, which faced the street.

. The first thing that caught my eye was Jayell and Phaedra, lying bound and gagged on Mr. Teague's bed. Mr. Teague and Tio sat on the couch, a dog boy's pistol at the back of their heads. Doc Bobo sat in a wingback chair, his fingers steepled under his nose. The door closed softly behind us, and I turned and looked up into the face of Clyde Fay.

"I told you, no noise," Doc Bobo said.

"Couldn't help it," said Bubba White. "The Indian got away . . ."

"What!"

"Thanks to him!" said Bubba, shoving me forward.

"Ahhh, yes, the loft rat." Doc Bobo pressed down the tape around his bandaged nose. "Well, he's the one I wanted." He smiled at my surprise. "Makes no difference about the Indian," he said. "If I know him, he's in Carolina by now." He dropped his hand and cocked an eye at Bubba. "The boarders?"

"They tucked in for the night."

Doc Bobo nodded once. "Well"—he pulled himself to his feet and looked around—"I believe now, Mr. Teague, you and I can conclude our business." He opened his coat and pulled out a sheaf of legal papers. "We'll just get your signature on these and we'll be done."

He stepped closer and extended a fountain pen. Mr. Teague sat staring at the floor.

"Come now, Mr. Teague, I'm going to take you out of all this grief. You don't need this; a man your age needs to be relaxing, enjoying himself."

Mr. Teague looked up. "You need to be in hell, nigger."

Doc Bobo drew back and his hand smacked hard across the old man's face. "I've had enough of that, you damned old piece of white trash—and I'm through wasting time with you! Fay!"

Clyde Fay crossed the room and seized Tio by the throat and lifted him in the air like a puppy. He stood holding him at arm's length, strangling him with his hands. I lunged forward and felt hands grip me.

Mr. Teague started up and Bobo shoved him back on the sofa and brandished the papers under his nose. "Sign 'em, or see his neck get wrung like a chicken!"

His face white, Mr. Teague fumbled the papers in his lap. He took the pen and scribbled his signature.

"All five copies." Doc Bobo smiled. He put his fists on his hips as he watched the old man sign. Tio was gagging, struggling for breath. "Don't know why I didn't see it before," said Bobo. "Could have saved everybody a whole lot of trouble. But it wasn't until I saw you buck up in defense of the boy that I saw the key to you, Mr. Teague."

Mr. Teague scribbled on the last page and shoved the papers back at Bobo. "Now, for God's sake, let him down!"

Doc Bobo checked the signatures. He turned to Fay and nodded, and the giant let Tio drop to the floor. Mr. Teague got up to go to him, and when he passed Doc Bobo, the undertaker looked at Fay and nodded.

I watched in shock as Fay's hands closed on the back of the old man's neck. Straining with the effort, the black man turned and lifted him off the floor and threw him full force headfirst into the wall.

Mr. Teague lay crumpled like a doll. A pool of blood slowly started to ooze from his head.

I couldn't move.

After a moment Tio went and knelt beside him. He lifted the bleeding head and cradled it in his lap and sat looking down into the small, drawn face. "Ah, little man," he whispered, "Little man . . ."

"You didn't have to kill him!" I screamed at Bobo.

"Kill him? Why no, the old man simply fell down the stairs. It happens all the time. Just as boys tend to wander and their bones are sometimes found in creeks and abandoned wells. Bring them!" Tio and I were seized and dragged toward the door. Doc Bobo leaned over Jayell and Phaedra, struggling on the bed. "Don't worry, you won't be harmed. You and the old people will only be kept out of sight until our big weekend celebration is over, then you will be free to go where you wish, to tell any story you like."

44

THE APE YARD STOOD WAITING IN THE SMOKY, BRICK-red dawn. There had been rain in the night, and when the first hazy slivers of sunlight began to worm their way through the trees beyond the river, heavy black clouds still lay banked to the south. Silent lightning licked at the distant earth.

Doc Bobo's voice rang through the quiet, "Get 'em out! Get 'em all out here!"

Tio and I stood beside him on the steps of the Rainbow Supper Club and watched the dog boys move from house to house, kicking in doors, snapping orders, herding people into the streets. We watched as they stumbled out, hesitant, frightened, dodging the swinging belts, moving along the ridges and clay paths toward us in the lower end of the hollow. The hillsides filled with them, hundreds of them, old people, sleepy children stepping tenderly with new-awakened feet, families clinging together, people swinging down from porches, pushing through weeds and around the little brown shacks, under clothes left on the line overnight, soot-grimed and speckled with rain. Slowly they gathered above us, lining the banks and ridges, and stood waiting in the earthen light and smoke of breakfast fires that rolled heavily over the rooftops and climbed along the hills.

They stood and watched and waited, in the smoky, brick-red dawn.

The dog boys came back to the supper club and stood in the yard and on the porch, about a dozen of them, vicious-looking, muscular men, some with shoulder holsters protruding from their expensively tailored jackets. On the hill across the road two more were coming down the slope, driving before them the

387

boys from the job: Carlos, Skeeter, Jackie, Willie Daniels. Simon and Loomis struggled to carry Speck Turner between them, his head bleeding. The dog boys whipped them all to their knees on the bank and came to the porch.

Doc Bobo waited for silence.

I looked at Tio. He kept his eyes on the ground before him. He seemed oblivious to all that was happening.

Doc Bobo stepped to the center of the porch behind us and lifted his voice for distance.

"Did you think," he shouted, "that I could be stopped so easily? Did you think *any* man, black or white, could stand up to Doc Bobo? Let me show you, let me settle your minds this morning!" He pulled the sheaf of papers Mr. Teague had signed from his pocket and walked slowly the length of the porch, holding them aloft. "This is a signed bill of sale—for the property once owned by Alvah Teague." He waited for that to take effect in the hills, for the shifting, murmuring, repeating of his words to die down. "Later this morning I will take part in a momentous occasion for our town, the celebration of the one hundredth year of our granite industry, during which I will be presented to our distinguished guests as the first black member of the Quarrytown Granite Association.

"Because, Monday morning we will begin work on a brand-new quarry, right here in the Ape Yard only a short distance from the county's first quarry, and the first in the history of this granite industry to be owned by a black man!" Doc Bobo folded the papers back into his pocket. "Truly, a momentous occasion. And beginning Monday morning, that store will be removed, and those ridiculous structures"—he turned and pointed to Wolf Mountain—"will be pulled to the ground! There will be no more interference with our way of life in the Ape Yard. Doc Bobo is your friend here. Your only friend!

"Let them pass their laws, let them make their promises, they will raise no more false hopes here. They

388

supposedly set us free before there was a granite industry in this town." He ran his eyes along the hills. "Are we free? We have pulled ten thousand tombstones from under this ground, and if we set one at the grave of every broken promise to the black man there still would not be enough! White men's laws are for white men's purposes, not for you and me. We have survived in the Ape Yard because we make our own laws. We have looked after our own.

"The old ones know what I mean. They know better than to lift their hearts in hope, and have them crushed again." He turned to look across the yard and road at the shop boys kneeling on the bank, down at Tio standing below him. "It's the young who buy the dream. Because they grew up in the *peace* Doc Bobo brought them! They don't remember the innocent black man who was burned on the square as I do. They don't know about the night riders who used to come through the Ape Yard on Saturday night shooting out windows for fun. They don't know those horrors because they don't happen anymore! Thanks to Doc Harley Bobo!

"They are ready to mix and mingle, to turn a black man against his brothers—like these two right here. This is an example of the future if we let it continue . . . a black boy raised by a white man, spoiled and deceived by a white man's lies, a born troublemaker and a disgrace to his people . . . and a sorry, trashy white boy who thinks that lily-white skin is a badge of distinction giving him the right to attack and humiliate any man, no matter what his rank or position, so long as that man happens to be black!

"Their kind will not be tolerated in the Ape Yard!

"I will show you that now, young people." He motioned to the dog boys and they began filing up the steps and into the supper club, taking off their metal-studded belts as they came. "I will show you that once and for all, and when that is done we will climb those slopes to take part in the celebration of the town. I will expect to see every black face in this hollow on the square and cheering when Doc Bobo, on your behalf, accepts his place of honor. And if there are any among you who entertain notions of creating further trouble, I want you to look closely at these two, and those kneeling on the bank, when we are done with them. As they pass you in the streets in the future, look at them, and remember!"

Doc Bobo turned around to those in the supper club. "Open those windows and let them hear it, and take your time."

That was the way. Nothing in the sunlight for Bobo. Give them only screams to take with them as they climbed the hills to do his bidding, to take to their beds that night, to boil in their dreams and allow their imaginations to do Bobo's work. Later they could see the result. He was so careful in his staging, in his use of terror against ignorance. Bobo was a master.

"The black boy first," snapped Doc Bobo.

Clyde Fay took Tio's arm and led him through the door. Two dog boys walked to either end of the porch with pistols drawn, letting them hang loosely at their sides. A third stood at the door, waiting.

The Ape Yard waited, under the flares of sun that streaked through the morning shroud to the iron-rich clay of the slopes, bathing them all in a reflected red earthen light.

When he was ready, when there was not a movement in the hills, Doc Bobo turned to the dog boy in the door and nodded.

The dog boy relayed the signal inside.

A moment later screams began, starting low, then rising rapidly to shrill, piercing shrieks, the echoes bouncing off the silent ridges and ringing through the hollow.

Then, through the numbness of shock, I became aware that they were not coming from inside the supper club but arose from somewhere else. Heads were turning in the crowd. Arms lifted to point. Doc Bobo stepped to the edge of the porch, looking up toward the Ape Yard rim.

45

BEYOND THE LAST HOUSES ON THE UPPER RIDGE, A
blobby shadow was descending through the red earth-
en light. Down the terra-cotta slopes he came like
a charging primeval beast, jumping, bouncing, clearing the rain-gutted trenches, howling that inhuman
cry.

Heads poked out of the supper club's windows. The
dog boy on that end of the porch, recovering, raised
his gun and braced it against the post. Doc Bobo was
on him. "No shooting! No shooting!"

On the Indian came, leaping from bank to bank,
dead-on across the grassy knolls, sliding down the clay.

"Stop him!" Doc Bobo shouted to the frightened
people clustered along the way. "You better stop him!"

Jojohn built his speed, dodging through the little
brown yards and grappling hands, feeble hands, un-
willing hands, brushed aside with exploding howls.

He burst through the plum thickets onto an apron
slope, then off a high bank to the flat below, hit the
ground rolling, then was up again, hatless and running,
a flicker of khaki through the pines. He circled the
marsh beside the supper club and could be heard
smashing through the tall reed-thicket, straight on,
roaring his coming.

Dog boys were crowding to the door of the supper
club. Doc Bobo glanced around at them. He beckoned
to the one at the other end of the porch.

"Cannie!"

When the man came, Doc Bobo had him drape his
jacket over his pistol. He looked nervously up toward the fairgrounds. "One shot," he said, shaking his
finger, "one shot."

The dog boy knelt and propped an elbow on one knee.

Em Jojohn broke the clearing, the dog boy lowered his chin, sighting, and when he did I whirled and threw myself straight on top of him. The gun exploded in the jacket.

The Indian came pounding down the clearing, white-eyed, bellowing. He cleared the low steps and dived, landing inside in a crash of men and furniture.

Scrambling to my feet, I ducked into the darkened supper club, watching for the furious dog boy to come after me and at the same time trying to stay out of the commotion inside. Through the window I could see Doc Bobo setting the two on the porch to guard the crowd.

The mill-house dance floor was a churning, tumbling pile of arms and legs, with Em in the middle and dog boys, struggling, diving over each other to get at him, making fierce, guttural sounds in their throats. They were rolling across the floor, smashing, tearing clothes, gouging; it was as though Em was being devoured by a many-armed, furious beast. He was fighting defensively, rolling away, trying to get out from under, and they were falling on him from all sides. The walls echoed with the struggle, tables toppling, faces flashing in the light streaks. It seemed the room could not contain the savagery.

Suddenly a man squawked like the hogs I had heard in the slaughterhouse, and the Indian rose to his feet.

And the sight of him was incredible. It was Jojohn in a fury I had never seen before, fighting as I had never seen before.

A head taller than his attackers, he stood against the bar and moved his powerful body in a continuous destructive rhythm, bobbing, weaving, fighting for footing, windmilling blows at the heads below him as though he were demolishing a wall. The mob lunged and dived in upon him, arms thrusting, making a shock of contact, falling away. Others jumped in over those broken, winded, trying to crawl away from the flying boots; they crowded in, bumping shoulders, working to get him, fighting not on orders now, not for fear of Bobo, but in the evangelism of the violence itself. The faceless mob converged upon the furious, battering giant at the bar in an exaltation of fury. Still he stood his ground. A dog boy in a checkered coat arose behind Jojohn's head. The Indian turned and drove a fist through the man's breastbone. A man with a misshapen jaw kept leaping and screaming dementedly, swinging in over the crowd. Jojohn found him and smashed his face. He hit the jukebox and toppled to the floor, amid a pile of blood and black flesh and bright-colored rags.

Em's shirt was hanging by the seams, white bone showed through the skin of beefy knuckles, his right eye was closing, his hair was corded in sweat and blood, but still he swung from side to side in that curious dance and knocked them away as he had kicked bottles from the circle at Dirsey's.

One by one they crumpled, bleeding, crawling over fallen bodies to get clear of the churning above them, the boots that stomped at the fallen injured.

As the fight wore on, Em showed signs of weakening. His shoulders swung heavily, his breathing grew loud and rasping. He was taking more blows now, sometimes staggering, but each time bouncing off the bar in new roaring rage at those who leaped in to the seeming advantage, still swinging to that instinctive rhythm, without style, without aim, eyes wide and staring, reacting to flickers in peripheral vision. Still he fought and cursed and roared.

As men dropped away the pace of the fighting slowed, until there were only two left, powerful men, experienced alley fighters who loved to fight, and it became a slugging match. They shuffled before him trading punch for punch, trying to wear him down. But Em stood high in his awkward stance, fixed them with his good eye and swapped with them great, shocking blows.

It went on for several minutes. At the edge of his strength and will, Em was sagging slightly now, rocking away from those punishing fists. Still he kept

393

swinging, often missing, but maintaining a staggering balance and swinging. At last the man on his left went to his hands and knees; Jojohn's boot came up under his stomach with a force that lifted him off the floor. But the one on his right, a short, heavy man built like a wrestler with batwing muscles standing high through the torn shirt behind his neck, swayed and grinned in a violent stupor and kept coming back as if he had never known pain. He was a thrusting shadow, grinning and silent, rocking lightly from side to side and uncoiling his ebony arms with terrible force.

Em grunted and absorbed the flashing hammers. Occasionally he connected, and only then, with the smack of flesh and the awkward lurch of the black man, did the force behind it show. The man kept tearing away at his middle, Em's flesh jumping under the blows, and the Indian took the punishment, holding firm. He would not be worn down.

And then at last there was a subtle change in the black man's drive, the rhythm faltered, there was a tempering of his fury, and when that happened, something in Jojohn renewed itself. It was what he had waited for. The animal look returned to his eyes, a flicker of savage joy. He stiffened and began pile-driving blows until he broke the other man down. The Negro stumbled and grabbed Jojohn around the waist. Throwing an arm under his chin, Em straightened and broke his neck.

He released the body and let it slide to the floor. He looked about, at the wreckage, the fallen bodies.

The jukebox lay on its side, making a rhythmic clicking noise. Em turned for the door and stopped, clutched a post and slid to one knee.

"Em! Watch out, Em!"

It was Tio, struggling behind the stairs. The boy went tumbling across the floor. A shadow moved out from the stairs, lengthening until it lay before the kneeling Indian. Em raised his head, squinting, blinking away blood.

Clyde Fay stood watching him, the smile tight on the slit of his mouth.

Em moaned in the effort to rise. A jack boot cracked across his chin and sprawled him on the floor. Again he tried to get up, and Fay seized the post and whipped out a flying kick that sent him backward through the door. He hit the porch on his back and toppled off onto the ground.

Fay was beside him. He kicked again, but this time Em managed to block it with a forearm and kick Fay's other leg out from under him.

From the startled murmuring which arose from the hills, there now came screams and cheering.

Fay rolled away and onto his feet and stood watching as Em pulled himself painfully up the side of the porch. Then he pounced in and away, and a long gash appeared in Jojohn's cheek. Em looked surprised and rubbed it with the back of his hand, and for the first time seemed to see the knife. Fay darted in again and blood oozed from a rip in the Indian's sleeve.

Then Fay went after him, lunging, cutting him off as Em dodged around the yard, trying to avoid the flashing knife. But it was too fast. Fay was an expert. The shaggy giant stumbled and roared as the blade flicked out again and again, each time opening new fissures in the old china skin. Fay circled gracefully, springing in and away, avoiding the Indian's clumsy swipes, the grin tight on his face, enjoying but checking himself, prolonging the kill like a cat.

With a howl of frustration Em lurched away and clutched at his neck. Fay stamped his heels. A little joy dance. It was death and he was in the thrill of it. Em watched the knife point, flicking slowly, dropping his blood. The thing was eating him and no way to stop it. He drew a tattered sleeve across his face, smearing blood. Fay leaped in and lay a slash across his thigh, just below the crotch. He looked at the place and at Jojohn, his eyes shining with malevolent glee.

395

Em stood looking back at him. Slowly something began to change in his face. He seemed to be drawing in, concentrating something within him.

Then, raising his head, he fixed the black man with his good eye and began to shuffle cautiously forward. Fay backed down the yard, feinting, bouncing away.

Still the Indian came. He closed in, watching the knife, hands hanging loosely at his sides. Fay checked his bluff. He drew a line of blood across Em's forehead. Jojohn shook it off and continued his advance.

Fay danced lightly backward, watching the giant move toward him, puzzled, staying on his toes. Em kept moving him down the yard and into the shadow of the supper-club porch. When Fay's back touched the porch rail he froze; the smile slipped from his face.

Em strode quickly forward, dropping low, tensing. Fay glanced for an opening, but the Indian was raising his hands to his sides, as though he were cornering a wild animal.

Fay's reaction was instantaneous. He tucked low in a sweeping, coiling motion, and the knife blurred straight for Jojohn's throat.

This time the Indian didn't dodge.

Standing flat, focusing hard with his good eye, he swung his left hand over, flat and straight. The knife went to the hilt through his palm.

Having thus anchored it in his flesh, he closed his left hand on the knife, wrenched it away, and in the same motion stretched himself to his full height, puffed his cheeks, and with a great, contracting movement of his entire body, he windmilled a massive right fist with sledge-hammer force.

Fay buckled, his eyes bulging froglike from under his caved-in forehead, dead before his back hit the ground.

Em hung over the black man's body, spent, shaking, blowing blood and saliva. He turned and sank to his knees, his face lifted, eyes closed, bathed in the purple of his blood.

There was silence. The yelling in the hills had

stopped. The Indian knelt in the sunlit yard drawing his breath in great, heaving gasps.

There was that and the wash of the river.

46

I BECAME AWARE OF MOVEMENT ALONG THE PORCH. The two dog boys who had been guarding the crowd were edging toward the other end, their frightened eyes darting. Suddenly they sprang over the far rail and took off down the road toward the river, knees high, pumping hard, their shoulders jerking as they ran.

Doc Bobo stood in the yard, turning, looking at Fay, at Jojohn, at the figures disappearing down the road.

There was a soft, rustling sound. He turned and looked up, and stood transfixed.

They were pouring slowly down the hillsides, down the banks, filling the paths, brushing through the brittle weeds—hundreds of them, clay-colored people with raw, expressionless faces.

Doc Bobo turned, circled, watching them close from all sides.

"Listen to me!" he shouted. "You better listen to me!"

A chorus of voices began rising along the rocks. Feet shuffled faster. A black-and-tan mongrel got caught on the road before the crowd; he ran in circles before them, barking, vicious, hunger-ribbed, rolling his eyes, then found escape by leaping a gulley and galloped away up the road.

Doc Bobo shouted, commanding them, then suddenly broke and ran for his car.

At that the crowd charged, their cries filling the air. They jumped from the banks to the top of the Continental, pounding it with rocks and sticks, and others rushed in to the sides, kicking, scraping, hammering with their fists. The limousine squatted under their weight as they flung themselves on it, burying it with their bodies, pounding at the doors and windows, climbing over one another like a horde of rabid squirrels, with still more pouring down from the rocks.

The engine started. Wheels spun helplessly on the clay. Then they were rocking it. Louder and louder their wails climbed the Ape Yard walls. Louder and louder grew the pounding.

The Yard was swarming with people. Trying to reach Jojohn, I was jostled and fell. Then someone was beside me, pulling. It was Tio; we fought for footing, lost in the wild motion and suffocating heat of the mob. All I could see was people, pushing, shoving us closer to the action taking place at the car.

Then there was a surging of the crowd and I saw that the green limousine was being lifted and turned, moved out into the deep-rutted road.

Tio and I were carried along with them, across the branch and out of the reed hollows to the main road up the Ape Yard, lost in the midst of the shouting, heaving mob, marching to the pulse of mindless rage.

The procession moved higher into the streets of the little tilted shacks, leaving Fletcher Bottom and surging up through the steep cut banks, the car limping on twisted wheels as they shoved it over the ruts.

Over the crowd came another noise. The honk and thump of bands moving out from the fairgrounds. In the distance I saw the glint of sun on horns, the flash of white boots and batons of plumed, high-stepping majorettes, tractors pulling floats.

Now the mood of the crowd was changing. They began marching to the band music; some of them started to sing. They pushed along with joyful abandon, laughing, shouting, Speck Turner and Carlos dancing on the jouncing roof.

At Cabbage Alley the procession turned and moved off the road and up the long, sloping granite apron to the wire fence that surrounded the Poncini quarry. Here the pace quickened, moving easily up the

398

graveled slope. The flimsy wire was stomped down.

As we drew near the edge, noses twitched, women turned their faces away. The stench was sharp and acrid in our nostrils. We had smelled the stinkhole all our lives, but it had never seemed so foul. It was as though it were coming alive and waiting, its diseased fumes boiling in anticipation.

I could see the dark bottom, where the sun had not yet descended. There were scurryings below at the approaching din, splashing things and flittings.

There was a groan from the crowd and the green Continental nosed out over the ledge. Doc Bobo's face was at the window in a sweat-glistening foxfire of terror, contorted, silent-screaming behind the thick, tinted glass. The front wheels dropped off and the car bellied on the rock, throwing off sparks. The window was opening; Doc Bobo scrambled to crawl out. The car tilted, wavered, then came a final shove and it went toppling into the dark, fetid night of the quarry.

After a moment came the heavy splash, the sound of it washing up the walls to mingle with the lung-rending, deafening cries of the crowd assembled at the ledges.

Then Skeeter was waving frantically for quiet, staring down. A hush fell.

Far below in the reflected granite light a dark form could be seen, thrashing, screaming. Miraculously, somehow Doc Bobo had not died in the fall, and he now pulled his broken body through the floating filth, struggling furiously to save himself.

As the crowd watched in horror, he splashed along the granite walls, scratching at the sheer stone face, his terrified screams rising to high-pitched, futile squeals.

It went on for several minutes, until at last, his strength exhausted, he slipped beneath the scum-choked surface.

Someone touched my shoulder. It was Tio, pointing. It took a moment for me to make the Indian out, he looked so small in the distance. Then I saw him, a dark thing clinging to the side of the slope at the far lower end of the hollow. Slowly, painfully, he pulled himself upward, scratching for footing in the shadowy crevices, reaching out for a clump of roots. We watched in silence as he inched higher and higher, until he made the rim and drew himself over into the weeds, then struggled to his feet and, like any wild, wounded creature, lumbered toward the waiting woods.

It was just after sunrise.

Jayell, Phaedra and I stood before the nearly finished house the boarders would occupy and waited for them to finish their inspection. Mr. Burroughs, dressed in his best Sunday suit, lunged up and down the yard looking at his watch. Mr. Rampey dozed at the wheel of the loaded school bus.

After a week, the Ape Yard was pretty much back to normal. The celebration that had gone on for three days, with crowds milling and carousing in the hollow under the watchful eyes of state troopers and national guardsmen, was over. The town itself was still jittery, but the riot the centennial celebrants had heard was erupting that day never spilled out of the hollow. The centennial festivities were ruined, to be sure, and the mysterious upheaval was widely reported by the visiting press, but was unanimously interpreted as a juke-joint fracas that got out of hand. The dignitaries were hustled out of town and the city fathers went about shushing rumors and urging a return to calm. Inquiries into Doc Bobo's disappearance met empty faces, shrugging shoulders. Sheriff Middleton and FBI agents were still poking through the hills trying to piece together the story, but were getting nothing but vague replies and contradictions. The people were interested only in getting back to their jobs at the quarries, at the mill, in climbing to Cooper

Corner in hopes of a day's labor to put something on the table that night.

The Ape Yard was peaceful. People came and went, bowing respectfully to the officers as they passed.

The Poncini quarry sat quietly in the sun.

Mr. Burroughs paced. He twiddled his fingers. Finally he lunged through the school-bus door, seizing the horn with both hands and holding it for a full thirty-second blast, scaring Mr. Rampey half out of his wits.

Boarders began emerging from the house and groping their way down the steps.

"You can just stop that, Horace Burroughs," scolded Mrs. Cline, "I'm nervous enough as it is."

Mr. Rampey put his head out the school-bus door. "Look Horace, I'm the driver. If you want the horn blowed . . ."

"Bo-o-oard!" Mr. Burroughs urged them. "Bo-o-oard!"

"I still say Esther will choose the corner room," said Mrs. Porter.

"We agreed now," said Mrs. Bell, "Esther can have whichever room she likes." She turned to the others. "Did everyone get a good look at everything, so we can describe it all to her?"

"That's why I'm taking pictures," said Mrs. Cline, winding her Kodak. "Oh, I forgot to get one of the outside!" She trotted up the road, looking for an angle.

"But if we're leaving now," said Mrs. Bell, "when will you have time to get them developed?"

"There'll be time!" wailed Mr. Burroughs. "It'll be a week before this crowd gets off!"

"Jayell," said Mrs. Metcalf, taking his arm, "I hate to say it, but I may be allergic to that paint you're using in there. I got real dizzy-headed."

"Oh, damn," said Jayell, "I'll bet they're using the wrong paint. I got special nonallergenic paint for this house. Don't you worry, Mrs. Metcalf, I'll have it all redone while you're gone."

"Oh, thank you," said Mrs. Metcalf, *greatly relieved. "You know, not everyone understands about my allergies, Jayell."*

"I do," nodded Jayell *sympathetically, "I do."* He helped her aboard the bus.

Mr. Burroughs turned to Mr. Rampey. *"Lester, would you kindly give your horn another squeeze for me?"*

Mr. Rampey obliged, and revved the engine a couple of times to boot.

Farette shooed Ruby on the bus ahead of her. *"Get on, Ruby, I can't stand this racket!"*

"You sure you counted them lunch boxes right, now?"

"I counted 'em," said Ruby. *"Wait a minute, I left my pocket book on the steps."* . .

"Woody!" shouted Mr. Burroughs. *"Where's Woodall?"*

"He's tryin' to find the door on the other side of the bus," called Mr. Rampey, *"you better come around and get him."*

"Jayell," said Mr. Jurgen, *"I don't like to complain, but don't you think those steps are a bit steep for these old people?"*

"I think maybe you're right," said Jayell. *"I'll take care of it."*

One by one they got aboard the bus and selected a seat. That is, all except Mrs. Porter, who went from one to another trying to find one that would suit her for the long ride, and figuring which side the sun would be on so it wouldn't shine in her eyes. Mr. Burroughs came around the hood leading Mr. Woodall, who eyed the elusive door as though suspecting some vague conspiracy. He broke free and hastened through it before it could get away from him again.

"You sure you won't come with us, boy," said Mr. Burroughs.

"No, sir," I said, avoiding Jayell's and Phaedra's eyes, *"but you be sure and give Miss Esther my love."*

"I still think it's foolishness," said Mrs. Cline, huffing up the incline with her camera, *"to just go barrel-*

ing off up the country without even lettin' anybody know we're comin'!"

"They'll know when we get there," said Mr. Burroughs, "get aboard, please."

"What?" laughed Phaedra, incredulous. "You mean they don't even know you're coming? Why, what if that son of hers won't let her go?"

Mr. Burroughs jutted his head forward, lowering his brows menacingly. "Then it'll be his duty to try and stop us, won't it!" He swung aboard the bus as Mr. Rampey scraped his way to low gear. "My most fervent prayer," he roared above the noise, "is that the son of a bitch will try!" And with the long sweep of an executioner's arm, he shut the door with a bang.

The bus rattled off down the hill—narrowly missing trees and dodging workers, hats and handkerchiefs waving out of the windows—and assaulted the Atlanta highway.

Jayell shook his head. "God help anybody that tries to stop that crowd."

"You know," said Phaedra, "I think I understand it now, for the first time."

"What's that?"

"Why young girls fall in love with old men." She made a little growl in her throat and turned a mischievous smile on a puzzled Jayell.

I was walking the bike cart around from behind the lumber pile. Jayell came to take a handlebar and help me.

"Well, Earl," he said, "I guess there's no changing your mind?"

"No," I said. I got aboard the bike.

"I still don't understand why you've got to go," said Phaedra, "just when things are finally working out."

"They've worked out for you," I said. "You've all got what you wanted. I still don't know what I want, and I just want to bum around awhile and try and find out."

"At fifteen?" she said. "Come on, Earl."

"I know . . . I—I just don't want to stay here any

403

longer." I rocked down on the starter and revved the engine, eager to be away.

"But what about school? There's a law, you know."

"There's plenty of time," I said, "and I know how to stay away from the law." I grinned at Jayell. "They won't even know I'm alive."

"Well," said Jayell, "your life's been so screwed up to this point it's no wonder you don't know what you want to do. Go on, look around, Early boy, it won't do you any harm. There's a thing inside all of us trying to tell us what we are. You listen to yours. You'll know in time. But do think about school again. I don't know what life's got for you, but it's not here in these quarries and mills. Maybe you'll find it there. Besides," he added with a wry grin, "you can take my word for it as one who knows—you'll never make a living with those hands."

"I'll remember that," I said, grinning.

I shook hands with Jayell and grabbed Phaedra and kissed her hard on the mouth and rolled off down the hill.

The store was stripped of its merchandise. Every shelf was bare. The meat cases and drink box stood empty, their doors thrown open and airing. The vegetable bin held only a few scattered pods and shucks. Balls of trash littered the floor.

Tio brought out a box of groceries and set it in the cart. "That's all I could put aside," he said. "Maybe last you a couple of weeks if you eat light and stretch it."

"They really cleaned you out, didn't they?"

He shook his head. "I never saw anything like it. They'd have bought the kitchen stove if they could'a got it. It'll take a month to get the place restocked. You need some gas? Here, pull over to the pumps and I'll squeeze you out what's left." . .

"I don't need any. Got a full tank."

Tio looked me over. He peered in the cart. "You got a coat? You gon' freeze on that bike come winter. I got one upstairs I never wear, I'll get it for you."

404

"No, I'm all right." I pulled Em's old army blanket out of the cart and showed him where I had cut a hole in the middle to make a poncho out of it. "See? I'm just fine."

He thought a minute and took off his trademark, his hat with the square holes in the crown, and set it on my head. He stood back and clapped his hands. "Now ain't you some dude!"

"You'll be dead of pneumonia in a week," I said.

"Well," he said, folding his arms, "which way you goin'?"

It came to me for the first time that I hadn't even given it a thought. I thought quickly, as Tio would expect at least a direction. I looked around, trying to visualize land beyond the familiar terrain, realizing for the first time how small were the borders of childhood.

"Just away will do for now," I said...

Tio shook his head. "I might'a known." He was about to say something else when he was interrupted by a shrill, panic-stricken cry from the rear of the store.

"T-i-ooooo!"

Racing around the corner together, we came upon Mr. Teague, his head bandages loose and hanging, dangling upside down with his legs caught in the automatic freight elevator that had risen to the second floor.

Tio put his hands on his hips. "Mist' Teague, you sposed to be lyin' down!"

Tio went to the derrick and began shifting levers and sorting chains. "I told you not to try and work this thing. What you call yourself doin' anyhow?"

"Tryin' to get that load of produce off this dock before it rots, like you were told to do an hour ago!"

"I told you I'd get it in," said Tio petulantly, paying out chain. "Don't know what I'm gon' do with you."

"You're going to kill me, that's what!" cried Mr. Teague, groping frantically for the floor. "You will succeed where Bobo and all his cutthroats failed! I have every confidence!"

"Well, you two don't need me anymore," I said.

"Hey," called Tio, "if you—uh—happen to run acrost anybody we know, tell him I said hello."

"I'll do that," I said, backing. It was hard enough, leaving, and he wasn't making it any easier...

"And—if you ever need anything—well, you know where we live."

I waved, and rounded the corner.

The trees whipped by in the morning hills, making the sun flash and sparkle as it came chasing and dancing like a hound along the crests of the smoky ridges. The road swung perilously around the tight, narrow curves, but I held the throttle wide open, even through the blinding pools of fog that still lay deep in the hollows. The aged bike trembled and shuddered with the strain as we severed the mists of the Georgia hills and lunged through the breaking morning.

Away now. Just away, and quickly.

For already they were fading, those times of childhood creeks, of gulley fortresses and vine-covered banks, of blue steel dawns and amber afternoons.

Had they been real, those bright, illusive images that drifted, even now, so distantly across my mind? Was there ever a time when I actually touched them —and was so sure they would never end? Or were they only dreams—as Jayell said, the ravings of angels, a kind of lyric madness that flashes for a moment, and fades with the echoes of their cries.

Only dreams?

That gave Jayell the courage to build his fantasy village, his place, in a conformist world he couldn't accept? That made Mr. Teague and Tio beileve they could keep their small world intact amid the change that erupted and swirled around them? That stirred Miss Esther and a house of forgotten old people to do battle with time itself?

Only dreams, with which an Indian opened to sunlight and whistling adventure and unthinking joy the shrouded mind of a sick and frightened boy?

406

If so, could I stay there and watch it all fade away? Could I be there for the world, that might already be on its way, that my friend, Em Jojohn, had died?

No, I had to be gone while those houses still stood at Wolf Mountain, while the old folks still pulsed with their thunder and fire, while TEAGUE & SON'S *grocery still thrived.*

Let Jojohn always be free in my mind to wander his rainswept highways and holler down his ghosts, to pamper his fraudulent stomach (and fight and love on his own terms too!), to sleep where he could, leave when he would, do his crazy dance and chant his wordless song and kick off his boots, on the proper excuse, to feel the dew and get his bare feet in the earth.

Away now. While I still dared to believe in dreams. While I still could hear the angels cry.